PURSLANE

PURSLANE

By BERNICE KELLY HARRIS

CHAPEL HILL

*The University
of North Carolina
Press*

The characters in this book, both their names and their personalities, are fictional. No resemblance to living persons or their families is intended.

T ryL c

PURSLANE

"The common purslane [pusley, U. S.] is
...an annual...used as a pot herb, for
salads..."   —Webster

I

"Oh my darlin', oh my darlin',
Oh my dar-r-lin' Clemintine,
You are lost and gone forever—"

THE SAD FINALITY OF THE SONG, the gloomy blue haze yonder above the Neuse River, the wood dove's lonesome call from the huckleberry swamp, the weariness of a long Monday were suddenly too much. The boy Calvin, drooped listlessly astride old yellow Nellie mule, gazed forlornly into the blue river vapor with the eyes of a wanderer who yearns for a haven beyond his reach.

Beside John Fuller on the wagon seat, his wife Dele looked up when Calvin's song ceased abruptly and studied the set of the boy's head. She also looked toward the river haze lying above the pines and sighed.

Seated flat in the wagon body, the girls Letha and Kate removed their heavy padded gloves made of old stockings, Letha examining her hands after a day with the hoe and Kate eating the last biscuit from the dinner basket. Nannie Lou was letting her bare feet drag over the cool weeds in the road and communing with Nature...

...The cumulus clouds of sunset,
The gossamer wrap of evening
Fringed with starry gems...
Fringed with star...

...No, the words were gone. Almost the beautiful thoughts had trembled into rhyme when... What was a little cotton? Ah, how little they understood. Papa had scolded, and Mama had watched her like a hawk afterwards because she had chopped up a whole slu' of cotton while her mind soared up in the clouds... or what's a heaven for? Some day these songs she was composing among the cotton rows would bring more money than the whole lower field put together, and then they would be sorry. She would build them a three-story brick mansion, with Brussels carpets so soft they'd mire up to their knees when they walked on it, with electric lights, with fine furniture and a water closet. And she'd hire a cook and a butler to do all the work so they could sit on the porch—the front veranda—and talk polly-wogs all day. She might have to give Mama some fancy work to keep her hands still. And the cousins—Christine and Lessie and Margie and Aunt Sugar's girls, who bragged because they didn't have to work outdoors and were all time passing by where she was chopping cotton, with their parasols h'isted—some day she would pass them by in a rubber-tired carriage with her black coachman whipping two fine gray horses and silk tassels flying! ...

> *Fringed with starry gems*
> *The moon, a big pearl button*
> *To fasten...*

John Fuller drove up the lane home. Calvin drew water for the mule trough, fed Nellie and Daisy, and shucked corn for next day. John brought two buckets of swill from the kitchen and watched the shoats scramble for it—twelve hams and spareribs and sausage and chittlin's—he knocked the sausage and spareribs of the lustiest from the trough so the little runt could eat—not much account, the runt, but a feller got used to the little rascal.

With the milk bucket on her arm, Letha stopped at the corner of the porch for a pink rosebud; furtively she wore it in her hair to the cow-lot. Dele hastily made a fire, fried some shoulder, baked clabber biscuits, and left Nannie Lou to tend the oven while she pulled some young pusley for the cow; old Bess liked green stuff same as folks.

Kate lifted the dasher from the churn, ran her finger over it, and licked off the milk. Churning was her practice period. Some days it was Sunday school pieces; others, revival hymns; occasionally, love songs; and today, "Clemintine"...

> *"You are lost and gone f'rever,*
> *Oh my dar-r-lin'..."*

The lyric floated through the kitchen door toward the lot. Dele interrupted and sent Kate hurriedly to the pantry for some scuppernong preserves while she herself took up the butter. The men came in to supper; one pan of biscuits had burned while Nannie Lou was frolicking with Nero. Dele ate the burned biscuits.

The Fullers always ate in heavy silence unless there was company. Observations were made by the head to the foot of the table if a cow needed salt, if Grandpa had shortness of breath worse than common, if Preacher Rafe's mule broke into the dunghill corn patch, if Sim had another spell. Nannie Lou's face burned down to her feet then; for Perrie was Preacher Rafe's boy, and she still cried when they teased her about Perrie.

Calvin bolted his supper and left the table. The supper dishes washed, the milk set to clabber, a pan of gunjers * made for tomorrow, Dele slipped into the shed room to get some smoke-rags from the blue chest. The bee gums must be robbed as soon as Uncle Wes could catch up with his plowing. He always took honey for folks; the bees never stung him.... Calvin was lying across the bed staring at the ceiling. Dele lingered at the chest. If she knew what to say—a neighborhood singing, a Sunday with Aunt Nettie, who kept a boarding house in Raleigh, the Sunday school excursion to Morehead City, hopeless as that was—these crossed her mind. She closed the chest, with the smokers in her arms.... Oh, Calvin.... At the door she hesitated.

"Anything ail you, Calvin?"

_____
* Molasses cookies.

3

"No'm."

She shut the door softly. On the back porch John was soaking his tired legs in the foot tub and rounding out the day with a chew of tobacco. Dele sat with him, shelling garden peas in the dark to send Aunt Cynthy.

Blowing out the light, Kate was soon asleep. Letha, in her rough-dried unbleached domestic nightgown, was patting buttermilk into her complexion and counting nine stars her ninth night. Nannie Lou from her bed near the window was feeding her soul. Ah, the moon, a virgin bright—Nannie Lou was vague about virgin: it meant a girl, a maiden with a lamp; five of them were wise and five were foolish....

Sweet gem in the cheek...no...in the crown of night,
Thy radiance guide the lonely path that I must
  trod...no...thy radiance guide my lonely way,
Thy calm breathe through the noisome day....

Some day her pen would carry her far....

Pig, pig—wooie. Pig, pig—wooie! ...Chick, chick, chick, chickee! ...Here, Nero, here, here! ...

  "Why do you wait, dear brother,
    Oh why do you tarry so long?
    Your savior is waiting..."

Kate would sing those persuading songs first thing. The noisome day had begun.

"Nannie Lou, where's my penny? You got my penny out of this drawer."

"I never, Letha."

"It's gone. I got to mail a card. You bought a pencil at Uncle Millard's Saturday."

"Mama give me a penny."

"All right. I'll just go ask her."

"It was one I saved, I reckon." But Letha was already half downstairs.

4

When her sister had crossed the back porch, Nannie Lou tipped quickly down the steps to the trunk where her Papa kept the Sunday school treasury. Snatching a penny from the box of pennies, she closed the lid. Wait. She would need another pencil soon. Two pennies would be missed no more than one. Safe again upstairs, she slipped a penny in Letha's drawer and picked up a card with Letha's hand-write on it: "Are you still in the land of the living? Be sure to come to church Sunday. We may have a Sunday school excursion soon. I hope I can go. You be sure to plan to go too. I have lots to tell you. As ever, your friend, Letha." If Papa knew she wrote to that Victor Parrish! Let her tell about the penny, and she'd tell about this card Letha was fixing to slip in the mail box. Maybe the mail man would bring The "Blessed" Farmer, as Kate called it today, and there would be another poem to add to her collection. Cotton or no cotton, she would think up poems today. The pencil must be taken along so the words would not escape as they did yesterday.

Breakfast over, the dinner basket packed, the morning chores completed, soon after sunrise the Fullers climbed into the wagon and started for the lower field. On the way Dele kept looking toward the east, where a strange cloud hovered. All morning she chopped ahead of the girls as John and Calvin sided the cotton behind them. Under his big straw hat Calvin's eyes stared dully at the furrows. A silent morning among the cotton rows.

... You're worth two of her, Calvin—Dele went over the words row after row, knowing she could never speak them, for all her practice— No boy's got your looks. You always had looks from a baby up. She's not pretty and no bigger'n a washing of soap. The world's full of girls, pretty ones. Let her go, Calvin....

Calvin plowed on listlessly, as stolidly silent as Nellie mule. The offer from that Alabama minor baseball league no longer lured.

John stormed at Daisy now and then and "confounded" her when she stopped to seize a luscious tuft of grass. When he said that ugly word, the girls glanced at their Mama's face. She winced, but never once looked up from her hoe. Tonight she would ask him again not to say "confound" before the children. John, between confoundings of the "infernal varmint," was harvesting the crop...a bale to the acre, plenty corn in the crib for the stock, hominy and meal for the house and a few barrels to sell, four barns of tobacco on an early market...he might bank two hundred dollars or more clear of debt if no doctor's bills came in, and in a few years there might be a way for that gal to get her schoolin'. There was going to be some weather. Rain-seed in the east, a queer look about the sun all day, and—Daisy jerked her head to one side and was again confounded.

Letha, as she chopped, was walking up the hill to the church in her new flowered lawn with the black velvet bows. Furtively she searched among the boys standing under the trees near the church door. There was Victor. Her card had brought him. Cautiously she smiled and bowed and gave him a look...

"On the cross He sealed my par—don,
Sealed my pardon, paid the debt-t-t-t..."

She would enjoy putting the alto to that today. Somehow she must manage a few words with Victor after preaching...

"And made me free, and made me free..."

They must make plans to be together. Papa was unreasonable. It made them love each other but the more....She beat the rest out and turned to chop the next row. Dele silently stooped to pick out two huge bunches of wire grass Letha had left, straightening to look quizzically at the sun.

Kate jogged along, not thinking much, looking often at the sun, which moved slowly under those funny looking

6

clouds toward twelve o'clock, and making frequent trips to the spring for cool water.

> *. . . Dawn with its mist and dew*
> *Paints the celestial blue*
> *With rosy spangles bold*
> *And an orb of burning gold. . . .*

Nannie Lou meant to hold that rhyme. With the water jug she slipped away hurriedly to the spring and, unfolding her paper, added a rubber tire to her carriage and silk tassels flying in the breeze. Kneeling, she drank the cool spring water, pausing to study her face in the mirrored surface of the pool . . . "I baptize thee, my brother and my sister" . . . as soon as the water roared in her ears, she jerked her face from the spring. All the practice in the world would not dispel the dread of the watery grave, inevitable as Fate, that disturbed the most inspired moments. Filling the jug, she placed it on her shoulders and slowly, with dignity, climbed the hill. . . . In the cool of the evening Rachel came to Jacob bearing upon her shoulder . . .

> *In the cool of the eventide*
> *Dear Lord abide;*
> *In the glow of the waking dawn . . .*

"Nannie Lou, come on back to this cotton patch!" Shut up, old Letha. Ah, how little any of them understood. No thought but dirt and cotton and grass. . . .

> *Dawn with its mist and dew,*
> *Paints the celestial blue . . .*
> *An orb of burning gold . . .*

Sustained by money and fame down her vista of years, she placed the jug in the moist earth under the persimmon tree and took up her hoe; her Muse was soon dust. . . . She began to add a chapter to her novel, subtracting less cotton in this

7

simpler literary effort.... Geraldine—should she be Swannanoa?—Swannanoa's heart was breaking. Tonight was theirs alone. He would live in her heart to eternity, but tomorrow she must send him away, not dead, but dead to her, lost and gone forever.... Kate was leading the way to the persimmon tree; it was time to eat. Ah, no thought but food!

In the shade of the persimmon tree lunch was unpacked and spread on a tablecloth, just like an Easter picnic: fried chicken, boiled eggs, biscuits buttered and sprinkled with a little brown sugar from Uncle Millard's store, light bread, watermelon pickle, gunjers. Nannie Lou ate six biscuits. Less restrained in the open than at home, Kate and Letha grew almost lively over their food when John had finished eating and had rolled over for a nap. Calvin showed little relish, but he ate.... Oh, eat, Calvin. No girl's worth good vittles. We can have a right good time, just us.... On an impulse Dele started to tell about the time Aunt Puss cooked the craw in the chicken—she could tell it funny, the girls said —but Calvin unobtrusively slipped down the hill toward the spring pool. Dele ended her story abruptly, while the girls stretched themselves in the shade, Kate for a little nap, Letha to daydream, and Nannie Lou to fondle her pencil; it felt good in her hand even when she relaxed from literary pursuits.

Dele, breaking biscuits for Nero, gazed fixedly at the rim of trees where Calvin had disappeared. Presently she took the water jug and went casually to the spring. Calvin was standing there, staring into the still water. In silence she handed him the jug to fill, while she searched under the pine straw for heart leaves and wintergreen to go in a salve she made from Grandma's receipt, for insect bites and fall sores....

John gave the signal to resume work. There might be some weather before night. Early in the afternoon a thin haze settled over the field. The girls began to lean on their hoes, vaguely uneasy. The mules grew restless and nervous. Dele kept looking at the sun in silence. Even Calvin showed interest in the stilled light. John spoke ever more kindly to his mule; he began to call her gal.

The light waned gradually; a strange half twilight descended. There was only a fleece of a cloud, and yet the sun … John hitched Daisy to the wagon and tried to keep his voice straight as he said, "We'll go home now. I don't know what it is."

"It might be an eclipse." Dele was calm.

Nero whined mournfully and stayed close to Nannie Lou as the twilight deepened.

"I've seen eclipses all my life, but I never saw nothin' like this." John touched Daisy gently with the reins.

"Le's go to Grandpa's," Letha suggested.

"Look, stars! See if you can count nine, Letha," Kate laughed.

"I wouldn't talk, children. Can't tell what this is. It's the Almighty's works." John's voice echoed in the dusky stillness. The wagon wheels sounded unwontedly loud in the silent ride home.

Oh dear Father—Nannie Lou could never say God—forgive my sins of omission and commission. Dear Father, I love Thee. I praise Thy great name. Save us. Forgive me for taking Thy pennies. I have sinned and am no more worthy. Save us, dear Father, and I will go to the foreign fields and make Thy great Name known among the heathens from the rivers to the ends of the earth. …

Almighty God, I have sinned—John pleaded silently with Deity—I have used words contrary to Thy will. Spare us, and I will keep my tongue undefiled before Thee. Spare us, God Almighty. … He slapped the reins over Daisy's rump. "Get up, gal." His voice was almost tender.

Kate nibbled on the last gunjer in the dinner basket.

9

Calvin prayed to Milly. Oh, Milly, are you thinkin' of me? I wouldn't care what happened, just so we was together. Oh, Milly, le's don't let them part us."

Dele picked the pine straw from heart leaves and wintergreen and mused over the ingredients of Grandma's salve, remembering how it had cured the fall sores on Calvin's legs when he was a little boy.

At home the chickens had gone to roost, the cows were lowing at the lane gate. Inside, the house was hot and still. In Mama's room the family gathered and sat waiting. Nero kept licking Nannie Lou's hand, as she sat bowed humbly in the half light, furtively watching Papa's face as he studied the sky and made it promises. Dele rolled rags into smokers for the bee gums.

"We could sell some honey. Town folks think well of it, Nettie says. I'm certain we could sell five dollars' worth," Dele mused over the rags.

Nobody commented. Honey seemed such a trivial thing. Dele rolled another smoker. "Five dollars would pay for a family ticket to Morehead. The children really ought to see the ocean." (Calvin might get to see Milly.)

The twilight was lifting a little. "I aim to take 'em on the excursion, unless Providentially hindered. All of us—if we're spared till then."

Dele worked steadily in the sickly light. When the sun shone normally again, she saw a new light in Calvin's eyes and presently she heard him romping in the front yard with Nero, and laughing. She lifted her heart to Deity then.

II

THROUGH THE NEIGHBORHOOD there had been characteristic reactions to the eclipse. At Uncle Hen's, his wife Aunt Puss, who was Dele's sister, hovered flutteringly over her brood of girls in the darkest corner of the hall, assuring them that they were all going to be destroyed—Julie, Margie, Christine, Lessie, Annie Laurie, Tiny—in a pile! Uncle Hen stood on the porch watching and waiting for he didn't know what next. It might be a tornado working up, or an earthquake like a few years ago. Well, everybody had to go sometime one way or another. He wished they-all were over at Grandpa Pate's—his wife's father was on the best terms with the Almighty of anyone Uncle Hen knew. It wasn't until the sun was beginning to brighten again that he thought of the almanac.

Uncle Israel, Dele's brother, told his folks not to be afraid; he felt sure this was only an eclipse. His boy Swade bet Grandpa Pate would know for sure. Uncle Israel was reminded then that there was a way to find out; he told the boys to get the almanac. Robin and Swade struck a match to look for an almanac, but their mother had burned it because she didn't want almanacs hanging below her mantel like the rest of the Pates—like Sugar Pate! It was too old-timey, like roadcarts and surreys. She glanced from her window toward the shelter where the outline of their fine new carriage showed through the dimness.

When Aunt Sugar, the wife of Dele's brother Seth, saw the darkening sky, she hurried to her fireplace to consult the almanac that hung on a nail below the mantel. "Yes, that's what it is, an eclipse," she told Maud and Bettie, who had been ripping up flour sacks for everyday underwear. Uncle Seth sat on the front porch steps alone, watching the sun through a piece of brown glass he had picked up. He always stayed by himself, out of Sugar's way. The kinfolks thought of him not as Uncle Seth but as Aunt Sugar's husband; her sons, too, were not so often called Ekie and Buddy as "Aunt Sugar's boys." Ekie, slipping around the house from the back porch, joined his father and was timidly directed to look through the brown glass at the sun, when Aunt Sugar bounced out the door.

"You Ekie and Buddy! Drop that glass and get back in that back porch."

"We just want to see the sun—"

"The sun ain't none o' your business. Get back to them peas!"

Uncle Seth walked off in the twilight to Grandpa Pate's. To Grandpa he would always be special, for Seth was his first-born, child of the beloved Rachel. For hours the two men in loving fellowship often sat together, not talking much but never tiring of each other. Aunt Sugar, jealous of this bond, early in her married life had determined that her sons should not be papa-boys. That course she had pursued, would pursue! Seth didn't try with his boys often, but an eclipse—

With the waning sunlight Grandpa Pate became lost in the past. He mused over the last eclipse: Rachel was living then; Seth was a little fellow; Millard was the knee-baby; Sad was in the cradle, and Job—at first Grandpa had had to fight the bitterness that rankled against Rachel's last baby, that had cost her life, but the years had brought the conviction that "He doeth all things well." Sarah had been a good wife to him, a good mother to Rachel's four motherless ones no less than to her own—Wes, Dele, Emmie, and Ben, poor fellow, who had died up yonder in Raleigh, where his wife Nettie had dragged him. Bettie, too, had made little difference between Rachel's and Sarah's children and her own—Puss, Israel, and Lina. Five sons and five daughters living—but Rachel gone since the last eclipse, Rachel with her ready laughter and the twinkle in her eye.

"Come in, Seth. I was settin' here thinkin'. I recollect one time when you was just a little fellow, just could talk, that we had an eclipse of the sun. Your mother smoked a piece of glass for us to see through."

"And I kept sayin' 'I can't shee-it, I can't shee-it'?"

"Yes; it tickled your mother. She always had that for a by-word after that."

"I remember it, dim. You stood me up on the watermelon scantlin' and held the glass to my eyes. Long time ago it was as I remember."

"Yes, it was a long time ago. Your mother had just fixed some catnip tea for Millard—"

"I loved that cough syrup she fixed out o' butter and sugar and vinegar and herbs."

"Your mother was good with herbs. No doctor couldn't beat her. I recollect the time you had pneumonia and the doctor gave you up. She went out in the woods and gathered alder and poplar leaves and wrapped you up on 'em and cooled the fever out o' you. She doctored the whole neighborhood. Then she was taken, and all the doctorin' couldn't save her."

"I use to pick out a certain star and imagine 'twas her lookin' down. Look, yonder's the one—" Uncle Seth suddenly flushed a little in the deepening twilight, for he hadn't meant to think out loud that way.

"She looked at the sky a lot. She knew all the signs. Yes, she's somewhere up there. As my breath gets shorter it seems closer. No, she don't seem far. Rachel's up there, waitin'." Grandpa often thought aloud these days.

Grandma Pate bustled into the front porch with some glass she had smoked for Grandpa. He shook his head. "No, Bettie, my eyes is too old now."

Uncle Seth saw something in Grandma's eyes that vibrated some deep vague hurt in herself. "I want the glass, Mŭ," he said. Grandpa had taught Uncle Seth, Uncle Millard, Aunt Sad, and Uncle Job to call their two step-mothers "Mŭ." "Mother" had been for Rachel.

Grandma went back into the house where her unmarried daughter, Aunt Lina, was trying by lamplight to finish a

13

dress for Aunt Nettie, whose boarders in Raleigh gave her no time to sew. "Leave your machine, Lina, and look at the sun through this smoked glass. It has been a long time since we had an eclipse."

"I want to get these seams felled and Puss's waist cut out by night."

Felling seams and cutting out shirtwaists for her sisters, Aunt Lina found sunrise, sunset, and eclipses all about alike since the Spanish-American war.

Mr. Tom Smith, who was nervous in the dark since his wife's death, left his house and hurried over the branch to Grandpa Pate's to see what he thought of all this. He passed Cousin William, who was all the hired hand Grandpa had for his patches and who kept plowing in the half light, and hurried to the house. Aunt Lina had just left her seams a minute to peer through the smoked glass when Mr. Smith stepped up the walk. For the first time, Aunt Lina popped into his mind; he had been considering Babe Landers and Essie Pear, widows—but a virgin—yes, he definitely would consider Aunt Lina.

Mr. Bill Wall and his wife Miss Charity sat on the back steps, close together, expecting the earth to shake any minute, when Mr. White came to borrow a plow point. "Scared? Hell, naw!" Mr. White was the hardened sinner of the neighborhood who found all sorts of beams in the church's eye. "Let the hypocrites be scared!" Mr. Bill and Miss Charity breathed easier when he left, and moved a little closer together.

Aunt Mary, Dele's sister-in-law, rushing home from Uncle Job's pond, where she had caught a nice mess of fish for supper, found her husband sitting on the little bench under the well-oak.

"Wes, what is it?"

14

"Nothin' to hurt nobody."

They sat together through the eclipse, just being still and knowing that He was God. Then Aunt Mary cleaned her fish for supper.

Preacher Rafe Bliss was wholly confident and unafraid. He was patching the fence through which his mule had broken into John Fuller's field, when his wife, Miss Katie, and Perrie left their weed-chopping and hurried into the pasture. Mr. Rafe laughed patronizingly. "There are people right here in this neighborhood that will believe this is the end of time. Oh, the ignorance, the superstition abroad in the land!" The end of time was too long in coming for Miss Katie.

Old Mr. Penny knew what it was at once; he always knew things. Old Miss Becky, his wife, saw Sally Baker, who had been dead thirty years, walking around in the back yard; Miss Becky had expected something, for the witches had bothered her again all night. Cousin Sim, who marched his folks up the road to hear what Mr. Penny thought of all this, marched them right back when Old Miss Becky told him about the dead woman in her yard.

Uncle Job, Dele's brother, reminded his household that thus would Judgment Day come, like a thief in the night; for they knew not the day or hour; let them watch, therefore, so that they all might be found ready, whether it should be noon or night; let their lamps be trimmed and bright, filled with oil like the five wise virgins; Aunt Lessie, his wife, soothed by the softened light, laid her head back on her chair tidy and napped before Uncle Job finished. Ellis, who was going to be a preacher, saw his mother and thought of the sleeping disciples in the Sunday school lesson. "Can ye not watch with Me a little while?" Thus today did they

15

sleep, when the power of the Lord was being manifested outside. Aunt Lessie suddenly started in her sleep, dreaming she had scorched one of the six starched shirts she had just finished ironing when the light began to fail. Her eyes opened anxiously and were comforted by the six immaculate shirts hanging on the chair ready to be folded and put away.

Aunt Cynthy had been picking geese all day. This would give them a whole summer to grow more feathers before cold weather. With a goose's head held tight under her arm, she was plucking the downy feathers into a sheet spread on the floor of the back porch. She was startled at the increasing darkness when she looked up from her goose and saw there were no clouds.

"Millard, what you reckon—"

"Judgment."

"Oh, Millard!"

"You done anything mean today?" Her husband's voice was accusing.

"I reckon we all—"

"You stripped them geese right naked. How'd you like to be stripped? And I saw you hit one goose when she squirted on you. How'd you like—?"

"You don't think it's goin' to be a earthquake then?" Aunt Cynthy was further reassured when Uncle Millard joked with Cousin Ashley, who ran into their yard scared to death.

"Wh-wh-what is i-i-it?"

"Judgment. The sinners are goin' to be parted right and left!"

"D-d-do you r-r-reckon—?"

"Hadn't you better give me that quarter you owe me before—?"

"Th-th-this is all I h-h-have, b-b-but if you—" Cousin Ashley emptied his pocket.

16

Uncle Millard laughed then. Cousin Ashley never could keep up with whom he owed. Aunt Cynthy made her husband give the money back before Cousin Ashley left, reassured about the eclipse.

Garland Miles, his father, and Cousin Nath were shadding at Neuse River when the sky began to darken. They rowed to the bank and hurried toward home, for fear their women folks might be upset. As they passed Cousin Nick Pate's, they saw the women on the front porch looking through opera glasses that the aunt from Philadelphia always included in her trip South. The men bowed and hurried on. The Philadelphia aunt turned from the sun and trained her glasses on them an instant.

"The eclipses we have in Philadelphia are so much more spectacular, don't you think, Joyce?" She looked critically skyward.

"Perhaps it's because the lights are turned on that the darkness seems so much more emphatic," Miss Joyce thought, watching this southern sun a little apologetically. "My first proposal came during an eclipse."

"I know. James Monroe MacWilson. Joyce, he has the most charming son, marriageable, too." She glanced toward Milly, whose eyes were fixed on a star.

"James always said if he ever had a son—"

"Well, he has one—money, position, everything, with it. If you let Milly go home with me—"

"Next spring. I want her to have one more winter with her music."

"Are you sure that Raleigh teacher is competent? We have such splendid musicians up North."

"The finger technique is faulty, but—Milly does play well."

"Our family was always musical. Milly isn't a Pate. Not at all! You have much to be thankful for, Joyce."

"Sometimes I—I fear it. Water seeks its own level, you know, and blood—"

"Oh, blood will tell, our blood! Forget your fears."

"There's an uncouth young fellow—" Miss Joyce lowered her voice. "It's nothing, perhaps, but if we hadn't discovered that she was meeting him around in the neighborhood—Mr. Pate had to take a firm hand. I think she still moons over that youth."

Milly, in the hammock at the end of the porch, was mooning now. Yonder was a faint flicker of a star, their star: they had picked it out one night at Cousin Maggie's from a whole skyful of stars. "Look at our star and make a wish, hard, and it will come to pass." Was he wishing right now, hard, wishing they might go on the excursion together? ... Oh, Calvin ...

"Wait till she meets young James MacWilson. Don't wait too long to send her to Philadelphia."

"Yonder comes Mr. Pate. I hope he had no further trouble with that tenant."

"Joyce, his tenant houses are disreputable. I always thought a southern plantation had whitewashed cabins, with clean, smiling pickaninnies singing spirituals in the yard. These Ne-groes are not clean, and they don't smile or sing. If James Mac—"

"Oh, I'll see that the cabins are painted before he comes and that the tenants are clean and that they sing spirituals for the wedding," Miss Joyce laughed as Cousin Nick hastened up the walk to join the ladies in the dim light.

Jessie, John Fuller's negro tenant, was taken with a violent ague in the cotton patch. The white folks could say it was because he had been scared to death, but Jessie knew what ailed him. He had been conjured once before. Argo had never liked him since he had told Mr. John that Argo's crowd was roguish, and Argo was the one that dropped that meat

18

skin at his door. Jessie had found it with three pins stuck through the center when he walked out his door early that morning, and he had been sick at the stomach ever since. Breakfast and dinner were omitted; he grew worse. As the day advanced Mariah and the children began telling him he didn't look right. The rooster kept crowing before the door; a rabbit ran across the end of his row to the left.

When the light began to fade into a hot greenish twilight, Jessie staggered to the house and crawled in bed. Mariah hung quilts over the little windows, buttoned all the doors, and started praying, while the younger children set up a terrified wail.

"Do, Jesus! Do, Jesus! Don't let 'em git us. Do, Jesus! Don't let dem Yankees come dis way, do pray! Don't let 'em git us."

"'Tain't Yankees, 'Riah. I's conjured. I knowed it all day."

"Do, Jesus!"

"Yes, I's conjured. I found It at de do' dis mornin'. I's tricked, for fair."

There was no supper at Jessie's that night. The family sat huddled together in the room opposite Jessie, while he muttered strange gibberish and begged Mariah to get the trick taken off him. They did not even know that the sun came out again before setting, for they had made night of their quarters and were afraid to look out. When they awoke the next morning and saw the sun in the right place, Mariah fed her family and offered a bottle of chill tonic to Jessie.

"No, I can't swallow. My th'oat's closed on me. I's tricked. I's goin' to die if it ain't tuk off."

Finally Mariah set out for Old Miss Becky's. When she reached the back gate, she heard the old lady talking shrilly to somebody on the porch. Inside the yard, Mariah saw that Miss Becky was alone.

"How'd dey git away 'thout me seein' 'em, Miss Becky?"

"Who?"

"Dem you was talkin' to."

"She ain't gone nowhere. There she is."

Mariah's eyes grew bigger and bigger as she looked around and saw the porch empty except for Miss Becky. "Whur?"

"Speak to her. You'll have to raise your voice."

"Do, Jesus!"

"She's lookin' at you now. She sees you. What you want?"

Mariah wanted just to leave that place. If a ha'nt was that close by, she was needed at home right then. "Seein' folks I can't see. Gi' me de Yankees!" Mariah hurried through the yard.

"I know what you come for."

Mariah stopped at the gate and looked back.

"Speak out."

"Jessie—he's tricked." Mariah fearfully searched the peopled space.

"I knew. Tell him to find some hog's hair under a rock soon as the moon comes up."

"Yeb'm."

Miss Becky closed her eyes and was silent so long that Mariah eased through the gate, thinking that was all.

"Tell him to take three hairs, just three, hide 'em under the doorstep till day, and then go throw 'em in running water."

"Yeb'm."

"Yes, that's Jessie's wife. Yes, her name's Mariah," Miss Becky told the empty chair.

Mariah left that place.

The nearest sure rocks Jessie could think of were down at the side of Mr. John's smokehouse. Crawling out of bed, he reeled along till he saw the rocks lying white and ghostly in the moonlight. Under the very first rock he found hog's hair. Selecting three hairs, he reeled back home, hid them under the doorstep, and went to bed comforted. If he could just live till morning!

As soon as the rain-seed showed pink in the east, Jessie went as fast as he could toward Rocky Branch. Then he threw the three hairs into the run of the branch; strength came back to him; his head cleared and his steps became firm and steady.

"Fix me a bait o' hog meat, 'Riah," he called as he neared his shack. "I's cuored!"

III

"Who's goin' to empire?"

"Le's get Cousin Sim."

"Yeh, he calls 'em fair."

"Come on, Cousin Sim. Call 'em for us."

"Me?"

"Yeh. Come on."

"All right. If I can suit you. Play ball."

During "Confurnce," which had just adjourned after a lengthy session, Cousin Sim had been calling "Strike one—ball two" even during the prayer. The nine players, who had to sit through a sermon and a Confurnce Saturday afternoons before a ball game could be started, had shifted their positions impatiently while Uncle Israel made a report on his negotiations with the railroad company and announced that a vote as to whether the Sunday school wished to go on the excursion to Morehead City would be taken tomorrow. Then the vigilant committee reported the case of an intoxicated member who was sorry and asked to be forgiven; Uncle Job had given an account of funds collected for new tin dippers; and outside across the road the Cale Springs nine were noisily warming up. That crowd had to be licked good today—to learn them a lesson—Garland and Swain, the Pate's Siding battery sitting together on the back seat, had whispered as they planned the pitches and line-up, conceding that the game would depend mostly on Calvin and how he was batting today.

Calvin had sat on the end of the bench, his mind divided between the impending game and Milly, who was sitting with her father and mother, Miss Joyce and Cousin Nick—the only married folks who sat together in church—and the aunt from Philadelphia. If only Milly would stay and watch the game, Calvin had mused, he would knock the ball clear to the woods. Oh, Milly. . . .

When the preacher had finally dismissed his flock, the team had hurried to the schoolhouse across the road from the church, whence, after they had donned work shirts and home-made baseball pants, they emerged to face the enemy nine.

With the small children, the women, impatient to be at home about Saturday night suppers, looked on in silence—not knowing when to cheer anyway—from buggies and surreys in the church grove. Only Aunt Sugar definitely began to assemble her family as soon as church was over. Her boys, crouched behind a group of men at third base, were expertly watching the pitches and calling strikes, balls, and "fow-els" ahead of Cousin Sim—safe for the duration of the game, they hoped. But Aunt Sugar found them.

"You Ekie! You and Buddy come on. Right now!"

The boys, sullen and humiliated, rose to follow, looking back with yearning eyes toward the diamond.

"No Lot's-wife-in' about it, either," Aunt Sugar warned as she led the way to the surrey. The sulky eyes of the boys smoldered with disappointment as they were borne through the dust out of sight. At home they slipped across the pasture to the tobacco barn and pitched the stocking-thread ball to each other, meanwhile watching for the first buggy to appear over the hill and bring news as to who beat. Uncle Seth watched, too, from the corn crib.

Back at the game, the men stood, or squatted for the most part, near the home plate, while the girls, sitting under the church oaks just across from the diamond, added their "keen hollers," as Uncle Hen put it, to the lustier rooting of the masculine fans. Letha, dressed in a new dotted percale, moved with Julia away from the shrill voices under the oaks, over to a top buggy near the well, where she watched the game quietly and with a studied detachment. Victor was playing with the Cale Springs boys. With a Ty Cobb stance he picked up his bat and struck out.

Kate was foremost among the hearty rooters. "Catch him out, Garland!" she shouted to the lanky catcher behind home plate. Garland caught the batter out and grinned toward the trees.

"That one's got on his mama's shirtwaist. Look!"

"Yeh. He's mama's boy. He can't knock nothin'."

"Watch him open his mouth every time the ball comes toward him."

"Don't swallow the ball."

"He's hungry. Hits like he didn't have nothin' but soup for dinner."

"Take more'n soup to beat us."

"S-o-u-p, C-o-u-p, SOUP! SOUP!"

Calvin, in center field, was watching a carriage in the edge of the grove, where Miss Joyce and the visiting aunt from Philadelphia were waiting with polite patience for Cousin Nick to finish talking with Uncle Israel about trying to get the Governor to speak in the neighborhood. Cousin Nick, after keeping a governess in his home for years, had suddenly affected a great concern in the public school when the Governor opened his campaign for education. The women on the back seat of the carriage were discussing fashion trends.

"Black marquisette skirt with folds of taffeta around the bottom, a taffeta petticoat, and a china silk blouse would do for traveling, too, Joyce."

"And a pink muslin for dress, with black lace appliqué around the yoke. I saw a model at Stronach's—"

Milly, on the front seat alone, was looking steadily toward center field. . . . Do you see me, Calvin?

Calvin saw her. . . . Are you looking at me, Milly? Stay till the game's over, and I'll knock a home run. If you're just looking, I can do anything. Then after the game I'll pass by your carriage and take off my cap, I don't care who sees it. . . .

"Fow-eld out. Who-o-o-oo! Three out. Who-o-o-oo!"

"They must've eat chicken for dinner," Cousin Nath observed to Uncle Hen as the Cale Springs player was called out.

"Whings, at that, the way he tried to fly to first when Calvin done had him out in center field!"

"Knock her away, Calvin!"

"Hit it, boy!"

"Pitch it to him there!"

"Ball three." The pitcher wanted to argue with Cousin Sim about that one. Cousin Sim changed it to a strike. "Ball two, strike one."

Then Calvin knocked a home run. A home run was defined not by boundaries or distance, but by the player's ability to get home on a hit. The ball went clear to the woods.

"What's all the shouting over?" asked the Philadelphia aunt, looking out from the carriage, startled.

"It's a home run." Milly's gentle brown eyes looked dreamily toward the home plate, with a glint almost of maternal pride in them. "He had an offer from a league in Alabama."

"Who, pray?"

Milly flushed, but she answered steadily, "Calvin."

"The Fuller boy." Miss Joyce looked significantly at her companion and then called politely to her husband, "Mr. Pate, excuse me for interrupting, but—"

Cousin Nick left the Governor with Uncle Israel and

24

hurried to his wife, apologizing for the delay. The carriage left the grove briskly and was soon enveloped in a cloud of dust. A pair of wistful eyes peered through the dust to catch a last view of the ball game before the carriage turned into the river road.

Uncle Millard, who had slipped out of Confurnce, as soon as his name was called, to go to the siding for the Saturday box of fish, drove up and was soon surrounded by the men who had to make the important choice between trout and croakers for Saturday night suppers. From among his fish Uncle Millard took several pieces of ice and told Cousin Ashley to fix a bucket of ice water for the players.

"But don't stutter in it," he cautioned.

"A-a-all r-r-right. I-I-I w-w-won't."

"Victor's shirt-tail's out, Letha," the girls under the oaks called to Letha, so aloof in the top buggy with Julia. "You'll have to re-tail it."

Letha disdained a reply. She and Julia were making plans for the excursion. They did hope the Sunday school would vote in favor of the Morehead trip tomorrow.

Nannie Lou was improvising...

> *Here's to our baseball nine,*
> *How each at bat does shine,*
> *Swain in the pitcher's stand,*
> *Sees that Cale Springs is fanned;*
> *Garland behind the bat,*
> *Catches the balls so pat;*
> *Calvin—*

Nannie Lou hesitated. It seemed like bragging to praise your own brother. Still, Calvin—

"So-o-u-p, C-o-u-p, SOUP! SOUP!"

Calvin had knocked another home run.

25

IV

SUNDAY AFTERNOON Mr. Tom Smith drove his rockaway purposefully down the lane into Grandpa Pate's grove, tied his horse to the sycamore with a flourish, shook down his breeches leg, which had caught under his knee, and marched to the house. Grandpa, after a nap, was sitting on the front porch reading his Bible; Grandma, her hands folded in her lap, was listening to the promises of "many mansions" Grandpa read off with such confident assurance, the cadences of his voice soothing, pleasant on her tired old ears. The lusty cries of three sets of children had made an aged voice restful and easeful, like sweet oil in aching ears.

Aunt Lina sat listlessly on the bench by the window, planning a new way to make a dress for Nannie Lou. Trading in Raleigh the other week, she had picked up a remnant of pretty lawn that close cutting might get a dress out of for a child. Dele didn't have much time during the summer to sew, on account of the field work, and she couldn't get the girls' dresses to hang level anyway. Pink was becoming to Nannie Lou. Yonder came old Mr. Tom Smith. He was so tiresome. Father always had to lie down after he left.

"Good evenin'."

"Good evenin,' Mr. Smith. Come in."

"How are you all?"

"Just tole'able. How are you?"

"I'm well and hearty. How are you all?"

"Have you a seat. Hand him a palm-leaf, Lina."

"Much obliged. It is hot for the time o' year. You all well as common, I s'pose?"

"Yes. I have shortness of breath right bad at night, but I do along pretty good in the day. A man can't complain."

"What I used to tell Eveline. She had shortness of breath bad just before she died. A man can't complain, but it does leave him in a bad fix."

"I'm willin' to suffer shortness of breath, if the Lord wills—"

"I mean a man without a wife's in a bad fix."

"Yes." Grandpa looked at him suddenly. "Yes, he is."

"A man can't complain, but he don't hardly know which way to turn."

"No. No, he don't."

"Them that ain't been through it just don't know."

"I know."

Grandma looked quizzically at Aunt Lina. She knew some things, too.

"She's been gone a year now. She always told me she wanted me to get somebody to stay with me. Children needs a mother."

"Yes. Yes, they do."

Grandma moved restlessly in her rocker.

"A man can't complain, but a woman does make a sight o' difference in a house."

"Yes, a woman even lights the lamp different, and it burns better for her."

Presently Mr. Smith wanted Aunt Lina to play her guitar and sing some. She went at once into the shadowy parlor. This was escape. After a song or two she would slip on her hat and run across the branch to Dele's before anybody else came. Mechanically she picked out a chord; once she had touched the guitar lovingly.

"Come back to me, sweetheart, and love me as before;
Come back, back to me, sweetheart, and leave me never more.
In life's dull pathway, the sun no longer shines.
Come, love, and meet me, in the shadow of the pines."

She was not conscious of the words she sang, easing from one thing to another just to get through—

> *"Sweet bunch of daisies*
> *Fresh from the dew,*
> *Darlin' I love you,*
> *Will you be true?"*

"Sing 'Baggage Coach,' Miss Lina."
There stood old man Tom Smith in the door. Well—

> *"As the train sped onward,*
> *A husband sat in tears,*
> *Thinkin' of the happiness*
> *Of just a few short years.*
> *Baby's face brings mem'ries of*
> *A fondest hope that's dead,*
> *But baby's cry can't awaken her*
> *In the baggage coach ahead."*

Mr. Smith took a seat just inside the parlor door, crossing his leg. It wouldn't do to stop now and get in a talk with him. Maybe he'd go after one more. She didn't remember that he ever cared anything about music.

> *"While shot and shell were shriekin'*
> *Upon the battlefield,*
> *Our boys in blue were fightin'*
> *Their noble flag to shield.*
> *Came a cry from our brave captain,*
> *'Look, boys, the flag is down,*
> *Who'll volunteer to set it up again?'*
> *'I will,' a brave voice shouted,*
> *'I'll bring it back or die,'*
> *And plunged into the thickest of the fray.*
> *He saved the flag, but gave his young life*
> *All for his country's sake.*
> *They brought him back and softly heard him say:*
> *'Just break the news to Mother;*
> *She knows how dear I love her—'"*

Mr. Smith blew his nose so loud Aunt Lina was startled. She had momentarily forgotten him; her thoughts flashed back to 'our boys in blue,' to one boy in blue. She hurried into another chord.

"I wandered down by a little babblin' brook,
Its every ripple speaks of thee,
Then, too, the flowers drooped their heads
In sympathy with me, Marguerite—
If all the world were mine to give,
I'd proudly lay it at thy feet.
But oh, the thought you'll not be mine,
Will break my heart, Marguerite,
Mar- guer- ite!"

Mr. Smith moved the toe of his shoe up and down approvingly. "Bluebell," "Just As the Sun Went Down," "Dolly Gray," were concluded. How long was he aiming to sit there anyhow? Why didn't he go back on the porch? She'd sing herself out of breath before she'd get in a talk with him. Mercifully Babe Landers walked in, just as she was beginning to get hoarse. Babe was surprised to see Mr. Smith; she hadn't seen him pass her house! In a short while the Widow Pear walked in, very much surprised to see Mr. Smith, for she had not seen him pass!

When the kinfolks began to come in, Uncle Millard walked by the parlor door, paused, and entered.

"How are you, Millard?" asked Mr. Smith.

"Peart. How are you?"

"I stay about the same. A man can't complain. I do get lonesomer all the time. How are you?"

"I reckon I'm on the mend. I hope you're well."

"In body, yes. A man can't complain as long as he can eat three meals a day. But my mind does stay tore up about the children, all time scared they'll get sick or somethin'. You're well, I s'pose?"

"All except a little touch of smallpox that's come back on me. I've been itchin' the last few minutes. A man can't complain though—"

"No, a man— Smallpox? What did you say about smallpox?"

"I itch. If it ain't smallpox—"

"Smallpox?"

"Le'me show you."

But Mr. Tom Smith didn't wait to be shown. He had always been a little afraid of Uncle Millard's scars anyway. He tumbled out of his stool-chair and paused on the porch only long enough to grab his hat, not shaking down his breeches leg, which had caught under his knee. While he was opening the lane gate, Widow Landers called to him from the front porch to wait, let her ride if he didn't have a load.

"He'll have one when Babe Landers gets in," the Widow Pear snapped.

"And smallpox by bedtime!"

"You don't really think the itchin's a sign of anything, Mr. Millard?"

"No. Some folks just give you the itch."

Aunt Lina, who didn't laugh or cry at things, laughed then at Millard's foolishness.

V

IT WAS THE day of the excursion. The neighborhood turned out early in wagons, surreys, and top buggies. With loads of watermelons piled near the railroad to be shipped, Pate's Siding looked like a village market-place. Everybody, dressed in Sunday clothes, carried great boxes of food and fruit; a few mothers toted satchels. Uncle Israel was in charge of arrangements. He had engineered this trip to Morehead City through strenuous opposition. One faction had objected because the Sunday school had never been on an excursion before; another, because the ocean was dangerous; cost was mentioned; others spoke of train wrecks; Uncle Job thought it was too worldly.

The tickets were five dollars a family, whether the family was twelve or two, through Uncle Israel's maneuvering; he had chuckled a little when he left the head official's office, for the railroad company was bound to lose money at Pate's Siding. Aunt Puss and Uncle Hen with their six girls were the first to climb into the train.

"Why, you could see the pure trimmin's on their drawers," Aunt Sugar whispered behind her palm-leaf fan to Aunt Cynthy and Aunt Nettie.

"It's like skinnin' the cat, all right," they agreed, dreading their turn.

Aunt Sad and Miss Jennie, who had made a bargain to stay close together all day, backed away from the high steps.

Perrie, the preacher's boy, had gathered the cousins over behind a box-car, promising some fun from that angle. "Side-show, free!" he had whispered around. "Stack-poles, knittin' needles, splinters—yonder's two put on upside down."

Aunt Sugar spied the boys. "Come back here!" she screamed when Maud started to swing into the car.

"But Mama, they said 'all aboard.'"

"Let the men—and them boys—get on first!"

An appeal to Uncle Israel fixed it. The men and boys were ordered into the car first, then the girls, last the women, who refused to expose themselves before their daughters. Perrie and the cousins hurried through an adjoining car and jumped out the door to peep again from behind the box-car at the girls skinning the cat. The women were a pretty good circus, too, when the wind ballooned their skirts away from them like tents.

Miss Jennie, the last to get on, while trying to hold down her skirt dropped the shoe-box full of her funny little pies

31

and cakes. She and Aunt Sad, delayed by their attempts to blow some of the grit off the food, found the seats all taken; they stood meekly near the door without speaking for a mile or two. Then Uncle Wes made them take his seat. Missing Julia and Tiny, Aunt Puss sent Uncle Hen through the car to collect them.

"Puss is always losin' a youngun," Cousin Nath observed to Uncle Millard.

"Give her time, and she'll lose her mind," Uncle Millard dryly predicted. Years and years later she did, and had to be drawn out of the well in the lot. Uncle Millard began to review his experiences in the pesthouse in Raleigh.

Swains from the little towns strutted up and down the aisles, winking at the girls. "I love my wife, but oh you baby doll." ... "That one with the brown eyes is over pretty." ... "Yonder's the tootsie-wootsie I'd like to stroll through the shady lanes with." Soon the country boys began strolling the aisles, timidly at first. In cars where they were not known they were soon winking at the girls and snatching handkerchiefs from their laps; they thought they were acting rowdy like the town boys.

There was little chance for the girls, under the watchful eyes of mamas and papas. When the town fellows stumbled over parasols stuck out too far in aisles, there had to be a little talk for politeness' sake, in spite of parental vigilance. Unabashed, declaring his preference for the fair sex, Cousin Maggie's city beau sat with her all the way, those around him listening intently to his bits of information about the briny deep. Aunt Mary silently wondered if there were many fish in the ocean. Presently Julia, who was regarded as fast, slipped out with Letha into another car to speak to some girls they knew. Their beaux were waiting for them. Holding hands under Victor's hat, Julia and Victor courted the morning out, carefully watching the door against spies.

Milly's parents, scorning excursions, had yielded at last

32

to their daughter's tears and sent her along under the watch-care of the aunt from Philadelphia. Her eyes still swollen a little from weeping, Milly sat very still by the window with her guard. On the back seat, poignantly happy just to be in the car with her, sat Calvin. His eyes never left that little blue hat with the plaid band around it. It was not necessary to see her face; he knew it by heart—the gentle brown eyes with yellow flecks in them, the smooth olive skin, the sweet-est mouth on God's green earth. Oh, Milly....

Aunt Nettie told for the dozenth time about the raise her son Dwight's boss man had given him in the candy factory in Raleigh. Aunt Sugar, as usual, discussed last year's teacher and wondered who would board this year's. She supposed it would fall on her again. She did hope the new teacher wouldn't take two pieces of fry on her plate at one time. It had been whispered around that maybe Airy Pate wanted to board the teacher this fall. Since that new carriage, she thought the preacher and the teacher all ought to go to her.

Aunt Lina helped her married sisters with their babies, while pantries and gardens were discussed all around. Black-berry, huckleberry, apple, and plum preserves; watermelon pickle, cucumbers in brine; no variation in content and receipt, only Miss Jennie, rather flushed in the telling, spoke of some apple pickle she had tried by a receipt in The Farmer. A smile went around. Bound by routine and habit, they let new country pass swiftly by the windows and clung to the known. Dele looked often at Milly.

Pointedly Uncle Israel called attention to counties and towns through which they were passing; the differences in crops, soil, cultivation, the trucking section were cited; but the Pate's Siding men only glanced indifferently out the window and returned to their own cantaloupes, cotton, corn, and tobacco. Cousin Nath asked Uncle Wes how was his cat crop. People were always dropping cats on Uncle Wes.

Fascinated by the train luxuries, the little boys spent the

morning turning spigots of water-coolers, filling up with ice water, and going to the men's room. Between drinks, Fatty ate bananas and apples. The little girls thought every river they crossed was the ocean, and at New Bern, where the Neuse is impressive, they grew so excited that they flew to their mamas, who were excited too. Uncle Israel took this occasion to educate his kin by reminding them that big oaks from little acorns grow: this was the same Neuse River that the boys went shadding in back home. The kin did not believe a word of it; they cringed away from the train windows toward the aisles and grew very quiet till the bridge was crossed.

At the outset of the trip, Nannie Lou communed with Nature from her window, but the new scenes checked the literary impulse. The child was almost pretty today, Dele noticed, her brown eyes shining, her cheeks flushed, her face alive.

Not once was Milly free of the guard. Sharp eyes from Philadelphia followed her when at last she walked down the aisle speaking with different groups. Never quite reaching the back of the car, she drew near enough to smile at Calvin. Then he started walking the aisle, pausing always near where Milly happened to be. Once he touched her arm in passing.

"Excuse me."

"Certainly."

His heart leaped. They had spoken again. It was still only morning.

Arrived at Morehead, families ate their lunches while Uncle Israel prepared for them to cross the sound. Not a woman could be persuaded to get into the motor launches and sailboats to ride on that ocean. It took a lot of effort before the fathers would consent to take the children to see the Atlantic, and Uncle Israel was bound the ocean should be witnessed. With a toss of her head, the aunt from Philadelphia stepped into a launch about filled and ready to motor across the sound. Milly suddenly decided in favor of sails. So it chanced that Calvin and Milly crossed the sound together.

Noting that the side on which she sat dropped down level with the water, Nannie Lou quickly crossed to the higher side, followed by others who believed their weight was unbalancing the boat. Seeing one side still near the water level, they knew the boat must sink before that expanse of water could be crossed. Restrained terror froze a boat-load of excursionists into grim silence.

... Dear Father, let us not turn over in the water. Please, dear Father. Forgive me for loving my paper-dolls. Only save us, and I will serve only Thee. I have sinned. Please forgive me for kicking cats. Oh, dear Father, please save us, for Thou art good and all-powerful, all-merciful and mighty....
Nannie Lou in a tight place always tried flattery.

Others were saying it their way. John repented of the "confounds" in yesterday's tobacco field, thought of Daisy and Nellie safe in their lot at home, their joyful whicker at his return—if he returned.... Grant it, Almighty God....
The stolid patience of the mules, the little runt, the fat shoats, Nero.... A man was a fool to leave home— Oh, God Almighty, watch out!

Calvin asked for nothing. He had everything. He did not know the boat dipped heavily on one side. He saw only Milly's little brown hand trailing in the water.

Safely across at last, the excursionists wandered over the sand, collected shells as Uncle Israel told them to do, watched with shocked interest the bathing suits—Uncle Job began to shape up some remarks on worldliness for next Sunday—wondered at the ocean, not quite believing it. Milly and Calvin strayed off unobserved. They sat on the white sand. Philadelphia was far away; heaven, very near—a heaven of blue water and glistening sand and a little angel with a blue hat on her head. Calvin's heart ached with happiness. Tomorrow this time they would be apart. Oh, Milly....

"The water looks green."

"Yes, it does."

They stared at the waves coming in, crying to each other without a voice. The tenseness of a chaste passion quivered between them. Gaiety, laughter, flippancy, wisdom, balance —youth and age—passed along. These two were lost in a world where youth is too young and too old.

"Isn't the sand white?"

"It hurts your eyes it's so white."

Milly gathered a handful of glistening sand and let it trickle through her little brown fingers.

> *"Little drops of water,*
> *Little grains of sand—"*

She started lightly, but subtle tragedy entered her tone.... Oh, Calvin, do you remember? Under the sweet gum ...

> *"Make the mighty ocean*
> *And the pleasant land."*

They smiled. Their eyes were too sad and desperate to sustain the smile.

...Oh, Milly, you're the sweetest thing God ever made.

...Calvin, I'll never love anybody but you. They'll never make me love anybody but you.

"I wish we could see over that hill." Her eyes turned wistfully toward the ocean.

"Le's run climb it."

"The waves would bring us back."

If only the waves wouldn't bring them back and they might sail over that hill far from everything, everybody, just the two of them so that they would be together tomorrow, the next day, forever. The first day he would just look at her; she'd laugh and he'd laugh because tomorrow they wouldn't be apart. The blue water brought startlingly before him the blue vapor above Neuse River and her father's big white house near by, so aloof, so shut to him. Tomorrow this time he would be driving old Nellie along the tobacco rows, the hot sun burning through his blue chambray, his fingers stained and sticky, the sweat pouring along his body—and miles away the blue haze, tantalizing reminder of their apartness.

The afternoon was passing.

In her handkerchief she had tied three shells. One she handed to him; it was pink and gray.

"Keep it. It says things."

"What does it say?"

She looked down, making little graves in the sand.

"What does it say?"

"Oh, a lot."

"Name one thing." He was whispering.

"First you would put it to your ear and listen. Then—"

"Then?" If he could ease his heart with words....

"Oh, Calvin."

"Tell me."

"It might sound like the roar of the ocean at first, but listen close and it will say—"

"Milly, what on earth are you thinking about?" There was no brotherly love in the eyes of the aunt from Philadelphia, as she examined Calvin. "I've looked the beach over for you. Come on!"

"This is such a nice spot. Couldn't I sit—"

"No, you couldn't. Look yonder at that cloud." They looked.

"The boats are ready to cross, and in two minutes we'll be left. Come along."

A heavy roll of thunder emphasized her words.

"It's thunderin'!" Calvin was surprised at the sharp flash of lightning that tore from the black bank of clouds.

37

"I should say it is, and has been a half hour. Hurry!"

There were no more words. Thus in the twinkling of an eye the world ended. Milly was snatched into a launch which motored away from Calvin, standing forlornly in the sand. John led him like a little boy to the sailboat. Among the excursionists fast filling the boat, there was subdued terror. Many were in a state of incoherent prayer. When the rain started to fall Nannie Lou began rather wearily to tell Him how good He was, how merciful, how mighty—wondering subconsciously what it would take to satisfy Him. A terrific crash of thunder reproved her. She made a vow, covenanting with Him to join the church this coming August meeting or He would be welcome to strike her dead....Please dear Father, save us....One by one she began to drop, placatingly, the pretty little shells, so laboriously gathered from the sand, over the side of the boat into the water....Take all, take my life and let it be consecrated Lord to Thee....

The landing was prosaic enough; but the reunion gave the women, who watched from the wharf in an agony of anxiety, an idea of what it must be to be There. Little was said, but wives walked closer to their husbands along the gangplank to safety—and the husbands let them.

That ride across the sound was the source of many a tale in years to come.—"Water on every side, and fallin' from above. The cap'n shook his head when the waves washed over the side into the bottom of the boat ankle-deep." In time it was knee-deep.

The excursionists settled wearily into their seats, and the train at length pulled out of Morehead City. Aunt Mary had found some good fishing ground during the day, if ever she should get back down here. Aunt Puss had lost the knee-baby and raised right smart excitement. Miss Charity had had a violent sick headache all day. Miss Jennie and Aunt Sad hadn't seen anything special. Aunt Sugar had seen A-Plenty and was whispering aloud the worst of it. Uncle Millard

38

observed to Cousin Nath that Sugar's mouth looked like it was full of nest-eggs, and Cousin Nath told Uncle Millard he dared him to ask her if she had a foul taste in her mouth. John soon discovered he was bound to have a chew of tobacco, though there was no place to spit, with the rain pouring in the window he raised experimentally. Uncle Wes pushed a cuspidor toward him.

For a while the lustier youth paraded the aisles, winked at the girls, sang snatches of "The Good Old Summer Time" and "Coon, Coon, Coon." Uncle Job stopped that and was about to make some remarks about this being a Sunday school excursion, when Uncle Israel tactfully suggested that singing might wake the babies sure enough.

The odor of over-ripe bananas and cantaloupes, of tired wet bodies, sour babies, train smoke, and disinfectant stayed in Sunday clothes for days—Cousin Nath at church the next Sunday said, "Umph! Smells like Morehead in here"—Babies cried, were fed. Men laid their heads on the hot velvet seats and snored. Women, cramped and crowded, arranged what comfort they could for the little ones. Cousin Maggie's beau from the city talked most of the way, as lively as ever, naming the five oceans, the continents, and declaring three fourths of the earth was water. Uncle Millard expressed surprise and doubt, baiting the young clerk, for Uncle Millard was well-read; he had been in the pesthouse and in Norfolk, where there was water, and he took two papers.

The storm followed the train and raged increasingly as it approached Pate's Siding. Above the sound of the locomotive there was the dull roar of thunder; the lightning tore the opaque blackness outside. As the train stopped, a cloud opened. Families, unloaded to the mercy of the elements, were separated in the dark confusion. Uncle Israel's voice could be heard in the lull of the thunder: "Everybody hunt first shelter—Ishmael's, Argo's." These two negroes lived near the railroad, and thither the excursionists ran.

A few pressed on farther to Aunt Emmie's and broke into the house through an unfastened window, Aunt Emmie's folks having stopped at Ishmael's. Among these were the aunt from Philadelphia and Milly, who were given the parlor bed because it was the nicest, with its tufted counterpane and its red peacock pillow-shams. Aunt Sugar, who took the job of hostess on herself, piled the little girls in Aunt Emmie's room, where from the mantel little Essie—dead these two years—looked pale and placid in her coffin below a crown of cape jessamines from Dele's bush and a cross of roses. Aunt Delight in her stiff taffeta, which folks claimed could be heard rustling through the halls when the house was still, eyed the little girls from her easel in the corner. Not many steps from this very room was the graveyard, grown over with sassafras bushes and grape vines, where before Nannie Lou was born Aunt Delight had been put—and had not stayed. Ghostly footsteps through the front hall, pausing at the door, passing up the stairs, had been heard by some of the most reliable folks in the neighborhood. Aunt Emmie heard it frequently in the daytime as well as at night; it was company for her, she said.

Nannie Lou was the first to hear it—footsteps in the front hall, faint, but unmistakable, tipping, tipping. The little girls lay breathless, smothered under the quilt with which they covered their heads. Later when they came out for breath there were the steps again, pausing before their very door. Then silence.

When Calvin followed the crowd to Ishmael's, his eyes sought eagerly among the faces for one face. She was not there. Slipping out unnoticed, he ran through the wind and rain to Argo's. There the excursionists were huddled together on benches, boxes, chairs; some were standing, as Argo's seating capacity was pitifully limited. Calvin's restless eyes sought for one face. Escaping unobserved, he dashed through the downpour to Aunt Emmie's. There was no special purpose in his search; he yearned to be under the roof that sheltered her. Everything was quiet when he entered the front hall. Tipping, tipping, he observed that all the doors were closed. He sat in the dimly lighted front hall. Suddenly his eyes fell on a crumpled white object lying near the parlor door. She had taken the pink shell out of that handkerchief. He smoothed and laid it away in his pocket with the shell.

Then She was in the parlor. Drenched to the skin by the cool rain, he lay in warmth at the parlor door and slept a little. He could not know that a carriage with its negro driver had borne Milly away in the storm before the bed inside had been touched by her sweet weight. The parlor was empty all through the night.

VI

Two days after the excursion Cousin Sell arrived in the neighborhood. Aunt Nettie had warned the kinfolks on the train Tuesday that they just as well look out for him; he had put up on her in Raleigh long enough, and she had already told him straight out to come to the country for a while, the first passing! Uncle Fonnie was the first passing; on Thursday he took a load of cantaloupes to Raleigh; and Cousin Sell, who after missing supper and breakfast at Aunt Nettie's was hanging around the market in the hope of catching a ride to the country, climbed quickly into the wagon. He looked out of place on the wagon seat amid country produce, for Cousin Sell had an air of the stock market about him for all his worn clothes and empty pockets and homelessness. A gold watch and chain, the perennial white shirts, intimate talk about the steel outlook and trade treaties with Japan, about the families of the President and the Governor, about travel and train schedules and hotel accommodations and foods with strange names, were bound to make an impression.

After all, Cousin Sell was good company; his first appearance in the neighborhood always occasioned a little stir of excitement, particularly among the children, who could listen by the hour to his stories of the fascinating places he apparently had visited—of Norfolk, which was reached by a big ship just like on the ocean, where sailor boys walked the streets in their blue uniforms in peace times as well as war, where the eating places served lobster and oysters on the shell and deviled crab just like in novels; of Asheville, where the mountains were so high that trains in the valley looked like toys and people like dolls; of Roanoke Island, where Virginia Dare in the history book was born and her gravestone stood; of Morehead City, where the Atlantic—but Cousin Sell couldn't tell them anything about Morehead now, for, just think, they had been there and had seen the pure ocean!

Neighborhood men listened with patient interest to Cousin Sell's logic about rich people in cities, who bought cotton on the board, one hundred bales as quick as one—gambling, Uncle Job called it, and a tool of the Bad Boy—and who invested in Bethlehem steel and made fortunes by closing out when she was two points up; about Congress and senators who got the trade treaties through and declared war and lived a high life up there in Washington with their butlers and bodyguards and wine and society women, on the people's tax money, too.

Less patient were the women who had to cook for Cousin Sell—he wanted hot suppers on account of his dyspepsia—clean up his room, wash his other white shirt, draw fresh water for him, sweep out his dirt, sit in the straight chair while Cousin Sell rocked, hear his advice on how to cook, watch him look askance at their oven-baked corn pones as he suggested salt and eggs for their corn bread, and beef sometimes in place of so much hog meat, and a variety of vegetables instead of the inevitable boiled cabbage and potatoes and beets. They bore with him for a few days because their

42

husbands urged patience; after all, what he didn't eat the pigs would, and there was plenty for Cousin Sell and the pigs too. But the women had their own sly ways of moving Cousin Sell on somewhere else. Taking his other shirt under his arm, he then rocked on another porch awhile, waited for other women to draw him fresh water, looked askance at other tables of boiled cabbage and potatoes and baked corn bread. If he stayed too long, the women were not above serving the dishes that Cousin Sell despised and hiding the fried chicken and the pies in the safe, so that their families could go in between meals and help themselves while the guest belched the unrelished food as he sat in the rocking chair on the front porch.

Aunt Puss tried this once when Ca'line was staying with her. Ca'line, coming in at twelve o'clock from the field where she had been grassing cotton without stopping even for a drink of water, was shown the peach pies and the chicken stew in the safe, which the family could have after Cousin Sell left the table. Uncle Hen was working at Uncle Millard's that day; so when Cousin Sell sat down to the table of women folks he glanced toward Ca'line and jocularly called on her to say grace, knowing she didn't know one and he did. "Thank the Lord for dinner, and we got it hid," she rattled off. Next morning Cousin Sell tucked his other shirt under his arm and went to Dele's.

When Aunt Emmie about supper time on Thursday after the excursion saw Cousin Sell climb out of the wagon with Uncle Fonnie, she hurriedly made a fire in the kitchen stove to scramble a few eggs, fry a piece of shoulder, and make hot biscuits to help out the cold vegetables that were to do for their supper. She was not glad or sorry to see Cousin Sell; it made little difference to her when he came or went, only he did eat a lot of butter, and she had a use for her butter money. It counted up right slow selling just what she could get to town by first one and then the other. If the two pounds she sent to market today brought twenty-five cents, that would be another half dollar. Two pounds next week would add still another half dollar to the little heap of nickels and dimes in the sideboard drawer. If Cousin Sell stayed a week, though, it would take one of the pounds or more, for he wanted butter three times a day, even with corn bread at dinner. It couldn't be helped.

"Your butter's nice, Cousin Emmie," he told her at supper. "In the city you don't know whether you're eating cotton seed oil or—"

"What?" Uncle Fonnie looked up from his cold vegetables.

"Why, yes, Fonnie; they make butter out of cotton seed now and—"

"For folks? I thought cotton seed was for cows."

"They call it margarine, and it passes. After it's colored up I bet you'd think 'twas butter."

"No siree. They wouldn't fool me with no cotton seed hulls or oil. The cow is good enough for me."

"Well of course I like country butter better, if I know where it comes from. Now this is nice butter." He cut a generous slab from the molded sheaf of wheat and inserted it in a hot biscuit. "But not all country butter is nice."

Aunt Emmie knew just by the way he buttered another biscuit that he was with them no telling, and she would never be able to get rid of him by hurting his feelings or making him mad as did some of the women.

"This red gravy's nice too, Cousin Emmie. They make a milk gravy up in the West you ought to try sometime. Brown your flour and pour in rich cream or milk—"

"I've never learned how to fix up nothin' fancy—just plain cookin'."

"Oh, well, country cooking's all right. Pass the butter, Cousin Emmie. These little thin pats of butter they dish you out in the city don't hardly grease the roof of your

44

mouth. More butter and less style suits me. By the way, Fonnie, did you know steel shot up last week?"

"Shot what?"

"Why, it jumped up two points at the close one day. If you had five hundred shares you'd be in ten thousand dollars. A thousand shares—figure it up."

In the comfortable rocker on the front porch, Cousin Sell continued estimating potential gains on the stock market and debating whether it would be wise to turn loose for twenty thousand dollars on a bullish market. Fed well, buttered, contented in the serene atmosphere of this country home— Cousin Sell sensed antagonism even while too broad-minded to notice it—he mentally lengthened his stay, oh indefinitely. He had never spent a night with Cousin Fonnie and Cousin Emmie before; why, he couldn't quite— Oh, yes, it came to him now; there had always been sickness here when he was in the neighborhood, and the other cousins wouldn't let him put up on Cousin Emmie, as they called it. Years ago there had been the old consumptive woman, Aunt Delight, and later the little girl whose death had almost cost Cousin Emmie her mind. Yes, it came back to him now. These people were lonesome without their little girl; they would welcome his companionship; it was more satisfactory to have fixed headquarters too, with meals—oh, yes, out among the country kinfolks, but a bed he could call his own when night came. He was settled for the summer. Cousin Emmie made nice butter; it wasn't as good quite as Cousin Dele's, but superior to the puffy looking pats that Cousin Puss always set before him. He paused in his discussion of profit and loss when he heard the gate in the back yard creak on its hinges and footsteps approach along the walk toward the back door.

"Somebody has already heard I'm in the neighborhood," he thought, his heart warming to the approaching welcome; of course he could spend a night out now and then if they insisted. There were steps on the back porch now. It might be Cousin Millard; he always seemed to enjoy talking about the stock market and the government. Why didn't he knock?

"Emmie, if Cousin Sell's ready, le's go to bed. I'm gettin' sleepy. I started to town at three o'clock this mornin', Cousin Sell, so you know—"

"Somebody's on the back porch."

"No, I reckon not."

"Yes, they are; I heard the back gate click and somebody walking—"

" 'Twa'n't nothin'."

"But Cousin Fonnie, I heard steps out there. I wasn't dreaming. Suppose you go see—"

" 'Twa'n't nothin'. Emmie'll fix your bed—"

Cousin Sell left his rocker and walked around the house to see for himself. The porch and yard were empty.

"Well, I certainly thought— I still think—"

"Right up them steps. Emmie'll show you. Hope you sleep good."

The house was built with one story and a jump which was reached by a narrow stairway. Cousin Sell examined his room and liked it; it was cool and quiet—there were so many noisy children at all the other houses in the neighborhood— and the bed looked soft and inviting. He undressed and knelt at the bed to say his prayers. It added to his well-buttered feeling to kneel, unless he was too outdone with Providence and the kinfolks. It had been several nights since he had knelt at Cousin Nettie's. Cousin Emmie might be Cousin Nettie's sister, but she would never tell him the supper was all gone or there was no breakfast for him. He thanked Providence for that and extinguished his light. After pushing back the curtains, he stood for a few minutes at the window to cool off. His eyes turned to the barn, where the cow that gave the nice butter was peacefully resting in her humble stall; to the garden, where unmistakable cabbage and onions and potatoes row on row foreshadowed coming dinners;

46

across the field to the clump of bushes that marked the graveyard, shrouded now in moonlight. Cousin Sell turned quickly from the window, climbed into the middle of the feather bed, and was soon asleep.

He awoke startled some time later, instinctively listening tensely. He could not remember having heard anything, nor could he recall any fragment of dream that might have aroused him. Yet he was certain there had been some disturbing sound. The silence only intensified the certainty, so definitely did it have the quality of a pause. While his ears were still strained at attention, there was the sound of steps in the hall below, then on the stairs, slow cautious steps that seemed not to be getting anywhere, only endlessly climbing.

"Rats." Cousin Sell assured himself and tried to relax into his feathers. But he soon found himself listening again. That was certainly like a woman's walking, in low-quarter shoes, an old woman. Rats could raise a lot of fuss in the dark. Of course it was rats. The steps, more definite and measured, were in the hall upstairs, approaching his door. Cousin Sell sat up in bed waiting. No, that was not rats; somebody was walking down the hall, pausing now at his door.

"Cousin Emmie?" There was no answer. He swallowed and called a little louder. "Is that you, Cousin Emmie?"

Then panic rushed over him as he remembered that the door was unlatched and that there were no matches or weapons at hand against burglars. His first night in the country to be faced with— A call downstairs might precipitate a desperate move on the part of the intruder in the hall outside. A decision had to be made. He could not lie here and wait to be broken in upon; he certainly could not sleep any more with somebody prowling around in the house. With the blood pounding at his temples in his effort to ease soundlessly out of bed, he crept toward the door and found the latch. He snapped it shut and stood wondering what would happen next. Whoever was outside knew now that he was awake, that he was up, with only a thin door separating them. All was quiet; his ears ached with the strain: not a sound from beyond the door. At the continued silence his reason told him that the footsteps were a trick of his imagination; all old houses have strange noises at night that in the day-time pass unnoticed—the creaking of a board, the shrinking of timber, rats, the wind blowing loose shingles. There was one match left in his pocket; he lighted the lamp and deliberately, challengingly walked around in the room, making quite a bit of fuss himself; he moved a chair across the floor, the table away from the wall. Silence answered his challenge.

Well, he would just end it. Lamp in hand, he unlatched and opened the door. The hall was empty. Nothing was disturbed. The old chest piled high with quilts, the broken spinning wheel in the corner, the little high-chair were just where he had observed them as he came up the stairs at bed-time. It was well that he had not called to those downstairs, for Cousin Millard and Cousin Hen would have a great logic going all over the neighborhood about his getting scared his first night away from town.

It was one o'clock, five hours still to sleep unless Cousin Emmie got him up before light to eat breakfast like the rest of the neighborhood. That was good-tasted butter on the supper table; he liked his butter molded, too. Latching the door and blowing out the light, he rolled over into the feathers, determined not to notice any more noises. He was about to persuade himself back into sleep when his ear again picked up the sound of walking on the stairs. A board shrinking; he would ignore it. City noise didn't bother him at all. After all, the country was a pretty dull place, so still and quiet; the walking continued. At Cousin Nettie's and Dwight's there was always somebody coming in, the boarders kept interesting talk going, and there were policemen about. Of course the table fare was right dull at times; country folks did have plenty to eat. Fonnie had told him at the market today, yesterday now, that he was looking right ga'nt, and no wonder the way Cousin Nettie had cut him down on vittles. Cousin Emmie and Cousin Fonnie were right good folks, dull of course, but he would keep them company till— That was not a board shrinking. It might be a loose shingle or rats, though. That smart-aleck boarder knew when he joined him on the porch that he had gone without his supper —kept telling about filet of trout with butter sauce and sweet potato souffle and deviled crab and— That was not a loose shingle. Just as well face it. It was footsteps, somebody walking outside his door. No use to deny it any longer. No rat in the world could make that sound, and no timber, however old the house. The steps were—inside the room. The door had not opened; he knew that. It had not opened; yet there it was—definite walking on the floor of this room. The steps appeared to be advancing toward the window across the room. Without stirring, for he seemed suddenly helpless to move or to speak, he tried to peer through the dimness of the room to discover What was walking. Then the steps seemed to turn toward his bed, and there was the swish of silk skirts as plain as daylight. Somebody sat on the side of his bed.

He did not know how he got through the door or downstairs, and he was not conscious of his incoherent cries for help until Uncle Fonnie joined him in the hall downstairs and wanted to know what in the world ailed him. Cousin Sell told his story, urging Uncle Fonnie to get a lamp and gun and go after whoever it was upstairs in his room. By that time Aunt Emmie had thrown on a dress over her nightgown and had lighted a lamp. To humor Cousin Sell they went upstairs and searched everywhere; there was no trace of any intrusion; nobody had sat on the side of the feather bed. If he thought he had heard the swish of silk skirts—

"But I know somebody was in this room." Cousin Sell stooped to look under the bed.

" 'Twa'n't nothin'."

"But it was. I heard 'em walking up the stairs, then in the hall, then in this room, then they sat on the side of this bed—" Cousin Sell glared at his dull cousins.

"Just steps," Aunt Emmie observed quietly.

"As plain as mine and yours."

"Go on back to sleep and don't worry no more."

"Go to sleep with somebody prowling round in the house?"

"It wasn't anything to hurt you."

"I wouldn't stay in this room another hour—"

"One room's as good as another—in this house."

"If you had heard what I heard—"

"We hear—walkin', if that's all, any time."

"You mean—?"

"Day or night. You hear the back gate click and then steps—"

"And you've never found—anything?"

"We've never seen a thing."

"How you could go to sleep—"

"It's nothin' to hurt nobody. We don't notice it."

"It's company," Aunt Emmie said as she and Uncle Fonnie started down the stairs.

Cousin Sell sat in the hall outside their door the rest of the night, refusing to let them blow out the light. Next morning with his shirt tucked under his arm, he went to spend some time with his Cousin Dele and Cousin John.

VII

UNCLE MILLARD, DROPPING his plow handles, left his mule to graze on wild strawberry vines and sheep grass that covered the ditch bank and walked through the apple orchard toward the Fuller grove. He stopped to pick up a handful of June apples, pocketing a big red one to take home at dinner time to Aunt Cynthy. At the corner of the house he paused, on his way to the bee gums, when he saw that Dele's green porch rocker was occupied. Cousin Sell, arriving early, had been received casually with scant attention, since it was the day set to rob the bees and everybody was hurrying to finish the regular morning work. John had howdied him and said go in. After greeting the women in the kitchen, where ham was already boiling in the dinner pot, and stopping at the water shelf for a fresh drink, Cousin Sell had seated himself contentedly in the shady corner of the porch, pulled his hat over his eyes, and yielded to the overpowering drowsiness that had dogged him since last night's wake.

Uncle Millard recognized the sleeper and chuckled to himself. "Havin' a nap in the broad open daytime?"

Cousin Sell woke with a nervous start. The sunshine reassured him, and he arose to shake hands. "How are you, Cousin Millard?"

"Well as common. How long you been in the neighborhood?"

"Just got here. That is, I come from Raleigh with Fonnie Bundy yesterday and spent the night there."

"Spent the night with Emmie and Fonnie, did you?"

Cousin Sell was alert to the twinkle in Uncle Millard's eye and spoke guardedly. "Yes, I did."

"Must o' left there early this mornin'."

"Not early the way you country folks get up. How's your garden this time?"

"Cabbage and potatoes and beets a plenty. You'll be around to see us one night I reckon?"

"Yes. After I stay some with Cousin Dele and Cousin John I'll visit you and Cousin Cynthy a while."

"A while? I thought you was just makin' it one night around."

"No. I'll be in the neighborhood some little time before I visit my kinfolks in Northampton."

"You stayed just one night at Emmie's. Goin' back there tonight I reckon."

"No." Cousin Sell spoke shortly.

"Didn't you sleep good?"

Cousin Sell shifted his chair farther in the shade and spoke of the fluctuations in the stock market.

"You're nappin' mighty early in the mornin'. The ha'nts must have rousted you at Emmie's last night."

"Somebody walked all night up and down stairs." His cards were on the table. Uncle Millard would hear about it anyway.

"So they run you away." Uncle Millard laughed dryly. "Well, you can hear walkin' at my house too, day or night."

"I never heard nothing at your house I couldn't make out. Cousin Cynthy makes the best peach preserves I ever tasted. I'll say it behind her back or to her face."

This time Uncle Millard laughed heartily. "All right, Sell. Come on and help us peach it any time you get ready, if you don't mind footsteps all over the house all hours."

John Fuller came across the front yard on his way to the bee gums at the edge of the grove. Mosquito netting fell from his broad-brimmed straw hat over his shoulders like a veil; his hands were covered with coarse home-knit white gloves, and his pants were carefully tucked into his shoe tops. Uncle Wes, dressed in his usual everyday clothes with no protecting net, gloves, or coat, followed, carrying a knife and dishpan. Dele hurried across the grove with lard stands and smokers, rolls of rags made from old shirts, tied around with strings and smeared lightly at one end with tar so that when lighted they would smolder and produce a thick pungent odor.

It was Letha's week to clean up. Having made all the beds, spread sheets on the company mattress for Cousin Sell, swept the floors, clayed the hearth, set a vase of pink roses on the hall table, Letha had the rest of the morning to sew on the new flowered lawn that she would save to wear the first Sunday in August. Around the flounces of the skirt she carefully tacked black velvet ribbon, glancing out the window toward the bee gums now and then, preoccupied with pleasant fancies. Victor had wanted to hold her hand on the train; he had placed his hand between them on the red plush seat, covering it with his straw hat and whispering urgently, "Le's play hands." Boys did that to try girls, and no boy should ever say Letha Fuller was fast! But once she had let Victor's arm touch hers several minutes before she moved to the end of the seat: her arm had tingled for hours afterwards, and something like a blush had gone all through her. Victor had begged her to let him kiss her when they got off at the siding; they would hurry off the train ahead of everybody, there were box-cars—he would manage if she just would. She had told him she just couldn't; she wished she could, but she just couldn't, she really couldn't. He was going to anyway, he said, and there had been the wondering breathless excitement of waiting. But the storm had prevented the stolen kiss; the lightning was too terrifying and too revealing, and Aunt Sugar was too close. It was wrong to kiss a boy anyway; she would never be able to look Mama in the face again. If she had known Victor was going to take her handkerchief she'd have carried the pretty drawn-work one on the excursion. Victor might not be at church any more till the first Sunday in August, but they'd manage to have a few words together at the well between services and plan when they'd meet again. He promised to send her a card next week. This flowered lawn had made up pretty. She held its sheerness over the new corset-cover with the lace and insertion around the neck and arm-holes; yes, it did show through pleasingly. If Victor sat just behind her in church he would get the effect. Victor was a close observer; sometimes his eyes lingering on her bare throat and on the ribbon in her corset-cover beading made her feel red all over. Victor

53

knew a lot about girls; he was always trying to feel some-body's pulse; Julia said boys did that to find out if girls had Certain Times on them. On the train he had whispered, "There goes an East Raleigh woman," though the woman had looked like anybody else, unless her cheeks were pinker and there was more fruit on her sailor hat. Maybe they would sit on the same bench at August meeting and sing out of the same book. . . .

> *"I've wandered far away from God,*
> *Lord, I'm coming home;*
> *The paths of sin too long I've trod,*
> *Lord, I'm coming home."*

That had a pretty alto; some pieces didn't. Victor had never heard her try to sing alto. A bee buzzed into the upstairs window, hovering momentarily over the flowered lawn, and out again to real flowers.

Kate paused at her churning to taste a crumb of butter from the dasher. It had come, ready now to be washed and salted. A cake of fresh rich butter melted between hot bis-cuits, spread with warm white honeycomb oozing yellow honey, was good enough supper for anybody, and if Cousin Sell was looking for fried meat tonight— She would gather her butter on the dasher, wash the churn things, and run yonder to see how nice the honey turned out this year before going into the garden for the vegetables for dinner. She wished it was her cook-week all the time. Tomorrow she'd try a marble cake for Sunday like the one Aunt Airy had on the excursion. It had been almost like an Easter picnic down yonder at Morehead City, except that there had been a lot more water than at Uncle Job's pond; Miss Jennie even car-ried her funny little pies and cakes along. A lot of water was all right to go to see, but vittles tasted just as good at Whiteoak or Uncle Job's pond as at the ocean. The nautical note, however, crept unconsciously into her usual Gospel Hymn singing over the churn dasher....

> "*Oh, she never returned, oh she never returned,*
> *Her fate 'tis yet unlearned;*
> *But for years and years there are fond ones watching*
> *For the ship that never returned.*
> *Oh, she never returned ...*"

Immediately after breakfast Calvin and Nannie Lou had left the house to finish worming the dunghill tobacco. One job had been as another to Calvin since the excursion. The field of green tobacco undulating lightly in the morning breeze, the gray soil underfoot, the wood dove's plaintive call were green ocean waves, glistening sand and pink sea-shells, and Milly's voice in his ear. It was unreal like dreams or stories in books; yet just three days ago they had sat in the sand side by side, close enough for him to see the soft brown lights in her eyes, those little freckles over her nose, the sweetest mouth God ever made. She had really given him a pink shell—it was at the house under his pillow—and said it would tell him things. Just three days ago they had really looked at the blue hills of water and shared the impulse to run away from the glaring sand and people and get lost together out there beyond those waves and never never come back. He wouldn't let anything hurt her. She was so little and sweet. He pulled the head off a fat green worm at the end of a row and stood erect to ease the catch in his side. His eyes turned instinctively toward Neuse River miles away, marked faintly now by a grayish haze above the trees. It drew him this morning like the restless ocean waves. She was there. What if he should leave everything and go straight toward that blue haze and Milly? What was to keep him away from her when he loved her so hard he would rather die than even one of her little brown fingers be hurt? ... That blue fog kept them apart, the big white house, their fine carriage horses, his sweaty faded shirt, hands sticky and gummed and stained with tobacco, these green worms. A sudden pain stabbed his left side.

Nannie Lou was hurrying out her row. There were only two more apiece, and Calvin would help her finish. She just had to get to the house by the time Uncle Wes came to rob the bees. Warm honey right out of the gum was the best of all, and there was always the chance that a bee might finally sting Uncle Wes. Cousin Sell would be full of stories, too. He always praised her poetry, and there were lots of new ones he hadn't read. The ocean made pretty poetry; there were still those stubborn lines to finish. . . .

> Glistening white sand along the shore,
> Stirred by yon waves forevermore,
> Blue sea, pink shells and foam. . . .

A line next ending with "free" or "knells" or "roam." She buried a big fat worm and trampled his grave to make sure he stirred no more. When nobody was in the field with her but Calvin, she always killed worms the nicer, if longer way. Letha would have told on her; Kate would have made fun, for she did not mind pulling worms' heads off any more than a man. She did hope Kate would stay out of worms till her cook-week was over and Mama was making biscuits again.

"What ails your side, Calvin?"

"Nothin'."

"You been holdin' it like it hurts."

Calvin helped her out the last row, and she turned quickly toward the house. He climbed over the fence into the pasture, and Nannie Lou saw him stop at the sweet gum thicket. She knew why, but she'd never tell. When were those initials carved on the sweet gum anyway, in Milly's handwriting? Cousin Nick and Miss Joyce used to let Milly visit around in the neighborhood Sunday afternoons when they thought she was still a child. Nannie Lou recalled that fall Sunday after dinner when they had all gone to ride pine saplings in the pasture and Calvin had fallen in the branch trying to reach a wild flower Milly thought was pretty. She remembered it especially because next day Calvin had a chill that went into pneumonia.

Nannie Lou jumped across the ditch, pausing to gather a cluster of sumac blooms to decorate for a wedding; one of her paper-doll family was going to get married after dinner today. Circling the lot fence, she saw Uncle Wes, without a sign of mosquito netting over his head, stooping over the bee gums. She hurried to the grove.

John smoked the bees from the top of the gums, while Uncle Wes cut the honeycomb from the sides and lifted the racks out into the lard stands, white combs packed with golden honey. In some of the gums the honey was as dark as blackberry jelly, but it tasted all right. A little bee bread was taken; this could be strained for medicine; honey and alum soothed many a sore throat in the winter time. As soon as a lard stand was filled, Dele rushed it away from the restless bees into the kitchen where Kate helped her sort and pack the honey into stone jars and store it in the pantry. Some of the choicest comb was put in dishes for Grandpa Pate, Aunt Cynthy, Miss Jennie, Miss Charity, and any other neighbors who might like a taste. The choicest bit of all was left in her own safe for Calvin, who had been a little puny since the excursion. Jessie's folks liked the dark kind best, and a big pan was set aside for them. Uncle Wes and Aunt Mary didn't eat honey, for all his helping with the robbing.

The bees from one of the untouched gums took today, of all times, to swarm. They circled around John's head threateningly and stung him on the hand when he removed his glove to taste some honey. Uncle Millard and the women folks beat tin pans, hoping to persuade the bees to pitch, while John prepared a new gum, rubbing it with beeswax and bruised peach leaves inside. Finally the bees pitched on a

57

damson limb, a compact dark cluster hanging like a bag from the tree. A table, covered with a sheet, was placed under the damson tree, and the new gum was lifted to the table. With a turkey wing John brushed the compact cluster from the limb upon the table, hoping they would approve the new home. They finally accepted it. Other bees were beginning to appear excited and disturbed, but Uncle Wes finished without getting stung.

Cousin Sell, deep in his interrupted nap, was aroused by the rustling of—was it taffeta skirts in his very ear? After a nervous start the sunshine was again reassuring, but there was still the rustling—it was a stinking bee in his hair! Without thinking, he crushed the hat tight on his head and immediately felt the smarting sting of the spiteful bee on his neck. Another insistent buzz to his right; two, three, heading his way. He slapped at them with his hat and hurried out of the rocker and the shady corner down the back porch steps and broke into a trot down the hot road.

"Ha'nts rousted you last night, and now the bees—" Uncle Millard called after him.

Cousin Sell kept trotting.

"The sun's shinin' too hot, Sell, for a city feller—"

"Dog-gone it, let it shine!"

"All right, if you say so." Uncle Millard chuckled and turned to Uncle Wes. "Wes, le's me and you get us some bee gums—or ha'nts one. Save rations."

Uncle Wes closed the top of the last gum and went back to his plowing. Dele prepared a mixture of vinegar and soda to put on Cousin Sell's bee stings.

VIII

ACCORDING TO SUNDAY bargains made down the railroad bank after Sunday school—the boys always laughed at Fatty, Cousin Sim's boy, who had to run down the railroad bank as soon as the last song was over and rarely got there quite in time—the little boys of the neighborhood were going blackberrying early Monday morning. Now that base-ball season was here they had to have a ball; the ravelings from old stockings wound around pine bark would no longer do. It had to be a leather ball like the big boys played with this summer, and a leather ball cost money. If nine of them picked two quarts or more of blackberries apiece—but who would buy their berries, practical Swade wanted to know of Aunt Sugar's boys, who had almost tremulously offered the suggestion. Fatty, relieved now of his urgency, said his Papa was going to take a load of snaps and truck to market Tues-day and bet he'd sell their berries and not tell a soul, either. Of course Cousin Sim would!

"Cousin Sim's the very one. He don't think they's no harm in baseball." Ekie and Budy were articulate in excitement.

"Who does?" Robin could drawl scornfully, for Uncle Israel encouraged his boys to play ball.

"I'll pick my two quarts."

The "Me too's" tumbled over each other.

"I'll ask Papa and let you know this evenin'," Fatty prom-ised.

"Cousin Sim's the best empire of anybody."

"Sure is," was the unanimous verdict. Fatty could tell him, what they cared.

Through dense briar patches, over rough rail fences, along marshy places at the wood's edge, in snakey thickets, from the railroad swamp all the way to Becky's Hole nine little boys slipped furtively, trusting no risks, tearing bare legs and arms and pants on briars and rail fences, killing snakes and hornets and lizards that got in the way, plunging unexpectedly into yellow jackets' nests, tormented by biting flies, subjecting flesh to red-bugs and ticks, pricking fingers with sharp thorns, and staining hands. Not that the stain mattered: it covered a lot of dirt; but it was a guilty stain, at least to Aunt

Sugar's Ekie and Buddy, who on the way home thought of gathering and offering to their Mama a pail of dew berries that grew along the hill road, in case she wanted to make some dumplings for dinner. Aunt Sugar didn't want to fool with any dumplings today. They could eat their dew berries raw. Where had they been all morning anyway? They could just get their caps and walk down the road to Dele's for a mess of honey; Dele had told her at Sunday school yesterday they had robbed the bees last week and would send her a dish of honey the first passing.

Dele, dishing the honey from a big stone jar, told the boys to stay on and eat dinner; she'd make it all right with their Mama. She was having blackberry dumpling today. They watched her spread a flour sack on the table and sprinkle flour on the big green bottle with which she rolled the dough for the dumplings. On the round of dough were placed the berries and a little sugar; this was then rolled into an oblong shape, wrapped and tied in a clean white muslin cloth, and dropped into a pot of boiling water. When it was done, Dele removed the "baby," as she called it, carefully unwound the cloth, and smothered the boiled dumpling in a sauce of brown sugar, butter, and nutmeg. Aunt Sugar's boys said it was the best dumpling they ever tasted. Cousin Sell admitted it was good, but he liked the way they cooked dumplings in Northampton County—baked with a lot of butter inside.

Tuesday morning long before day Cousin Sim and Fatty with their load of snaps, squash, cucumbers, beets, apples, and blackberries started to Raleigh. Fatty lay in the wagon body by the blackberries and finished his nap, while Cousin Sim, giving the reins to his mule, nodded on the wagon seat most of the way to town. They went first to Aunt Nettie's, for she often bought neighborhood produce off the wagons and sometimes asked kinfolks to come eat dinner with her after they had sold out their load, particularly if they had given her bargains in her purchases. "Twenty-five cents for butter? Why, I can get all I want up the street for twenty-two cents," she had told Uncle Fonnie last week.

Aunt Nettie appraised the blackberries hesitatingly. They were beautiful berries all right. Yes indeed, eighteen quarts could be used for jelly and jam and blackberry cobbler all right. Her boarders liked something sweet for breakfast. They were big nice berries all right. Eight cents a quart? She should say not! Dwight's wife, who came out to the wagon from across the street, should say not, too! There was a subtle hint that, since blackberries cost nothing but grew lush and ripe for the plucking, the country cousins might just say it with blackberries sometimes, especially since they often put up on the city kin for dinner when country produce was brought to market. Dwight's wife remembered that picking blackberries was fine sport; when she was a girl she had visited her grandmother's farm and had gone black-berrying one day: little pink sunbonnets, black plump berries in shining pails, cool green grass underfoot, sweet wood's odors and fragrant winey smell of crushed fruit, honey bees collecting nectar from wild flowers, warm sunshine and pure fresh air—nostalgia for the fine sport of girlhood was in the city woman's eyes, staring at the plump berries in the too pointedly gallon measures.

DeWonner, Dwight's eleven-year-old son, standing at the side of the wagon while his women bargained over the country truck, was thumping blackberries toward a certain bush in a neighbor's yard to see how near he could hit it how many times in succession. Fatty said quit, but not impressively enough. DeWonner stopped to observe how come the blackberries theirs if they didn't plant them or plow the bushes or anything but just pluck the berries off when they got ripe by themselves? He thumped a plump berry right in the center of a white rose.

Cousin Sim replied with an invitation to come to the country and pluck all they pleased; he would be back in another

61

day with more garden truck and berries to sell: ample time in which to pluck plenty of jelly and jam and blackberry cobbler. DeWonner, at his arrogant insistence, was packed among the empty measures at the close of the day and dispatched to the country in the interest of jam and jelly. Those cheeky cousins, asking eight cents a quart for that which cost them not a penny, which was as free as the air they breathed!

Early Wednesday morning the freckled-faced country cousins took DeWonner blackberrying. He was enchanted over the fat seeded berries hanging luxuriously in clusters and staining the tin pail a rich Burgundy—row on row of dark reddish jelly in white paraffined glasses to spread on buttered bread next winter after school. A bumble bee zoomed smack against his head and scared him from the lush briars. If it wasn't a sting it was a bad smart all right; he believed he had been stung, didn't care what Fatty said. Fatty got so tickled he had to run behind a bush quick. At the next briar thicket the thorns caught DeWonner's stockings and shirtsleeves, and when he seized the bush to pull himself loose the thorns pricked his hands and got his fingers full of "splinters." That ugly stain on his hand would never come off, he was told; he would have to wear it to church and up town and everywhere. Crossing a reedy marsh to blacker berries beyond, he mired into black mud and had a time churning out; then the the hot sun caked the mud on his stockings, which felt very messy and heavy. There was too much walking over rough ground; he thought all the berries were in one patch.

As DeWonner seized handfuls of berries from the thicket near Becky's Hole, he suddenly felt something touch his foot; glancing down quickly he saw with horror a black snake coiled near and sticking out its neck at him. He splashed through the water, spilling his berries in a broad jump toward the road. All the boys gave him handfuls from their buckets then and let him have the shady patch at the edge of the woods. There he got into a wasps' nest and was chased clear across the field by a mad wasp. For several minutes he picked berries in peace, only the sun was too hot on his back. At the other side of the clearing there appeared to be nice bushes; it was a long hot walk across plowed ground, but when he drew near and saw some big clusters in the shade he was heartened. At the first handful an odor so overpoweringly sickening struck his nose that his stomach almost turned over. He called to Fatty across the field to hurry there quick; he was afraid to move for fear of getting into he didn't know what! Fatty came and found the dead snake some of the boys had killed on Monday.

"Wonder the buzzards ain't found him."

"What are buzzards like?"

"Hain't you never seen a buzzard?"

"Course I have, only not close by."

"Little buzzards are pretty. Want to see some? Do, come on; I know where there's a nest."

Fatty led the way back into the woods. When DeWonner saw the little buzzards and was told that the old mammy buzzard would bring the little fellers some of that dead snake for their supper, he heaved loud enough for Swade and Ekie to hear. They came running and on learning the trouble added to buzzardana the information that the old buzzards ate dead snakes and truck and "vomicked" it up for their little ones when they got home. DeWonner lost his breakfast. Running away from the boys who stood eating berries as they appraised the buzzard's nest, he found enough berries to fill half his bucket.

Moisture began to trickle down his back, over his face, under his pants. The woolen trousers were chafing. He scratched gently; the chafing got worse. But he kept on plucking berries. At the end of the morning, he triumphantly carried two big pails to the house. The boys wanted to know what he was walking so "spraddle-leg-ged" for. He confided that he had heat between his legs. That could be easily remedied; he was only "galled-ed"; they got like that a heap of times. Blades of green corn rubbed on the spots affected were prescribed. DeWonner tried it.

That was when the grown folks got into it. The child was put to bed, and pulverized wood from a rotten stump, sifted through a muslin rag, was dusted on the affected parts. By that time the red-bugs, firmly entrenched on his legs and ankles, were beginning their torture. Fatty gave him a pretty glass marble.

Five quarts—forty cents' worth—of berries were taken back to the city on Thursday for jam and jelly and black-berry cobbler; thirty-five cents' worth of medicine was bought for the fevered victim, including a dose of castor oil for his upset stomach. Cousin Sim observed dryly this was about breaking even, with a slight margin of profit.

IX

MISS JENNIE HUMMED her funny little monotone at her morning's work. Her step was a little brisker, her movements more purposeful, her eyes brighter, and her voice cheerier as she called Fido to his bowl of mulberry pie that hadn't turned out as good yesterday as the receipt sounded. For Aunt Sad had told her Sunday to come spend Wednesday at her house, and days at Aunt Sad's were always red letters in Miss Jennie's life.

After clearing the table and covering the dishes with a white cloth, scalding the fly trap and baiting it with molasses, pouring a gourd of water in the chicken trough, and adding water to the tin cans in which the legs of her safe stood ankle-deep, Miss Jennie took the window sticks out and propped them securely over the bottom window sash, before re-arranging her hair in a figure-eight at the back of her head and pinning on her black sailor. Last of all she tied the white apron, with the crocheting at the bottom, over her black skirt, and then hoisting her parasol she set off up the road.

Aunt Sad took her at once into the kitchen and let her help with the dinner; they could talk freer, working. As she rolled the Irish potatoes around in the tub with a rock to break the skins, preliminary to scraping them with a knife, Miss Jennie told about a story she had read in Kind Words, and from that it was a natural transition to the receipt for stickies that she had found last week in Farm and Hearth. No, she hadn't tried it yet; it took so much butter and sugar, and she happened to be out of spices right now, too. Aunt Sad, singeing a chicken she had just picked, suggested that Miss Jennie try stickies today; there was plenty of butter, sugar, and everything she would need in the safe. Pinning a blue checked apron over her white one, Miss Jennie with sparkling eyes went happily to work. She rolled her dough very short, with more lard in it than she ever had to use at home, into small thin rounds, on which she spread butter and sugar copiously; after sprinkling ground cloves, mace, and nutmeg lightly over the top, she folded the dough into oblong rolls and baked them a golden brown in Aunt Sad's nice oven, without having to shift the pan from bottom to top to bottom grate or blowing off the ashes as in the oven at home.

"It says use these in a saucer with any tart fruit in season, preferably tart, anyway." Proudly she displayed her rolls.

"There's enough gooseberries ripe if they'll do. Go yonder, look by the smokehouse bush—"

"I'll go gather a pailful."

When Miss Jennie returned with the gooseberries, Aunt Sad had dried out a piece of bacon left from yesterday's boiling and was lifting into the hot grease in the frying pan a flesh-fork full of stewed cymblings; with onions sliced into the pan she began the tedious hot work of browning the mixture. Between stirrings she spread the white damask over the dining table, although Miss Jennie begged her, as was custom, not to put on the Sunday cloth just for her. Not much of the white showed by the time the platter of chicken fricassee, browned squash, buttered potatoes, green snap beans with slices of ham on top, red beets submerged in vinegar and sugar, stewed tomatoes, pickles, preserves, hot biscuits and corn bread, peach pie and gooseberry rolls, a dish of cup cake, the caster in the center with its vinegar cruet, salt and pepper, were placed on the table.

Neither of the women ever ate very much, but something in each was satisfied by the hot and tiring preparation and the appraising pause when each woman looked over the food and saw that it was good. Then Aunt Sad lifted the dish of snaps to start the meal.

"I know Jimmy's grace by heart, but I never believed in women tryin' to take a man's place." Aunt Sad always prefaced the meal thus.

"I know you miss havin' somebody to say grace." Miss Jennie always responded to her cue thus.

"Nobody but them that's been through it knows how bad it is."

"I missed Pa a heap. I still miss him. But I know it is bad to go through, with a husband."

Miss Jennie had been among those who had seen Jimmy's death five years before as a blessing. "Sad couldn't hold out much longer to wait on Jimmy," the neighborhood women had whispered, not adding that Jimmy's querulous complaining and crabbedness were wearing Sad down quite as much as the physical wear and tear of lifting, rubbing, washing for the invalid, preparing an exacting diet, and sitting up nights. But Aunt Sad was left pretty blank; Jimmy's going had not wholly taken the purpose and direction out of her life, for it had given her a grave.

"Have some cymblin's. This is the way Jimmy use to love them, and I always took a whole mornin' to fix them right—"

66

"Have you ever tried bakin' them in the oven? It's not as hot and tiresome, and they taste—"

"No." Aunt Sad was almost sharp. "This is the right way. Jimmy wouldn't touch them unless they were browned on top of the stove in dried-out meat grease."

"Your beets are bigger than mine. I haven't had any but twice this summer, and one time I tried a new way—buttered them when they were hot, and I declare they didn't taste bad. I had read—"

"This is the only way beets is fit to eat, plenty of vinegar and sugar and pepper. Jimmy wouldn't touch them if they wa'n't fixed like these is today."

"Everything's mighty good. Seems like these is the best snaps I ever tasted."

"Jimmy always wanted them cut up fine like this; the seasonin' went through them better, and he never thought they was fit to eat unless the grease stood a half-inch deep all around the dish."

"'Tis better—if you have the meat."

So was the hunger of two, without direction toward appeasement, satisfied a little by musing over food that memorialized other appetites than their own.

"He use to hunt up my cookin' at picnics and August meetin's and wouldn't touch nobody else's, unless Dele's now and then."

"I remember. I use to try to get him to taste my dinner, but he was always full he said, and then I'd see him ease over toward your vittles—"

"Well, I learned how to fix things his appetite called for. When we was first married he use to come in the kitchen and tell me how his Ma fixed things for him—"

"And what was it you said the time you walked in on him?" The conversation always headed this way.

"Law, that!" Aunt Sad laughed mirthlessly. "I was so bashful I was even ashamed of my own self when I first got

67

married. Men folks ain't ashamed, Jennie. They soon strip off before you the first night—"

Miss Jennie's little ears pinkened, and the pulse quickened in her throat as she aimlessly played with the vegetables on her plate. Aunt Sad absent-mindedly forked a beet from the dish as she went on.

"Jimmy just soon to anyway. But I turned my head away or left the room when he got to his pants—at first; you get over that. But you know, Jennie, I never did get use to a man havin' hair on his breast, and I wouldn't look at it—till Jimmy got sick." Aunt Sad smoothed a wrinkle in the tablecloth; she was again rubbing a poor white body.

"And then you walked in on him—"

"That was the week after we got married. Jimmy was in the kitchen washin', standin' there stripped naked as my hand, when I walked in to cook supper, thinkin' he was at the lot. Seemed like I couldn't move, but I just started hollerin', 'Don't look, don't look, don't look!' And all the time my eyes was set on him there, naked as my hand."

"Then—" Miss Jennie's voice was hardly audible as she shifted her snaps to the other side of her plate.

There was a meditative pause. "Well, I was broke from then on, though I never did get use to the hair on his breast." Some day Miss Jennie felt sure Aunt Sad would reveal just what did take place in the kitchen that day. "But law, after you live with a man awhile his body don't seem no stranger than your own, hair or no hair."

They washed the dishes, filled the cooler with vegetables which they let down with a rope into the well, and sat on the back porch awhile to continue the idyl. It ended today as always in a pilgrimage to the graveyard. With parasols hoisted, they bore to the shrine a weeding hoe, a water bucket, and an armful of roses. At the churchyard they made the usual rounds, the usual comments.

"'Annie and Fannie, born December eight, eighteen

eighty-five; died July tenth, eighteen eighty-seven.' It was their second summer; they had cholera morbus I remember." They walked sadly away from the twin headstone over to where Grandpa Pate's two wives "rested in peace" under a gnarled oak. " 'Rachel, wife of Calvin Pate, born eighteen thirty, died eighteen sixty-two. Henceforth there is laid up for me a crown of righteousness. R. I. P.' . . . 'Sarah, wife of Calvin Pate, born eighteen thirty-nine, died eighteen seventy-seven. She hath done what she could. R. I. P.' "

"Mr. Calvin Pate will go right here, and then Miss Bettie next to him. I hope she'll have something pretty over her, too. She's a good woman; she's raised three flocks of children."

"Yes, Jimmy thought a lot of her."

" 'O for the touch of a vanished hand, and the sound of a voice that is still' is pretty, and it's not on a single tombstone. Ain't it pretty?"

"Yes, that's all right. This here grave of old Mr. Batten ought to be fixed up. It's caved in bad. Look, you can see the edge of the coffin."

The women mused sadly by the neglected grave. "Old Mr. Batten use to bring me red-streaked candy when he'd come to sit with Pa till bedtime. It was pitiful to hear him tell how bad he missed 'Sweet Betsey,' as he always called her."

"And spit worse'n a goose. But he was a good man."

"You can't even make out the words on Miss Betsey's tombstone, it's so old and black now." Miss Jennie stooped to pull up the weeds at the foot of the grave.

" 'Elizabeth– Eighteen seventy-eight– She is–precious– rubies.' I can make that much out."

"I wouldn't want to be weather-boarded up like this, would you?" Miss Jennie stepped around a grave and peered through an opening near the roof of a miniature wooden tent where a single grave piqued the curiosity of the neighborhood. "I rather have the sun and rain and moon on me."

"Maybe she rather be shut up though."

"Do you reckon—?" Miss Jennie would not say it. It was well enough to speculate at home on back porches whether this stranger had been a good woman or not, but here awe and pity overcame curiosity.

Aunt Sad was less reticent. "What did a strange man bring her here for—in a strange graveyard where she had no folks —and put her away without any preacher or song or mourners?"

"They said the man cried like a baby."

"Yes, Jimmy said he did. But no women folks here and no funeral— Job was against puttin' her here, in spite of all the man said about the body couldn't make it no farther, and Jimmy said he was with Job till Wes said something about 'a stranger and ye took me in.' Wes never was one for sayin' verses, but seemed like that time he just spoke out before he thought and then walked away to let them do as they saw fit. Well, here she lies."

"Le's put one rose on her grave."

"We can't. There's no door. She's shut up."

"I can reach my hand through here—" Aunt Sad handed her a bud.

"Emmie keeps little Essie's grave nice. She's goin' to put a little angel here soon as she saves enough butter money to buy one."

"Those little shells look sweet around the grave. She brought home a satchelful from Morehead City. Essie was a good child."

"Yes, she was a good child. This tombstone over poor Willie is going to fall if it ain't tended to soon. 'Willie Pate, aged twenty-two, died eighteen eighty-nine, son of Millard and Cynthy Pate. How many hopes lie buried here.'"

"That sounds like they believed Willie did kill himself."

"I reckon we all believe it a little, but it's best just to let it go as a huntin' accident. It's the only way to stand it."

70

"What poor Willie could want to die for— He was a good boy."

" 'Eveline Smith, wife of Tom Smith— Sleep on, beloved, sleep and take thy rest—' It don't seem right though for Ev to be lyin' down restin' this time o' day, dressed up in her Sunday black dress, when she never stopped stirrin' till sundown and up before day feedin' pigs and choppin' cabbage rows and—"

"She was a good woman."

"Yes. She wanted Jimmy, and tried mighty hard to get him when we was girls together, but she made Mr. Smith a good wife, yes. And now already he's gettin' frisky and real mannish at church Sundays, when—"

Aunt Sad suddenly turned away and hurried to her own grave, a refuge and an anchor. With the hoe she worked the violets she had planted around her square, while Miss Jennie went to the well in the church grove for water to fill the vases half buried on the mound. She wet her handkerchief and washed off the lettering, reading as she worked: "Jimmy Pate— There shall be no night there." Aunt Sad placed the roses in the vases and involuntarily smoothed with her hands the sand above the body she had soothed so many times on the bed at home.

"It looks so nice to see husband and wife lyin' side by side, with violets all around, takin' the rain and the sunshine together," Miss Jennie observed wistfully, as she polished "no night there." But she was not depressed as she walked slowly back to her cottage at sundown, albeit she would have to take the weather alone. It had been such a pleasant day!

X

A FEW DAYS AFTER the excursion Calvin was taken with a chill in the tobacco patch. The doctor said lungs again. Dele knew it was heart, too. Twice she had nursed Calvin through pneumonia; this time Milly would have to help. Nannie Lou was hurried off with a note to Uncle Wes. It was the only secret Dele ever had from John. How Uncle Wes managed it and under what difficulties the girl escaped from her parents' strict vigilance, Dele never knew. Ruthless now, she did not care. Milly came early a hot July afternoon, sat by Calvin, and put cold cloths on his head. He knew her touch on his forehead and opened his eyes.

"I still got the shell—under the pillow."

"I'll tell you what it says"—Dele was at the well after cold water—"It says 'I love you.'" Her lips were close to his ear. "They'll never make me love anybody but you." Then he closed his eyes under the pressure of her little brown fingers.

Calvin was sitting up when August meeting started. Dele packed the dinner and got her family off to services early every day, hoping this year Nannie Lou would join the church. The girl was miserable. There was the vow she had made on the sailboat, or He was welcome to strike her dead. Then when Calvin's fever had gone to one hundred and four, she had reiterated her promise to be a foreign missionary, if only, Please Dear Father, Calvin would get well. From day to day she postponed her trip up to the front. Then Friday came, and the meeting would break. After all, she was only eleven; one more year could not matter with Him. She would study her Sunday school lesson, read the Bible, put aside her paper-dolls, and write more religious poetry, songs of praise, she promised Him during the lunch hour Friday, watching anxiously meanwhile the racks sailing threateningly in the sky. During the afternoon sermon a thunder storm gathered, and when the last invitation was given and "Just As I Am" was being sung, a gloomy dusk settled over the church. Four girls and three boys went up, accompanied by a reverberating crash of thunder. Nannie Lou wanted her Mama. Tears came easily when they sang, "Oh, Lamb of God, I come, I com-m-e"—; even if the

72

skies had been blue and Mama had been close by and nobody's fever had been one hundred and four, who wouldn't have cried when all the women in the church were wiping their eyes? Now she choked and swallowed and finally sobbed convulsively. Her Sunday school teacher, hurrying to Nannie Lou from the front seat where she had just led one soul, embraced her and wanted to know if she didn't want to go, "without one plea," and give the preacher her hand. Led by the teacher, Nannie Lou went "just as she was," and there was another sweet session over one sinner that repented.

Back at home, Nannie Lou hurried to the looking glass. She felt pale and holy, and if inward change were reflected in her face— Yes, the roses were only faint in her pale cheeks, the eyes were a deeper brown, the very countenance kindly and gentle. "Dear Jesus, take me, use me, I am Thine, In this dark world, Thy little light to shine."

Dele, rejoicing silently that all her family was in the ark of safety, cut the last ham, made red gravy, filled the honey dish, and let Nannie Lou eat all the hot biscuits she wanted. Only, Nannie Lou ate cold corn bread and buttermilk, denying herself, as was fitting.

The aunts marveled at the change in Nannie Lou. Why, the child even looked different out of the face since she became a Christian. The child overheard them. Liveliness gave way to quiet meditation; her face reflected an inner light, according to mirrored reflection. She read her Bible often and spoke kindly to the cats. Promptly at ten every morning, with the sweeping and hearth-claying over, she sought the darkness of the clothes closet and had a sweet hour of prayer through most of August.

During the days before baptizing Sunday, the paper-dolls troubled her. Every one—collected from catalogues, a few furtively from Pilgrim's Progress, and secreted between the pages of Bundick's Temperance Lectures—was dear to her.

She had promised Him to destroy them. They became her
secret sin. The last Saturday in August she burned every
paper-doll, her tears frying upon the stove into which she
was thrusting so much of her happiness. At first there was
exquisite suffering over the sacrifice and an added sense of
pale holiness. Then as the bitter loss grew on her, she felt
vaguely mad at Somebody, cut the prayer sessions for two
days, and kicked the cat all she pleased. Two days before the
dreaded watery grave yawned before her, the petitions were
renewed.

XI

THE HOT AUGUST stillness was ripe with the odor of curing
tobacco. Oak and hickory logs, old fence rails, and scantlings
were piled at one side of the tobacco barn, just down the hill
from the Fuller house; these were shoved at intervals into
the furnace to keep the fire at an even temperature. A shelter
projected over the furnace side of the barn, one side of which
had been weather-boarded to the ground for protection
against rain. In this corner had been built near the ground
a broad shelf on which were spread quilts and pillows.
Planks had been nailed between the posts supporting the
shelter roof, which together with two splint-bottom chairs
served as rude seats for those who fired the barn or visited
there. The ground under the shelter was swept as clean as a
floor. Up the hill to the right was the peach orchard with its
luscious yellow clear-seeds and big red presses flavoring
the air, and opposite was a watermelon patch where fat,
grayish green-veined melons lay turned up to the sun. The
winey aroma of ripe grapes in purple clusters on vines
behind the woodshed was mingled with that of the full-
bodied curing tobacco and the warm fragrance of the
peaches.

Letha, who was tending the fire all day Saturday, called
Calvin from the fodder field on the rock hill to come see

74

about the heat. With the tobacco leaves inside so dry now, she was cautious; for if one leaf fell from the stick on which it was strung, and touched the hot pipes, it would burst into flames and light the whole barn. Calvin looked at the thermometer through the little glass window in the door and added logs and rails to the furnace. While waiting to test the heat further, he walked over to the melon patch, stooped to thump several melons, selected one not marked with the cross which indicated John's choice for seed, and burst it open on a fence rail. From inside he gouged the red mealy heart still warm from the sunshine and ate it quickly, spitting the black seeds from his mouth. Calvin looked again at the thermometer and the fire and hurried back to the fodder field.

Since he had been able to work again, although John urged him to take it along slow, Calvin had driven himself tirelessly, almost feverishly. He wanted to do a man's work, to harvest a big crop, to help get something ahead, to live different, to see his family independent, his women folks free forever of field work. He did not analyze his ambition and hopes, kindled into a blaze by Milly's visit when he was sick and her words in his ear, "They'll never make me love anybody but you." Sometimes in a sudden gust of depression he wondered if it had been fever or a dream or if she really had said, "They'll never make me love anybody but you." Then with morning, rested and buoyant again, he reveled in the heartening assurance of those words which he knew he had not dreamed; unnaturally articulate, he would sit on the woodbox while Dele kneaded biscuit dough for breakfast and ask her at intervals the details of that visit which had changed the world for him. Had Milly worn a pink dress? Had she put the cold cloths on his head herself? Had she stayed two whole hours? Could Dele remember anything else Milly had said? Had Dele left them together a whole half hour? That alone proved Milly had said That: they were alone together, and she couldn't have gone away without saying it. Not one syllable of what he had said to her would come back to him, but Dele always assured him that he had opened his eyes and smiled at her as she was leaving. Dele did not smile in the telling. After these little talks with his mother, Calvin could hardly wait for breakfast to be over before he was hurrying to the field—to get something ahead.

Dele in silence watched him anxiously and knew nothing to do. Twice she had tried to keep him out of the hot fodder field with lighter jobs in the shade, but he had finished these in hectic haste and joined the fodder pullers. This year Jessie, who was the fastest fodder hand in the neighborhood, had to race to beat Calvin. When the others paused in the shade to cool or sat under a persimmon tree to eat watermelons, Calvin seemed impatient about the time they were losing.

"You've got me whupped down, boy. Don't go have pneumonia no more," Jessie told him daily now.

How Milly was related to his ambition to get ahead, or just what he hoped, he could not have put in words. Somehow hard work and a good harvest would bring them closer: he would be able to give her something: doing a man's work would make him older and more forward: they might be able to buy a horse—if he had a horse he might go to her house some Sunday, he would go there! A horse could be bought maybe if crops turned out extra good, and with a horse to ride on he would go there! He left the other fodder pullers and didn't even stop to holler—to "crow," they called it, at the cow's tail—at the end of the row, but hurried into another.

After supper on Friday night he had gone briskly to the tobacco barn to take his turn sitting up. John, who was beginning to watch him anxiously, too, had followed and told him to go to the house; the women folks were going to sit up tonight. But Calvin had stayed; it was his turn, and he

76

was going to stay. Kate could come keep the fire the fore part of the night, then call him, and he'd stay awake till day. Decisively he had lain down on the pallet, and John had walked slowly to the house, puzzled; the boy had never argued with him before.

On Saturday night they killed the barn of tobacco. With the guano sack of ice Uncle Millard had saved for her from his box of fish in the afternoon, Dele froze a gallon of custard flavored with crushed yellow clear-seeds and took it to the barn. Setting an iron pot to boil over the fire, she shucked and silked twelve roas'n' ears. Kate had dressed three young roosters to barbecue over the coals; and she was basting the chickens, placed over a wire rack, with a sauce of vinegar, red pepper, and butter when Aunt Cynthy and Uncle Millard got to the barn.

"A good smellin' night." Uncle Millard sniffed it in. "Don't know which smells the loudest—the ripe peaches and watermelons or baked tobacco and hot vinegar."

"You!" Aunt Cynthy almost caught her breath; she never said things like that, but Uncle Millard had been teasing her all day about Cousin Sell and the peach preserves he had eaten the last jar of when he was at their house. She had preserved a gallon Saturday morning, and Uncle Millard declared he was going to invite Cousin Sell home with them from Sunday school tomorrow.

"Me? Why, Cynthy, I just washed and stripped to the bottom. If you smell me—"

But Aunt Cynthy hurriedly sent him to the corn crib for some shucks in which to bake ash cakes to go with the barbecue. She had seen her mother make them many a time, and she had promised to learn Kate how.

Letha and Nannie Lou came, bringing dishes, spoons, a jar of watermelon rind pickle, a plate of sugar cakes, the butter dish, and a bucket of ice water. While John, Calvin, and Uncle Millard took turns at the freezer, Aunt Cynthy and

Dele mixed corn meal with water, wrapping the little cakes of dough in clean corn shucks and covering them with ashes in the smoldering furnace.

"I saw the preacher's mule flirtin' over the fence with your pea-vines this evenin', John."

"If I have to put up his stock another time—"

"Don't it cost you as much to feed 'em in your lot as it does in your field?"

"I'm goin' to charge him next time, what I am."

"You just well charge it to Providence."

"I'll law him, preacher or no preacher—"

"Did you know he spoke to Job and Israel about lettin' him help in the meetin' the other week?"

"To be sure not!"

"He named it to 'em. I saw him standin' under a mulberry in his pasture one day makin' some fancy pulpit gestures. Perrie tells around that his Pa practices up his sermons on his cows and mules and hogs."

"Perrie hadn't ought to sass his Pa like he does. Why, one day—"

Nannie Lou, holding the bowl of sauce for Kate, reddened at the mention of Perrie and shrank into the shadows behind the furnace. She didn't hate Perrie; she didn't hate anybody since she had joined the church. But oh, if only Perrie's father would move away and never come back and she would never have to hear the name of Perrie again! She loved everybody of course. It couldn't be wrong just to wish people somewhere else. It couldn't be wrong either to eat a hearty meal tonight. That chicken smelled so good browning over the coals, and chickens were made to eat. Were they though? Didn't chickens love to live just as well as folks? Well, they were dead now, and she as well eat. Next week she would eat cold corn bread and buttermilk. September wasn't far away now and baptizing Sunday. She very humbly and kindly held the bowl of sauce near Kate.

"Sugar give Cousin Sell a hoe and told him to chop down some weeds in the garden, after he had been at her house three days."

"He left of course."

"In a hurry. Between the ha'nts and bees and Sugar, I reckon Sell thinks he's havin' a right smart hard time in the neighborhood this summer."

"Sell's good company, if he is lazy. I wouldn't mistreat him."

"Me neither."

Aunt Cynthy and Dele exchanged glances.

Kate dipped her basting mop into the vinegar sauce and moistened the roasting chickens, now a golden brown over the coals. Dele arose to lay a cloth on the benches, placing on it a huge platter of roas'n' ears boiled on the cob and rubbed in butter and salt, pickle, light bread still warm from the oven, and sugar cakes. Aunt Cynthy brought her plate of ash cakes to the board, as Kate after a final basting lifted her chickens to a dish and the men set the freezer of cream near the improvised table.

They laughed and talked and ate with relish—washed and dressed in clean clothes, a week's work behind and Sunday's rest and fellowship ahead, pantry shelves loaded with good food for Sunday, stacks of fodder harvested and cotton cracking open in the fields, another barn of tobacco well-cured and ready to grade for market, scuppernongs ripening a little, sweet potatoes grabbled ahead of the season and sweetening in the sun, everybody well.

At the very heartiness and well-being of the group Calvin was unaccountably depressed. There was in his sudden unhappiness something of physical reaction after a strenuous week's work his strength was still unequal to; much more, of the emptiness of Sundays which brought fellowship with kinfolks and neighbors to the others and only hungry looks toward where Milly sat in Sunday school to him; a little, of

unconscious impatience at the very heartiness and content-
ment with this way of life, emphasizing the bitter difference
between his and hers. He could not visualize Milly at a tobacco barn: she did not fit in with barbecue and ash cakes
and corn on the cob and quilt pallets. Dressed in cool white,
on the back seat of a carriage, or in a little brown coat, under
a sweet gum tree, or in a blue dress, on the white sand, or
at the piano her little brown fingers touching the white keys,
or by a bedside in pink and white . . .

His eyes across the lantern light were despairing. Dele
yearned over him and knew nothing to do. No, he couldn't
eat any more ice cream. Dele laughed lightly with the others
when Uncle Millard told Kate he had found a barbecued
craw in one of the chickens, but her heart was not light.

XII

THE FIRST SUNDAY in September stood for something as
definite as the Rubicon, Waterloo, Perga in the Sunday
school lesson. It had always been baptizing Sunday at Pate's
Siding. During August, five little girls and three little boys
had looked forward to September with mingled emotions.
The boys, who had been slipping in Uncle Job's pond and
in Becky's Hole since they were knee-high, assumed a cocki-
ness that did not at all reassure the little girls, with only a
bathing background of big white bowls and zinc tubs. But
the girls kept the dread in their hearts and assembled last
summer's white dresses, white hair ribbons, white stockings,
and their aunts' wool shawls against inevitable September.

Among the candidates were Aunt Puss's third girl, who
had left the mourners' bench and had stayed away two years
when a wasp got after the mourners and frightened the
epileptic one into a fit; Uncle Wes's youngest boy, who had
been persuaded by a personal worker to give up his sins and
"come then and join this holy band"; Fatty, who joined be-

cause the church gave picnics and excursions and things; the three who had bargained to be saved the same afternoon; Robin Pate, who was going to be an engineer, and Nannie Lou. Ellis Pate, Uncle Job's boy who was going to be a preacher, assisted.

Dele assembled her family for an early breakfast of fried chicken, broiled ham, blackberry jelly, and clabber biscuits. A husky grace trembled from the head of the table. Nannie Lou could not eat; she had not been hungry in a week. The old gray suitcase that had never been farther than Uncle Job's pond was carefully dusted, and the white lawn with the val lace yoke, the bleaching underclothes with the hamburg trimmings, and the patent leather slippers were placed therein. The candidate was assisted into the white piqué with the little eton-jacket effect, white stockings, and Letha's discarded white ribbon in her hair. There was so much white in the day that cape jessamines and pale cold hands and little Essie's white coffin kept intruding strangely into Nannie Lou's consciousness.

On the way to the pond, with old Daisy officiating between the shafts of the surrey, Dele from the back seat with the older girls kept telling Nannie Lou nervously over and over to shut her eyes on "the Holy Ghost," to hold her breath and give up—not struggle and try to fight her way out like Kate did her year. John looked down once and said, "There's nothin' goin' to hurt you, Sook."

Calvin, making his first appearance since his illness, was so hungry for sight of Milly that he grew impatient at the slow procession ahead of them. Dele could not tell him what the neighborhood now knew, that Milly had practically been locked in since her visit to Calvin had been found out. He would hear soon enough.

The Fullers arrived at the pond, the scene of Easter picnics, egg hunts, fish-fries. But there was no trace of the earthly today. A Sabbath hush rested over the solemn pines, the still water, the subdued congregation, the meek mules and horses tied to the pines. The candidates were grouped apart, their mothers hovering near with shawls on their arms, while they waited for the youngest Martin boy, who didn't have a mother. He came at last, his father holding on to the flour sack that had his dry clothes in it. Under the preacher's instruction and eye, the little boys took the girls' hands, and he led the motherless one to the water's edge while the congregation sang "Shall we gather at the river?" The clear sopranos, Dele's alto, and Uncle Israel's tenor, a few aging gallant basses floated out in unearthly sweetness over the placid water. The preacher read and prayed. Aunt Emmie, who cried at every baptism since her little girl had been buried, was leaning against a pine trying to sing, though the tears were spilling over her Gospel Hymns—"Gathered with the saints at the river"— The mothers were faltering; the fathers' voices were steady enough, but their song books shook a little.

They had no Greek lexicons, no Baptizos, no mode consciousness in their experience. Like their fathers—gathered at the "beautiful, the beautiful riv-er"—they were born into the world, were baptized, died—the eternal simplicities. They would no more have argued over immersion than over being born or dying.

The preacher entered the water; the white-stockinged legs of the little girls followed, the boys awkwardly holding to their hands.

> *"What can wash away my sins?*
> *Nothing but the blood of Je-sus"*

sang the faithful as the candidates advanced toward the stick that had been placed at the right depth for the tallest. The little boys had slyly wrested their hands from the girls'. The largest girl was unfolding the shawl for the smallest. The preacher raised his hand in benediction, the burial was negotiated, and the child came up strangled, but with that clean baptized look. Other shawls were unfolded and held in readiness. Nannie Lou was next. Her breath came fast; she swallowed at the lump in her throat; she folded her arms, drew one last long breath on "Holy Ghost"; she was going backward, her eyes shut tight after that one glimpse of fathomless expanse of water she was being lowered into.... A mighty rushing of waters blotting out the earth, a red darkness—surely this was the end, and she would never see light any more, nor hear the sweet commonplaces of life— the rooster crowing, Nero's bark, the dinner bell, Mama's voice. Her hands were about to snatch after reality, to struggle against the weight that deafened and held her, but a tired voice from her past droned above the mighty roar in her ears: "Don't struggle and fight like Kate did." Suddenly there was a great quiet; a brightness flashed into her wet face; she coughed some of the weight from her chest while somebody wrapped Aunt Cynthy's shawl around her shoulders. The world looked sweet and clean.

She glanced toward the line of black skirts and white shirt-waists and flowered lawns yonder against the pines, and her heart lifted. It was over. She felt light; a song danced in her heart; she was sure her countenance shone. Jesus was her Saviour; there was fried chicken, ham, cabbage, pound cake, cucumber pickle in the cupboard at home—she didn't mean to think of eating, dear Jesus, but she had been baptized on an empty stomach, and anyhow when she was happy she always thought of eating. She was happy now. It was over. Would Jesus please not be angry at her gladness that the water part of it was over? True, there was the dressing part of it ahead—stripping before Aunt Sugar and all of them, when she even darkened the room always before her own nakedness. True, there was the wine part of it—the cup that brown and black mustaches (the white ones were worse, for they showed dirt), lips that timed their final pi-too-ees with

83

the diapason of the organ invitation to "come we that love the Lord," and Miss Charity's pale sickly mouth would press before it was passed to the children. But the wine part of it was not immediate.

The right hand of fellowship was. Nannie Lou rather enjoyed standing in front of the pulpit in her white lawn and blue sash, her hair interestingly wet, her countenance shining —she could tell—while the brothers and the sisters (uncles and aunts in everyday life) filed by. Some shook her hand heartily; Cousin Maggie's beau who usually went to church in Raleigh whispered, "God bless you"; others merely touched her hand a bit bashfully, a pale hand-shake. It was rather nice and important to be saved—till Mama and Papa came along. They gave her an impartial hand-shake just like they did all the others; she could trust them not to stop and hug somebody like Aunt Puss did her girl. But somehow when those calloused hands touched hers she wanted a lap to cry in. . . . Dear Jesus. . . .

In the afternoon when the cousins came and would play as usual, Nannie Lou watched them from the bench under the sugarberry tree. She could not play somehow as long as her hair was wet—damp even.

XIII

SEPTEMBER BRIGHTENED INTO harvest. White fields, ripe fodder, red apples, golden scuppernongs, black bullaces defined the farm and kitchen work. There was Sunday school for diversion from the hot fodder fields, the back-bending over cotton rows, the jellying and preserving, the wrapping and spreading of winesaps in the cuddy; and there was one unforgettable circus, when Dele, the girls, and Calvin saw their first elephant. Long before day they ate breakfast and were off on the twelve-mile ride to Raleigh behind old Daisy. Leaving the surrey at Aunt Nettie's, they squeezed into a crowded street car for the fair grounds where a new earth awaited awed eyes, accustomed to the tameness of farm mules, cows, and pigs. So it happened that the ocean and the elephant were added to their experience the same year.

John had stayed at home partly to finish shingling the kitchen and partly to keep an eye on his fodder and corn fields adjacent to the pasture of Mr. Rafe. This neighbor was a retired preacher who farmed and had bad luck with his fences. By the time he got around the mending of the vulnerable jambs, a cow or a mule had found another place to break out. John had never been in a lawsuit; none of his folks nor Dele's had ever been a-near a law court except for a little jury duty. But when a man tried every other means to prevail upon the preacher to keep his stock up— Just last week Mr. Rafe's mule had broken into the young pea-vines, and in complete exasperation John had warned the preacher through Jessie that the next offense meant— Law. It was a secret from Dele; without confiding in her, he had consulted Cousin Nath, who was a magistrate, and had learned the proper legal procedure. Secretly the witnesses were lined up; Jessie had been carefully coached for his role as star witness. For many nights now, John had lain awake going through the trial and his testimony, and a spice of excitement was in the day's routine. For pure cussedness Mr. Rafe's mule took to walking up and down by the pasture fence next to the pea-vines without once testing the fence that would have yielded to a gentle kick. But John remained alert and kept going over his grievance in magistrate's court.

The shingling had been finished, and for an hour John had scanned the bend in the road for a glimpse of Daisy and the familiar surrey. It looked like the younguns would have enough circus by now; Dele was just about as bad, waking him up mornings before day to tell him the children ought to see lions and elephants. What's an elephant? ... Well, the roof wouldn't leak any more. Maybe he ought to walk over to the young pea patch, though if that mule had broken through he surely could have seen it, being on top of the kitchen all day as he had been.

Jessie interrupted his train of thought. "Mr. John, we wants de day off to go to Piney Grove tomorrow."

"Hanh?"

"Yessuh. De white preacher's goin' to swap us a sermont for a day's cotton pickin'. De meetin'—"

"What preacher?"

"De preacher down de road. De meetin' breaks tomorrow, and Mariah's bound to see Duck come th'ugh."

"What's he goin' to preach about?"

"Mendin' de walls o' Jerus'lem is his tex' he told me, and—"

"He better stay home and mend his fences, don't he's goin' to get lawed—'stead o' sermons to you niggers."

"Did you ever hear, Mr. John, how come de mule and cow and pig breaks out de pasture?"

"Sorry fences. You're witness to it."

"Why, it's 'cause he tries out his sermons on his stock, how come dey breaks out. He can raise a whole crap o' hell when he gets het up. How come we want him at Piney Grove."

Daisy's joyful whicker sounded near the lot gate. The girls had brought the circus home with them—the lions, the bears, the elephants. Nannie Lou was most impressed. "Why, the elephants were so big they could blow you down if they snorted at you; they could suck little children up in their snouts and squeeze grown men to death. If one should get loose from the circus—"

John checked the excited chatter and sent his family to bed. There would have to be some early rising next morning, with a whole day's cotton picking behind. Dele slept with satisfaction, for all day Nannie Lou had been a little girl— she was usually too growny—and Calvin had seemed to have a good time.

Night settled over the farmhouse. The tired family slept fitfully, an elephant stalking now and then across their dreams. John woke on the crest of a profound snore to a faint but disturbing sound somewhere. He soon defined it as the bleating of a calf in mortal distress. An almost human quality in the cry hurried him out of bed and into pants before all his faculties were fully alert.

Out the back door, he picked his way gingerly over the rock pile near the chimney. The thin agony of the calf's bleating ceased abruptly as he approached the barn lot. Suddenly near the road he stopped dead; his heart began to pound painfully; cold moisture gathered at the roots of his hair. There silhouetted against the lot fence stood—an elephant, huge, sinister, holding in his snout the inert and dangling calf. Poor little calf. He would never forget that picture. The massive bulk of beast moved forward. So did John. His instinct took charge of him; he fled with winged ankles toward the house, remembering that the front door was locked. There were no rocks in his path this time. If only the elephant didn't beat him to the back door he would have a chance.

He dashed in at the back, locked the door, woke Dele, and panted out incoherently their peril and the urgency of getting the children upstairs. He began moving trunks against the doors, between his commands to the family to hurry upstairs unless they wanted to be squeezed to death like that poor little calf out yonder. If only the ax were in the house so that they could knock down the stair-steps if that elephant should break down the doors and try to ascend! Next house he built would have narrower steps. If day ever came they could holler to Uncle Millard to get up a posse and kill that elephant.

Right now the elephant might be in the yard waiting, or in the shadow of the smokehouse, yonder behind the sumacs, or at the very door. All night the tense excitement held the

Fullers, though John once or twice had to scold Dele away from the windows where she went to investigate. Exhaustion finally closed their eyes, and by dawn all were sleeping soundly except John. In the clear light of day, he felt a little foolish. Unbarring the back door, he peered out cautiously. He ventured on the back porch, into the yard, the path of the night's race. The rocks were there this morning all right.... What was that half-eaten bundle of fodder doing yonder in the road? Did elephants eat fod— He turned and started to ease back to the house when he heard Jessie limbering up on revival hymns in the lot as he separated Bess and her calf. Jessie knew good and well they had been parted after he milked old Bess last night. Miss Dele would wonder how come there was no milk this morning.

John walked quickly to the road. There were tracks, very clear and unmistakable tracks.... Then, the dead calf was the bundle of fodder, and the elephant was the preacher's old mule. Jessie launched the story, and gradually the "elephant" traveled over the lower end of Wake County. For months John could not go to town that he was not quizzed about the last elephant he saw. Once there came by mail a clipping regarding the escape of an elephant from way off yonder.

The lawsuit was dropped.

XIV

"THOSE FALL SORES HAVE run on long enough. They've got to be healed up. It's too cold without shoes and stockin's now, and stockin' dye won't do for fall sores. Step across the branch to Grandma's and get some salve," Nannie Lou was instructed early one morning in October.

"Can I stay all night?"

Letha immediately told Nannie Lou that she could not. Dele followed her out the back steps and added that she might stay if she would be smart. "Mind you walk in the sand in the middle of the road, don't you'll get the toe-itch, let alone dew poison in those sores."

Down the hill bordered by the apple orchard— Grandma and Aunt Lina had to have a lapful of those winesaps. Slipping across the pea patch covered now with dew-laden grass sparkling in the morning sun, she pulled the red lusciousness from the lowest limbs and filled her little plaid gingham skirt. Along the road the sumacs hung with reddish purple berries, which Aunt Puss made her children eat to keep them from wetting the bed. Nannie Lou tasted the rough sourness, carefully avoiding the cow itch vine.

Near the branch the leaves of the poplar tree were turning to gold. What a pretty color for a hat to wear with the new brown worsted dress! Spilling the apples in the goldenrod by the road, Nannie Lou dashed through wet tickle grass and dog fennel to collect a handful of the gorgeous leaves. With a few thorns from the hog-apple bush she pinned together the leaves and fashioned a colorful fall bonnet, across the top of which she placed a dog fennel frond for a willow plume. In the branch water she noted the effect.... The willow plume drooped gracefully over her white brow as he leaned toward her and poured burning words of love into her shell-pink ear. "Oh, darling, you're the sweetest thing God ever made."

A big toe suddenly itched. The mirrored surface was quickly disturbed by a fat brown foot washing off the dew. Drying the foot on her underskirt where the wet would not show, she gathered the apples and ascended the foot log. Below there was a river deep and wide; all that separated the little girl, so bravely making her way to bring succor to her ill family, from a watery grave was the frail bridge beneath her tiny feet. Would she make it? Five lives were at stake on the one side, and on the other—the salve that would save them from a horrible fate. Darkness was all around; only a dim light from the moon showed where the bridge was suspended, the bridge that already was tottering from her frail weight. Pale but determined, the heroine pressed on and at last reached the other side.

A bullace vine, where nature had fashioned a seat exactly to fit a little girl, tempted Nannie Lou from her brave mission. She sat there and ate bullaces and talked to the birds. She threw a handful of fruit at a flock of sparrows until she heard the familiar "Per-chic-o-ree, per-chic-o-ree" and recognized a thistle bird. "Where's your yellow coat?" she demanded.

Nannie Lou opened the lane gate and hurried to the house. Grandpa was sitting on the front porch in the warm sunshine, his big black hat pulled down to shade his tired eyes, his cane lying at his feet. On through the hall where Nannie Lou had written on the wall in pencil, "This is a house," as soon as she could form letters, which had been allowed to remain, out the back porch where the shining oak water bucket and the white gourd invited a drink, into the back yard. The sugar maple would soon be leafless now, and the green grass where the cousins had played "pretty girls' house" and "red statue" all summer would soon be as brown as the thistle birds.

Grandma was at the well, stooping over the curb. Oh, if the cat had fallen in again! Oh, she did hope— No, with a long-handled hoe Grandma was carefully scraping moss from the sides of the well. "Let down the sweep just a little," she instructed Nannie Lou over her shoulder, "so I can put the moss in the bucket."

When she had gathered her specimens, she raised the sweep and removed the moss in a tin basin. "I'm fixin' to make some fresh salve, and you can go to the woods with me if you'll walk in the dry places." They took along the stone jug to bring home some spring water.

In the woods they first scratched away the pine straw to find the wintergreen. These beautiful white-veined plants

90

were placed in the tin bucket, and heart leaves were added, together with other aromatic herbs. Last of all they went to the sweet gum trees and with a sharp knife scraped the hardened gum into a box, Nannie Lou collecting for herself a big chew of the gum. Filling the jug from the spring, they returned to the house. Grandma carefully washed the herbs, placed them with the sweet gum and the well moss in an iron pot, and boiled them in spring water for several hours. Straining the essence through a muslin rag, she added mutton suet and fresh unsalted butter. When it was cold, it was a soft brown paste that smelled good enough, Nannie Lou thought, to salve an angel's wing. Grandma knew it would cure fall sores on many little brown legs.

As the evening waned, Nannie Lou began to look often toward the fringe of woods beyond which was home. Suppose a run mad dog was to bite Nero while she was away, or Mama was to get bad off in the night. She grew very quiet; around sunset she went out and sat on the back doorsteps. About her supper preparations Aunt Lina called her in to give her some biscuit dough to cut with a thimble into a little pan of doll-baby biscuits for her supper. Then she was sent to the dairy to open whatever jar of preserves she pleased and to cut some of Sunday's cake. Nannie Lou kept telling herself at the table that she didn't want to go home, that she was happy, that she was eleven years old anyhow, that it was great fun to be staying all night at Grandpa's, that day would soon come. She glanced out the window toward home. Everything was blotted out—only darkness, layers and layers of it. Suddenly she could not eat; the ham and red gravy, the biscuit and peach preserves were scarcely touched. There wasn't anything the matter; she just wasn't hungry. No, she couldn't eat any cake. Grandma talked on about tomorrow's plans, about getting some corn to mill. Nannie Lou knew she couldn't stand it any longer; she laid her head on the table and cried and cried. There wasn't anything the matter that she knew of; she was just crying to be crying she reckoned.

Grandma smiled at Aunt Lina and was in favor of putting the child to bed and letting her cry it out.

Aunt Lina rose from the table quickly. "There'll be plenty to 'cry it out' over later. I've got to go to your house to see your Papa about taking some corn to mill for us, Nannie Lou. Want to go?"

Nannie Lou wished she had wings to get there faster.

XV

ALONG THE LONESOME country road Esther Cole dully appraised her school community and found no pleasure in it. The farmhouses for the most part needed paint; a few browns and grays showed flat and drab in the October sunshine. Dog fennel and may-pop vines were powdered with dust. Here and there patches of brown broom straw waved listlessly when the little puffs of wind blew yet more dust on the goldenrod, now subdued and sad under its gray veil. Plump ears of corn nestled against dry stalks in corn fields, and the wind rattled tan fodder stacks. It was to be a dry, brown world for seven months, for all her months, the new school teacher sighed from the back seat of Uncle Israel's carriage. At one of the low rambling brown houses with a long ell, several girls were peeping from the windows. (Aunt Puss had ordered the children not to peep when the new teacher passed, all the time peeping herself when Uncle Israel's carriage came into sight.) What dullness, what mediocrity these brown houses sheltered, what ignorant patrons, what stupid children! She was shown the gray, weather-beaten school building and across the road from it the church. She sat up surprised at the white paint and the trimness of the church house, and as she stared a youth came down the steps and tipped his hat toward the carriage.

"That's Job's boy that's goin' to be a preacher," Uncle Israel volunteered from the front seat. "Job's my brother."

"Where does he go to school?"

"He still goes up here, but the teachers always make special classes for him. He's a good boy. He's our janitor and won't have a cent of pay for keepin' the church clean. Want to ride?" he called to the boy across the church ground.

"I'm not through, much obliged." Miss Cole looked back and saw him drawing water from the church well.

The ride came to an end before a plain gabled two-story frame house, painted white with green blinds at least. Inside everything was neat and well enough appointed, and her room looked restful and clean. The landlady was fluttery and might be a nuisance. (Aunt Airy appraised the trunk the colored men brought in and was pleased to see that her boarder was pale and stylish looking. She had dreaded walking into Sunday school with her tomorrow for fear that Aunt Sugar might make unfavorable comparisons with the teacher she had boarded last year, but now—she looked the new teacher over again carefully—she was reassured, for this was the most stylish teacher they had ever had. She'd hint that she'd better wear her best dress tomorrow.)

Miss Cole unpacked, hung her dresses in the closet, poured water into the pink-flowered bowl, and after a bath lay across the big feather bed to rest awhile before supper and try to forget. But there was no forgetting, it seemed. The loneliness, the aching desolation of her life, swept of all that had given it meaning, crushed her no less in this unfamiliar strangeness than at home. This "change of scene" might only add to her wretchedness, so empty did the horizon appear. Well, here she was, cut off from the things that would keep her forever reminded, and maybe she could forget by filling her mind with addition and subtraction, the continents and oceans, wars and kings and queens. She *would* forget; at least she just would not remember; if she couldn't look forward, she just wouldn't look backward. There should be no people now, none at all. She would live mechanically in this rural setting, which would not demand too much of her. There must be lots of sleep, for the long wakeful nights, the empty awakenings. Lately she had tried attaching herself to a cloud, spreading herself upon its fleecy softness and floating, floating, floating— She grew drowsy on Aunt Airy's feathers.

During the first days in her strange environment she lived as mechanically as the clock's ticking—eating, but scarcely knowing what she ate; talking, with no interest in what she said; teaching, with no conviction about what she taught; sitting with the family, but far away from them; not sleeping soundly, but no longer struggling against wakefulness; looking often at an empty finger.

The first change intruded imperceptibly, a faint stirring of eagerness during the dull day for the physical comfort of her room. A fire would be burning; there would be a subtle fragrance of fresh air and sunshine, a dish of mellow wine-saps, big old-fashioned pillows, a throbbing stillness. More decided was her stirring of interest in people. She had un-peopled her world, she told herself dramatically, except for automatons to minister to her exigencies, and no one could enter. But Ellis Pate entered definitely the first month. At first none of the plain, ordinary children who thumped their book sacks on each other's heads and watched her with in-scrutable eyes, who wanted her to play "fox-in-the-wall" and "King William" with them at recess, who brought out-rageously difficult problems for her to solve, or who kissed the tiny tracks she left in the sand, made any difference to her. But the big boy who never left his desk at recess, who could read Latin almost as fluently as she herself, who never mingled with the other pupils, whose dark eyes disturbed her a little, began to make a difference. He was a model pupil; bright, attentive, courteous among a room of boisterous

94

youth; often he flashed her a quick understanding look when some boy made a ridiculous answer to her question and then flushed furiously. She began to help him at recess, to lend him books, to miss him if he was late.

Secretly she was soon watching his reaction to the other pupils, to the girls. Daily as she entered the school room the blackboard was filled with fortunes:

Swith Williams   —*love*
Kitty Banks   —*love*
Nannie Lou Fuller—*marry*
Petrie Bliss   —*marry*

The wide-awake little Fuller girl, her cheeks burning painfully, always erased her name and then cried behind her book, Miss Cole noticed. Ellis's name was never coupled with a girl's; his cap—he always wore a hat, however—was never hidden; nobody ever sat with him, and he walked alone. The teacher mused often over him. He was eighteen, only five years younger than she herself. The boy must be terribly lonely to suffer such chilling respect from the others, she thought.

Ellis Pate was indeed lonely, without knowing what ailed him. His abnormal adolescence had fastened on him strange complexes that made him an outsider among the healthy young animals of the neighborhood. He knew he was different and alternately felt ashamed and proud of it. Uncle Job, like Hannah in the Bible, had dedicated him before he was born, and his boyhood—almost his babyhood—had been designed toward the high calling. There had been a few toys in his life: little iron banks to save pennies for Sunday school, little wooden blocks to build churches with steeples, little red wagons to haul in wood for his Mama, but no foolish jumping jacks, dominoes, air rifles, knives, or marbles like the other boys had. Early he had learned to run in and ask if he might play "King William" or "stealing sticks" or "pretty-bird-in-my-cup" on Sunday afternoons with the little cousins and to accept the verdict that it was wrong to kiss or steal or lie even in play and that his God saw him no matter what he did. When that idea first took hold of him, for days he was ashamed of his anatomy and was constantly wetting his little pants rather than expose himself before the All-seeing Eye. He never did strip and go in the pond like other boys. In his middle teens he did try for a time to be of the robustness of his fellows, to fit into the pattern, to have adolescent friendships. But when he entered a room, all the robust rural gaiety of a lively neighborhood ceased suddenly; even the grown folks switched to serious talk when he appeared, to Sunday school matters, when he wanted to hear about coon-hunting. The boys were no less shy of him than the girls. So he had gradually withdrawn into his studies and accepted his loneliness, though he often felt namelessly restless and hungry.

When Miss Cole began to offer him help at recess he remained impersonal, with a detached courtesy that intrigued. This was the way she wanted it. Paradoxically, in proportion to his increasing detachment she began to try to tempt his unawareness into recognition of her as a person, a woman-person. He remained aloof. Had the maelstrom of bitterness through which she had been swept fundamentally altered her so that she repelled? She did not guess how intrigued she was until one night in early November. At school that day some of the boys asked her if she had ever been snipe-hunting. She had never heard of it. Wouldn't she like to go? At first, no. Then she temporized; she was afraid of guns; what was it like anyway?

"You don't have to take along no guns—just sacks. All you do is sit and hold the sack open, and the snipes will come."

"Don't you bait them?"

"No'm, they just go in the sack. Snipes are thataway."

"Foolish snipes!"

96

"Yes'm. All you have to is hold the sack open and wait."

"Sounds easy. But what would I do with a bag of snipes?"

"Bring 'em home."

"Are they good to eat?"

"Why—uh—"

"Yes'm," Robin spoke quickly. "I'll eat all you can catch."

"Yes'm. That's right. Robin loves snipes."

"Le's get up a crowd and go, Miss Cole."

"Yes, le's. Girls and boys. Please do, Miss Cole."

Her eyes unconsciously turned to the corner where Ellis was reading. She did not understand the quick look he flashed her, but it was not detached. Perhaps he would like to go.

"All right. Get up your crowd and come by for me to-night, early, mind you."

Again Ellis looked at her significantly, with a half-smile playing around his mouth. The children were jubilant. A crowd of girls and boys called for her soon after supper. A month ago she would have been bored, but now she joined them almost gaily, looking around expectantly. Ellis was not in the group.

When they reached a clearing in the woods back of Uncle Israel's house, Robin handed her a guano sack and instructed her just how to hold it. She was not to stir from that spot; they had given her the best stand, she was assured; if she held the sack open long enough, the snipes would just fly in. All that was required was patience.

"Where are you going?" she called to the group when she saw them hurrying into the woods.

"We all have to be stationed at different places. We'll see you later."

With that they disappeared. This was the first time she had ever been alone in the woods. It was early; the moon was shining; she was not afraid. The young people could not be far, even though they were strangely quiet, as much fuss as they made at school! Of course there had to be silence or the

97

snipes would be frightened away. Perhaps that was it. Last November this time! It had been a night about like this, crisp clear, and cold but not too cold to stand on the porch looking at the stars and drinking in the wine of words. Inside a piano was playing, and somebody next door was singing "One Little Word." They had laughed when the song floated out to them:

"Too late, too late, all our fondest hopes are dead;
One little word, that word was never said."

"Too late yourself!" he had challenged the lilting soprano across the hedge. "It *has* been said." And he had snatched up her hand and kissed the ring in the starlight.

Suddenly she shifted the sack so that the moonlight fell full on her hand. The finger was empty all right. And the sack was empty too.

"Miss Cole."

The low voice startled her. "Yes?" She looked around quickly.

"It's me." Ellis Pate cleared the space between them and stood by her. His voice was toned to a whisper.

"Oh! Ellis."

"Yes'm."

"I didn't realize you were along."

"I'm not. I mean I came by myself."

"Stay here and help me hold this bag. Snipe-hunting's too lonesome."

"Miss Cole, let me have that sack, and you come on with me."

"All right. Where?"

"Back to the house."

"And leave the crowd here?"

"They've left you already. The girls are back at Uncle Israel's, and the boys have gone bird-blindin'."

"After snipes?"

98

"After real birds. It's a sin the way they hide in bushes and—"

"I don't understand. They said they were going to catch snipes—"

"There aren't any snipes. It's just a joke; they think it's funny to leave you in the woods by yourself waitin' for snipes, but I don't."

"I see. That's what they mean by 'leaving somebody with the bag to hold,' I suppose. Well, I guess it is funny in a way. I'll go give them their laugh."

"Couldn't you slip in your room the back way so nobody would know and let them keep on waitin' for you? They'll finally come after you if you keep stayin'."

"Capital! I'll do that. Ellis!" She turned to him impulsively. "Did you walk or ride?"

"I rode."

"Buggy?"

"Yes'm."

"Where is it?"

"In Uncle Israel's grove."

"Come on. We're going to ride over to Nannie Lou's to sit till bedtime. She has begged me so often to come."

His chivalry touched her. The boy had sensitiveness. She would cultivate him. She caught his arm to steady herself as they hurried over the corn rows toward the grove. Undiscovered, they drove off together.

Dele met them at the door, surprised and wondering how they happened to be together, but cordial. The girls ran to change their dresses when they learned it was the school teacher. John laughed heartily over the snipe-hunt, and Nannie Lou promised not to tell the children at school where she had gone. In spite of Miss Cole's liveliness, the conversation was strained. They listened politely to her account of a fox-hunt she had participated in once, but without offering to tell of similar experiences. Calvin started to mention a

99

coon-hunt some of the neighbors were planning when Ellis interrupted to ask John if he knew where the preacher was going to stay Saturday night. From that the talk turned to the last sermon and the report of the vigilance committee last conference. Kate, to relieve the tension and because she was hungry herself, brought in some late pears from the cuddy and showed Miss Cole how to try her fortune with the seed.

"Let me try your fortune, Ellis," Miss Cole challenged.

"I haven't any." He blushed so that she gave it up.

In the buggy again she took the reins from him and lightly tapped them over Uncle Job's horse. "Let me drive. Get up—What's his name?"

"Bob Glenn."

"Last year I rode behind a horse named Esther."

"That's your name."

"Yes. The horse was named for me."

"Esther's in the Bible. It's a pretty name."

"It does well enough. I'd prefer Eloise."

By this time she had Uncle Job's Bob Glenn in a spirited trot. Ellis felt a little uneasy, a little sure that sin would find him out.

"Such an exhilarating night. Crisp, cold, a perfect moon—"

"Are you plenty warm?"

"Chilly a little. Pull the robe up."

He tucked the buggy robe around her feet and slipped it over her lap. The buggy seat was narrow; they had to sit close together, their arms and shoulders touching. When his side of the buggy bumped suddenly into a deep rut in the wheel track it threw her toward him; his arm crushed her breast. He felt strange.

"Excuse me." He knew Who was watching.

"Excuse me yourself. The driver should watch the ruts. Slow down, Bob Glenn."

"I don't think I ever saw a night just like this one."

"It is—different from most nights."

"The heavens declare the glory of God—"

"What made you decide to be a preacher, Ellis?"

"Papa always planned for me to."

"How long ago?"

"Ever since I was born."

"I mean, when did you know?"

"Always, I suppose. I promised when I was fourteen."

"You never played around with the other boys?"

"They didn't like to play with me. I don't like them either."

"It's pretty lonely, this business of trying to live up to people's plans for you, isn't it?"

"Not since school started—this year."

"Ellis, I'd like to help you. Could you stay a half hour after school and let me teach you to declaim?"

"That would be too much work on you." His voice was trembling with eagerness.

"I'd love it."

"I'll stay."

"Monday then." She gave him the reins. "I'll teach you the funeral oration and then 'Spartacus to the Gladiators.'"

They drove on in silence till they reached Uncle Israel's. With a note of wonder in his voice after he had helped her out of the buggy, he said, "I never knew nights could be so pretty."

"They can be even prettier, Ellis."

He didn't know what she meant. He didn't know what this strange embryonic ecstasy swelling up inside meant either. It kept him awake.

XVI

As HARVEST GREW lush Calvin's hopes, so flourishing after Milly's visit, began to fade. Calvin liked picking cotton and leaving the white fields black, gathering the winter apples and storing them in the cuddy for long cold nights, stacking the fodder into brown shocks, threshing the black peas, cutting the cane for the sorghum—if some day he would be doing these things for Her. But in October the season began to lose its meaning. Twice at Sunday school he had seen Milly, but she had dropped her eyes before the importunity in his. Knowing now about the punishment she had suffered because of her visit to him in August, Calvin made no attempt to speak with her.

The cane-mill was set up in the Fuller grove to grind the neighborhood's sorghum. Garland Miles, who lived up the lane from Milly's home, brought his cane, and, while he stayed to watch the syrup cooking, told Calvin he would slip a note to Milly. Painstakingly Calvin wrote: "I have the shell. Does it still say the same thing? I'd die if it didn't. Can't you let me know some way?—Guess who."

Through the week the acrid sweetish odor of boiling syrup filled the air as the mules patiently turned the mill to grind the cane juice into the cooking vat. The neighborhood children gathered after school to play on the heaps of refuse and to sample the hot sorghum. Nannie Lou, engrossed with her studies, the fall activities, and collecting a new set of paper-dolls, still took time to interpret Nature to her generation. She tried to cultivate a melancholy mood which would make her see eye to eye with the poets who moralized on the decaying season—"The melancholy days are come the saddest of the year." The truth was she found fall gay and gorgeous, the happiest time of all. Yet in her desk, a cracker box set up by her bed, there were lines lamenting the death of the flowers, the last leaves on trees, the shortness of life ...

> *My heart grows sad, my eyes grow dim,*
> *For the blighting hand of the Reaper grim*
> *Is laid on flower and leafy tree,*
> *And the hue of decay is on hill and lea.*

But in spite of death and decay in the cracker box, she led the gay games around the cane-mill and invented new ones after "red statue," "pretty girls' house," and "snake-in-the-gully" were stale.

After his note, Calvin was feverishly restless till the following Sunday. He dressed early that morning and walked the mile to Sunday school an hour ahead of the surrey. After classes Milly's eyes fluttered toward him once, but fell immediately to her song book. That Sunday, dinner was gall. Calvin joined the neighborhood young folks on a hack-hunt to Rocky Branch in the afternoon, because there was nothing else to do and he was too restless to remain still. Letha had written Victor about the hacking, and he was waiting for the party at Three Pines. Nannie Lou made up her mind to tell, for Victor said her teeth looked like grubbing hoes, right in a crowd, too, every time he saw her, and she was tired of it! While the others wandered off in groups or couples to gather hacks, ride the pine saplings, roll down the hill, catch fish—it wasn't fishing to use their hands, the little boys argued—Calvin strayed down to the falls pool where he sat studying the cool depths and musing on what Milly would do if he should fall in and drown. Would she cry over his body and cling to him till they tore her away so they could put the dirt over him?

"Penny for your thoughts." Margie had been trying for several minutes to think of another way to begin.

Calvin looked up without interest. "Where's the crowd?"

"Left me. Gone way down the branch." She sat opposite and made him eat hacks and hog-apples from the branches she had broken. Fashioning little boats of leaves, she sailed them across the pool, Bogue Sound she called it, thinking of the summer excursion. Then she fancied a shipwreck, with all on board drowned except one couple who swam to a lonely island; his name started with a C, hers—he must guess. They had to make tents out of tree branches and eat berries and fish while waiting for rescue. But she helped him; she was not frail and weakly like some girls. What boys wanted to like girls that couldn't do anything but fancy work for, she didn't see—did he? All the time Calvin's thoughts raced on: "If only me and Milly could sail away and get lost. If only it was me and Milly." He walked off and left Margie talking.

When the crowd assembled with their branches of purple hacks to take home, Letha was missing. They waited a half hour; then, as night approached, warning calls rang over the hills. A search through the rocky recesses of the branch and woods was made, shouts becoming increasingly frantic as no answer came. Frightened and subdued the young people hurried to the Fuller home to give the alarm. For the first time Nannie Lou was conscious of love for her sister; all the way home she furtively brushed away tears. Even Kate stopped eating hacks and walked silently behind Calvin.

White-faced but very calm Dele met them at the road. They were to hurry along home and not worry any more. Letha and Victor had run away and got married. News had come a half hour ago. Alone with her family, Dele had Calvin go for Uncle Wes. John in a wild state had gone off in the pasture by himself and had forbidden her to follow. Somebody must try to calm him. Uncle Wes would know what to do. Calvin involuntarily shared his father's anger; yet it emphasized the hopelessness of his cause with Milly. Her father would feel that way too. Until now he had never thought of his love for Milly in terms of running away to get married. It fascinated and repelled; the idea lodged and was something to muse over.

Dele set her children at the ordinary tasks. She herself, for the first time in her life, absent-mindedly gathered pusley for her cow on Sunday. While Calvin fed and watered the stock, she milked the cow in Letha's place, seeing with relief Uncle Wes walking casually down the pasture lane as though he might be going for a tooth-brush.

104

The table was set as usual, only Dele carefully removed Letha's chair and plate the girl herself had laid at noon. For a half hour they waited for John. Finally he strolled in, grimly silent, took his place at the head of the table, and said grace almost as usual: "Oh Lord, make us thankful fortheseandall-Thyblessin'sforCri'sakeamen"—with the sling at the outset decreasing into a whispered amen. Casually Dele spoke of the corn-shucking set for Friday and planned the supper. Kate, always ready with a menu, made suggestions, while Calvin—sensing his mother's anguish in this inane discussion of food—spoke of making another barrel of beer for Christmas. He and Nannie Lou could gather the persimmons after she came from school one day; there should be enough scattering persimmons, even this late. Nannie Lou went out behind the wash-house and vomited as quietly as she could.

Suddenly a step was heard on the front porch, in the hall, across the back porch, a familiar impossible step.

"Aunt Cynthy comin' to sit till bedtime," Kate observed. Dele knew who it was even before she looked up and saw Letha in the dining room door, hesitating and wretched. Nobody spoke at first; then John, following his family's gaze, turned around, sprang from his chair, and harshly ordered Letha out of his house forever. Dele rose.

"I never got married. I run away, but I couldn't do it. I never got married. I couldn't. I—"

Desolate, white of face, she stood repeating the words. John knocked over his chair and left the room and the situation to Dele, while he sought the cow-lot. Absent-mindedly he fed and watered the stock. Calvin, touched strangely by the desolation of his sister, hurried into the front yard. Nannie Lou ran out to feed Nero and to hide again behind the wash-house. Pushing Letha's chair to the table, Dele served her plate and made her eat as she skimmed a pan of milk into the churn. Letha could not swallow; she just sat and stared, while Kate reached over and ate her second slice of pie.

After the rest had gone to bed, Letha crept out on the back porch where she knew Dele would be sitting. Desperation had made the girl articulate. Dele winced in the dark as the story was poured out. What a different bedtime Letha had planned! They had meant to spend one night in Raleigh at his aunt's, then go to his father's to live. She fully expected to marry him; she cared enough to run away. But when they reached the magistrate's she just couldn't. Every corner at home, every pot and pan, the cow, old Nellie and Daisy, the red plush album on the parlor table got in her way. And she just couldn't. She had begged Victor to come back home and ask for her. He wasn't allowed in her yard, he said, and besides if she did not love him enough— Oh, she did, she told him, she always would; she couldn't bear to give him up, only please— He had ridden off and left her standing in the road. She had walked two miles home. Now she was afraid he wouldn't look at her again, and how could she stand it! Dele knew from that hour Letha was an old maid. How well she understood the girl's panic. Once she herself—but she closed two doors and went in to John.

During the days of preparation for the corn-shucking, Dele saw that Letha had plenty to do. At night she pleaded with John to be kind to their daughter, to speak to her. Once when he was present she spoke shortly to Letha, who apparently was not scouring the water bucket to suit her mother. John looked up almost angrily at the impatience of the words. Rather gruffly he told Letha to leave what she was doing and go wash up the jugs for the persimmon beer. Almost she washed them with her tears. The kinder everybody was the sorer grew her heart. Now she believed she would run away with Victor anywhere, give up anything, only why couldn't he ask for her? She knew she had lost him, though she slipped a note through the mail begging for his forgiveness, for a chance to explain things. There was no answer. In almost no time he was courting a girl in his neighborhood.

Calvin and Nannie Lou gathered the ripe persimmons and locusts, packed them in the molasses barrel with a few sweet potatoes, covered the mixture with water and broom straw, and waited. Later they would heat some rocks to drop into the barrel, and by Christmas the beer would be ready to draw. There was still enough in the other barrel for the corn-shuckers.

By Friday the corn was arranged in huge mounds, with chairs placed around the heaps for the shuckers. The men gathered early in the afternoon around the plump tan-sheathed ears of corn, joked lustily, wise-cracked a little naughtily, sang, yodeled, and shouted over the red ears. In the kitchen the women were preparing great platters of savory chicken slick, fresh backbone from one of the shoats John had butchered the day before, sweet potatoes, fruit pies, collard greens seasoned with hog-jaw and red pepper, potato pudding, turnips. The girls frisked back and forth with huge pitchers of persimmon beer; Uncle Job asked them to bring him a glass of water. Then Cousin Nath pretended the beer had gone to his head and acted drunk, to the great merriment of the crowd, who knew that a whole barrel of their kind of beer would not intoxicate. The girls, lingering while the boys hunted for red ears, were finally called back to the kitchen to peel the syrupy batises,* to open stone jars of cucumber and pear pickle and grape and fig preserves. Letha stayed with the women and never showed herself at all before the men.

When the table groaned to the right volume for the women, the men came in and were served, not too obtrusively, for some were ill at ease with the girls watching them eat. By lantern light the men finished the shucking and then came to the house to sit by the open fire and plan their next year's crops, while the women across the room raised biddies, planted gardens, and bragged a little on their children. In the kitchen the young folks pulled stewed sugar and molasses

* A variety of sweet potato.

into ropes of taffy. Over a pan of stewed molasses Kate and Garland became conscious of each other. The syrup stuck to their fingers however heavily they were buttered, and Garland finally whispered to Kate that he was some kind of stuck on her.

Calvin did not share the light gaiety of his friends. The days were very dull. Almost every Sunday now he saw Milly at Sunday school, but she continued to avoid his eyes. The Sunday after the corn-shucking, when he came home more discouraged and gloomy than usual, Nannie Lou slipped a note in his hand. At the sight of the writing, Calvin turned weak as a woman. Into the darkened parlor he hurried with his treasure. For several seconds he sat close to the window, raising the shade just enough to give a dim light, almost dreading to open the note. If it was bad news—he drew the shade to darken the room more; even if the news was good, it would take such a little time to read it, and it would be so long before another note. On a page from her Sunday school quarterly—she had torn John the Baptist's head off—she had written: "No change. Will see you soon somehow. Don't answer. I'll explain everything. M."

At dinner he gave his chess custard, always his favorite sweet, to Nannie Lou. He said he was full without sweet'-ning. Calvin was indeed full.

XVII

ON A THURSDAY afternoon late in November Kate Fuller, with her nightgown wrapped in The Progressive Farmer, walked the mile and a half to Aunt Puss's house in response to a note from Margie inviting her to come stay all night. There she found Aunt Sugar's Maud, and Kitty Banks, who were also going to spend the night. Kate, greeting the girls, hoped Aunt Puss was going to let them all sleep in the front room where there were two beds, so they could lie awake and talk way late in the night. Kitty knew the most shocking things about married life, and it was always interesting to speculate together on what they didn't know and Kitty couldn't tell them, in the dark where blushes couldn't be seen. Everything that could be picked up from brothers or the older women about neighborhood boys was confided during these occasional midnight sessions. The little boys, who went in swimming with the older boys in Uncle Job's pond, often artlessly told Things that made their sisters almost faint with delicious shame.

"We're going to help you cook supper." Kate rose when Aunt Puss got a match from the mantel and started toward the kitchen.

"No, you all stay in here and—"

"We're not going to let you make company out of us."

"I don't have nothin' to do but make biscuit and fry up some sausage. I got vegetables enough done from dinner and a big potato puddin'—"

"I'll fry the sausage."

"Sit down. Many younguns as they is here—"

"Well, just so you won't go to no trouble, Aunt Puss."

"And don't put on a tablecloth for us. We're used to oil cloth—"

"Lessie's done fixed the table. Now hush."

"Please make home folks of us, Miss Puss."

"I will. Get up there on the organ stool and play and sing some, and I'll go tend to my kitchen works."

Maud played the organ, while Kate and Kitty sang "Marguerite" and the current parody on "Hiawatha."

> *"Oh, the lady in the boat*
> *While afloat*
> *Caught a goat.*
> *Did she hold him?*
> *Well, I reckon she did."*

Seeing Margie pass the window with the milk bucket on her arm, they left the parlor and joined her at the cow-lot. Uncle Hen, feeding the stock, began joking with the girls and declared he was going to take them snipe-hunting after supper.

"I rather go possum-hunting, myself. Let's get up a possum-hunt," Kate suggested, thinking maybe Uncle Hen would take them through the woods near Garland's home.

"Yes, do." Kitty thought maybe Mr. Hen would take them through the woods near Swain Williams' home.

"Yes, do." Maud, away from Aunt Sugar's vigilance, wanted to go in any woods at all.

But Uncle Hen wasn't going to have Aunt Sugar on him about taking a pa'cel of girls off to the woods in the dark. "The wind's blowin' up too sharp for possums. No, it's snipes tonight or nothin'."

"You don't catch us holding no sacks for no snipes."

Laughing, Uncle Hen left the lot and went to the wood-pile to cut an armful of lightwood splinters to start morning fires.

"Listen, you all," Margie told her guests on the way to the house, "I've got something planned for us to do tonight."

"What?"

"Guess."

"Go on, tell us."

"Set the dumb table."

"The dumb table?"

"We've talked about it a lot of times. Le's do it."

"Law, Mama would skin me if she was to find out—"

"What does Aunt Sugar care?"

"She just don't believe in such. She says it's a sin to try to find out the future. Still, I don't see—"

"Mama don't think much of setting the dumb table either. I remember once when Letha and Cousin Maggie talked about it, she said she didn't believe in meddling with the unnatural. I don't see no harm myself. It would just be in fun."

Margie stopped and looked steadily at Kate. "You don't believe there's anything to it?"

"No, do you?"

"If it was tried right—"

"I'd be bound to laugh though."

"No use to try it unless everybody will promise faithful not to speak or laugh till—"

"Till what? Go on."

"Till—something happens."

"If Mama heard about it—"

"She won't. We're not going to tell a single soul, ever. Everyone has got to promise faithful not to, whatever happens."

"Aunt Puss will tell, Margie."

"She's not to know either."

"Right here in her own house?"

"We'll use the old kitchen out yonder in the yard. I got the things slipped in there ready. I'll tell Mama we want to pop some corn and maybe make popcorn balls. She won't bother us noway."

"You don't really think—anything will happen?"

"Who knows? There's strange things in the world."

"I've heard the wind always starts blowing."

"And blows so hard nobody has ever had the nerve to keep on."

"Old Miss Becky tells about a girl one time that kept on. She set the dumb table, prepared, without speaking, the supper, and sat down by the empty chair to wait. She looked up at the window, and there she saw the head of a white horse. In less than a week she was a corpse, and a white horse drew her hearse to the graveyard."

"Oh, but you're not supposed to see horses. Miss Charity declares to right now that she set the dumb table when she was a girl and that Mr. Bill appeared in the door plain as life and then vanished soon as she spoke."

"Gives me a cold chill to think about a gray horse and a hearse at the window."

"It will be your future husband, if you do it right."

"Law, Margie does believe in it."

"Will you all promise not to laugh or speak or tell anybody ever, no matter what?"

"I can if the rest can."

"I will."

"Me too."

"Suppose Garland was to appear and take a seat by you, Kate, and—"

"He could have the supper. I'd heel it away from here without stopping to say howdy."

"And suppose Deck Williams—"

"You'd have me to shroud, sure."

"What you reckon you'll see, Margie?"

"Oh, I hope he'll have brown hair and brown eyes and be tall and slender with—"

"Calvin's the only boy with brown hair and eyes."

"No use for anybody but Milly to see Calvin," Kate laughed.

At the supper table Uncle Hen told the girls to pitch in and help themselves, assuring them there was plenty of it such as it was. Which reminded him of the time Cousin Nick went off to see Miss Joyce, when he first started courting her. "He took a feller along that knowed how to do 'mong the big dogs and told him to kick him under the table if the feller saw him do anything wrong. Well, they had butter in them little plates at everybody's place, and Nick he thought he'd praise the somethin' t'eat, and so he told 'em the butter was mighty good, what they was of it. The feller kicked him under the table, and Nick busted out with: 'I mean they's plenty of it such as 'tis.'"

The girls had heard this yarn all their lives, but they laughed heartily.

"Now Nick's so proper I reckon he cuts a blackeye pea into, 'fore he'd take such a big mou'ful."

"So proper he's got above his own folks, him and his proud family."

"Milly never has acted above any of us," Kate defended. "She use to spend the day with us when we all were little—and would now, if they'd let her."

"What's Milly? Everybody's always got Milly in their mouth! She's nobody's pretty girl sure thing!" Margie flushed after she had blurted out the impatient words and Uncle Hen had eyed her speculatively.

"Margie's queer," Kate mused to herself. "She's the only girl round here that's got no use for Milly."

After the supper dishes were cleared and the family and guests had talked around the open fire awhile, Margie rose, telling her mother of the plans to start a fire in the old kitchen and maybe pop some corn and make popcorn balls. Each girl shivered a little in the brisk breeze as she left the back porch and hurried through the yard to the old kitchen some distance away. The darkness seemed full of a strange quality tonight, which added to the lure of this forbidden adventure into the unnatural.

Cold air rushed out at them from the unused kitchen as the door was opened, extinguishing the match Margie struck on the wall inside. Involuntarily each girl looked toward the window, a gray twilight square in the dense night of the room, and almost feared the grayness would take form and become a horse's head. Finally, Margie lighted the lamp, and in silence the girls made a fire in the big fireplace and started their supper preparations. After hanging a heavy coat over the window, Margie mixed corn meal and water for the ash cakes; Kate heated a griddle for the scrambled eggs; Kitty set the coffee pot over the coals, while Maud spread a white cloth on the crude board. When the food was cooked, water was poured over the fire and the lamp-light turned low so that the room would be shadowy.

Each girl placed her own—and another's—plate, knife, fork, and cup on the cloth and two chairs side by side at the table. Not a word was spoken, though at the outset Kate had almost snickered out. The seriousness of the others, however, and the queerness of the occasion sobered her. She would show them she could hold in too and keep the pledge to remain dumb during the supper. Margie, very intent and solemn, bent over her ash cakes, while Kate took the eggs from the griddle and Maud dished the thin slices of broiled ham. With a start, they paused in their work when the door rattled suddenly. Listening breathlessly, they heard the wind shake the door and window and howl around the house and down the chimney. So—the wind *had* started blowing! Where would this end?

The girls avoided one another's eyes, which were beginning to show the strain and a little fear, and following Margie's example continued the preparations. Like the cry of some living thing the wind began to wail outside. Kate half wished she were at home in her warm bed, with Mama downstairs and the sure walls of their house around her. Old Miss Becky believed in spirits and things, but of course— Well, who knew? The door, shaken viciously as though by human hands, opened abruptly, and a wild gust of wind blew across the room. Kate instinctively ran to shut and latch the door, and just in time she checked an impulse to break the silence which was beginning to hold them like a spell. No, if they could she could!

Each plate was served, and the girls sat at the table by the vacant chairs—waiting. Margie, looking a little pale in the dim light, kept her eyes on her plate. An urge to talk suddenly possessed Kate, and she opened her mouth to tell her companions she liked hot vittles herself, and her future husband could take his cold if he— But she seemed unable to make a sound. Again she tried; if she said any words apparently nobody heard her, for the faces around the table remained set and intent. Only the wind broke the stillness. Suppose they were all stricken dumb for trying to solve the mysteries of the unnatural world. Her name was easy. If she couldn't say "Kate"— She would. "K-K—"

Before the word was articulated, again the door blew open, and a cold blast swept through the interior; the lamp-light flickered out, and the room was in darkness except for the faint embers in the fireplace. Then Kate found her voice and yelled for the matches. Maud shrieked in terror, declaring she had run against somebody when she arose to hunt the match box. When the lamp was lighted again, they saw that Margie was crying.

"Margie, what is it?"

"What's to matter?"

Margie continued staring at the window in silence. The girls fearfully followed her gaze. The old coat had fallen to the floor, leaving the window uncovered.

"Reckon she saw—something?" Maud whispered.

"I latched that door. How'd it blow—? I thought I did."

"Margie, what you crying for?"

"Are you—scared?"

"Oh, it—it ain't nothing but the wind. Le's go to the house and—"

"Margie, come on. We're going to the house."

Finally, Margie like somebody in a dream rose and went with them. Safe in the two beds in the front room, they planned their "first nights" with their future husbands. Kitty made each girl take an eyelash and rub it several times in the palm of her hand.

"It's gone," Kate said, searching her palm.

"I must have rubbed it too hard," Maud added, searching her palm.

"I didn't try it." Margie was sitting on the side of the bed staring at the window.

"They're the first words your husbands will say when you go to bed your wedding night," Kitty informed them.

Margie never would tell what she was crying about.

XVIII

REPORTS OF A STRANGE animal discovered by hunters in the Sally Baker woods had for days enlivened neighborhood talk. The animal had not been seen by any reliable witnesses; Cousin Sim, who was given to having spells and to seeing things, had declared around that he had seen it one night, that it was the size of a dog and had eyes like balls of fire and was white as cotton. Uncle Millard said he reckoned it was Cousin Sim that was white as cotton. Several men had heard the unearthly cry of the animal, which Uncle Hen believed sounded more like a little baby crying than anything he could think of, a piteous disturbing cry in the darkness. Uncle Millard added that Hen had heard so many younguns crying in the darkness in his lifetime no wonder the woods sounded full of them to him. The cry had followed the hunters for an hour, sometimes startlingly close and then fading into a thin wail; but though the night had been fairly bright and the men had carried lanterns it had remained, in spite of efforts to locate it, only a haunting voice.

Old Mr. Penny reckoned it was a pant'er, but whoever heard of a pant'er round there? Uncle Hen knew it couldn't be a little baby, but still— Garland accepted it as some strange animal he'd like to have a hand in catching. Cousin Sim held to his belief that it was a ha'nt, and for his part it could take the Sally Baker woods; he had no use for it a sure thing! Calvin said nothing, but he sort of felt sorry for a thing that cried like it was lost. John laughed at all the theories and remarked dryly that it was likely too much hard cider. When

116

Cousin Maggie's beau heard about the strange animal during his Sunday visit, he was greatly amused and asked to be taken along on the next hunt. He had always planned some-time to go coon-hunting, and he could arrange to spend a night in the country and take the early train back before the store opened. None of the clerks in the store had ever been coon-hunting.

John had just poured another mound of sorghum on his plate with which to finish his buttered biscuit—he couldn't seem to come out even tonight, for the sorghum and but-tered biscuits would not give out together, he was remarking to Kate at his right—when voices in the back yard inter-rupted. Hastily sopping the syrup, which again had been miscalculated and called for another biscuit, John left the table and went to the door.

"How about a little coon-hunt tonight?" Uncle Hen chal-lenged.

"Coon-hunt?"

"They're gettin' sassy, botherin' late corn and stuff around."

"Tell me the coons run you fellers out o' the woods last time."

"Nothin' never run me out. When that baby-cryin' started, the dogs took and left, and dog if I can tree a coon."

"Maybe they'll leave again."

"Not hardly. Old Brown's along, and old Brown stays with 'em. Want to go?"

"Who's along?"

"Me and Millard and Sim and Garland and—" he lowered his voice to a whisper, "Maggie's town feller. You and Calvin get your ax and gun and come on."

John went back into the dining room where Dele already was piling up dishes. "Dele, me and Calvin's goin' with 'em coon-huntin'. I don't know what time we'll get back."

"Well."

With guns, axes, saws, lanterns, and lightwood knots to be lighted in emergencies—Garland had a jug of cider slung over his shoulder—the men cut across the huckleberry swamp straight toward the Sally Baker woods.

"Here," Cousin Sim remonstrated, "you told me you wa'n't goin' to hunt in this ha'nted woods tonight."

"You go yonder and set on Sally's grave till we come back, if you rather," Uncle Millard retorted. Cousin Maggie's beau laughed heartily. He'd tell that one to the clerks tomorrow.

Old Brown just then picked up a hot trail in the field bordering the woods, and leading the other dogs he plunged into the thicket. The coon ran through the underbrush to reach the gum where four little coons were waiting for their supper of corn and acorns. But the dogs were too close. With desperate speed the coon tore through the brush and jumped upon the trunk of a gum to temporary safety. Up the tree out of reach of the dogs she paused an instant against another and more desperate race. Jumping several feet in the opposite direction into bushes that broke the fall, the coon was away again toward home. At the gum the dogs began to bark frantically, triumphantly, urging the hunters on.

"They've treed him."

"Old Brown gets 'em every time."

"Now," Uncle Hen told the city guest, "you're goin' to see somethin' pretty."

"What?"

"Just watch the dogs. Sometimes the coon puts up a mean fight."

"Le'me there with my ax. Then you all can saw the gum down." Garland cut diligently and was relieved by the others with the saw.

The tree began to waver; reluctantly, as though with one final effort at steadying itself, it turned on its side and fell. the excited dogs barking wildly sprang to seize the coon which the hunters hastened to force out. But there was no hollow; the tree was empty. The dogs could not believe it. Their exultant cries turned almost to sobbing; they were helpless and pathetic in their frustration.

"Shucks, that one was too slick. He just marked this tree."

"Of course. Sassy booger!"

"Marked it with what?" Cousin Maggie's beau wanted to know.

"A lead pencil," was Uncle Millard's answer.

Old Brown had already recovered and was smelling around the tree. In a flash he had picked up the scent and was on the trail again, the other dogs behind him. This time the men were more alert, determined not to let the coon outdo them again and mark a tree on them.

When the dogs treed the second time, Garland lighted his torch and turned it full upon the tree. The coon's eyes shone out of the hollow at the top like two coals of fire and then disappeared. Seizing an ax, Garland began cutting, and soon the tree was tottering. With gun barrels the coon and her little ones were forced from the hollow and quickly snatched by the dogs. She growled and fought gamely.

"Listen at the old scoun'el sayin', 'Don't tear my jacket, don't tear my jacket!'"

"I say so too. I'm savin' all the coon hides. Some money in 'em. If nobody wants these—" Garland interposed to save the coon's "jacket" from the dogs. "You've had your fun. Turn loose now. And go find you some more."

Garland passed the cider jug around, inviting everybody to take a swig. Some of them wet their throats just to be sociable, but John told them he had a sweet goosel where cider was concerned and couldn't use hard. They stood under the trees telling hunting yarns, laughing, joking, and teasing one another, and unconsciously reveling in a way of life that permitted men to get off together like this.

Soon the dogs were on the trail of another coon. "The old

daddy this time," Uncle Millard observed. "Run away to save his hide. Now—"

"The male and the female mate together, then, in the same hollow and—"

Uncle Millard interrupted the clerk. "He helps her make the nest, but she lays all the eggs."

The hunters, cheered by the cider and the fellowship of the hunt, went after the dogs, urging them on. The scent was fresh, the dogs, eager and excited, pressed toward another gum where other coons might be waiting breathlessly. Suddenly an unearthly cry agonized the air, wailing piteously somewhere above the heads of the hunters. The dogs stopped dead in the chase and sniffed the air uncertainly. Then as the cry again shattered the air around them, they slunk back toward the men, whimpering and cowed. Only old Brown stood his ground, but he did not advance, and he dropped his tail ready to retreat. The hunters instinctively sprang quickly away from the trees around them into an open space.

Calvin was slow to move. He looked up wonderingly. "Pore thing," he thought before moving toward the others.

"The varmint," Uncle Hen whispered. "Close. Everybody be quiet."

Breathless they waited, hoping to be able to locate the creature from its cry. Watching the trees tensely, they stood for minutes in silence. Only silence answered them. The trees were motionless in the still night air.

"I feel like it's watchin' us. Le's move on."

"But if it was a pant'er it ought to be killed, Sim."

"Somebody shoot and roust him out o' his hidin' place," John suggested.

Garland raised his gun and shot toward the trees from which the weird noise had seemed to come. The hunters waited. Only the echoes responded.

At last the men resumed their way through the woods, but with a wariness that took the edge off the hunt. They were

120

crossing the log over the run of the swamp which bordered the river woods when the strangely human wail again seemed to shatter the air above them. Cousin Sim, who was midway across the log, lost his footing and slipped into the water. Scrambling out hurriedly, he squeezed the water from his trousers as he ran to join the others, who were standing very still, their faces turned upward. With lanterns and pine knots another search was made, to no purpose. There was an oppressive silence.

"Le's leave here. It'll follow us all night."

"I reckon we just as well. But I'm in favor of comin' back in daylight and seein' what's in this swamp nohow." Uncle Hen sounded outdone as he dropped his lantern to his side.

"You won't never see It in no daylight." Cousin Sim was shivering. "It's a ha'nt."

"It's some kind o' wild varmint, but I never heard nothin' like it." John was impressed.

"I suggest we go back to the house. We've caught the coon." Cousin Maggie's beau's face looked white by lantern light.

"Why, you've not seen no coon-huntin' yet. Le's show him some. We're goin' down toward the river now."

Garland called the dogs and struck out toward the thick river woods. Cousin Sim followed hastily, though the others lingered, reluctant to leave the creature's identity unsolved. Presently Garland stopped.

"Look yonder."

"What's a light doin'—?"

"Is the woods afire?"

"Looks like a ball o' fire—"

"Oh, that's a jack-o'-my-lantern."

"Yeh, that's what that is."

"Looks like the elements is ha'nted tonight."

"They's no harm in jack-o'-my-lanterns, Sim."

"No. Not a bit."

"They's harm if you follow one. I've heard—"

"I've followed many a one."

"I've always heard they'd toll you on and on and on and on till you never could come back."

"I come back. You can't get no closer to the things, no matter how fast you go nor how far."

"I don't want to get no closer. They's things in this world that ain't none o' my business, and jack-o'-my-lanterns is one!"

"It's a strange looking light." The city man was staring straight ahead, his face whiter than ever.

"Oh, it ain't nothin' but Sally Baker huntin' her a coon. They say she used to cook coon muddles by the potful, and she comes here now and then to hunt her some young coons like she use to."

"Who is Sally Baker?"

"We passed her grave a while ago."

Calvin had kept his eyes steadily on the bobbing light. "I always wanted to follow one." He was hardly conscious of speaking aloud. "And find out—"

"Listen! The dogs has struck another coon. Come on. They're hot."

The men turned toward the river woods. Calvin hesitated and then impulsively went in the direction of the dancing light. He did not understand nor try to analyze his impulse nor why it seemed important for him to follow. If he could touch it! It must go somewhere. Maybe it just danced around awhile and burned itself out. Then it would fall, and he would know. Let it lead him on and on and on and on. In the end he would know.

He was barely conscious of the ground he was covering, so intent was he on the luminous sphere. It grew brighter and then without warning dipped behind some scrubby pines. Eagerly Calvin ran toward the thicket. It was farther than he had thought, and he was panting by the time he approached the pines. Disappointed, he saw the light dimmer now but definite still bobbing along nearer the ground apparently a hundred yards away. The pines had merely screened it from view. It was low enough to touch with the naked hand if it remained at this level. Calvin bounded over the dry underbrush two hundred yards; the light remained a hundred yards ahead. It did not appear to be moving now, but rather hanging like a ball of fire in an open space ahead. He covered the ground rapidly, but although he could not see any motion he drew no nearer.

With his eye he marked the spot where the light seemed to hover. There was a single tree near by in case his eye miscalculated the distance. Almost warily he approached; the sphere grew brighter, and for a minute he believed he was going to reach it. His eye had fooled him again. Touching the tree, he noted that the light was still many yards farther on. Yet it was closer than it had been at all. Like a small moon it burned a hole in the dark blanket of pines. Would it burn his hands?

Calvin stood for an instant gazing, fascinated by the bright luminous mystery unlike any light that lamp-oil or lightwood fire could make. It was motionless against the cyclorama of trees, within reach almost. He would know if it was a fire that warmed, and he would tell Milly. He would never, never tell anybody but Milly, and she would never tell. Nearer and nearer he eased, his eyes marking the goal. He sprang forward, every energy bent to his purpose. Stumbling over a stump that coon-hunters had left some time before, he fell flat on the ground. When he arose, the jack-o'-lantern was dancing dimly in the distance. Lured by his recent apparent nearness, he quickly followed. Through thorny brush that tore his clothes, over soft earth in which he mired, over dried reeds and cattails and swampy lowground he went on, not realizing how many miles he was covering. The light disappeared now and then, only to bob up in a new and nearer place. At last it vanished altogether, leaving Calvin standing on a slope fringed with low pines. He waited, watching expectantly. It was gone.

After an interval of waiting Calvin realized that the hill on which he stood sloped toward the river not very far away and that he was near the border of a wide field. When he saw lights in a house set in an oak grove across the field, he started. Intuitively he knew that he was on the border of Cousin Nick's plantation and that one of those lights showing faintly through the trees was shining on Milly. Forgotten now was the jack-o'-lantern as he gazed across the intervening space and tried to imagine where in the house Milly would be at this hour and what she was doing this very minute. Was she at the piano, or had she gone to bed? Was she asleep? If she knew he was this near, near enough to hear his voice if he should call across the field to her— Yet he never felt farther away. This physical nearness only emphasized the distance between them. He might go closer, close enough to see which rooms were lighted, to see her maybe through the windows, but she would not know he was there; he could not let her know. A great depression suddenly overpowered him; he felt alone and lost, as lost as that wild thing in the woods.

The lights from the big white house held him; he could not go nearer, and he could not turn back into the woods to join the hunters. Oh, Milly....

If he just lived in a big white house too and could ride up to her door, and she'd stand waiting on the steps in her blue dress, and he'd take her on his fine horse and they'd ride away, on and on and on and on. It never occurred to him to wish that she dressed and worked like his women folks; he could not identify her with any other setting than her own.

While he stood musing, he was startled to hear voices behind him. Retracing his steps, he was soon able to recognize the voices and lanterns of the hunters who were approaching the edge of the woods. Joining them, Calvin found that

124

Cousin Maggie's beau had been hurt; misjudging the direction of the fall of the tree in which the dogs had treed another coon, he had been pinned under the limb of the falling tree. Uncle Hen and John had made a saddle of their hands and were carrying him, since he declared he could not walk. Uncle Millard, who had been entertaining the city guest with more stories of Sally Baker, had little faith in the injury and was chuckling to himself at the procession. They realized when they reached the slope that they were on the border of Cousin Nick's plantation, and they did not relish seeking help from him. There was a temporary halt.

"We can't go there in these clothes."

"It's the only house close around here."

"I sure can't tote him all the way home."

"Still, we can't go there."

"Nick'll treat us all right."

"It's the women folks. None of us ain't fit—"

"We won't see them nohow. Come on. I'll go to the back and ask Cousin Nick to take him to your house in his carriage."

"We'll have to, I reckon, all these miles from home."

Calvin followed the group across the field. It was like walking in a dream, so unreal was the situation. Even when Garland had walked across the back yard and called Cousin Nick, Calvin still had the feeling that the lights in the house would presently begin dancing away from him and the whole scene would vanish into darkness or the tangled fringes of a dream. He had never walked in his sleep, but it would be like this.

Cousin Nick opened the back door and came out upon the porch. He was cordial enough and readily agreed to see that the injured man reached Uncle Hen's safely. As an afterthought he asked the hunters to come in. Calvin, his worn everyday clothes torn by thorns, stayed in the shadow of the boxwood bushes near the back gate. He heard Miss Joyce inquire of Cousin Nick from within what had happened. Dressed in purple linen, she came out on the back porch, lighted the gas, and brought from the dining room a silver tray on which were a dainty linen napkin and a cut-glass goblet of cordial for the accident victim. She gave Cousin Nick directions and then withdrew into the house, while he stepped across the yard to summon the negro driver.

Somewhere within was Milly. The silver tray, the cut glass sparkling in the gas light, Miss Joyce in her purple linen, the white palings around the well-kept yard, the brief glimpse of velvet rugs when the door was opened, of handsomely papered walls—all these shut him out so definitely that Calvin wished he had gone on back home through the woods alone. Weighed down with the heavy hopelessness of it all, he joined the hunters who, after the carriage was dispatched, decided to return home by the shorter woods route.

Milly, standing at her window upstairs, almost cried out across the darkness as she saw the hunters turn into the field. At the gate there had been one to whom she had called wordlessly, who was touching her across the moonlight, to whom she was pouring out her heart.

Oh, Calvin, don't hide. I love you ragged, tired from the hunt, dirty from the plowed ground—any way you are. Let me rest you, let me rock you, let me rub the tiredness away, let me wash your feet, let me, let me, let me—anything—just let me, let me— Her tenderness was so tangibly pulsating, their closeness so real, their union so much surer than flesh that it was like taking sacrament at church; she had touched something deeper than she understood.

XIX

A FROSTY MORNING in late November, John, rising early to peep out at the weather, saw that the snow clouds which had hovered close over the earth for days had given way overnight to a clear sky of cold stars. Stimulated by the biting air and the prospect of favorable weather for the hog-killing scheduled for today, he aroused his household to activity. A fire was kindled under the big wash pot, a hole dug in the stiff ground adjoining the smokehouse, into which the hogs-head was tilted; and while the water heated, the butcher knives were given a final whetting on the grindstone at the well. Breakfast was eaten and the table cleared by lamplight.

When John, Calvin, Uncle Millard, Mr. Bill, and Jessie started with the sharpened butcher knives and an ax toward the hog-pen, Nannie Lou hurried breathlessly into the hall closet and stuck her fingers in her ears until the piercing squeals accompanying the butchering should be over. John stood for several minutes looking over the fence at his pigs. The little runt he had protected so many mornings from the greediness of the other pigs had grown as sleek and round and peart on his feet as the rest, the little rascal! That shoat he had nursed through that barb-wire snag, the big hog he had been proud to exhibit to his Sunday visitors, the fat pigs he had toted so many buckets of swill, thrown so many watermelons to—he loved them all, but to a purpose that was about to be fulfilled. So, without flinching, he led the men into the pen; the hogs were thrown on their backs and held while Jessie slashed their throats with the butcher knives. As soon as two were killed, the carcasses were dragged to the smokehouse, where they were plunged into the hogs-head of boiling water and scalded before the hair should set. From the water, they were lifted upon planks, the hair was picked, and the skin scraped till it showed pink and clean in the early morning light. Carefully rinsed off, the hogs were hung by their feet to the gallows, while Uncle Millard and Calvin split them open and the other men continued the butchering. The viscera deposited on the table in the wash-house became Mariah's job. Ca'line, who was staying a few days at Dele's, hurried in to help rid the chitt'lin's. A homeless waif of sixty, distantly kin to all the Pates, a perennial trial and joy, Ca'line went from hog-killing to hog-killing, always seeking the hardest jobs. Her life had been spent in a succession of homes where she exchanged the last ounce of her energy for food, clothes, and snuff. She had done the work of a man, without any wages at all, since her father's death when she was a girl—broadcasting manure, mauling wood, ditching and hoeing, plowing, picking cotton, pulling fodder, most of it self-imposed. There was no stopping her once she set her head to a job, however strong the will of her "hosts" was to make her work light. Difficult to live with because of her headstrong disposition, her tendency to color facts to suit herself, she had lost a few good homes—an experience that profited her nothing. Buffeted by ill winds all her life, she was hard to the core of her tight, shriveled little body, with no softness or defensiveness about her. There was something undefeated and undefeatable about Ca'line. Just now she was making her home at Uncle Israel's, where Aunt Airy treated her like a servant when Uncle Israel was not around.

"Gi'me here a-holt o' them hog guts," she ordered Mariah. She tackled them roughly as she had always tackled life. "I got 'em to rid, don't they'll be no chitt'lin's here."

"Don't break 'em, Mis' Ca'line, do you'll have de biggest mess to be shore."

"I've been in hog works all my life!" And Ca'line broke a chitt'lin' and had the "biggest mess to be shore."

The gut-fat to be rendered into lard next day was placed in a tub and washed, while the guts were emptied, turned, washed through many waters, and salted for further soakings on succeeding nights.

"They ain't a house this side o' the river I ha'n't had a hand in their hog-killin's, Mariah Sanders."

"Ever holp Mr. Nick down on de river?"

128

"Naw." Ca'line spit into the fire. "I wouldn't work for that 'er woman."

"I would. Ev'ry house on deir place is painted white, ev'n's to de co'n crib and de back-houses."

"Don't make 'em set no better." Ca'line broke another chitt'lin'.

"Me and Jessie went over de river a-Sat'day to see his folks, and when we pass by Mr. Nick's we see dat lady o' hisn standin' dere in de wind a-tellin' dem niggers how to put dat white paint on."

"Must be 'spectin' some of her fine folks from up North."

"Is or ain't, she's shore purtied up dem tenant houses round dat place. I never lived in a painted house in my life. I wisht I could take a peep inside 'em."

"You better wisht you could take a peep inside their meal gum and meat box. You can't eat paint."

"Nob'm, but I shore wisht I could live in a white house one time."

Calvin, who had just brought another tubful to the wash-house, lingered by the fire listening to the women. It was true: even the tenants on Cousin Nick's plantation shared the appearance of well-being, of a better plane of living. The colored women that Miss Joyce always brought along to the revivals to serve the dinner and wait on her family always wore spotless white dresses and white caps; the black driver was as well-dressed as most of the Pate kinfolks; all the tenants on that river farm somehow had an air and took the shine off old Jessie's crowd, as the sleek, high-stepping carriage horses in the church grove took the shine off old Daisy and the homely surrey. His Papa was too easy, Calvin mused, with Jessie. Jessie farmed about as he pleased, planted cabbage in the cotton rows, corn-field beans among the corn, used fertilizer in his garden that was needed for the tobacco patch, got the mule and wagon about when he pleased, spent the few dollars from his share of the cotton on candy and cake and Santa Claus. He had been with them twenty years and had never made enough to repair his house, let alone paint it; it was sagging in the middle, the steps were rotting, the chimney leaned away from the dark weather-beaten walls, a ragbag was stuffed in a broken window. There had always been plenty of food on the table and enough rags to cover their naked, but never any money to improve the shack that housed them, never any money to improve their own house, Calvin thought a little bitterly. Cousin Nick got a lot out of his tenants. And what a pretty picture the plantation made with its big white house among the oaks, the white cabins nestling at its knees against the background of pine forest!

When Ca'line went to the well for another bucket of water, Calvin turned impulsively to Mariah. "Miss Joyce was havin' the place painted up, was she?"

"She was dat, wid a big fur round her neck and her hands stuck in a fur muff."

"Was anybody else— Did you see—anybody else?"

"I see de cook in a white dress cuttin' octobers in de back yard. Dey tells me dey puts flowers on de table reg'lar as vittles."

Flowers, silver vases, polished tables, women with their hands in fur muffs—Milly. "Wasn't somebody on the front porch, or maybe at the window?"

"No, suh, I never seed none de rest excusin' de workmens. I did hear de piano playin' in de big house when we went by—dat sad slow musit dat make you want to cry and don't know what over."

"Couldn't you see through the window—how she looked?"

"I couldn't see th'ugh de lace curtins, but I 'spects it was dat little pale-faced gal playin'."

Ca'line reëntered the wash-house. "You better get back to your hog works 'stead o' runnin' off at the mouth, Mariah Sanders."

"Yeb'm, I is. I was jes' a-tellin' 'bout seein' Mr. Nick's lady out a-bossin' de job in her furs and a-steppin' round in de cotton patch like a puore queen. She walk like dat all time, dey say."

"She walks like she's got corners to it," Ca'line snapped. Calvin went reluctantly back to his work. Mariah just four days ago had been close to Milly, close enough to hear her playing sad music, close enough to bring him a message from her if she had known.

At twelve o'clock the men came in to dinner. Ca'line pushed her chair in by Uncle Millard who sniffed at her several times and edged his chair away.

"Ca'line! you smell."

" 'Tain't nothin' but hog mess on my apron."

"Get out o' my nose and go to the kitchen."

"If you'd worked in hog guts all day like I have—" She continued eating as Uncle Millard scrouged in on the other side of the table.

Next morning Uncle Millard helped the men cut out the meat, heaping the kitchen table with scraps of ham and middling for sausage meat. Dele fed the sausage mill with the trimmings, with sage and red pepper, seasoning the ground mixture in the wooden tub to taste. The chitt'lin's, rinsed and soaked through many waters, were held open with bores home-made from basket slats and stuffed to hang in long festoons from the smokehouse loft. Ca'line tended the fire around the pot of lard, watching the bits of fat browning into luscious crisp cracklings, her favorite fresh. The livers, haslets, a part of the backbones and spareribs were given to the neighbors and Jessie. The pigs' feet, ears, and other portions of the head were boiled to make souce meat, which, sliced and placed in a crock of vinegar, made an appetizing accompaniment to collard greens.

John and Kate feasted on chitt'lin's, boiled till tender, browned, and treated with vinegar sauce; the rest of the

131

family preferred hog brains, tenderloins, johnny bones. Ca'line served herself from the lard stand where the cracklings were stored for crackling bread, making her dinner and supper on salted cracklings and sweet potatoes.

"I spewed all night long," she announced at the breakfast table.

XX

TWO WEEKS AFTER hog-killing, Jessie early one Saturday morning appeared suddenly at the crib door where John and Calvin were shelling corn to take to mill. He fidgeted with the button on the door several minutes without speaking. Then he climbed into the crib and abstractedly shelled a few ears, tossing the corn cobs toward the stables.

"You got plenty meal on hand, Jess?"

"Meal? Yes, suh." He studied the ear of corn. "Plenty meal."

"I got hungry for some yellow corn bread with my backbone and turnips. Send one of your younguns down, and I'll give you a peck o' yellow meal when I get back from the mill."

Jessie was silent. Calvin lifted one sack of shelled corn on his back and went to hitch Daisy to the wagon.

"I'd like to give Mr. Rafe a peck or two; he's had so much hard luck lately with his corn. But it's too common to give a preacher."

"Yes, suh."

"You better put your crowd in the cotton patch today while it's fair. I'm goin' to give you the scatterin' cotton. Ought to be a hundred or two pounds, hadn't it?"

"Yes, suh."

"Enough to help out with your Santy Claus. Ha'n't that big old outside thing found out yet?"

"Naw, suh."

"Well, let 'em believe in old Santy long as they will. I didn't know for sure till I was nearly free."

John closed the crib door and turned to draw water into the horse trough. Jessie followed him uncertainly, his head hung down.

"Children now'days find out; they're a heap forwarder than when I was a boy."

Jessie leaned on the well curb.

"You can get that other hog's head to cook with your collards, whenever you want it. Dele's savin' it for you."

Jessie remained silent.

"Where's your lip this mornin'?"

"Mr. John." Jessie pulled himself up from the curb and faced his landlord. "I've decided to move."

"Move?" John lifted the bucket of water to the curb and stared at his tenant.

"Yes, suh. Move."

"What you talkin' about, Jess?"

"It ain't nothin' you done, no suh. You been good to we all a many a year, but— Yes, suh, we fixin' to move I 'spect."

"Where to?"

"Mariah's tuk up a notion she want to live clos'ter to de river." He gazed deep into the well. "Dey's nice fish in Neuse River I 'spect."

"You're goin' to farm with Nick Pate. Is that it?"

"Well, yes suh."

"God A'mighty!" John looked around quickly to make sure no women folks were about the lot.

"'Tain't dissatisfaction wid you, Mr. John. We jes' decided we want to live wid Mr. Nick."

"Them whitewashed houses has played the wild with you niggers!"

"We ha'n't never lived in a white house befo'."

"When you movin'?"

"Next week."

133

"Well, it's a free country."

"De folks from 'crost de river's a-comin' to see us a-Christmas, and Mariah want to get settled in de new house—"

"All right, Calvin. I'm comin'."

John climbed into the wagon and with Calvin drove off in silence down the road, Jessie looking after them crestfallen and helpless. After a mile John cleared his throat.

"Jessie's a-leavin' us."

"Yes, sir. I overheard."

"Well, it's a free country."

"There's plenty you can get in his place all right."

"Yes." The silence between them was broken only by the wagon wheels crunching in the sand. "Plenty."

A fierce loyalty suddenly burned in Calvin. So, Cousin Nick thought he could toll folks' tenants away with a little white paint. Made light of the sagging roof and broken windows to Jessie, no doubt! Belittling his Papa to the neighborhood! Till this, Jessie's shack had no more been noticed than the dead hickory that had always stood at the forks, but now it would be pointed out; the rotten steps, the shackly chimney, the rag-stuffed windows would be in everybody's mouth. No wonder Jessie left John Fuller. Nick Pate kept his tenant houses up to scratch.

"I use to try to keep them window lights in, but that pa'cel o' younguns chunked rocks so bad a-playin' hail-over I give up," John mused, hardly conscious of speaking.

Calvin's face flushed from the resentments aglow within. Nick Pate with his four tenants taking the only one his Papa had!

"Jess was with me when you was born. . . . Well, it's a free country."

Calvin without realizing it moved a little closer to his father. He would break his neck but what his Papa should find a good tenant. He would save that scattering cotton himself, every lock of it, and he'd use a little white paint, too!

134

When they reached Bland's Pond, one customer, already ahead of them, gave up his place, since he lived close. Calvin, refusing his father's assistance, shouldered the sack of corn and stepped into the mill house to have it tolled. John leaned against the door in the sunshine opposite the man from the Baptist Center neighborhood.

"How'd crops turn out down your way this year?"

"Just common. Cotton's too low and cotton goods too high, though, like always. Folks in my neighborhood is wantin' to see the Democrats go back in awhile."

"I don't know. I'm a Democrat all right, but I always favored a Republican at Washington and a Democrat at Raleigh. Makes better times. Them Northern millionaires is Republicans, you know."

"Just same, I want to see Williams Jennin' Bryant go in there one time."

"Bryant's a good man, but Wall Street don't like him. If they was to squeeze down on us like when Cleveland was in there— I reckon you know what folks's cotton sold at that year."

"Well, they're goin' to do the South like they please anyhow. I don't reckon me or you either one would know no difference who was in the White House."

"No. Farmers is clear out of it, any way you take it. What ever become of that farmers' union you fellers round here joined?"

"It didn't amount to much except a few picnics and a little public speakin'. You fellers wouldn't come down and co-op with us."

"We never join nothin' up our way but the church. The union was talked around, but we concluded it would take the farmer's privilege away. Better let a man tend his crop to suit hisself."

"I joined. It looked like a good thing, only the farmers wouldn't stick together and do what the speakers told 'em to. It died down after that last picnic here at Bland's Pond. You all still like your preacher?"

"Some does, and some don't. He's a good man."

"We're still out of a preacher at Baptist Center. How much you all pay yours?"

"A hundred and twenty dollars a year, ten dollars for every trip, five a sermon."

"We promised a hundred, but we fell behind. Preachers have to live same as folks."

"We got a preacher up our way that needs a church. His corn was all nubbins this year, his pigs all died on him, his mule got lame, and he didn't make but two bales of cotton." John spit out his tobacco. "He needs a church."

"Yeh, I know about him—talkin' about Preacher Rafe Bliss, ain't you?"

"That's right. He can preach too."

"Whyn't you all call him?"

"Well, he was raised in our neighborhood for one thing, and then we got a preacher, too."

"We don't need no broken-down preacher. We want a live, wide-awake man."

Inside, Calvin watched the miller raise the gate to start the mill wheel under the house. He helped fill the hopper and stood watching it feed the corn to the huge mill stones that crushed the grain into meal, vibrating the house with their power. Through broad cracks in the floor, he could see the water, lying deep and still until the great wheel churned it into foam. There was a faint pleasant odor of warm crushed grain as the box was filled with golden meal. (*Their* meal, if they ever had anything as plain as corn bread on their table, would be white.) Today the pond, bordered by willows and scrubby pines, looked cold and bleak in the winter sunshine—no jolly picnic groups under the trees, no fishing along the banks, no rowboats to trouble the still water, no happy couples to stroll through the woods paths. (Jessie was

136

deserting. He was like one of the family. Jess and Mariah, gone?)

Remembering Ca'line's orders to bring her back some tooth-brushes, he left the mill and climbed the slope into the woods, his feet slipping on the new pine needles carpeting his path. (Yes, Ca'line should have her tooth-brushes, his Mama should have some wintergreen to roast in the oven for her chickens, and his Papa should chew all the tobacco he wanted! He hoped he would take a chew right in Cousin Nick's face.) A black gum, gray and leafless in the chill air, caught his eye. He stripped a dozen twigs, trimmed them the size Ca'line liked for her dipping, and dropped them in his pocket. Plunging deeper into the woods, he discovered under the pine straw some fine wintergreen. In his quest for more, he strolled farther than he realized. Presently he heard men's voices just beyond a thicket of young pines. Startled, he stood motionless, listening.

"I'd like to get a-holt o' some yaller corn," one of the men was saying. "Yaller makes better'n white."

"I been aimin' to see what color the toll is up at the mill. But white goes right good to thirsty mouths."

"Yeh, I ha'n't heard no complaints. But the lumber man wants good whisky and will pay for it."

Calvin knew then he had stumbled upon a still. He was afraid to move. If the men discovered him he wouldn't have a chance; they'd shoot him down and move their still and nobody would ever know how it happened. John had always warned him when he went hunting that if he ever did run up on a still to get away as quietly as he could and never to say a word to a living mortal about anything or anybody he saw. Once Cousin Sim had tried to tell about stumbling upon a still, and John had hushed him up; he refused to hear a word of it. Calvin knew if he could get beyond that cleared space he had just crossed without being seen he could ease his way back to the mill safely. But there were dried branches and dead leaves and a broken tree trunk to pass over. As he made his way back, the blood pounded painfully in his ears; he felt that he was being watched, followed maybe. Nearing the thicket of gums, he heard the snapping of dry twigs behind him. He ran the rest of the way.

When he reached the mill, John was lifting the sacks of meal into the wagon. The miller looked at him curiously. "Had a foot-race?"

"No. I hurried because I stayed longer than I meant to and—" Calvin had to stop to catch his breath.

"And went farther than you meant to?"

"Just up there in the woods, after tooth-brushes."

"Tell me there's a blind tiger over toward the creek woods, but I—"

"I didn't see any signs," Calvin assured the men around the mill.

On the way home John eyed him sharply. "You didn't run across—nothin' in the woods?" He knew from the boy's face he had found a still.

"No, sir. Not a thing but wintergreen."

John knew the boy could be trusted.

Next morning after Sunday school Cousin Nick edged his way around to John to hope there would be no hard feelings over tenants. He had never thought of bothering anybody's tenants, but Jessie had come to him asking to move to the river plantation and declaring he was leaving his present home anyway. Unless it was perfectly agreeable though—

"It's a free country." John took a chew of tobacco right in Cousin Nick's face.

XXI

A FEW NIGHTS before Christmas Dele awoke startled from a fantastic dream. She had been walking on the church grounds, which turned out to be Midway at the Raleigh fair, and while the preacher inside was trying to shout above the noise outside, bells were ringing and fakers were hawking along Midway. Dele, struggling desperately to get to the church to hear the preacher, broke through the rim of consciousness and realized something was amiss. A farm bell was ringing somewhere, and muffled voices registered dully on her confused brain. She sat up when she was fully awake and at once distinguished cries of, "Fire! Fire!" Springing from the bed she dashed to the window, thinking first of their own roof and then of Aunt Cynthy's. Something was afire down the road. Red flames shooting upward were eating a hole in the darkness. It was in the direction of Mr. Rafe's. Yes, it was his place burning up. And he couldn't get a church, and he had just lost his lot of hogs! Quickly arousing her household, she hurried into a dress and heavy cloak and followed the men to the fire.

The old storehouse where Mr. Rafe kept the two bales of cotton that constituted his money crop had been burning some time before it was discovered. Neighbors who gathered first threw buckets and tubs of water on the blazing building, more in sympathy with Mr. Rafe's desperation at the loss of all he had worked for during the hard year than hopeful of beating the fire; it had too much headway, though they fought on after they knew their efforts were futile. Water was poured on the roofs of all the other buildings so that there would be less danger from the sparks that were flying everywhere. Calvin and Cousin Ashley stood on the porch and kept the top of the dwelling house soaked, while the women drew water and relayed buckets to them.

The old oak that had stood a hundred years lifted its fiery arms against the sky, as tongues of flame shot up from the walls of the storehouse. A vague anger burned inside Dele, drawing water at the well and gazing at the destruction. Fire was so wasteful and disorderly, so final. That oak she had watched turn green in the spring and brown in the fall, gray and bleak in the winter or covered with ice and snow—soon it would be just dead ashes. Change disturbed; she loved the seasons as they came, once she got into them, but approaching transition always depressed. She didn't want destroyed even ugly old buildings she was used to.

Mr. Rafe, after the first frantic appeal to the neighbors to save his cotton he had worked so hard over, became resigned and calm. "It's the Lord's Will," he assured his wife, whose face was set and stony. At that instant the well ran dry. There was nothing to do now but stand and look. "The Lord loveth whom He chasteneth," Mr. Rafe replied to the commiserations of the women. It was his most forceful sermon, for he was practicing what he had preached at others through the years. His wife sat on the kitchen steps and looked very chastened indeed.

It was Miss Cole, the school teacher, who first suggested a pounding at Sunday school the next Sunday. Although the idea was new, there was whole-hearted approval, and plans were made for the neighborhood to assemble with their "pounds" at Uncle Millard's on Tuesday night. Miss Cole had been careful to explain that just a pound of anything would be adequate, but when the neighbors left their vehicles at Uncle Millard's to walk the short distance down the road to Mr. Rafe's, they were carrying bulky packages that weighed many pounds.

"Uncle Job looks like Christian in Pilgrim's Progress, with that budget on his back," Nannie Lou said to Christine, who was a little sulky tonight.

"Everybody'll laugh at mine, I know. Mamma made me bring a pound of soap when I wanted to bring apples."

"All her lye soap got burned up in the storehouse. They'll need soap, too."

"What's in yours?"

"Black warnuts. She can use 'em in cakes Christmas."

Garland declared the jug he carried was filled with hard

cider for the preacher's Christmas. Cousin Ashley wouldn't tell what was in the box balanced on his shoulder. "I-i-it ain't n-n-nothin' to e-e-eat, nor n-n-nothin' to wear. G-g-guess again." The children guessed wrong all the way to the preacher's house.

"What you got in your bag, Ca'line?" Uncle Millard wanted to know.

"Same thing you got in your'n," she snapped.

"I sure would love to know what's in that little teeny package Cousin Nick sent. It weighs just a pound. We tried it on our scales."

"Why couldn't he come and join in like the rest?"

"Well, it's right far for him."

"Right far for Garland, too, but he's here you see."

"He had some attraction besides the preacher. He's keepin' close to Kate tonight. Look."

"This is as much fun as Santa Claus, ain't it?"

"It's a whole road full of Santa Clauses."

"Won't the preacher be surprised?"

Mr. Rafe opened the door to Uncle Israel's knock. He was surprised.

"My friends! My friends!" he exclaimed as the neighbors filed in with their gifts. Whatever speeches had been planned went unsaid; everybody choked up a little in the lamplight, blinked moisture out of eyes, and wordlessly laid their offerings in the hall. The gaiety had given place to solemnity. They would have gone back immediately, not quite knowing pounding etiquette, but Mr. Rafe and Miss Katie, with the gracious hospitality that was about all they had salvaged from more genteel days, brought out trays of apples and made everybody take one while they looked over the gifts.

Miss Jennie had brought a Bible; nothing else was good enough to take to a preacher. "Law, he's got a dozen," Aunt Cynthy whispered to Dele. Dried apples from Aunt Sad, a gallon of vinegar from Aunt Sugar, a box of fat lightwood splinters from Cousin Ashley, sorghum from Garland, sacks of flour, of sugar and coffee, hams, sides, sausages, all varieties of fresh butter, eggs, chickens, stands of lard, were among the "pounds." Everybody moved a little closer when the preacher came to Cousin Nick's package. It was a pound of money! "Nickels," Aunt Sugar observed aloud. John explained that he and Dele had left their "pound" tied outside. It was a nice shoat they had raised to sell; they had reasoned the preacher would like to have something alive, something to feed, same as folks.

Cousin Maggie called on the school teacher, who had studied elocution and could make cold chills chase up and down young spines, to recite. Throwing her handkerchief on the table, she stepped into the center of the group. "I shall read for you 'Pyramus and Thisbe,' the tragic story of two lovers of long ago."

"Where's her book?" Aunt Puss whispered.

"Why, Puss, she learns pieces by heart; she's educated."

The attention was open-mouthed. At the end, a sigh unconsciously went out from the women.

"She takes off a man one minute and a woman the next. How she does it—"

"Made me feel like cryin'. It's a sad piece."

"Why, Letha, don't you know every word of it was made up? They ain't a bit of it so."

"I felt like the lion was so. I thought he'd grab me every minute."

"Made cold chills go down my back, too. How she does it—"

"It's elocution," Cousin Maggie informed them.

Next Miss Cole "read" an Uncle Remus story that brought gaiety back into the evening. The men liked that one.

"She takes off a nigger all right."

"Yes, education's a great thing—learns you how to talk right and wrong."

142

Uncle Hen chuckled. "I thought the old fox had him one time."

"That kittle of water had me fooled, too."

"I was hopin' the rabbit wouldn't get throwed in the briar patch and tore up, though."

"But the rabbit wanted to get throwed in the briars so he could run away. Rabbits use in the briar patch you know."

"Well, it could've been that. Hadn't thought of it in just that light."

As the neighbors rose to go, Mr. Rafe raised his hand signifying that they were to join him in the long-metered Doxology he was quavering into. A little awkwardly because of the nigger piece they had just laughed so heartily over they followed:

> *"Praise God from Whom all blessings flow,*
> *Praise Him all creatures here below,*
> *Praise Him above, ye heavenly host,*
> *Praise Father, Son, and Holy Ghost."*

They filed out quietly, solemnly.

"Looked like we was braggin' on ourselves a little," Garland whispered to Kate.

"Well, just one thing was lackin'," Uncle Millard remarked after they had gone up the road some distance.

"Looked like they was some of all there to me—even's to a live pig," Uncle Hen answered.

"No. One thing was lackin' that ought to been included."

"What, Millard?"

"A fence. Somebody ought to give a fence to keep that live pig out o' John's patches."

John grinned sheepishly in the moonlight.

XXII

KATE AND CALVIN took more interest than usual in Christmas preparations. Holly, cedar, and mistletoe were brought from the woods and made into wreaths and garlands and stuck over every window and picture in the house. Letha complained a little because after all holly would only dry up and have to be taken out as soon as Christmas was over. Listlessly she helped her mother stuff sausage, make souce and liver pudding, bake pound, fruit, and layer cakes and cocoanut pies, barbecue spareribs, bake hens, and grate a huge spicy potato pudding for John, who thought little of fancy Christmas cakes.

Nannie Lou still believed in Santa Claus; at Christmas the poet and novelist receded, and she was a little girl, so excited and happy that she could barely sleep. On Christmas Eve night Uncle Millard and Aunt Cynthy came up to eat oysters with them and to slip the Santa Claus confectioneries to Dele, who had traded eggs for them. After supper Uncle Millard told ghost stories till Nannie Lou was afraid to go to bed. Soon after midnight she awoke and begged Kate to go downstairs with her to see if Santa had been. When they neared the fireplace where the stockings were hanging, she stumbled over a terrible form stretched before the hearth. With a suppressed scream she ran back to bed, where she remained smothered in a quilt till nearly day. John chuckled heartily as he climbed back into bed and realized how blank Christmas would be when all the children found out about Santa Claus.

It was a vase and a ring just like one Nannie Lou had wanted in J. Lynn's catalogue, besides oranges and candy and nigger-toes. Before breakfast she ran down to show Aunt Cynthy what Santa had brought and to take her an orange, and from there over to Miss Jennie's. Miss Jennie used to make funny little dresses for her dolls, and now she had some of her funny little cakes on hand and would have Nannie Lou taste while she went to get a box to put some of her Christmas cooking in to send to Dele. Nannie Lou threw the cake to Nero, who played with it and then hid it under the doorsteps. For that, Nannie Lou kicked him and as quickly stooped to kiss him.

In the neighborhood yards the smaller children were blowing horns and pulling little wagons around while they stuffed confectioneries all times of day. At noon the Fullers turned their surrey in at Grandpa Pate's for Christmas dinner. Five sons and five daughters, seated at the right and left of the old patriarch, felt a momentary tug at their emotions as they noted his increasing feebleness, though he was trying to carve the turkey as usual. Grandpa Pate had a noble face, with firmly outlined features, high forehead, clear blue eyes, and closely clipped white mustache and beard. Laying his carving knife across the dish, after the family had assembled, he closed his eyes. All the sons bowed their heads when they said grace or prayed, but Grandpa with steady assurance raised his, whenever he lifted his voice toward God.

"Almighty and loving Father, we are not deserving of Thy manifold mercies. Thou hast led us through another year, and we walk in love and in peace before Thee. I beseech Thy continued mercies upon these my sons and daughters, upon their children, upon the sick and suffering. Be their meat and drink as Thou hast been mine, and they shall not hunger nor thirst. Then when Thou art done with us here on earth, take us all to Thyself in heaven. Amen." Grandpa slipped the gizzard over on Uncle Seth's plate.

Uncle Job cleared his throat and blinked away the moisture in his eyes. There was a momentary silence, broken by Grandpa with, "Hen don't like turkey, so pass him the corn bread, Lina." Everybody laughed, and Christmas dinner was on. Aunt Lina waited on the table. With the help of colored Eldorado she had prepared the feast, and her eyes looked completely tired now. She was still beautiful, though the gray showed in her hair that once had been gold—like the streets of heaven, Eldorado said often. In the plush album on the parlor table there was a picture of a handsome stranger with honest enough eyes that intrigued Nannie Lou and the other nieces.

"Aunt Lina, who is the man with the uniform on?" they asked too often.

"A man I used to know."

Beyond that they could not pierce her reticence. There was a sort of legend among the nieces that this was a soldier beau Aunt Lina caught when she used to sew for Miss Trixie in Raleigh and that he had fooled her. They studied her face with the frank interest of youth when she sang with guitar accompaniment the war ballads, and once they had seen her break down in the middle of "Dolly Gray" and go to her room where she shut herself up for hours. After that Aunt Lina never did cry any more even at funerals where everybody cried. Once when Nannie Lou had slept with her, she suggested by way of comfort that maybe the soldier in the album had been killed in Cuba. Aunt Lina had not answered.

Uncle Millard near the foot of the table was telling about the Christmas dinner he ate in the pesthouse years ago, declaring it was fried dog and mouse stew with a slice of boiled mule. Aunt Puss begged him not to begin trying to turn her stomach or she would be bound to leave the table. Uncle Millard added barbecued cat just to test her. Then he recalled the time he and Uncle Hen had gone off together to see some girls and all they had given them for supper was dead turkey and dead pig. Aunt Puss screamed then, but she sat tight in her chair. Reminiscing, John went back to the first Christmas he and Dele had eaten in their brand-new little cottage before even they had a pigpen—fried rabbit and batis potatoes it had been, and the sweetest vittles he had ever tasted. Which reminded Uncle Hen of the rabbit-hunt last fall. He had bought some pants from a bargain counter in Raleigh late in the summer and had them on when he decided to catch the rabbit that had been using in his late corn. Off he had gone through the dew, and soon he had been wet up to his waist. The pants began to stretch as they grew wet till two or three times he had to cut them off at the bottom to keep from tripping. Then the sun came out, and as the pants dried they shrank, till by the time he got home they were up to his thighs. Uncle Job did not join the laughter; he did not believe in stretching things. When Uncle Millard made a remark about dew and watermelons, too low for the women to hear, Aunt Sugar bristled and said she didn't see anything funny and asked for the gravy.

"I recollect one Christmas dinner during the war"—Grandpa's voice at once sobered the jocular—"One piece of fat meat, fat side, was all we had. It was good too—better than all this turkey and ham meat."

"That was the day you all sung 'Am I a Soldier?' on the march, wasn't it?" Uncle Job was definitely lifting the tone of talk.

"Every time I hear that song, the war comes back fresh as yesterday. 'Must I be carried to the skies On flowery beds of ease, While others fought to win the prize, And sailed through bloody seas.' The song sort o' kept the fat meat company, and we made for the Yankees like we was goin' to finish before night."

"We'll get all the family together and sing that song for you after dinner," Uncle Job suggested.

"Margie can play it. She's learnt it by heart," Aunt Puss boasted.

"Didn't know she could play anything but chopsticks," Aunt Sugar laughed. Aunt Puss bristled at that.

"Kate can play good, too," Aunt Cynthy declared, remembering the oysters last night. "They ought to ask her to be organist at Sunday school sometime."

"So many pieces she can't play. Now Maud, if she is mine, can—"

"Maud's taken music all her life. She ought to play," Dele retorted.

When they rose from the table, the men told Dele if she would have a soon supper and plenty of it they could make out. Dele smiled, for she knew her pantry was adequate for all the families she had invited to her table Christmas night.

While the older girls and boys ate, they made plans for the week. Aside from the suppers they would attend, they must have gatherings around every night or two. Tonight the boys were going to don old dresses and bonnets, disguising their faces and voices, and serenade the neighborhood; by bedtime they would have tasted everybody's apples and candy. One day they must all ramble down to Rocky Branch and climb the hills. Letha winced. Robin, suddenly remembering the hack-hunt, remarked that Victor would hardly join them at Three Pines this time, for he was getting married right after Christmas. "Did you ever get left?" he teased Letha. (Years later when the Rev. Robin Pate came back to preach the home-coming sermon at his mother church, Letha stubbornly refused to go to hear him.) The girls scrambled over the pulley-bone of the turkey, but it was Kate who pulled the long piece, tying it in her handkerchief to put over the front door at home.

"Old Garland will be the first to walk under it, bet you," Robin said.

Kate blushed. "You're so smart, don't you burn?"

"Old Garland says you're so sweet you're sticky."

"You're not sweet. You're a sour pickle, a whole jar full."

"Say, you learnt any new darlin' pieces to play for him Sunday evenin'? Tell me you've sung darlin' songs to him a-Sundays so much that he calls his sow and pigs darlin' a-Monday mornin' when he feeds 'em."

"Pity what you' as smart enough to have pigs."

"What's the sow for?"

"Robin! Robin Pate!" The girls left the table.

There was little of Grandma's gobbler left for the children. But there was an abundance of old bacon ham, barbe-

148

cued shoat, mutton, tom-thumb,* boiled custard, and cake
—cochineal, cocoanut, walnut, pound, spice, raisin, choco-
late, and jelly. Nannie Lou, having shown her ring around,
told of her encounter with Santa Claus; the little girls wondered Santa had not put snuff in her eyes. Christine had seen
Santa's track in the fireplace ashes at her house; others had
found reindeer tracks in the yards.

"Humph, billy goats," the little boys mocked. But they
proudly displayed knives and marbles and harps Santa had
left them.

There still were the serenaders to look forward to, and
brave threats were made to jerk off the door-faces † and see
who the serenaders were. Each knew he would sit close to
his Mama as always, or crawl under the bed when the weird,
fascinating beings walked in.

As soon as the little stomachs were taut to capacity, the
children ran around the house several times to settle their
dinner so that they could enjoy the black walnuts waiting in
the wood-house to be cracked. Some of the girls had brought
their dolls, and led by Nannie Lou they broke the ice in the
ditch behind the house and baptized them.

On Friday night of Christmas week Cousin Maggie was
expecting one of the rare visits from the city beau. She borrowed dishes and vases, a rug from Aunt Sad, a pair of
drawn-work pillow cases from Letha, a cake plate from Miss
Charity, and a cake from Aunt Lina. Cousin Nath said she
had so starched and ironed the house he couldn't stay in it.
When Garland heard of the prospective guest in their midst,
he bestirred himself and sent word all around there would be
a storm party at Cousin Maggie's Friday night; everybody
was to keep it a secret and bring along a sack of fruit or candy
for refreshments. Willing to help give the stranger in their
neighborhood a good time, the young people assembled

* Sausage stuffed into big intestine casing.
† Dough-faces.

under the hickory tree and moved on quietly from there to Cousin Maggie's.

"And didn't we surprise them!" Garland beamed on his companions several times during the evening, not reading the bored resentment on the faces of the victims of their hospitality.

The first game was "good morning." Margie made Calvin get out of his corner to be her partner. He had joined the party in a sort of desperate hope that Milly might slip away and come.

"Good mornin', good mornin', good mornin'," he went through the formula dully. "Can you make a cherry pie?"

"Can I take Milly's place?" Margie improvised.

"I never told you that," Kate shouted. She had whispered the answers to the girls, while Garland thought up the questions.

Next they marched to Jerusalem, and soon all the stiffness of the starched house wilted, as did Cousin Maggie when she saw the beau yawn behind his hand. After a round of "thimble," Kate was chosen to name forfeits for the bad guessers.

"Fine or superfine?" she had to know.

"Superfine. What must the owner do to redeem it?"

"Sit by him," Kate pointed to the city beau, "and make compound love." Julia took her handkerchief and made her declaration. Pretty soon the two went out on the back porch for a drink of water. Cousin Maggie was so mad she almost poked the fire out.

The game went on. "Fine or superfine?" Kate wanted to know.

"Fine. What must the owner do to redeem it?"

"Stand in the middle of the room and crow like a rooster."

Calvin was pulled forth from his corner. In the middle of an unenthusiastic crow he stopped very suddenly. The door had opened quietly, and Milly was entering.

"Go on, finish!" They teased him laughingly.

And Calvin crowed with enthusiasm.

"Fine or superfine?"

"Superfine."

"Let the owner get up there on the organ stool and play some talk music."

"It's needin' bad," observed Robin.

Maud took her brooch, but declared she couldn't play anything.

"She just wants to be begged," Swade said.

"No, I don't have my notes with me, and I can't play by ear." This was meant deprecatingly for Kate who did play by ear. With apparent reluctance Maud wound up the organ stool, pulled out and pushed in certain stops, adjusted the knee-swells, and went into "The Robin's Return."

Somebody called, "Fruitbasket!" and the boys hurried to chairs by their girls.

"Lemon side of a peach! Who ever heard of such a thing?" Robin wanted to know, looking at Kate and Garland. The organ drowned him out, but as soon as Maud paused for comment on her playing, he said: "The robin sure returned all over them keys. Let him roost now, I say."

"Play on," Garland by Kate insisted. "That was a over pretty piece."

Maud swelled into "Nearer My God to Thee," with variations.

Calvin, silent through the first solo, now spoke low to Milly. "Reckon it's goin' to snow?"

"I think it's too cold."

"What did Santa Claus bring you?"

"This bracelet, a pair of gloves, confectioneries. What did he bring you?"

"I don't hang up my stockin' no more."

"Feel in my sweater pocket and see if you don't find something."

There might not be a Santa Claus, but Calvin knew there were angels. From the pocket of one he slipped a tiny package and held it tight in his palm.

"Now you shut your eyes and hold your hand."

Between their chairs Milly slipped her hand, and a package was placed in it.

"What is it? I can't wait till I get home."

"A ring. Nothin' fine. I wish 'twas."

"Oh, Calvin."

"What's mine?"

"Scarf pin."

"I can't wait."

"You must put my ring on with a wish."

"In here?"

"No, not in here."

"Le's go get a drink of water." It was the boldest thing Calvin had ever said.

"All right." And Milly led the way.

The wind blew bitingly across the back porch where the water bucket stayed, but it was July again to the girl and boy.

In the dim light—Cousin Nath had hung a lantern on the hat-rack for the proprieties, knowing how thirsty young folks got sometimes—they stood and looked into each other's eyes. "I can't stand it you're so sweet."

"I can't stand it either, Calvin."

"What are we goin' to do?"

"I don't know." It was little more than a breath. She suddenly raised her face to his. Drums beat in his head, his arm trembled around her, his lips touched hers. The hall door opened.

"We'll have to go back," she whispered. They passed Robin and Swade at the back door. The boys wanted to know if the water was good. Returning to the parlor soon after Calvin and Milly had resumed their seats, they urged everybody to go get some of that good-tasted water. Calvin could not stop shivering, though he sat by the big oak fire. There were so many things that must be said, must be said, must be said, he kept repeating to himself while he sat close by her, their arms touching a little. Milly begged him never to doubt her, whatever happened. She wanted to write, to see him, meet him off places, but it was best to be careful awhile. Later—

Calvin saw a great purple bruise on her arm; it fascinated, held him. How did she hurt her little arm?

At first she evaded; then with the kiss between them she broke down and told him everything—how she had been almost a prisoner, how closely she had been watched, how she had been caught the night she tried to slip out and send Calvin a note. She glanced at her wrist.

"But it was the only time Father ever struck me, honestly, and if I had given him the note— I threw it into the fire, right in his face. I couldn't help it. They're good to me, Calvin, except—except about us."

"What are they so down on me for?"

"Nothing, only—only I love you so good."

"Not as good as I love you."

"Oh, Calvin, do you?"

"Better than Jesus Christ or—or God."

"No—don't." Milly shivered. "Love Them the best."

Maud concluded her variations of "Nearer My God to Thee." Kate rose to break up the storm party.

It was a relief, and it was agony to see Milly go—agony over what Milly might have to suffer, what Calvin must suffer before another meeting, relief to be by himself with the kiss. That night he re-lived those few minutes on the porch, touching her lips, crushing her to him, holding her. Flesh spoke; he could not sleep.

For days he was in a state of goose bumps. Often he slipped into the kitchen and sat behind the stove while his mother made biscuits or crackling bread for supper, confiding little things about Milly, about the bruise, about how much they thought of each other, how they didn't know what to do. He proudly showed his scarf pin, a pearl set in a filigreed heart.

"Why should they cut up, if I'm the one she likes?"

"It isn't just you, Calvin. It's us—not so much us as what we don't have. They feel above us, I reckon. They think we're just—pusley."

"How come? They're kin."

"Cousin Nick's kin, or was till he married that proud woman from Philadelphia. It's been a long time since I heard him 'cousin' any of his folks. But you're just as good as her; remember that."

"If I could start me a little farm, make some money—"

"I'll speak to your Papa. We rather you wouldn't like Milly, for they tell me her Mama's folks goes to theaters and plays cards—"

"Milly don't."

"We'll have to put up with it, if you feel that way; but go slow, and let things sort o' work out."

Then Calvin would eat supper in a little better heart, only to go to bed and toss restlessly till midnight. At the breakfast table where silence was the rule, he began talking; he took on himself all the out-door chores, made little shelves in the kitchen, mended plows under the wood shed, practiced throwing the baseball high into the December sky, dropped that suddenly to track rabbits—alternating between a reckless gaiety and deep grim silences. Dele thought he laughed too much and too little.

XXIII

BECAUSE EVERYBODY expected the serenaders during Christmas week the boys decided to wait till Old Christmas and thus take the neighborhood by surprise. They assembled at

154

Uncle Millard's to dress for the "serenade." Uncle Millard a little wistfully added touches to their costumes, wishing the boys would suggest that he join them, yet knowing it was the boys' night. After the serenaders were disguised in women's dresses, aprons, hats and veils, bonnets, and fascinators, Uncle Millard built bosoms on their flat chests and hips with cotton and old towels.

"Here, Garland, hold your head a little higher and you're Airy with that hat and veil stuck up there! Israel will be tryin' to go to bed with you."

"Shucks, I'm twice as tall as Miss Airy."

"I'm glad for my part women don't grow as big as you fellers. Do, they'd walk over us. Here, Ashley, hump over a little more and you're Old Miss Becky, with that fascinator over your head. But don't speak; do, you'll give yourself right away."

"I—I—I'll just a-a-act," Cousin Ashley promised.

"Altogether you're a right smart scary bunch o' ladies. I wouldn't like to meet you on a lonesome road a dark night."

"I—I—I'm a w-w-witch!" Cousin Ashley declared in a high falsetto, grabbing Uncle Millard.

"Now, Ashley, witches don't stutter. You keep your mouth shut or you'll spoil it. You're showin' right bad to be on the public road, anyhow."

"I—I—I'll sc-sc-scare 'em to death, w-w-won't I?"

"No doubt. Wait, Calvin, a little more bosom there. That's better."

As soon as the boys were out of the house, Calvin quickly slipped the padding from under his dress. He felt too tender toward womankind to wear a bosom lightly. Along the road the boys practiced in shrill falsettos what they would say at the different houses. They decided to serenade Old Mr. Penny first, as old folks would go to bed soon. When the door was opened to their knock, they filed into the bedroom where Old Miss Becky sat by a low fire nodding.

155

"Wake up, Becky. Here's comp'ny."

Old Miss Becky opened her eyes and stared at the "women" indifferently until she noticed Cousin Ashley. Then her face woke up; easing the tongs into the hot coals, she watched him intently. The boys put on their act, asking Mr. Penny all sorts of foolish questions in their shrill women's voices, while the old man replied in kind. Cousin Ashley, true to his promise, remained silent. Presently in the midst of the silly conversation, Miss Becky squalled out at Cousin Ashley: "Whyn't you speak?" Garland nudged him sharply in the ribs to remind him not to open his mouth.

"I know who you are. What you keep comin' back here for? What, in the name of the Lord, do you want, Sally Baker?"

Old Miss Becky's words more than her scream silenced the boys. They stared at her, as Mr. Penny tried vainly to re-sume the light banter, after a low deprecatory, "Aw, Becky!" The old woman suddenly rose with the hot tongs held aloft. "You've ha'nted me long enough. Get back to your grave, Sally Baker!"

"I–i–it's me!" Cousin Ashley screamed as he saw the tongs directed toward him.

"I know it's you! Just because you've been dead thirty year—"

With a terrified leap Cousin Ashley was in the hall, out the front steps, the other boys closely following. Nobody laughed—the weird little drama just witnessed had no funny edges for the boys till a long time afterwards. There were solemn assurances that this first venture would remain a se-cret among the serenaders.

A little subdued, the boys made hurried visits to several houses, where they were given candy, apples, and nigger-toes. Then they came to John's. Calvin had said nothing to his folks of the serenade; so they were startled at first, and Nannie Lou was deliciously frightened throughout the visit.

Dele knew Calvin in spite of his disguise and entered heartily into the spirit of the occasion, happy to see Calvin enjoying the play-acting.

Mis' Stewsticky introduced herself. "How's your husband and children?" John asked the giant of a woman.

"Up and about," Mis' Stewsticky replied in her shrill voice. "The baby's croupy though."

Kate believed to herself that was Garland Miles. "A few drops of kerosene on a little sugar's good for croup, Mis' Stewsticky," she ventured, watching closely.

"Oh, I give her hard cider and with-it."

"Garland Miles! Now I know you're Garland Miles!"

"You're wrong. Garland Miles went off tonight to see his girl. He's a nice young man, ain't he?"

Kate was less sure now who this was. If Garland had gone off to see a girl—she'd make Calvin tell her the truth, and if he had it would be cold coffee for Mr. Garland Miles.

"I—I—I'm a h-h-ha'nt," Cousin Ashley blurted out, tired of being dumb.

"Ha'nt, eh? How long you been dead, Ashley?" John wanted to know.

"Th-th-thirty year."

"You look it. Is it very hot where you been?"

But the serenaders shied away from ghost-talk, for there was the graveyard to pass and not much moon tonight. At Dele's request the "ladies" sang "Nellie Gray," shrilly and without much tune. Then the girls passed fruit cake and persimmon beer, and the boys crooked little fingers and mimicked fastidious ladies sipping tea. When they rose to go, Mis' Stewsticky decided to kiss the women folks good-by, and a merry struggle ensued. Even Dele had to run behind the bed to escape; and in spite of Kate's efforts she was caught up with behind the door and given a resounding good-by smack, while the persistent "lady" received a stinging slap across her cheek.

At Cousin Sim's, Fatty—in the midst of the "ladies'" experiences with settin' hens, bakin' cakes, quiltin', complaints, and husbands—suddenly jerked up Cousin Ashley's skirt.

"You ain't no woman. You got on britches!"

"Fatty, where's your manners, pullin' up ladies' coat-tails!"

But Fatty, unimpressed by serenaders or Santa Claus whose whiskers he had peeped behind the past Christmas, ran into his mother's closet and reëntered as a very fat, pudgy little lady.

Aunt Puss's youngest girls were really frightened. Two of them ran under the bed when that strange array of women appeared. "Law, you've skinned your back-sides," Aunt Puss declared pulling out two of the terrified girls. "It ain't nothin' to be scared of." But Aunt Puss was a little scared herself, for it could be robbers dressed up or escaped convicts. It was with relief that she saw the last one out of her door.

As they approached the church, Garland, who was leading, suddenly stopped and looked fixedly toward the graveyard.

"What you see?" But by the time the question was asked the others saw what had given Garland pause. A bulky white object, formless and ghostly, stood motionless under a tree. In silence the boys stared, wondering if their eyes were playing tricks on them.

"Now, what is it?"

"Le's investigate," one suggested.

"It's one way of findin' out. Come on." But as they approached the gate to the graveyard, the white formlessness began to move slowly, to flutter toward them.

"It ain't nothin'. Le's don't bother with it."

"I never believed in no-such, but if they *is* ha'nts—"

"Th-th-that's what 't-'t-'tis." Cousin Ashley hurried to the road. One by one the others joined him. As they continued to gaze, undecided whether to go on or to out-wait the ghost, the fluttering whiteness, without appearing to

158

move, glided slowly toward the gate. Cousin Ashley struck a trot. Before they realized it, the serenaders were running at top speed up the road, now and then looking back over their shoulders to see if they were being followed. They decided in a world of ghosts it would be no fun to be women, with skirts in the way of a clean get-away. Cousin Ashley tore his skirt as he dashed into the gate at Garland's home.

Uncle Millard at the graveyard gate chuckled heartily, folded up his sheet, and started home, satisfied vaguely that the youth so gaily setting forth from his house on an adventure he was too old for had failed to meet his challenge to their bravery. His years sat less heavily on him on his way back.

Garland told the boys he would hitch up his father's surrey and take them all home if one of them would come back to spend the night with him. Nobody relished the thought of walking by the graveyard a second time. Let the horse and the ghost race it out! When they had crowded into the surrey, which Garland slipped out quietly from under the shelter, one suggested that just for the novelty of it they serenade at Cousin Nick's. The idea of seeing inside that river house—how they lived, what they would be doing, if they stayed dressed up all the time as was the general report—pleased the boys, bold in their disguise.

"Nobody won't believe we dared. Le's do it." It would be fun to tell Uncle Millard a great tale about bustin' in on the big dogs!

"I bet we'd lose our nerve at the door."

"When Miss Joyce looks straight at us—"

"Or Cousin Nick—"

"Shucks, I won't. I'll go in first," Garland promised. "I've been in. I want you all to see that big clock in the hall; it's taller'n I am. And the shiny piano spread out over half the room, and the velvet carpets, and the silk window curtains, and—"

"Drive on. We're goin'."

Only Calvin opposed the plan. He could not bear for his friends to appear ridiculous or to be hurt, and he did not want Cousin Nick's folks to appear cold and unkind to his friends. A sense of vague divided loyalties tormented him as he urged the boys to give up the idea. But lured by the challenge of the adventure, they drove on toward the river, leaving Calvin under the twisted oak at the forks of the road.

"We'll pick you up soon as the party breaks up," the serenaders called to him.

Calvin, since he could not enter that door as himself, would not sneak in under a dress. Some day he would ride up on a fine horse, and they'd let him in! After the boys were gone, however, his hunger for the sight of Milly swept over him overpoweringly, and he decided he must see her in any guise. He walked forward rapidly and was about to shout for his companions to wait, when the flapping of the skirts around his ankles reminded him. His sensitive nature shrank at the thought of showing himself ludicrous and crude before her, and so he went back to wait in stubborn tenderness under the oak.

The boys returned in a half hour with a great show of bravado. Oh, yes, they got in, saw the big clock, the grand piano, the shiny furniture, the gas lights, the silk curtains; mired up to their ankles in velvet carpets; sat on plush cushions and warmed by red coals in a grate; drank the best somethin' that had ever tickled their throats out of a silver pitcher and ate the shiniest red apples on a silver waiter they had ever seen their faces in! Yes, Cousin Nick's folks stayed dressed up all the time just like Sunday; Cousin Nick had on a collar and tie at ten o'clock at night, and Miss Joyce high heeled slippers and a rustling silk dress and jewels around her neck. She passed around more manners than they had ever sat with and seemed tickled a sight to see them. Not one word, by preconcerted plan, would the boys say about

Milly, and Calvin though piteously hungry to hear her name would not ask.

It was as they said: the serenaders after the first astonishment their presence evoked had been received graciously. Cousin Nick in a low-voiced explanation had assured Miss Joyce that this was merely a "serenade," quite a common custom in the neighborhood once; he had been on one or two himself when he was a boy.

Miss Joyce, staring curiously at the group of ridiculous "women," suddenly laughed. "How quaint. How old English!" she exclaimed and went forward to receive the serenaders with such grace and elegance that the boys became awkward and embarrassed out of their act. Miss Joyce, just before she retired, turned to her husband musingly. "Mr. Pate, more than ever I'm convinced that Sister is right. Milly *is* a hothouse flower among weeds."

"You don't mean—you don't think that young Fuller chap dared—"

"I rather think so."

"I'll send Milly to Philadelphia tomorrow. I'll not have that ordinary—"

"Not yet. In the spring. Unless of course something else happens."

"I'll take desperate measures before— I wish I had slammed the door in their faces."

"No." Miss Joyce was thoughtful. "It was wise to show them up—such uncouth, awkward fellows. I watched Milly. She was disgusted I think."

But Milly had only been sick with disappointment when she looked over the serenaders and sensed that Calvin was absent. If only he had been in the room, had stood by the piano, had sat in a chair by their fire, she would forever have had his presence to return to. There had been an opportunity in the hall for her to learn from Garland that, no, Calvin was not sick, that he was waiting at the twisted oak for them, having been ashamed to show himself in a dress. She was almost helpless in her tender impulse to rush to him, to comfort his loneliness, to assure him she loved him whether he wore a suit or dress or rags; he was hers, she was his, they were each other's forever and ever. In the throes of her passionate tenderness she slipped a shiny red apple from the silver tray into Garland's apron pocket and sent it to Calvin because she had to send him something, a sweet compulsion that almost sent her rushing into the darkness to find him under the twisted oak.

Calvin clung to the apple desperately. He could not eat it; he could not let it rot. As the days passed there were the unfailing signs of decay. In a strange mood, he buried it in the orchard. It might be a tree. It would always be a red apple her little hands had touched. He would forever have a presence in the orchard to return to.

XXIV

THE DAY THE Hewitts moved into Jessie's house, Nannie Lou was so excited over the prospect of white tenants that she hurried home ahead of the other children to hear about the new family and maybe to get a glimpse of them in passing. If there should be some girls her age, would she be expected to play with them, to take them to school? Old man Hewitt —they would have to call him mister since he was white— said, when he came from across Swift Creek looking a place to live, that there were several girls and boys in the family. If they looked like their papa—he had been ragged, greasy, unshaved that day and didn't look so much better than the scarecrow in the corn field.

Although Mr. Hewitt had made no complaint when he saw the poor shack that would house him, John felt that because his tenant was white the window lights must be mended, the steps patched, and some of the loose boards nailed up. Before Christmas Calvin had been going to break his neck but that there should be some white paint for the house, but the scattering cotton had gone to a happier purpose. Next year he would put a gold bracelet on that little arm or fasten a locket around her throat. His own throat grew tight at the thought of the sweet contact. No work would be too hard, no days too long, no sacrifice too much, because she had whispered in his ear Christmas that she was his forever, no matter what. Cousin Nick could not break them up now; she was his forever. It was like a precious physical thing against him, when he went to the lot to feed the mules, when he took the buckets of swill to the pigs, when he sat around the fire after supper with the family, gazing into the blazing coals and dreaming unbearably tender things about her.

So, with good heart Calvin had helped his father improve Jessie's house for the first white tenants that had ever been in the neighborhood. The newspapers from the inside walls had been scraped off and a coat of whitewash applied; a new mantel had been added; one room had been ceiled with rough boards, the roof patched, a new kitchen floor laid. The outside still looked like an old lady pulling up her skirts to squat down, as Uncle Millard, who helped them with the ceiling and flooring, remarked; but John had given up buying a suit of clothes he needed sorely, and he had no more to give up for improvements, even for a white family.

As Nannie Lou approached, she saw two streams of blue smoke curling over the house, cheering sight after the weeks of cold chimneys since Jessie had moved to the river farm. The faces of two little girls were pressed against the new window panes, pale, expressionless, with big staring eyes. Mechanically Nannie Lou bowed. Their mouths dropped open as the children continued to stare with dead, set eyes; they did not speak.

"There are two little girls about the fourth grade, I

bet!" Nannie Lou threw her books and wraps on the bed and joined the family at the fireplace.

"There are four little girls and a baby boy." Kate looked up from the yoke she was crocheting. "What there is of him, as Cousin Nick would say."

"And a grown girl." From Letha who was making lamplighters in the corner. "Plenty of her such as 'tis."

"Five girls?" Nannie Lou looked from one to the other.

"And four yearlin' boys," John added.

"Twelve in that little house?"

"Jessie had about twelve."

"But I didn't know white folks had so many children."

"Color don't have much to do with it." John glanced slyly at Dele, who flushed a little but did not raise her eyes from Calvin's shirt collar she was turning.

"Will I have to go to school with them? Are they like other folks?" Nannie Lou pulled a chair to the fire near her mother.

"You'll treat them exactly like other folks," Dele said firmly.

Already they had seen enough to know they had a pitiful crowd on hand. The Hewitts hadn't eaten in two days when they moved to Jessie's house, and the ragged clothes on their backs were all they possessed in the world. John had sent two wagons to move the furnishings, expecting to make a third trip for the family. One wagon had held their all: one broken bedstead, three mattresses, a few pillows, a pile of old quilts, a rusty stove and tin safe, a box of dishes and pans, four rickety chairs. It was hard to believe folks could live on that little.

"We ha'n't got nothin' but chil'en," Mr. Hewitt had said to John when he told him they were ready to fill the other wagon. They had made no complaint, and it was only when John asked them if they had eaten their dinner that the big girl admitted they hadn't had any dinner in two days. A week's provisions had been hurried to their shack before the wagon had been unloaded. Dele had sent all the cold food she had on hand.

"The big girl's name is Sally." Letha rose to place the finished lamp-lighters in the vase on the mantel and to make a fire in the kitchen stove; it was her cook-week.

Soon after supper there was a knock at the back door. Mr. Hewitt, in his flat, monotonous tone, wanted to know if the madam had a spoonful of medicine she could spare his old lady.

"What kind of medicine?"

"Something to stop fits. The baby was took bad right after supper—"

"Fits? You better let me ask my wife before— Will you come in to the fire?"

"No, sir."

As soon as Dele heard the man's request, she went to the door. "Is the baby subject to fits?"

"Not partic'lar. Not bad as this un."

"Has it been sick?"

"No more'n common. It's always been puny."

"How old is he?"

"A year or two."

"Your wife must have fed him something—"

"She just chewed his vittles too fast, I reckon. That back-bone tasted so good to the old lady she—"

"Backbone?"

"It seemed to turn on his stomach. He was stiff as a board and blue in the face when I left."

"We better go with him, John."

Dele selected two remedies from the medicine cabinet and joined John to hurry up the road. Mr. Hewitt followed.

Mrs. Hewitt sat with the scrawny little body relaxed on her lap. Dele made a quick examination. The baby was dead.

"He's quiet. I reckon he's better," the mother said.

"No." Dele took the baby from the mother's lap and laid him on the bed. "Mrs. Hewitt—" Dele couldn't go on. A little boy baby—

There was no outcry. The woman sat staring helplessly at Dele. The big boys arose and left the room quickly. The little girls gazed with big expressionless eyes at the strangers; one of them ran and hid behind the door. Mr. Hewitt walked to the bed and looked down at the baby, bewildered a little. Only the big girl covered her face with her apron and cried quietly in the corner.

It didn't make any particular difference where it was put; they were all scattered around and about and didn't stay long at a place anyway. No, they didn't care to take it in a church; they wa'n't fixed to go in a church. No, they didn't want a preacher; they never had a preacher. No, there wa'n't anybody to send word to. Yes, there was a nightgown clean that it could be dressed in; Sally had sewed a little strip of lace in the neck, and it looked enough like a dress. The boys could tote it to a grave somewhere; no use to bother with a team. If Mr. Fuller didn't mind letting it lie on a little corner of his land that wa'n't fittin' to tend—the last one was put under an old tree that had so many roots it couldn't be plowed under anyhow. He and the boys could nail up some kind of a box if there were any boards around Mr. Fuller could spare.

"I hate I got to put a coffin on you first thing." Mr. Hewitt spoke apologetically and a little fearfully. "Course we'll take it out o' our share."

When Calvin and John brought the little white pine coffin with the brass handles and placed the baby inside on white silk, the whole family gathered around and mused wonder-ingly, ill-at-ease. Dele and Aunt Lina had fashioned a tiny shroud out of some white muslin Aunt Lina had saved from other days and had slipped a cluster of pink geranium in the waxen hand. They had made a stranger of the baby forever.

Mrs. Hewitt, overwhelmed by the strangeness and the sudden realization of her empty arms, broke down and cried primitively, not covering her contorted face nor wiping her eyes at all. The little girls, scared by her outcry, crowded around their father, whimpering a little, staring at this fine strange baby that had once been theirs; one sat alone in the cold kitchen. Mr. Hewitt, his eyes moist, gazed pridefully at the store-coffin, and the boys wiped away furtive tears now and then; they could not look enough. Sally sobbed brokenly. Arrayed in splendor, this that had been just another dirty, crying baby to pet or neglect was now a thing of beauty, too valuable to bury.

Uncle Job conducted brief services at the grave in the churchyard. Aunt Cynthy had made a little wreath and a cross out of ivy and Christmas cactus that looked pretty on the little mound off there in a corner by itself.

Next day Dele and John took an inventory of everything they could do without. Many things they could not spare found their way to the Hewitts'. A bedstead, pillows, quilts, dresses, coats, stockings, underclothes were left at the tenant house amid the same listless wonder and expressionless stares that had prevailed. Sally brightened when she saw Kate's blue percale and timidly fingered it, even before Kate turned from the box of clothing to go back home. It did not occur to John and Dele to tell of the destitution of their tenants; it was their responsibility to be met somehow. They would meet it in time.

Word got around, however, and the generous impulse of the neighbors responded to the need at their door. It was chiefly through Miss Cole, who called with Nannie Lou one afternoon to see about getting the children in school, and Uncle Job, who began working on the Hewitts, as soon as they had moved, to induce them to attend Sunday school. It was only by relentless questioning that Uncle Job learned why they would not go to Sunday school; they had nothing fittin' to wear before folks. Coats, suits, dresses, hats, shoes, quilts, chairs, a mattress, feather bed, and dishes were contributed—all worn but still in use and for the most part needed. Aunt Sugar gave one pair of socks, though it was her opinion the Hewitts were John's business.

The Hewitts dressed up and rode to church on the one-horse wagon. Mrs. Hewitt refused to leave home, and the big boys ran away into the pasture at the last minute, awkward and shy in their new outfits.

"Them girls and old man Hewitt acted real nice, just like other folks," Aunt Puss assured Dele at Uncle Millard's that afternoon. "They sure did look nice."

"Everybody has been mighty good to them. We appreciate it."

"You ought to. Cynthy stripped me. I hunted my other long underwear all over the place last night, and 'dog if I didn't see 'em stickin' out old man Hewitt's britches leg at Sunday school."

"Out o' my britches leg you better say. Them was my britches till Maggie got stirred up over them Hewitts," Cousin Nath chuckled.

"Law, Puss gave away so much I started to collect the wrong children after church; them coats and things had me fooled."

"I can beat that," Cousin Nath declared. "I leaned over after classes and asked Sally Hewitt where was Garland today. She had on Kate's blue dress."

"That Sally is pretty. If she was fixed up—"

"Yes, she's pretty."

"She sure is pretty." The men were emphatic about it. The women were silent. Nobody was sure about the color of her eyes; some said hazel, others said gray.

None of the children would go to school in spite of Miss Cole's efforts. John wouldn't interfere. Maybe they would start in next winter when they were more used to the neighborhood. Uncle Job, encouraged by his success at persuading the Hewitts into Sunday school, went one night to read the Bible with them and try to explain the Way of Salvation. He took Ellis along to do the reading, while he outlined what they must do to be saved. The men had just come in from splitting rails and the women were cutting and bringing in fire-wood, but they listened politely, hiding furtive yawns, and promised to think about joining the church.

Sally Hewitt told them, all the time looking at Ellis, that she had been to the mourners' bench several times and she'd like to be baptized if they'd have folks like her.

"There is rejoicing in heaven over one sinner that repenteth. Of course we'll receive you."

Uncle Job arose to go, but Sally begged him to read one more chapter, all the time looking at Ellis. She opened the door for them at last, and Ellis saw that she had blue eyes.

The next Sunday Sally Hewitt, in Kate's blue percale dress, joined the church. She was received with rejoicing.

XXV

Toward the end of January there was a week of damp, chilly days with muddy skies that presaged sleet or snow. During the regular Friday afternoon exercises at school, Miss Cole kept anxiously watching the lowering clouds while the children said their pieces. Swain Williams was struggling on the rostrum with the hero at sea, declaring three times that "the boy stood on the burning deck," each time louder and more eloquently, before the children's suppressed giggling reminded the teacher to prompt the big awkward boy. From that hour he was Deck Williams to all but Kitty Banks; he remained her "Swain." Lessie recited her same sad piece about the little girl who from her fevered couch kissed her parents goodnight and breathed into their ears: "Be better in the mornin'—'by." Next morning the little girl was in

169

heaven, Lessie declared dramatically, trying to imitate the teacher's elocution and glancing around for possible wet eyes. The pupils were not impressed, though, for the little girl had gone to heaven so many times in Lessie's sweet sad tone. Fatty, his hand fumbling with a string in his pocket and his eyes heavenward, raced through his lines, with nobody knowing what he said. Ellis Pate always was heard in awed silence; this afternoon with "Spartacus to the Gladiators" he held his audience spellbound. Miss Cole forgot the skies outside and sat tense and thrilled while he spoke. What a joy those half hours after school had been, and how the boy had applied himself; every gesture and inflection was perfect; at least each was her own.

The debate on the taxing of bachelors over thirty years of age for the support of public schools was the feature of the program. So Nannie Lou and Christine, who upheld the affirmative side of the question thought, believing that their impassioned answers to their own questions were proof. "Shall the bachelors over thirty years of age be forced to pay a tax to support public schools? Of course they should. I say tax them! I say tax them off the face of the earth!" Nannie Lou sat down confident of the judges' decision. Larry and Swade defended the bachelors: "Shall the poor bachelors be taxed to support public schools? Of course not. I say no, they shall not be taxed." Larry even added to his proof: "No, a thousand times no. They shall not be taxed!" and sat confident that he had the judges. Miss Cole watched the skies again. Not liking what she saw, she cut the program short and dismissed the children that they might hurry home before the impending storm. She would keep Ellis a few minutes in spite of threatening clouds.

There had been so many days of heavy skies that the girls, unimpressed, played along on the way home, reluctant to part company since a big snow might separate them for days. Fatty, Aunt Sugar's boys, Perrie, and George slipped away to the railroad to steal a ride on the freight train when it slowed down to pull up the grade past the siding. Hubert, the model boy who had never told a lie, dutifully hurried home to fill the porch with wood. Larry walked home with Lessie and Bettie, carrying their book-sacks across his shoulders. Robin and Swade followed the girls to torment them with a dead mouse they had found in the cloak-room. "Deck," still burning, took Kitty home in his buggy. Ellis, for fear tomorrow might be stormy, hurried over to the church to sweep and dust for Sunday. He was out the door before Miss Cole raised her head from the book in which she was hunting him another declamation. Depressed and a little offended, she locked the door and went on to Uncle Israel's, hoping to sleep and forget awhile.

Nannie Lou rushed in where her Mama and Letha were putting in a quilt, to report excitedly that one of the new window panes at Jessie's house was broken already.

"Better wish the window pane was all. Old lady Hewitt—"

"Letha," Dele reminded her, "your Papa wants you children to mister them."

"Anyhow her leg's broken."

"Mrs. Hewitt's?" Nannie Lou didn't realize grown folks broke legs.

"So the doctor says."

"The doctor's been?"

"Yes. A coffin and a doctor's bill in less than a month."

"She didn't break her leg for pleasure, Letha."

"It's certainly no pleasure to us to see the paint money all goin' to the Hewitts."

"It can't be helped."

"I got enough of the Hewitts already. I wish Jessie was back."

"I rather pay for coffins and doctors' bills for the Hewitts than for my own folks. I'm just thankful we're all well." Dele vaguely felt that whatever they sacrificed for the ills of others was somehow a pawn paid to Somebody.... It was pneumonia weather.

"If Mrs. Hewitt's leg is broken, then where you reckon Sally Hewitt was goin'?"

"When, Nannie Lou?"

"I met her way up the road when I was comin' from school, with somethin' in a paper under her arm."

"Why, to be sure the girl wasn't goin' to try to plant that ivy in this threatenin' weather."

"What ivy, Mama?"

"Wednesday mornin' I gave her some cuttin's of ivy to root. She said she wanted to plant somethin' on the baby's grave, but I thought she knew better than to try to set it out now."

"And her Mama in bed with a broken leg!"

That was just what had given Sally her chance to slip away to the graveyard with her ivy. The men were penning cord wood, Mrs. Hewitt was sleeping, and the little girls were eating sweet potatoes by the fire when Sally eased out the back door and hurried up the road.

She had seen that all the other graves had bushes or vines growing around them, and she wanted theirs to look something like the rest before another Sunday. HE might notice. It had been this vague stirring in Sally after some outward semblance of conformity that had been responsible for Mrs. Hewitt's broken leg. Sally had noticed, on the nights she went to Dele's for the left-over cold food, how clean and orderly the kitchen always was and decided to make their house look that way, where it would show. HE might come to read the Bible again. So, on Friday morning she had lavishly soaped the floor of the bedroom, where they sat, and sloshed water around to rinse it, hoping when it was dry it would be a miracle of whiteness. Then if HE—she knew his name, but it wouldn't be said yet—should come again he would know they lived like other folks.

Soaping the floor, she mused over two unforgettable moments with HIM. At church last Sunday she had happened to sit next him on the bench, and during the prayer their arms touched. Sharp needles went up and down her arm. Then on Monday night as she was coming home from the Fuller place with a dish of backbone stew, he had overtaken her in his buggy and had stopped.

"Will you ride?" he had asked, and she knew that voice.

"Yes, sir."

"Oh, I thought you were—somebody else. Hop in if you want to, though."

She had hopped in, happy and breathless. They had to sit close together because the seat was narrow. He drove slowly, and once when the buggy wheel on her side slipped into a deep rut he had fallen over against her, his arm crushing her breast. The needles were sharper than ever, all over her body. And her throat was dry and tight all night.

At that point in her musing, Mrs. Hewitt had walked in from the kitchen and, not anticipating a wet soapy floor, had slipped flat on her back, one leg doubling under her.

Sally passed the sunken grave covered with thorny vines and came to their corner cut off from the other squares by dead leaves and dry grass. She stooped to plant the ivy at the head of their grave. Intent on making that mound conform to the general pattern, she did not notice the gray cloud sweeping nearer and nearer till the wind caught up the dry leaves and hurled them in her face. She looked up and was frightened at the gathering darkness. Suddenly she felt lost and alone in a world of dead people. The wind sharpening into a blizzard tempo roared across the churchyard, twisting the leafless branches mercilessly and showering her with icy drops. She arose at once and decided to seek shelter in the church. A blast of wind snapped a dead limb just above her head and hurled it toward her. Jerking her body from the path just in time, she fell over on the sunken grave; it caved

173

in with her weight. Ice began to pelt her face. In horror she tried to pull herself out of the grave. Her coat caught on the thorns and drew her back. She felt herself sinking deeper as she struggled. In blind terror she jerked her arms out of the coat, and finally scrambled out.

Instinct more than reason now guided her to the church through the blinding icy storm. Terrified and breathless she pushed the vestibule door open just as Ellis Pate, having finished his janitor's work, walked out of the church into the vestibule. He came to a dead stop, doubting his eyes. She rushed to him, clung tight to him, first in relief, then in ecstasy. He did not doubt her arms. She whispered incoherently words she wouldn't have dared under less dramatic circumstances. He held her.

In the dim twilight of the vestibule they forgot the storm outside, the Bible and pulpit beyond the church door, the waning day, home fires, All-seeing Eyes. He was no longer Ellis Pate, Uncle Job's boy, who was going to be a preacher; she was not Sally Hewitt, a white tenant's girl who wore such clothes as folks gave her and ate cold food they would have given to dogs. Their forgetfulness was not beautiful nor tender; they were primitive.

Next morning the world was covered with ice and snow, with big flakes falling steadily and the wind sweeping great drifts of the fluffy whiteness against out-buildings. The farmhouses framed in the snow were drably colorless, and the dismal nakedness of the trees was outlined by a coating of ice. From faded chimneys thin lines of gray smoke were silhouetted against a dirty horizon. The withered brown of cotton stalks was the only spot of color to break the monotony of white fields, a flat deadness everywhere. That was the world as Miss Cole saw it when she looked from her window and groaned inwardly. She saw Ca'line, her feet tied in old guano bags, scratching wood out from under ice and snow at the wood-pile. (There was wood on the porch, but

174

the hard way was Ca'line's way, and Uncle Israel couldn't keep her out of the stinging bitterness outside.) This snow meant little school for several days and a lot of Miss Airy. That snow could be waded through all right. Why couldn't she have Ellis come and bring his books so that she could help him all day? If only there were telephones! Perhaps he would think of it. She would get the cook (Ca'line's status had never been explained, but Aunt Airy had tacitly approved the teacher's interpretation of her presence in the house) to make a fire in the parlor, and there would be a very satisfactory session. He must think of it; she would will it!

But Ellis Pate was thinking of another session this morning. The snow was deep and the wind was cutting, he found by raising his bedroom window, but if it got no worse before night he could wade through it to the tobacco barn. It wouldn't be so cold inside with the door closed and his heavy old coat for cover. A fire might be kindled on the dirt floor; no, a fire wouldn't do. Darkness was better. They wouldn't be cold, anyway.

Dele, looking out her window, hoped the stock at the lot and the chickens were not suffering. It would be raw outside, raw for Calvin who lately *would* do all the feeding. Without waking John, she quietly dressed, slipping on his boots, an old coat, and a shawl over her head, and hurried to the barn to do the feeding and the milking herself. When the family awoke she had the fires going and some of the chill taken off the interior. The eggs and the canned fruit packed in cotton seed were not frozen, and there was plenty of sausage and ham in the safe without making a path to the smokehouse. Her men folks should sit by the fire today, pop corn, roast potatoes in the ashes, eat snow cream, and card cotton for her quilt if they got restless. Before noon Calvin got restless. With Nero he strolled off into the pasture to see if there were any rabbit tracks in the snow. Kate stirred the flaky snow into boiled custard and ate snow cream with

175

buttered popcorn all the morning. Nannie Lou transferred the beauty outside to her tablet. She would show this one to Miss Cole. Miss Cole was so sweet.

At Cousin Sim's, Fatty, pulling back the window curtain, gave a whoop and slipped out to the wood-house. He found a wide board and a little wooden peg to which he tied a string; Fatty was never without a string in his pocket. He whistled himself past his mother, who was slicing sweet potatoes to fry, and took several cold biscuits out of the safe. After scattering crumbs on the snow, he placed over them his board, resting one side lightly on the wooden peg. He held one end of string in his hand and stood on the front porch watching for the snow birds. They soon began to pick up the crumbs under the dead-fall. Fatty jerked the string and caught four; one was too badly mashed to use, but the others he carried into the kitchen for his dinner and hurried back to trap more.

XXVI

WHILE THE SNOW WAS thawing, Dele and the girls started quilting, and as soon as the road was clear Aunt Cynthy, Miss Charity, Aunt Lina, and Aunt Puss joined them around the quilting frames, adding their small neat stitches to the squares Kate had tediously sewed together. Kate wondered who would be the first to lie under that quilt.

"Had you all heard about Cousin Ashley's patent medicine?"

"What medicine, Kate?"

"Why, he saw some medicine advertised for stutterin', and he ordered after a bottle. He told Garland about it."

"That's what he wanted with the quarter he borrowed from Hen."

"And the quarter Bill loaned him."

"Papa give him a quarter; he knew Cousin Ashley wouldn't pay back noway."

176

"Not unless there was another eclipse or earthquake," Aunt Cynthy laughed. "He emptied his pockets last summer during the eclipse to pay Millard and never owed him a cent."

"Law, he can't keep up with who he owes money to."

"Ashley took a load of melons to town last summer for Hen and never has paid him a penny of it."

"I know. I let him have a load of chicken hens the same way. But he did give me and Millard a pocket handkerchief apiece Christmas."

"Well, Ashley's afflicted. I rather give him all my quarters and all my hens than to have a child of mine afflicted," Dele said quietly. "Pass me the thread, Lina."

"This side is ready to roll now, Dele."

The women rolled the wide border and sat again to put their fine stitches through the intricate pattern, the cotton batting, and the cambric lining.

"You think John's goin' to like the Hewitts as good as he did Jessie?"

"Well, they seem to be smart. The men are all time drivin' at somethin'. They don't knock a thing off for the cold weather."

"The women either; at least I see that big girl out in the weather right smart. I've seen her go toward the church twice lately."

"She has tried to fix up that baby's grave. Did you notice Sunday the ivy she planted on it?"

"No, the grave's so far down in the corner. I don't see where that girl's so pretty, do you all?"

"No." It was unanimous.

"Men have funny taste. Her face is too doll-baby, no expression in it, and her eyes— I don't like her eyes."

"They're like a cow's. She looks milky, like a cow, to me."

"Now, Sally's all right I reckon. She comes down here real often and asks me about things. I believe she's tryin'."

"The preacher seemed mighty pleased when she joined

the church. By the way, Dele, you still lookin' for the preacher to stay at your house next first Saturday night?"

"Yes, that was the understandin' last first Saturday."

"What are you goin' to feed him on?"

"Why, just like usual; ham, chicken, sausage, and truck."

"Sure thing I'd hate to feed him this time, after he's just been to Cousin Nick's."

"From what I hear Joyce don't set so much of a table. It come through colored folks, but I was told that all she had for supper the Saturday night the preacher stayed at her house was fried chicken, potatoes, and one lemon pie."

"They say she don't have more'n a piece around on her table. Right after she and Nick were married, Nick asked Millard down to eat oysters with him one night—to show off his fine wife, what it was for. The bowl of oysters was settin' right at Millard's place, so he thought it was his and pitched in and ate the bowlful. That was all there was except a fancy side-dish. Nick never has asked any more of his kinfolks down there to eat."

"That's what keeps Milly so thin; she don't get enough to eat."

"They want her to be thin and pale. That's the style. Look at the teacher."

"Yes, Miss Cole don't weigh but a hundred pounds."

"She don't eat nothin'. Airy says she hardly ever finishes one biscuit for breakfast."

"Sugar says who would eat but one of Airy's biscuits! Sugar's still miffed over the teacher boardin' at Airy's."

"It takes Ca'line to tell about the teacher. She went in one mornin' with her bed-stick to beat up the feather bed and scared Miss Cole, who was still under the cover. Ca'line can look mighty fierce, you know."

"She calls Ca'line the cook. But I don't fault Miss Cole for that; it's Airy's doin's."

"No, Miss Cole don't know no better. She must be a good

178

teacher; all the children likes her. She's learnin' Job's boy how to speak elocution. They stay after school every day."

"Ellis ought to make a good preacher some day. He's cut out for one."

"Yes, Job ought to be mighty proud of raisin' such a good boy; he won't even go to parties and gatherin's or play baseball."

"It ain't no sin to play baseball."

"I know it ain't, Dele. I just meant Ellis is too full o' religion to do anything worldly. He can teach a Sunday school lesson same as a man."

"And make a nice talk too. Last time he spoke it was like a sermon, with a text and all; for a young chap it was as good as I ever heard that Sunday."

"He sure did. Maggie's beau said so too, and he hears all the city fellers preach."

"Nettie says he's as good as anything they have up there in Raleigh."

"How many boarders has Nettie got now?"

"The same crowd. Cousin Sell dropped in on her last week; she said she'd keep him awhile, but for us to be lookin' out any time for him in this neighborhood."

"Millard likes to see him come, but I tell him if he had the waitin' on him to do the shoe would be on the other foot. I sure don't begrudge him his vittles, but he won't even draw a bucket of water."

"That's right—just sets and waits for the women to swing the chain for him."

"Have you planted your garden peas yet?"

"No; I always try to get them in the ground on Valentine Day."

"I'm goin' to plant my potatoes dark nights this year. Last year we put them in light nights, and the bugs eat us up."

"Millard don't believe much in old signs, but I can beat him with a garden every time. Last year I just let the moons go and planted my beans and peas on the waste of the moon. There was plenty of blooms, but that was about all. I'm goin' back to my old way this year."

"Beans will sure run to blooms and not half fill out. Like soap. Just try some one time on the wane of the moon and see what happens."

"I did one time when I was first married, and the cakes of soap shrunk up to nothin'. That learned me."

The quilt was finished, and the women looked on it with pride. As they rose to go, there was a general sigh of relief. The women had talked and quilted till night, leaving many fine stitches in Kate's log cabin quilt.

John, after Confurnce on Saturday, placed the preacher's satchel in the foot of the surrey and walked back up the hill to await his guest. A little self-consciously he returned with the preacher, who climbed into the front seat and gave unwonted dignity and importance to the Fuller surrey at the edge of the grove. Nannie Lou, on the back seat between Dele and Letha, kept her head turned stiffly away from the church, knowing that Christine and the other cousins were staring enviously and wishing the preacher were going to spend Saturday night at their house. Nannie Lou relished the sense of importance, the anticipation of the appetizing supper ahead, company talk around the parlor fire; there was just one part she didn't like, but her Mama might leave this out tonight—bedtime prayer and all that kneeling around chairs—when the preacher came.

Kate, sitting high on Aunt Cynthy's lap, was riding home in Uncle Millard's buggy, and Calvin had already started out walking home while the family awaited the guest, who had a certain amount of hand-shaking to do after each service. This provided the extra room in the vehicle. Kate was telling Aunt Cynthy about the cake that rose and fell and was too sad to put before anybody, much less the preacher.

"It looked just like Miss Jennie," Kate laughed.

"You women folks ain't go no sense. Sad cakes is the best kind," Uncle Millard insisted.

"I recollect Willie use to beg me to leave a streak of raw in the cake, whenever he'd come in the kitchen where I was bakin'. And seemed like every time the cake would turn out good because I wanted that raw streak in it for Willie. Now," Aunt Cynthy was suddenly wistful, "it ain't no trouble to make a failure." She glanced toward the graveyard.

"You don't never fail on peach preserves," Uncle Millard added quickly, touching his mule with the reins. "Least, Sell thinks you make the best—"

"Hush, Millard."

"Sell's stuck on the old lady's peach preserves, Kate. Last time he was at our house—"

"That'll do, Millard. You've told that enough." Aunt Cynthy was laughing now.

Calvin walked briskly over the frozen ground, seeing only Milly's eyes raised to his with that searching appeal. She had meant something special by that sudden look just after services, and Calvin was hesitating between elation at the certainty of a message flashed to him and distress at her pallor and the desperate pleading in her glance. It was possible that she would send some word by Nannie Lou; she had once, and that note had made a big difference in his day last fall. He would get the fires started in the house, and by that time maybe they would be home. The last first Saturday this time the preacher was riding toward Neuse River in Cousin Nick's carriage, sitting on the back seat with Miss Joyce, while Milly sat with her father on the front. Calvin had watched that carriage out of sight.

The conversation after the weather was passed on was a little strained as they rode along home in the surrey, but the preacher soon put things at ease by telling a joke on a fellow-preacher who had lost a set of false teeth in a pool and who recovered them with a piece of fried chicken. "They accuse preachers of making it right hard on young chickens, Sister Fuller. I reckon we're guilty."

Dele wondered if she shouldn't have killed a fryer instead of the fat dominecker hen, but Kate had thought baked hen with brown dressing and rich egg gravy would make a prettier dish.

At home the family sat together in the parlor with the guest a little while before Dele and Kate went out to cook supper and Letha to milk the cow. John would have liked to escape, but Calvin rose quickly after the women left and told his father he would attend to the feeding. Nannie Lou, enjoying the company-talk but afraid her father might slip out and leave just her with the preacher, hurried into the hall beyond reach of such an embarrassment. Breaking off hunks of the sad cake Kate had laughed so much over, she fed Nero and slipped back at intervals to the hall to hear what they were talking about in the parlor now.

In the kitchen Dele, after grinding a cup of parched coffee in the coffee mill, sifted the flour for the biscuits, mixing some extra lard with her clabber and salt and leavening so the biscuits would be nice and short tonight. Kate washed a link of sausage in hot water and cut generous pieces into the frying pan, slicing ham into another to broil. After the chicken and dressing were placed in the oven to be warmed, she opened three jars of preserves and pickles and cut the cocoanut pies and the pound cake. Kate never liked for much of the tablecloth to show, and finding too much white space near the foot of the table to suit her she added a dish of turnip greens left over from dinner.

At supper the preacher, relishing the fine meal the sisters had prepared, talked and laughed just like anybody else, adding a joke now and then. Nannie Lou, who had begged to be allowed to wait so she could eat more, listened in the kitchen and once laughed out louder than those at the table.

"One of my favorite stories," the preacher said, taking a

182

slice of ham, "is about the Carolina boy who was walking along the road with a bucket of berries. A lady from up Massachusetts way was driving along and slowed up to ask: 'Little man, what do you ask for your blackberries?' The little boy said, 'Eight cent a quart, ma'am.' The lady said, 'My goodness, don't you know if you had them in Boston you could sell them for fifty cents a quart?' The little boy replied: 'Yes'm, I reckon so—and if I had this here bucket of water in hell I could get a million dollars for it.'"

John laughed heartily; he couldn't wait to tell Uncle Millard that one. Dele did not think the preacher should have used "hell," even in a story.

"One time there were two little boys fighting when the Sunday school teacher stepped up," the preacher continued. 'Why, little man, don't you know you mustn't fight?' The little boy answered, 'Yes sir, but he hit me first.' The teacher reminded him that the Bible says to turn the other cheek. 'Yes sir, I did that. Then I remembered the Bible says that it is more blessed to give than to receive. So I let him have it.'"

Nannie Lou began to wish they'd hurry up; it was taking so long there couldn't be much food left. But there was still an abundance when she sat down at the table. With the dishes washed and the kitchen in order, the family again gathered around the parlor fire where the preacher told about his experiences on the farm when he was a boy and John related his elephant story. There was so much merriment and laughter that Nannie Lou began to feel reassured about the bedtime praying.

But at ten o'clock, Dele asked the preacher to have family prayer. She handed him the big Bible, and he read a Psalm, explaining and applying as he went. Closing the Book, he paused a minute in solemn reflection before he said, "Let us pray."

John and Dele immediately knelt at their chairs; Kate after a brief pause followed their example, for she was old enough now to do like the grown folks. Nannie Lou hesitated, and then her back stiffened stubbornly. The parlor was no place to read and pray; it was too intimate and solemn there. She just would not kneel, even if her Mama got after her later. What if she had joined the church? Kneeling in front of folks made her feel self-conscious and foolish. Peeping from between her fingers, she saw that Calvin and Letha also were bowed in their chairs and that only Kate was acting growny. Let her kneel!

"Bless this home, oh God. May it abide in Thy tender love and mercy, always safe and secure under Thy watch care so that no ill may fall suddenly or sorrow confuse. Bless the father and mother; may they be examples of piety and godliness—"

John knew Dele was thinking about his "confounding" the mules, and suddenly he felt resentful toward her and a little fretted—

"of Christian forbearance and good works and undefiled speech, abounding always in faith—"

John flushed; Dele had told the preacher to pray like that so it would hit him—

"and may the children in this home love and honor and obey their father and mother—"

Nannie Lou didn't like that; of course she loved and honored Mama and Papa, but he had no business preaching at her in front of God like that—

"so that their days may be long upon the land which Thou hast given them—"

Nannie Lou impulsively resolved to obey in the future better than she had in the past, for after all God did have the upper hand and could make her days long or short on this earth; she would rather mind Mama even if it did mean staying out of the sore-throat honey and other things than to live a short time on this earth—

"May they all live in brotherly love—"

184

All right, if old Letha would stop telling on her everything she did—

"and peace and unity, so that the example of this Christian home may bless the community and be a—"

Kate agreed with every word. It was nice having the preacher come and eat and pray with them. If she ever had a home she'd invite him to stay there a lot of Saturday nights. She'd have fried chicken and ham and barbecue and four kinds of cake and pickles, and the preacher would go home and tell his folks what a good table Mrs.—whoever she was— set. It would be nice kneeling like this in her parlor with the children and Whoever-he-was around her and a good break- fast planned for the next morning—

"memorial to Thy Name. Watch over us as we sleep—"

Letha suppressed a yawn and wished he would wind up so she could get to sleep—

"and may we meditate upon Thy goodness in the night watches—"

Calvin knew he would meditate upon Milly tonight. She had sent no word by Nannie Lou. He sensed her distress without being able to fathom it. There was something strained and worried about her manner at church this after- noon, her face was paler than usual, and the eyes she lifted toward him in that instant before her father hurried her down the aisle out of the church were sort of pleading and desperate. He had looked after her helplessly, hoping she would turn once more before she reached the carriage. What had she meant by that sudden flash of pleading? Her face was so white—was she well? If she should get sick— Oh, Lord, don't let her get sick or suffer or be hurt anyway; put it on me instead of her; she's so little and sweet—

"and wake to serve Thee in the new day. Keep us as in Thy sight, this mother and father, these daughters, this son. For Jesus' sake— Amen."

"Amen," Dele breathed softly to herself.

185

XXVII

A SUNDAY night late in February, Garland tied his mule to a cedar limb and was met at the door by Kate. But it was Calvin he came to see this time. When the two boys were alone, Garland told his news. Cousin Nick had found out about Milly's slipping away to the storm party at Cousin Maggie's Christmas; he had whipped her unmerciful, the wash-woman said, and had kept her locked in her room every night since. Milly had sent a note to Garland by the wash-woman, asking him to bring Calvin to the river bridge at ten o'clock. She would try to escape by the upstairs window and meet them there. If she were over an hour late, they must not wait for her.

Almost wild with excitement, Calvin jumped into Garland's top buggy and begged him to hurry.

"It's just eight o'clock. She said ten. Plenty of time."

Then Calvin, usually soft about dumb animals, vigorously struck the mule with the buggy whip and made her trot all the five miles to the river bridge. Having no watch, they were unable to guess the passing time. To relieve the tense waiting, Garland walked cautiously toward Milly's house to observe. Left alone on the bridge, Calvin was suddenly miserable and homesick a little. Home, his bed, old Nellie, Mama over the cook stove—the unchangeable, homely everyday— He thought the world and all of Milly, but what could they do? What did he have worth offering? Then her remembered sweetness overpowered him, her brown eyes with the yellow flecks in them, the sweetest mouth God ever made, her lips. What did anything matter just so they were together again? She would be like holding a dream in his arms. Was he here on the river bridge waiting for her, or was he in his bed at home imagining it all? Presently he would wake up and hear the chickens crowing for day; he would look out his window toward the blue haze over the river and wonder if she was dreaming about him. Almost startled, he saw the water below him, still under the moonlight. Leaning over the railing, he started, knowing the water was no dream. It made him vaguely sad—the water reminded him of the spring at the lower field, the falls pool, Rocky Branch where he had waded so often to catch minnows which his Mama had always tirelessly cleaned and fried for his supper, Becky's Hole where all the boys went in swimming; these were so familiar and safe, while this deep still river—he looked up to see if the blue haze toward which his eyes had so often turned hopelessly on his way home from the field would be visible here. There was nothing but shreds of fog, a few dim stars, and a big world. In the distance a train whistle sounded its lonesome station blow. A longing for companionship brought her back to him, the little brown fingers trailing the water from the sailboat, making little graves in the sand, offering him the prettiest shell, her fingers cool on his hot eyelids, the purple bruise on her little wrist, her lips warm and alive in the biting wind on the back porch. Oh, Milly.

Garland had nothing to report; everything was dead still up the road—no lights, no stirring outside or in. It was now after ten o'clock. You could tell by the moon. They would wait on awhile, though.

"Yes, we'll wait. She'll come. I feel like it. I didn't at first.

"It's a still house, all I know."

"You stay here and watch and let me go look. Reckon it's safe?"

"Safe as a graveyard. Just don't go too close; there's ghosts even in a graveyard."

Calvin hurried, on an impulse, to look at the tall white house when it couldn't help itself—like at a corpse, he thought, as the white gables loomed suddenly through the oaks of Milly's home. Somewhere behind those white walls she was awake, waiting her chance, preparing to come to him, scarcely breathing for fear that in the stillness Cousin Nick might hear her. That was her room upstairs facing south; she had told him once that she often looked out the south window toward where his home was and said her prayers that way. Was she at her window now, praying? He stepped into a clear patch of moonlight to reassure her. Let them see him! He had a right to the public road. Boldly he stood revealed, his eyes upon her window, silently calling to her. Once he was sure she was looking; so definite was the sense of her nearness that his knees grew weak. For her sake not daring to make any other sign, he removed his hat and stood an instant bare-headed in the cold February moonlight. Reassured, he hastened to the bridge to await her coming.

Garland shared his faith very patiently, but as time went by he became more certain that Milly would not come. The sensible thing was to go home and wait for better luck next time. It was twelve o'clock when they reached Garland's home, and though Calvin went at once to bed, he could not sleep.

Next morning at the breakfast table Garland's father a little casually announced that the hand from Cousin Nick's place had brought the news that Cousin Nick and Cousin Joyce had taken Milly to Philadelphia to stay with her aunt.

"When?" Garland wanted to know, dropping his knife on his plate.

"Last night on the nine o'clock train. Seems it was a sudden trip; at least he never asked the hand to look after his stock till after sundown."

"How long—oh, well, they'll be back in a week or two," Garland declared, picking up his knife.

"They will, but Milly is to stay; anyhow she took a big trunk along. Pass Calvin the preserves, Mama."

Last night at eight. At nine. At ten. She had not been looking out her window. The house had been empty. Calvin had held a dream in his arms: he had taken off his hat to a ghost.

While Dele was beating eggs for supper muffins, Calvin came in quietly and sat on the wood-box behind the stove.

"Rather have sausage or scrapple for supper?" she asked after a silence.

"Don't matter."

"Aunt Puss sent us a mess of fresh sausage—too much red pepper in it though." Dele felt thankful for the cold weather on their meat. They might be able to sell a few hams; Calvin could take the money and raise him some pigs to sell. It would soon be time to break up land: that put new life in everything, gave people another chance to try a little harder to get along, make better crops, save more—didn't Calvin think so?

Calvin wasn't thinking; his face was so drawn, he was drooped so hopelessly behind the stove that Dele was startled and thought at once of pneumonia. "Do you hurt anywhere, Calvin?"

"I can't stand it, that's all."

"What?"

"Milly's gone."

"Where?"

"Philadelphia."

"She'll come back."

"No. They've broke us up for good."

"If you and Milly— She'll wait."

"I rather be dead."

"That's baby talk. You and Milly's too young to get married anyhow."

"I don't care about the marryin', just so I could see her. She's gone. Out of my sight. Out of my reach."

Dele was sternly matter-of-fact, but her throat was aching like a toothache. "There's just one thing to do. Start you a little farm, save up what you can—we'll all help you—then ask her to—to come back. Your Papa's goin' to let you tend some little patches—"

"I don't want no farm. What would there be to think about in them long rows now?"

"About makin' a livin', that's what."

"Livin'? I don't want to live." He went out and stood aimlessly under the sugarberry tree. Then Dele saw him stroll off through the lot down the lane. Leaving Nannie Lou to watch the muffins, she hurried off into the pasture to drive the cows up the lane. When she saw Calvin climb the pasture fence and cut across the rock hill home, the relief was weakening. She was still further reassured when she noticed the freshly cut bark on a sweet gum tree; the gum, for which he had cut off the bark, she reflected, was a symbol of the dear homely things that made his words idle; he did want to live and to chew sweet gum! She never knew that she had stumbled upon a sacred place—a tree where once two children, retreating from the Sunday afternoon cousins, had carved M and C and where often since Calvin had found the two initials a comforting reassurance and a symbol of union. They meant nothing now. She was gone. Desperate, he had destroyed the carved witness of a hope dead since morning.

At the breakfast table next day, Dele was startled when Calvin handed Nannie Lou a half dollar—she knew it was about all the money he had—and told his sister to buy all the pencils she wanted. Holding tight to the money, Nannie Lou packed her book-sack and raced up the road to join her schoolmates. In the lapel of his everyday coat, Dele noted the pearl in its filigreed heart setting and was worried over her dish-washing; for the scarf-pin had been used only in his Sunday tie. From the kitchen window she suddenly saw the lean figure of her son slipping through the mulberry orchard with a gun on his shoulder. Something purposeful about his furtiveness sent cold terror to Dele's heart. She found John; he made light of her fears. But in no time he was moving through the mulberry orchard with the breechloader in his hand—to find him a young rabbit, he told Mr. Hewitt, who was sawing wood under the shed.

Dele went feverishly from one thing to another. She must have milked the cow, for she found herself straining milk in the dairy.

"What are you sweeping the yard on Tuesday morning for?" Letha setting the clay kettle under the doorsteps paused to ask.

The sound of a gun came from the woods beyond the orchard. Putting her brush broom down, Dele went to the well and drew bucket after bucket of water, filling the tubs and chicken troughs and water pails. From the upstairs window Kate wanted to know what her mother was going to do with so much water: yesterday was wash day. In silence Dele hurried to the wood-house and began carrying wood into the kitchen. She was still piling it around the stove when she heard John's voice outside. Suddenly she was too weak and blind to move.

"Here, put my gun up, Calvin. Calvin got the rabbit," John was telling Mr. Hewitt.

With dizzying relief Dele heard Calvin's step on the back porch. She walked out casually to get the rabbit to dress for his dinner. Afterwards she hid behind the wash-house and was violently ill, the first time since before Calvin was born. Later Dele saw the men at the lot talking earnestly.

"How soon can you get Calvin's clothes ready?" John asked her that night after supper.

"Why?"

"I'm going to let him try baseball awhile. I talked to Wes this evenin'. If Nick can send his gal off—Calvin can go down yonder and see how he likes that Alabama crowd. He don't have to stay."

"Does he want to go?"

"Carried away. I can handle the farmin' this spring. More in baseball than farmin' anyhow, if he gets in."

"The clothes part—I'll get them ready in the mornin', if only—"

John was soon snoring.

The blue suit was carefully pressed, the socks, handkerchiefs, and the three good shirts packed in the gray suitcase that had taken its last trip to Uncle Job's pond anyway.

"Don't bother nohow. I'll live in a baseball suit after I get there." Dele, turning the worn collar on a striped shirt, was glad to hear a new note in Calvin's voice.

Saturday night he left on the eight o'clock train from Pate's Siding. In his pocket were the ticket, bought with money John had borrowed from Uncle Wes, a little change from the Sunday school treasury, which would be replaced as soon as John could get a ham to town, and six dollars, Dele's egg money.

The family rose as usual next morning, milked the cow, fed and watered the stock—John threw an extra bundle of fodder to old Nellie, who would always remind him of Calvin—cooked breakfast and dinner, tidied the house, and were at Sunday school on time.

The first song was "What a Friend We Have in Jesus." Dele sang alto as usual.

XXVIII

THE SCHOOL YEAR was drawing to a close. The little teacher-pupil idyl that had budded in January had failed to flower as spring came on. For weeks after the snipe-hunt Miss Cole was intrigued by the subtle understanding she felt that the moonlight ride had established between her and Ellis Pate, and his increasing diffidence she interpreted as his effort to hide his real feeling for her from the other pupils. She was encouraged in this belief by his listlessness toward his school work. His Latin became less fluent, his algebra equations unbalanced, his dates in history confused, and even his declamations after school perfunctory. At first it was flattering. Miss Cole recognized the symptoms and was all gentle understanding. It was enough to keep their relations exquisitely subtle, she told herself as she applied lily-of-the-valley extract to her ears before starting Ellis on Patrick Henry's oration, without the complications of a finale. In these half-hours after school she sometimes imagined that emotion was about to tremble toward expression, and she grew surprisingly shy and unsure of herself.

The first cold breeze against the warmth that quivered between them was his announcement one afternoon at recess that he could not stay after school any more that week. She was surprised and hurt when he did not explain. The next week she waited for him to suggest the afternoon sessions, resolving not to mention resuming them and to remain just slightly aloof. When he continued to hurry away from school without glancing her way, she finally called him to her desk at the last recess one day to inquire coldly if he wanted to resume the declamations. He stammered confusedly that he had decided he better not stay after school any more, all the time flushing and averting his eyes. She hoped, flushing too, that his teacher next year would train him better than she had been able to do. But—but she must come back next year; what would they do without her, he wanted to know. She wouldn't be missed; it wouldn't matter to anybody whether she ever came back or not, she assured him. It would matter a lot; he knew it would matter a lot to him, he stumbled along more and more flustered. To him least of all, she declared over her shoulder as she walked away quickly to ring the bell for "books." For all that, he hurried away without a glance toward her desk as soon as school was dismissed.

The rest of the week she grew so cold and strange to him, so suddenly attentive to Deck Williams, that even the children noticed the change, and Kitty Banks got jealous of the teacher. One afternoon Nannie Lou had to remind Miss Cole that she had left out Ellis's Latin class. She was sorry she had forgotten all about Ellis; she'd try to remember next day. Next day she reproved him before the pupils because he failed to read his Latin correctly—and she forgot his history. Ellis's eyes began to take on a sort of left, lost look, and he looked more alone than ever in his corner. Often now, Miss Cole found him gazing at her in hurt bewilderment. The afternoon she handed back his English paper marked "Very Poor" on the outside—and it was very poor—he lingered at his desk when the other pupils marched out after school. She returned to the schoolroom to find the boy's head bowed on his desk, his face hidden, his shoulders very still and tense. Watching him as she wound the clock, threw the faded flowers into the stove, locked her "ponies" into her desk drawer, and furtively touched her ears with the lily-of-the-valley extract, she noticed that now and then he seemed to catch his breath convulsively.

"Ellis, are you sick?" There was no answer. She walked toward his desk. "Ellis, what's the matter?"

His shoulders shook spasmodically. She moved into his desk and put her arm around him. He sobbed unrestrainedly. She drew him close.

"What is it, dear lad?" she whispered, holding him close.

"I—don't—know."

And indeed Ellis Pate didn't know. He felt neglected, suddenly unimportant, discontented with himself, betrayed. There had been too many trysts too close upon one another, too devastatingly physical, too utterly cloying. His mind had dulled; he could not think out problems in algebra or memorize lines in declamations. He was humiliated at the futile struggle to concentrate on his studies; the conflict had made him wretched for weeks, and gradually he had come to associate Sally Hewitt with the humiliating change, with the teacher's disfavor and reproof, most galling of all. From active dislike he was beginning to despise the Hewitt girl, to loathe her, a feeling that was crystallized when he saw in the teacher's writing that he was a failure. He would never meet that girl again, he would never speak to her, he would pretend he didn't even know her, he would— But the resolution did not console; he felt desolate, blank.

"Tell me," Miss Cole was whispering close to his ear.

"I'm—just—miserable."

"Why?"

"I—don't—know."

"You may tell me."

"I—can't."

"Do I have anything to do with it?"

"You?"

"Yes. Have I hurt you?"

Here was something tangible, something to cling to. "Yes." He grasped at the grievance offered.

"My dear, my dear—don't you understand?"

He did not understand her words, but there was a quality in her closeness to him— How sweet she was, sweet as a flower there against him! He relaxed in her arms, comforted and soothed. It would be pleasant to stay like this, never to move away from such sweet nearness. She did not hurry him.

It wasn't till night that it came to him he was in love with his school teacher. Alone in his room, he picked up the declamation book she had handled so often and this afternoon had placed on top of his other books as he was leaving the schoolhouse and told him it was his to keep, in memory of the after-school sessions; the pages seemed to breathe out the fragrance of flowers. That was the way she was, fragrant like flowers. If only he could be close to her again like this afternoon. She was so sweet. She cared more about him than anybody else, but could she ever like him, That Way? He would try to make her. The rest of this year he would hand in perfect work, win her with fluent Latin translations, balanced equations, and faultless English papers, and pave the way for something rare and sweet between them next year. He could not of course say directly to her how he felt, how he would be willing to give up preaching if she would rather he would teach, how she could mold him as she would; but this summer there would be long letters to her, letters that would tell her All he felt for her. Then next year—he shut his eyes and imagined sweet sessions with her.

There was little time to be alone with her any more this term. Uncle Israel and Cousin Nick had finally been successful in arranging for the Governor to come to Pate's Siding for commencement, and Miss Cole rose to the occasion with all the elocution in her. The last afternoons of school were given over to the practice of songs, drills, and recitations that were to precede the Governor's address at eleven o'clock. Ellis, warmed by his secret love, was content to watch her as she directed the practice, to gloat over the rich future, to plan long love letters to her, to revel in the warm tender understanding that trembled between them....

There was no foreshadowing, those last days of school, of the miserable summer that lay before him, of the news that was to follow the mailing of his first love letter, the announcement of Miss Cole's unexpected marriage; nor could he know in this sweet new ecstasy that in a few months Sally Hewitt was going to have a baby.

XXIX

WHILE DELE AND the two girls did the hoe work, Mr. Hewitt helped John with the spring plowing, in Calvin's place. Nannie Lou, as commencement drew near, came home later and later from school. She had to practice the wand drill, her song, and "Over Hill and Dale," which she and Christine were to play first on the program. Ruefully one night after hearing the monotonous Secundo on the organ for an hour, John inquired how long it took a body to get over hill and dale. Dele, after a day in the field, used her nights sewing on the white lawn dress Nannie Lou was to wear on the stage and, when the rest were asleep, in writing to Calvin.

"Dear Calvin," she would painstakingly begin, "We are all well as usual. Papa and the Hewitts got the rock hill broke up today, and we shrubbed land. I dug up some of the sassafras roots, and we had sassafras tea for supper. I'm glad your board is good. I don't think I'd like the way they fix sallet, though. We have a nice chance of it. I put butter in one mess, but none of the rest would touch it. I'm going to send you some tea-cakes next baking. Aunt Mary came Monday, and I went with her to Job's pond. She caught a nice mess of fish. After church Sunday Nick Pate was around shaking hands and cousin-ing folks. 'How are you, Cousin Dele?' he said to me. He thought I'd ask him about Philadelphia I reckon, but I never. I did tell your Aunt Lina where Nick could hear it that you are knocking home runs every constant. The Hewitts are doing pretty good, but Papa misses Jessie."

In the same letter Nannie Lou took time from her school duties to enclose a few lines. "Dear Mr. Calvin: I miss you mighty bad. I'll be glad when you come home so I can go rabbit-hunting again. Miss Sugar still scolds at me when I go through her grove. I'm not even studying her old chickens and eggs. Good-by for this time, Your friend—Nero." ... "Dear Calvin: Guess what. I wrote a song about the school, and they are going to sing it before the Governor. I am going to play 'Over Hill and Dale' with Christine. The teacher wanted me to play Primo—that means soprano—but Aunt Puss sent word she didn't want Christine to play the bass. Mama is making me a white lawn dress with lots of tucks and lace in it. I wish you could be here to hear me play before the Governor. Yours truly—Nannie Lou."

At last the big day came. White dresses, wand drills, garden bouquets and dogwood decorations were in the March air. The little girls, uniformly white with rosettes of the national colors to wave at the Governor of North Carolina when they sang Nannie Lou's song, were sitting primly and haughtily in their desks, while the boys leaned back stiffly, eying the red, white, and blue rosettes on their lapels a little doubtfully. Nobody looked natural today in commencement grandeur. Reviewing the past months, Nannie Lou, tucked and important on the front seat, was suddenly sad, in spite of the duet ahead and the song poem and Easter Monday close by. Tomorrow she'd have to go to work, and her teacher would leave; suppose she didn't come back! School life had been great fun after all. There had been several afternoons when the school children had been marched across the road to the church to await funeral processions; the way the mourners "took it" had been an unfailing source of interesting recess discussions next day. There had been Friday afternoon programs, which Nannie Lou amid Dele's potted plants and much cedar had dramatically reproduced in the upstairs spare room for Mama and Papa and Aunt Cynthy and Uncle Millard. There had been the bean bag party which motivated many an exchange of notes, treasured long afterwards in top bureau drawers. There had been pranks, sitting in, spelling matches, an epidemic of itch—

Nannie Lou even warmed to her everyday and dull cousins, sitting near her now, yet so strange and aloof today. Crazy Pitcher Lola, so named because of her wild delivery at round cat, had been the target for many homely pranks because she was so good. Furtively watching the teacher's back, the children had almost daily taken Lola's shoes off her feet, the combs and pins from her hair, the safety pin out of her skirt and had thrown all out the window. Still Lola had never moved nor taken her eyes from her book. One day Nannie Lou, temporarily desking with her, had dramatized the current lodge initiation play by impersonating the goat of the "royal bumpus degree" and bumping Lola off her equilibrium —and the seat. Then there was Christine, who had gone into the miry field back of the schoolhouse one day after a book Nannie Lou had thrown far out and had plunged deeper and deeper into the mire. Aunt Puss, hearing the child's screams, had rushed to the rescue and had sunk into the mire hub-deep, as Swade put it later. It had been an unforgettable tableau that even now at this solemn hour brought an inward chuckle—to see Aunt Puss's white-stockinged legs churning the mud frantically and to hear her holler for Uncle Hen to pull her out or she would sink all the way to the bad place. Larry yonder, who always carried sweet betseys in his pocket, lurid prints to be transferred by benefit of saliva to readers, and pink candy balls from Uncle Millard's store to give the girls. Once he had given Lessie his papa's gold watch, but the papa had been unreasonable and had sent to Lessie's papa after his watch. Then on the back row—Perrie. Nannie Lou couldn't look that way; it made her stomach sick to hear his name. Let the other girls write notes to the boys—why, they even wrote their names on the walls of the little house down the hill. The unusual arrangement of "onlies" aided the swains in the expression of their preferences. The church "only," sheltered among the pines on the church grounds across the road, belonged to the boys during the week, but automatically became "Ladies' Only" on Sundays. The girls' school-week one in like manner reverted to the boys on Sundays. So on Monday mornings throughout the school year there had been waiting for the girls such Sunday-penciled legends as: "Julia Pate is so sweet"—"I love Kitty Banks"—"Lula Jones is a darling"—"Bettie Pate is the prettiest girl in school." Once when Nannie Lou had found her name, she had thrown a whole bottle of ink over it and later had to be excused from class to vomit.

There they all sat waiting the arrival of the Governor—Swade and Fatty; George, who had always answered "Imperfect" when the teacher called the roll to find out who had broken the rules against talking during the day and when asked how many times had always replied loudly "One" and *sotto voce* added "hundred"; Hubert, who had always answered "Perfect" and had been so; Deck, once too eloquent a Friday afternoon about a boy that stood on the burning deck; Buddy, the crippled one on whom no prank had ever been played.

Suddenly there was a flutter of excitement. Yonder came Uncle Israel's two white horses hitched to his carriage dispatched an hour ago to Pate's Siding to meet His Excellency, as the teacher called him.

Four things registered indelibly in Nannie Lou's mind that day: the Governor alighting from Uncle Israel's carriage, with all the kinfolks standing around in respectful silence while the teacher did the honors; the spot on the stage where he stood while the school children sang Nannie Lou's song poem—"The academy I love the best, In all the world it leads the rest," to the tune of "My Maryland" and amid the flutter of many rosettes; the Governor's story of the little boy who was so eager for an education that he went to school with only green apples for his lunch; and the bouquet of roses from Miss Jennie's garden that she had Christine take up to the Governor after the address. People laughed about that funny little bunch of common roses Miss Jennie thought up, and they bet among themselves that the Governor threw it out the train window. The following Sunday the neighborhood children walked up the railroad track two miles looking for the faded roses. They did not find them.

XXX

STREETS OF GOLD, starry halos, and white wings were accepted unquestioningly in all the Sunday school classes, but fish-fries among the angels would have brought heaven much nearer to the little girls and boys of Pate's Siding. The teacher of the corner class (later she became the wife of a teacher who eventually entered the diplomatic service) was getting her start in diplomacy by ignoring the restless excitement among her pupils as she described the beauties of immortality —the while her little mortals were pulling perch from Becky's Hole, hunting Easter eggs, and wading in Whiteoak.

After classes the annual wrangle over a place for the Easter picnic materialized. There were just two places—Uncle Job's pond and Whiteoak, the latter farther from home and so more enchanting. Uncle Israel was in favor of the pond; it was more convenient for everybody, and there would be a nice clean place to spread the dinner, whereas at Whiteoak there was so much underbrush that it wouldn't even be safe to make a fire to fry the fish over. Uncle Job quite agreed and added that at the pond it would be easier to keep the crowd together, whereas at Whiteoak the year the Sunday school did go there he noticed too much strolling off down the creek, especially on the part of the young people; in this day and time when the world was so full of material things of life and of worldliness and sin, it behooved the older generation to keep a watchful eye upon the young entrusted to it. At Morehead City last summer he had seen things—Uncle Wes, not even glancing at the eager faces of the little boys, quietly made a motion for Whiteoak, and Cousin Nath offered the second. The boys almost twisted off their little necks looking around to see how the grown folks would vote. Whiteoak won. Uncle Millard suggested that they make it an old timey greasy picnic, a fish-fry, hot hoe-cake, plenty of coffee. A gleam of joy leaped into Aunt Mary's eyes. She was ever the "compleat angler." Didn't she sometimes in her thinking swap the celestial harp for a reed pole and streets of gold for a creek? How she would keep the angels in fish! That Sunday afternoon she broke, as annually the Sunday before the Easter picnic, a Commandment; she dug a can full of worms for bait and all Sunday night caught chubs and pikes.

Next morning neighborhood baskets were packed with savory food, frying pans, corn meal, salt, and lard. New gingham dresses, little piqué bonnets, and gay straw hats were donned. It was a regular style show of its kind. Only Lessie failed to appear in a new gingham; she had clumsily torn her frock Sunday afternoon and had to wear her sister's piqué skirt and eton jacket.

Down the road went the procession of wagons filled with chairs or spread with a quilt over hay, of surreys, top buggies, and Uncle Millard's road cart—an intriguing vehicle, which two venturesome boys tried, as soon as Uncle Millard unhitched his horse, and got pinned under the seat when the shafts flew over their heads. Aunt Mary with her can of worms and her fishing pole went quietly and decisively down the creek where she sat patiently all the morning.

Robin early spoiled things for Nannie Lou; he had discovered Perrie in the act of trying to give her a pink ball of candy, and the teasing started. Overwhelmed as always by a strange shame when her name was coupled with boys, she ran and hid in the foot of the surrey. There were names she could not say—her own, Perrie's, and God's. "God" in her reading lesson had kept her at home more than once; always she looked ahead in reading class at school, and if "God" fell in her paragraph she quietly negotiated a change of seats with Christine and thus escaped Deity. Now she hid her burning face on the cool leather and dried her eyes on the little bleaching underskirt. Most of the children scampered away, intent on exploring the woods, hunting sweet gum, wading in the water, and bucking the boys that needed it. With Nero Nannie Lou finally walked off down the creek and communed with Nature.

> *Tender green of the budding year*
> *Bird song sweet upon the ear*
> *Starry blossoms here and there*
> *Gentle spring is in the air—*

It took her no time to compose these lines. Some day Robin would be ashamed that he had plagued her so. She would pretend she had forgotten.... "You used to tease me about who? Really I don't remember it at all."

Ca'line—ageless, colorful, original, too industrious to picnic—had brought along some unbleached domestic to sew her up a nightgown in spite of protests from the women; gowns were unmentionables even among cousins, except in sickness. Cousin Nath asked: "What you makin', Ca'line?" Quick as a flash she held the garment up in all its revealing proportions. "A cirkis jacket," she retorted, and the women turned their heads bashfully. Cousin Sim went to make a fire under the huge kettle to brew them all some coffee "strong enough to raise an iron wedge," he said. Old Miss Becky, her face corrugated with lines but her hair black as night still, pulled her wool cape around her thin shoulders and was soon dozing by the fire—for the witches had ridden her all night.

Aunt Lina began to squeeze lemon juice into a bucket of sweetened water. Squeezing lemons for the nieces and nephews had been as good as doing anything since the war in Cuba. Cousin Maggie and her clerk from the city strayed off down the creek carrying a buggy cushion, from which they meant to try their luck, as he put it, with the finny tribe. Only Aunt Mary caught any fish.

A scream from up the creek sent the women hurrying to trace it. Lessie and the white piqué skirt had fallen in the water, and though she had been pulled out by the frightened girls she was being chased through the underbrush by a wrathful sister. Lessie was pulled away from the piqué-owner's anger and dried at the fire. Miss Becky suddenly struggled with a witch in her sleep.

Meanwhile the boys were exploring the old Dodd mill and the deserted Dodd house, haunted and rapidly decaying. They drew funny pictures on the walls, collected dirtdobbers' nest-es, killed a mouse to torment the girls with, and left the Dodd house like scared sheep when they heard chains rattling upstairs.

Aunt Puss suddenly missed her knee-baby. The alarm was given: a lost child. Aunt Puss was always losing a child. In The Crystal Maze at the Raleigh fair, she had seen little Margie mirrored way off between two funny looking strangers and had shouted: "Law, Hen, yonder's Margie. Run get her," all the time holding tight to the child's hand. All activity was now concentrated on the search; only Aunt Mary fished on. After yards of trimmings had been snagged by underbrush, lisle hose covered in beggar lice, and the frying fish burned to a crackling, Aunt Puss suddenly remembered that she had sent Hen off down the creek with the knee-baby.

Cousin Sim hurriedly cleaned and washed in the creek the second pail of fish, amid little flutters of caution from his wife. He was wearing new trousers, which were proving to be two-way stretch. Already he was complaining: "The seat of my britches will be draggin' the ground by night," and he began to hold the slack up like a skirt.

At noon damask cloths were spread on the ground, and the women displayed their lunch—the usual boiled eggs and tom-thumb, ham, fried chicken, pickles, pie and cake. There were Aunt Airy's small cut biscuits very dainty among the robust broke-biscuits from other boxes. Aunt Sugar remarked low to Aunt Cynthy that Airy was about to get above herself since the Governor rode in her carriage—look at them biscuits please! Miss Jennie at the corner of the table was removing the little individual pies she had placed so proudly and yet with some trepidation in her shoe-box. She knew that her original cookery—she had little enough to originate with—was sometimes laughed at, but some day she would surely hit on something that everybody would like. ... "Oh, you must taste this. Wonder who made it. It's the best stuff you ever put in your mouth!" It might be these peanut pies today. She had found the receipt in The Farm and Fireside; they should be good.... "Oh, no, I don't mind telling you how to make them. Between two flaky crusts put parched peanuts, butter and salt, and a little flour." Unobtrusively from her corner she watched their fate. A sudden burst of lusty laughter sent the blood to her face, but they were laughing at Cousin Nath, she discovered, who had bitten into the cotton biscuit and was sputtering cotton and wit. Just then Fatty, a born pie-eater, grabbed one of the peanut pies, bit into it, didn't believe his tooth, tried again, and threw it disgustedly away. Pies belonged to be sweet; that's what Nero thought too, for after an experimental bite he dropped it right at Miss Jennie's feet. Her face burned painfully, and her eyes turned sick as she saw others tried and tossed to the dog and refused. Uncle Wes reached down and carelessly picked up one of the funny little pies, ate two, and called them good. When Uncle Wes died, Miss Jennie cried like one of the family.

From the common bucket with the common dipper, the children were drinking the lemonade. Cousin Maggie's beau, who believed in germs, declined to drink promiscuously. Spying a bucket of lemonade set aside among the boxes, he served himself and Cousin Maggie and was beginning the third serving when Fatty between bites into Dele's fat custard pie said: "The dog drunk out'n that one."

Aunt Lina started with a shoe-box lid full of lunch for Aunt Mary, who was getting too many bites to stop for dinner. Then in plain view of the men, Aunt Lina's bustle dropped to the ground. She stood paralyzed an instant, then grabbed the bustle, and ran. All afternoon she sat in a top buggy to herself.

After-dinner snuff for the women that used it, an egg-hunt for the children, and a nap for the over-fed men started off the afternoon. Mr. Miles stormed at the men a challenge to a foot-race. "Sleep on Easter Monday? You'd sleep at the pearly gates!" To the delight of the children he made every man race to the cedar stump and back, timing each runner. Cousin Sim, holding up the seat of his pants like a skirt, beat the crowd and won the plug of tobacco. Then he had a spell; seized with a rigor, his muscles drawn taut, his eyes walled back like death, he had to be rushed off to a doctor in Uncle Israel's carriage, with a spoon inserted under his tongue. Even Fatty stopped eating pie to stare open-mouthed with his companions, who had never seen Cousin Sim have a spell before and had wanted to. Aunt Airy looked the carriage out of sight; then she sighed a big disapproving mouthful. But she did not say anything.

To Aunt Cynthy Dele was confiding news from Alabama. "He knocked another home run yesterday—I mean it was the yesterday he wrote. The boss man told him fine work and to keep it up. He says they all treat him so nice, and he's enjoyin' it fine down there. He's goin' to send us his picture in a baseball suit before long." Aunt Sugar overheard and cautioned Dele to write Calvin not to forget to go to Sunday school, down there among temptations.

XXXI

DELE WAS EXACTING about her spring cleaning. Although her rooms were rigorously cleaned every day, when the twelve borrowing days in April were over, the ritual of house-cleaning was religiously observed at the Fuller house.

"How come them borrowing days, anyhow?" Nannie Lou wanted to know as she helped her mother polish windows.

"To kill up the old cows," Dele answered absent-mindedly, her thoughts on Alabama this morning.

"How come?"

"It's just an old sayin', that's all."

"I don't see how come the first twelve days called borrowing—"

"Old folks always claimed the old cows always kicked up their heels when March was over and boasted March hadn't got them yet. Then March turned around and borrowed twelve days from April to get the old cows anyway. Those twelve rough days are supposed to kill up all the old cows, the old folks always said, that had lasted through the winter. It's just a sayin'—"

After the windows were washed with hot water and kerosene, Dele built a fire under the big wash pot in the yard and heated water for the scalding and scouring she considered necessary. Around the wash-pot fire Kate burned the iron skillets, pots, and pans and polished them with ashes. The bedsteads were knocked apart and brought out to stand by the kitchen walls where gourdfuls of boiling water were poured into the crevices and over the slats, while the steads were rubbed with a mixture of turpentine and kerosene. Mattresses, feather beds, pillows, quilts, and woolen underclothes were hung on clotheslines, fences, and scaffolds to absorb the sun and air before being put on beds again or being packed away among garden herbs in the blue chest.

In the ceiled rooms, Dele, with her skirt tucked into her apron belt, carefully scalded down the walls with lye water. White sand from the creek was sprinkled on the floors. While Nannie Lou poured lye water from a dip gourd, Dele scrubbed the sand over the floors with a corn-shuck mop. When the rooms were rinsed with clean cold water they were sand-white, and smelled sweet and clean. The hearth, dog-irons, and fireplace were covered with white clay from Rocky Branch. A summer's supply had been stored in the smokehouse and the clay kettle filled for frequent use. The fireplace ashes were poured with the rest of the winter's ashes into the ash-barrel over which water was poured so that the resulting lye might begin to drip into the lye trough; with this drip lye, soft soap would be made.

Nannie Lou helped Letha polish the brass hooks on the

wooden water buckets, pewter casters, cutlery, and tinware with ashes, sand, and a corn cob; the wooden buckets, gourds, noggins, and chairs were also scrubbed to a clear whiteness.

The teester bed that had belonged to John's mother was always carefully handled on cleaning days. With the feller the ropes were twisted back in place and tightened with the wench. A mat of splints of oak or reeds knit together like chair bottoms was placed over the corded "springs," and upon this the mattress and feather bed were laid. Over it all went the homespun counterpane that John's mother had made on her loom, a huge bolster, pillows, and good-night and good-morning pillow shams. Starched scrim curtains were hung at the windows, a new muslin lambrequin spread over the mantel, white tidies placed on the rocking chairs, brick door-stops covered with fresh cretonne, and new rag rugs spread before the white hearths.

When night came, John tipped around cautiously on the white floors, a little uncomfortable in his own room at the new order and the cold clean fireplace.

Next day, the moon being full, Dele decided to make up the winter's supply of soap grease. She had learned from experience that to attempt soap on the waste of the moon was to have soap shrink and dry up. From the smokehouse she brought a lard stand full of scraps of old meat and emptied them into the pot with three boxes of lye, adding water as it was needed. As the mixture began to boil she stirred it carefully with the wash stick until the lye had eaten up the grease. It was tested for greaselessness in a pan of cold water, and then the liquid soap was poured into a tub to harden.

The odor of the hickory smoke and the acrid pungency of the boiling lye soap brought back poignantly to her mind the time Calvin had dropped his red cap into the pot of soap she had been making. The little fellow, only seven then, had started to plunge his hand into the pot after the stocking-cap he had thought so much of. Santa Claus had brought him the cap, and he had been told if he destroyed his gifts within the year that Santa would pass him by on the succeeding Christmas. She had found him an identical cap, which he had worn the day he was lost. Dele would never forget that day. There had been a heavy rain in the morning. It had been nightfall before she missed him from his museum in the woodshed where he had spent the afternoon. Frantic, she had followed his little tracks down the woods path that led to Rocky Branch, a raging flood after heavy rains.

Calvin had turned aside into a wet field and had mired. There was the struggle, molded indelibly on Dele's heart as well as in the muddy field. Deep in the mud there had been one small scuffed shoe with its broken strings. Hugging the boot close Dele had plunged into the woods pursuing the tracks and pleading with Deity. There not many feet from where the water ran swiftly into the falls pool she had seen the little red stocking-cap and the bewildered face under it. Though hopelessly lost Calvin had been sturdy and quiet enough. He had been looking for the rainbow; it had dropped down behind these trees somewhere; he had seen it plainly from the back yard at home after that last shower. On the way home they had gathered some pretty rocks for the little fellow's museum. Dele had been on her knees a long time that night.

His museum and graveyards. Dele used to hope that he never buried anything alive. There were those small graves in the jamb of the fence where the dead biddies, goslings, old Madge, Uncle Wes's stray cats, and once Letha's big doll with the yellow curls were given nice burials with flowers and pine-bark coffins and pretty rocks for gravestones. Aunt Sugar had told around the neighborhood that somebody had killed her sick guinea; if it had died on her premises it certainly could have been traced. Dele never knew for certain, but there had been a big funeral in the jamb of the garden fence that day.

The graves had been plowed over many times since those days, but Dele's eyes still turned wistfully sometimes to the fence jambs and to the shelf in the woodshed where Calvin had kept his rocks and bottles of worms and tadpoles, his snake-sheds and bugs and insects, patterned after the Museum in Raleigh that had so fascinated him.

And now the little fellow was a baseball player down yonder in Alabama, way across the miles—but she had stopped that idle calculating. From her apron pocket she took his last letter and, leaning against the oak near the pot of boiling soap, read again:

"The manager gave us all a big supper last night, but the barbecue didn't taste as good as they fix it at home. They cook different down here anyhow, and I've learned to like it, but not as good as your cooking. The folks here sure do treat us good. Somebody is always doing something for us. There's a woman named Mrs. Stuart next to where I stay that sure knows how to fix things to eat. She lives in a white house and has a yard full of flowers—roses and all kind of sweet-smelling things.

"Is Papa up with his plowing? I want to make enough money to help pay for somebody to plow in my place. Mrs. Stuart has a girl named Winnie. Her eyes are as brown as Milly's, but that's all."

Milly—Dele lifted her eyes and looked toward the blue haze above Neuse River.

XXXII

SPRING PASSED DULLY and slowly. Dele from her corn row watched expectantly the turn in the road where the mail man could first be seen. Feverishly she dropped corn from her apron pocket until he stopped or passed on by. The days after a letter from Calvin came, Dele worked very quietly.

Nannie Lou reckoned Calvin would get in the big leagues. Some day Cousin Nick and Miss Joyce—no, she shouldn't call her cousin—would be only too glad to welcome Calvin into their house. They thought they had sent Milly somewhere, but sure thing Alabama was farther than Philadelphia ever dared to be! She pulled the letter from her mother's pocket and mused over the Alabama postmark. Reckon the mail man had any more letters from so far—just think, 'way 'cross three states? Reckon Calvin wouldn't get rich and send for them all to come live in a mansion in Alabama sometime? Dele and Kate were reckoning silently these days, and since Letha seldom spoke anyway Nannie Lou sighed at the general unresponsiveness and directed her thinking toward the day her pen would bring money and fame. . . . He fell on his knees, worshiping, pleading. She held heaven in her hands, all the heaven his soul craved. Sorrowfully, sadly she shook her head. . . . Nannie Lou's heroines were always shaking their heads.

Garland was the only young man in the neighborhood who had a rubber-tired buggy. Kate couldn't wait to see it Sunday. Garland said last Sunday he wouldn't let her work in the field, but she should help him plant his corn and watermelons. They would have the finest garden in the neighborhood: egg plant, Brussels sprouts, endive, asparagus, rhubarb—all the strange things in the seed catalogues that nobody else had ever raised or even pronounced. Kate's dinner basket at August meetings and Easter picnics would always have the best-tasted food in it, and wouldn't everybody just flock around her corner of the table to get a sample of her cake and pie! They would name their first child Swannanoa Virginia— Kate absent-mindedly dropped a whole handful of corn in one hill.

Late that afternoon the native herb man came. John, disliking agents in general, had once put up a sign at the road: "No agents allowed here." It had attracted the agents so, each wanting to know the story behind the sign, that John in the end had taken it down. Following John, who did not stop his plowing, the herb man, after a preliminary pleasantry on the weather and the nice farming land, stepped in front of old Daisy.

"Barker is my name—Alfred Barker."

John slapped the rein over the mule's back and hurried down the furrow.

The agent trotted after him. "My name's Barker."

"I can't help it."

But when he mentioned indigestion, Dele entered the conversation. The result was she took the agency for the herb pills, receiving a trial box free and the assurance that she could make good money on her sales in the neighborhood. John was always glad that he let Mr. Barker spend the night, for after supper and during the periodical visits afterwards the agent played lively tunes on his fiddle and told jokes and funny stories about his travels over the state that made a bright spot to look forward to and back upon among the dull days. Next morning when Mr. Barker packed his medicine and his fiddle into his road cart and drove away, four pairs of eyes followed him wistfully. The herb pills proved to be good for many ailments; they became a family and neighborhood standby, and Dele did make a little money on her sales. After the pills had been tried on the neighbors, Dele sent Calvin a dozen, along with a box of tea-cakes she had promised him.

On Sunday afternoon Garland drove into the grove in his new rubber-tired buggy, tied his mule to a cedar limb, and tried to walk as casually as usual toward the house. He had to face a battery of eyes; for seated on the porch were Uncle Hen's folks, Uncle Millard and Aunt Cynthy, Aunt Sugar's boys. Garland eased into a chair among the kinfolks, glanced at Kate, and fanned vigorously with his new straw hat.

"Turning hot, ain't it?"

"Sure is," Uncle Hen agreed.

"Some rain wouldn't hurt."

"'Twould help," Uncle Millard then contributed, winking at Uncle Hen.

"Got your cotton in?"

"Some of it," Uncle Hen nodded. John, to whom the inquiry had been directed, grew very quiet among his company, who continued to discuss farming. The women on their end of the porch swapped settings of eggs, compared hatchings, planned gardens and offered each other pepper and tomato plants, exchanged flower cuttings, and watched their children playing in the grove. Kate, seated on the bench with Aunt Puss, gave her eyes and ears to the men's side of the porch, stealing a proud glance now and then at the rubber-tired buggy.

Toward sunset the leave-takings started. Uncle Hen had to arouse little Annie Laurie from her pallet; Aunt Puss went out to the rosebush in the back yard to get the baby's things; the girls had to be collected from the oat field where they were in the midst of a baptizing, with Nannie Lou as preacher; the boys were found in the apple trees eating green apples. Dele fixed that with a native herb pill all around. Garland told the boys do pray leave the apples to make cider of—for vinegar of course, he winked at Uncle Millard. After the horses were hitched to the vehicles, the men stood around waiting for the women.

"Well, you all come."

"Well, we will. You all come."

"Well. You tote the satchel, Lessie. Watch out there; don't drop it."

"You can get the red pepper plants any time. Just send."

"Well, I'll send Nannie Lou tomorrow."

"Well, good-by. You all come."

"We will. You all do the same."

"About the leghorns. I believe I rather have 'em mixed. They hatch better."

"They do for me. I'll get you a dozen first passin'."

"So do. Come on, children. Your papa's waitin'. Come, Dele. Come, Kate, you and Letha. All of you."

"We will. You all come."

"I will. You all come."

The first contingent left.

It seemed a long time to Kate before the porch was cleared. Garland stayed on. Lately he and his mule always remained for supper. Tonight John walked home with Uncle Millard and did not come back till after supper was over. So Dele had to call on Garland to say grace for the first time. He was ready. "Oh, Lord, have mercy on Jesus Christ, for God's sake," he intoned. It was satisfactory. The supper table cleared, Kate at last ushered Garland into the parlor, where she sat on the organ stool.

"How you like my buggy?"

"Fine. I know it rides good."

"Le's try it next Sunday. Can I bring you home from church?"

"With pleasure."

"Say, play a piece on the organ."

"I can't play worth anything."

"Yes, you can."

"By ear is all."

"Sounds pretty to me."

Kate wandered noisily over the organ keys, while Garland moved his chair close. "How about what I asked you?"

"I'm willin'."

"When?"

"You say."

"First Sunday?"

"It's all right with me."

"I'll ask him next Sunday. How's that?"

"All right."

"I got it all fixed. 'Say, Mr. John, me and Kate has decided—'"

214

"Sh—! I heard Papa come in the back door."

They sang a duet.

> *"Why do you wait, dear brother*
> *Oh, why do you tarry so long—*
> *Why not? Why not—?"*

About nine o'clock John began to walk back and forth to the water bucket. "Mighty thirsty," Garland whispered to Kate, adding aloud: "Need rain. Land's thirsty." Then the winding of the clock could be heard definitely in the parlor. "Slippin' up the hands on me." Garland found another hymn.

Shoes dropped with a resounding thud in the adjoining room.

"Climbed up on a chair to drop 'em that time." But Garland sat on. "Goin' to stay my time out."

At ten minutes of ten the time was out. The hall door opened. "Bedtime," John called, and immediately the clock struck ten.

"Um—humph. Moved the clock up like I suspicioned."

"Better go, Garland. I'll see you next Sunday. Le's keep on the good side of 'em."

"Well, good-by."

"Good-by till Sunday."

Kate rode proudly home from Sunday school in Garland's new buggy. After dinner, Garland with a meaning look toward Kate followed John very purposefully from the table. Mumbling something about helping drench a sick mule down the road, John broke away from his pursuer and hurried out the front door. Garland called to him to wait and let him help with the mule, but before he could get his hat from the rack John had disappeared. The supper hour passed. No John. Garland waited.

"He'll get back in time to call bedtime," he declared to Kate, who was beginning to get nervous.

When they heard the well chain rattle at the barn lot soon after supper Garland walked forth. John, on his way to the house, saw him too late. He started hastily back to the lot, Garland following rapidly.

"Mr. John, wait a minute. Mr. John!" There was no further escape. John turned. "Mr. John, me and Kate has decided to get married if you don't care."

"What's that?"

"Yes sir. We thought we'd get married the first Sunday, while the preacher's in the neighborhood, if you don't have no objections."

"You both's mighty young."

"I'm free. She's seventeen."

"I reckon you know what you're doin'."

"Yes sir. We think a heap o' each other. I know I do her. We want to make a start together. I hope you don't care."

"It's all right, I reckon. If you'll take care of her—"

"I aim to, yes sir."

"Turnin' cool, ain't it?" John was shivering as with a chill. "Why, I thought it was real warm this evenin'."

During the two weeks before the wedding, Kate was treated almost like company. Relieved of the field work, she spent her days washing, ironing, mending, and sewing on bleaching underclothes. Dele helped her with the tucking and ruffling at night, while Aunt Lina made the lawn dresses and the lace hat that constituted the trousseau. From her little store, Aunt Mary sent her a pair of bleaching sheets, Aunt Emmie two pairs of pillow shams, Aunt Cynthy a quilt, Aunt Puss a towel, and even Aunt Sugar a preserve dish. From Alabama came a half dozen fancy handkerchiefs. Letha contributed the hand-drawn pillow cases she had intended for her own bed—hers and Victor's. As Kate laid away in her small trunk the presents and her immaculate everyday clothes, smelling of beeswax and the hot iron, she felt very rich. In the trunk she scattered rose petals, adding fresh ones daily, as she took stock of her treasures. Dele tucked a box of native herb pills in a corner of the trunk.

On Saturday before the first Sunday Dele's kitchen smelled almost like Christmas. A huge pound cake, chess pies, boiled ham, fried chicken, and barbecued pork were on the menu. The preacher, Garland's folks, and some of the young folks of the neighborhood were to stay for the wedding supper and maybe sing some afterwards.

It seemed to Kate, who missed church that morning the first time in her memory, that four o'clock would never come. Washed scrupulously with John's shaving soap, which was the sweetest in the house, and dressed in her wedding clothes by three o'clock, she stood watching up the road for the rubber-tired buggy. "Ours, after today," she thought. As horse after horse was tied in the grove and vehicles emptied of the kinfolks who hurried into the parlor to get a good place, Kate began to feel a little funny, a little sick. When she sat down weakly on her bed, the familiar covers and pillows, a quilt over the foot of the bed surprisingly made her throat feel tight and her eyes moist. Each bed-quilt square brought a poignant memory: that striped piece like the shirt Calvin wore when he was baptized, the pink check from the dress she herself had worn at the corn-shucking, the blue gingham like the dress Nannie Lou had worn when she fell off the seesaw and broke her arm, the blue madras Papa had worn in the field so many days, Letha's dotted percale made so joyously for the last fair she had attended with Victor, the black and white calico Mama still wore to chop in, Mama who needed a dress worse than anybody. Her face buried in the quilt, Kate was suddenly sobbing. What did anybody want to leave home for? Why was she about to marry Garland? He was no kin to her. Why couldn't they just go on seeing each other Sundays, riding now and then from Sunday school together in the rubber-tired buggy, thinking of each other—and letting her work and eat and

217

sleep with her own folks? She just couldn't stand to leave them. If Garland would only take sick— No, she couldn't stand that either. But if only he would send her word—something. If four o'clock would just pass and he wouldn't come.

"Kate, Cousin Nick has actually come and brought you— Kate, what ails you?" Dele closed the door softly behind her.

"I—I feel bad. I think I—I—I'm goin' to have typhoid fever."

Dele studied the bent head a minute. Quietly she slipped downstairs to the pantry where the communion basket was kept. After pouring two table spoons of the sacrament wine into a glass and taking three grains of parched coffee from the coffee-mill, she hurried back to her daughter.

"Sit up. Take this. Do you hear me?" That tone of Mama's always availed. Mechanically Kate raised her head like a little girl. "Swallow it down. There. Now chew up this coffee and then spit it out. There. Blow in my face. It's all right. Now wash your face and rub some powders over it. Aunt Sugar's got sharp eyes—and nose."

"My knees feel funny."

"No, they don't. Straighten up!" Dele feared she had overdone the thing, for no child of hers had more than sipped the communion cup. "If you don't straighten up and act— proud before Cousin Nick and the rest, I—I'll whip you."

The kinfolks said it was a pretty wedding. Aunt Puss and Uncle Hen kept lingering over the presents, hoping they might get asked to stay for the supper after the rest left. Uncle Millard shook hands with the bride and groom and told them not to fight till they had to. Cousin Nath whispered to Garland that he had a ham of meat in his smokehouse for him. Cousin Maggie's beau wished the young couple a long happy life; Cousin Maggie, unwontedly wistful today, went a step further—she hoped the bride and groom would live forever and never die. Laughing then, Uncle Millard said Maggie had about covered the territory and all anybody

218

could add now was that all their troubles might be little ones. Leaving the preacher's side a minute, Uncle Job handed Garland a New Testament and told him to make a habit of reading a portion every night before he slept. Aunt Lina whispered to Dele she was glad the white lawn hung level.

"Her eyes look red to me. You watch," Aunt Sugar was whispering around.

More than red eyes bothered Dele. Kate was too lively, she was laughing too much. She edged closer to her daughter. No, they couldn't smell it, but even the preacher was staring at Kate. . . . Oh, Calvin, flew her thoughts to Alabama, I'm glad this isn't you. I wish you could have seen Nick Pate edge up to me and mealy-mouth, "Cousin Dele, I hope you're well. This is a happy occasion, Cousin Dele. Think of it not as losing a daughter, but rather as gaining a son." I wanted to tell him I've got a son, all the son I want, better than any son he'll ever have. I'll be glad when he gets out of the house. Oh, Calvin. . . .

At last the wedding guests were gone, and the supper was spread. It was a solemn feast, with the preacher present; but when the time came for the young people to accompany Kate and Garland to their new home they relaxed into their natural jollity. This buoyed Kate past the threshold of her home, the rubber-tired—"Ours, now"—did the rest, and before she had gone very far up the road, Kate "wouldn't not be married for anything," she kept telling herself. That was what she would tell Dele when she paid her first visit back home next Sunday, interminable interval.

The crowd had beaten the groom home (Garland admitting he had made his first ride in the dark with Kate last as long as possible) and had the house lighted for the bride. They sang and joked awhile and inspected the new little, rather empty, house, lingering in the bedroom and making wise remarks. Then Garland told them it was bedtime. Cousin Maggie and Julia put the bride to bed before they left. In her long bleaching nightgown, Kate knelt at the side of the bed; immediately she felt a little like typhoid fever or malaria—for she was hot and cold. Over the chairs, while Kate prayed, the girls spread conspicuously Kate's corset and underclothes. Julia tipped into the hall, and with a heavy masculine step and a man's whistle she approached Kate's door. With a bound, the bride sprang from her knees and jumped into the bed, turning her back to the hall modestly. Dully a bell began to ring in her ears, and as she turned farther on her side the noise increased. Stifled laughter drifted in through the open door and window, and she was about to crawl out of bed when Garland spoke close to her.

"Lie right still. I'll get it. Thought they was up to somethin'." And he untied the big cow bell from the springs. Then he blew out the light.

Kate wondered next morning if they still washed clothes at home on Monday.

XXXIII

NANNIE LOU GRIEVED silently for Kate. Even the melancholy poetry which began to have a way of turning into, "A place is vacant in our home, a presence loved is gone," was no longer a comfort. In the lonesome days following Kate's marriage, Nero was the refuge. Briefly at intervals there had been other dogs in Nannie Lou's life, but they passed. There would always be Nero; he was fundamental. Duke—useful, protective, driving the cows up the lane, watching the doorsteps—had had his day. Rover had walked up to the pulpit where the Rev. Richard Walker was preaching his farewell sermon and had offered his paw, as one Rover to another, Uncle Millard had said. For that Rover had had the neighborhood limelight all summer and a card from the preacher at his new field. Jennie, an unscrupulous hound, had been sold when she stole a boiling ham from the pot. Rosebud, a pure-bred fox terrier, had not thrived in her foxless environment. The goslings, too, had had their season; very cunningly Nannie Lou had taught them to eat from her hand and run after her. But the sweetest gosling had died and been laid away tearfully in the mulberry orchard, and the others had passed into goosehood. The little fluffs of spring biddies were seasonally dear, but in a twinkling they became somebody's Easter picnic, or hens.

There had been Madge's puppies. Old Madge, valiantly fighting a mad dog off her young, had been bitten and had to be shot. At Nannie Lou's pleading the puppies were placed under observation in the corn crib. Aunt Sugar had sent word to kill those dogs at once, but Nannie Lou begged so hard that the observation period had been extended. Furtively Nannie Lou evaded alert eyes, slipped through the snow, cautiously climbed through the door once a day, and had comforted the little orphans with cold biscuits and clabber. She had realized that any day the puppies might run mad, but they were so desolate without old Madge that they haunted her sleep. Anyway there were mad stones. In the end, while Nannie Lou had been at school, the little dogs had been killed and carried off in a guano bag to Rocky Branch. There was still Nero.

Nero was a small, curly black dog with no pedigree to speak of, but with what the teacher called personality. Lacking dramatic and swashbuckling instinct, he never jumped into water to retrieve a stick for Fatty or the other boys, nor stood on his hind legs to amuse his public. He might have tried to rescue a drowning child or kept a vigil at a master's grave, but drama passed him by; so he kept the even tenor of his way. Never puppyish and increasingly unplayful, he took his doghood seriously. His energy was always purposeful; he was not above killing a rat in the corn crib or catching a young rabbit for a meal, but he did it definitely, neatly and without a flourish.

Cast in unheroic mold—not small enough for the lap and not large enough to become the neighborhood huntsman—he was always his size with dignity. With aloof indifference he watched the bread-catching, paw-shaking, senseless retrieving of bigger dogs and with equanimity the kittenish antics of puppies, repulsing alike effusive overtures of his kind. No cringing, no wistful begging eyes, no greed over bones and biscuits for Nero. He ate his food fastidiously, without hurry and with just the right shade of polite gratitude. Scolded, he maintained a rear, elevated his tail a little like a standard as he walked away in silent dignity. His black hair was always curly and glossy; he offended not at all the most fastidious nose; from the dogginess of his kind he retreated. His stoicism was mingled with temperance. Once he tore his leg painfully over some barbed wire, and while John and Dele tended the wound he lay rigid and composed, but his eyes were full of tears. He had very human eyes with a special look in them.

One day Aunt Sugar sent word that Nero was sucking her eggs and would have to be shut up. Dele's hen nests were checked, and there were the tell-tale egg shells. Aunt Sugar sent word that Nero would have to be killed; he had broken up three more hen nests, and she couldn't stand it. A test became imperative. An egg was placed conspicuously in the back yard to tempt and trap or to prove Nero. In the house John and Dele, Letha, and Nannie Lou watched from behind various window curtains. Nero emerged from beyond the fig bushes, stopped to drink leisurely from the white pan that he affected, and walked serenely into the back yard —into his act. He noted the big yellow egg, without hurry took it into his mouth, and started to—none ever knew. In direct line of vision Nannie Lou, in the shed room alone, pulled back the curtain, gesticulated wildly, knocked the window a little, and caught the eye of the *persona dramatis*. He hesitated just an instant, flashed that special look toward the shed room window, elevated his tail like a standard, and marched to the henhouse to deposit the egg in a nest.

Word was sent to Aunt Sugar that Nero would not suck eggs, either! She sent word back that strychnine would tell. At that threat a couple of hot eggs were placed and held tight in Nero's mouth to teach him that eggs are hot numbers; he was then shown some broken egg shells in the nests and held over them for a sound whipping. He took the discipline in stride; reserved and aloof a day or two, he did not sulk, and he did not suck any more eggs.

It was long afterwards when Nannie Lou was in college that a letter from home told as casually as possible that a mad dog had bitten Nero and Aunt Sugar had had him killed. Among dogs Nannie Lou never again found that special look that was in Nero's eyes.

XXXIV

THE JULY DAYS lenghtened into August. It was revival week at last, and more than usual interest and concern were felt this year. On Wednesday John's surrey arrived early on the church grounds. A basket exuding the aroma of fried chicken, spicy pickles, warm crusty bread, and rich buttery cake was safely tucked in the foot of the surrey out of reach of ants; skirt bottoms were appraised lest underskirts showed, belts were adjusted, Daisy was tied securely to a limb, and the Fullers climbed the hill to the church. Uncle Israel's carriage and a few top buggies, from which protruded plump bundles of fodder, were scattered through the grove, and Uncle Hen's two-horse wagon was being emptied of its women, who were stepping gingerly from a chair to the ground and exposing lisle stockings and hamburg lace for all their pains. They hurried to the door to find that Uncle Job had just gone into his prayer, with "all the territory from the rivers to the ends of the earth" to be covered. He was pleading for those out of the ark of safety, when John peeped in and observed quietly: "It's Job. Just well's to take a chew of tobacco." And he did, timing his final pit-too-ee with the Amen.

Those waiting at the doors went in, men at one entrance, women at the other. Everybody was wearing her best lawn with val yoke and velvet sash. Piqué skirts and voile waists had done for Monday and Tuesday, but Wednesday was always special. Visitors from neighboring churches—Ebenezer, Mt. Carmel, Baptist Center, and even from Raleigh—would be present today. Cousin Nath, ever master of do, re, mi's, was beating time, and Maud was pumping "Higher Ground" out of the organ. Near the front sat the knee-pants boys where watchful eyes could see they did not whisper or stick pins in each other.

On the front bench sat Cousin Maggie and her beau from Raleigh, who had just whispered something complimentary about the fair sex, when the preacher announced "Stand Up for Jesus." These two, obeying what they interpreted as the pulpit's gesture to stand and sing, rose with two or three following their example. The minority seeing their error, sank quickly back into their seats, but Cousin Maggie and her beau remained standing like a duet, her face reddening and his jaw set to stand it through.

Cousin Nick, holding to Miss Joyce's arm, filed in behind their guests from the city. Very choice about where to sit, they finally chose a middle pew—after Joyce had shown off that purple silk, Aunt Sugar whispered to Dele, who all through the song was unconsciously standing up for Calvin instead of Jesus. Mr. Tom Smith, seeing that Aunt Lina was surrounded left and right, eased into a pew just behind her and nearly fanned the daisies off her hat. She suddenly wanted to fight the Spanish war all over. But her flare of anger subsided when the preacher asked Brother Calvin Pate to lead in prayer. Grandpa talked to God as though He was on the same bench. The congregation cried when he prayed; they knew that noble white head, that gallant soldier of the cross, that gentle patriarch could not be among the Amen-brethren much longer. "And let us be worthy to sail through bloody seas, to endure the pain, bear the loss, like true soldiers, oh Lord, till Thou art done with us on earth—" Grandpa led the congregation into his loved song:

"Am I a soldier of the cross,
A follower of the Lamb?
And shall I fear to own His cause
Or blush to speak His name?"

Then John prayed. Nannie Lou, bashful somehow to hear that familiar voice trembling toward God, shut her eyes tight and blinked back sudden tears.

The young preacher from Raleigh ascended the platform. ..."What will you do then with Jesus which is called Christ?" he asked the congregation. The scene of the trial was vividly, eloquently pictured; the crucifixion, poignantly presented. Surely the sinners would hurry forward at the first invitation. Then softly, persuasively the congregation went into "Almost Persuaded," and the children began to watch the aisles for the first sinner.

There sat Mr. White, stubborn, unrepentant after so many prayers, bearing down on an ungodly bass and armed for the personal workers with "I'm as good as the hyprocrites in the church." Cousin William, calm, unmoved, a good man, but out of the ark of safety, shook his head as Aunt Puss begged him to go up. Garland, in spite of wistful eyes turned toward him pleading silently, was not returning from his straying yet. No, he was not. Etta, Christine, and Bettie, all old enough to join the church but with bargains sealed not to join this year, stood firmly in their places. The congregation faltered into the last stanza—nearer and nearer that last sad wail, "Almost but lost." The mules were beginning to bray hungrily outside as the fodder hour passed. The preacher's face was taking on a drawn, hurt expression as the aisles continued to stretch empty before his extended arms. "Almost but lost! Will you come—just now?" he pleaded.

Nannie Lou began to wish that her sins had not been washed away last year in Uncle Job's pond, so the young preacher's face might light with joy over one sinner that repented. It wasn't fair to try as hard as he had and then nobody respond. Why wouldn't Garland go to the front? Her reproachful eyes glared at him singing "Doom comes at last" so cheerfully on the front seat. Only two more days, and the preacher would go away; she might never see him again, and oh— Suddenly the preacher halted the song to tell about a little bird that, tossed and driven by a storm, had flown straight one day to his breast, and he had opened his coat and given refuge to the storm-weary bird. "Just so," he assured Garland and Cousin William and Etta and Christine and Bettie, "may you fly to the bosom of Jesus, lover of your soul—"

> *"Jesus, Lover of my soul*
> *Let me to Thy bosom fly,*
> *While the nearer waters roll*
> *While the tempest still is high."*

How Nannie Lou wished that she, like the bird, could fly to Jesus' bosom, hide her face, and find refuge forever—though the bosom was a white shirt and blue serge.

Cousin William suddenly started up the aisle; the preacher met him with open arms; the sinner wept aloud. Oh, if only Nannie Lou might to his bosom fly and cry all she did want! Aunt Mary wiped her eyes; Aunt Emmie, Aunt Puss, Dele, all the women, Uncle Job, cried; the men blew their noses and cleared their throats loudly. It was a good hour of warm fellowship and spiritual feasting. Other sinners went up.

At last dinner was spread under the pine trees near the

226

road, and all ate heartily, for all the red-rimmed eyes and husky voices. Cousin Nick and Miss Joyce with their city company ate in their carriage, and Aunt Airy was about to take her basket over there to join them as they had invited her to do, when Uncle Israel broke it up. "Airy won't never know her place no more," Aunt Sugar remarked to Aunt Nettie, who had come to spend the rest of the week in the country. Big platters of fried chicken, ham, cakes, pies, pickles, butter beans, corn pudding, boiled cabbage, stewed tomatoes were placed on the white cloth. Kate watched with pride how fast her food disappeared; Garland wouldn't touch any other. Miss Jennie's heart sank as she saw her corner avoided again. When time came to pack the food away she took only a few of her things, pretending that there was little left. She had one sweet morsel to tuck away: the preacher had taken a piece of her black-walnut cake. Cousin William ate just one chicken wing from the table and then went off to sit under a tree by himself. On Airy's carriage steps Uncle Millard sat to eat a bowl of cabbage, corn, stewed tomatoes, ham, and chicken, placing his scraps by his side whenever he could catch Airy's eye.

Then to the well everybody went, where Cousin Maggie's beau and Larry handed to the girls many a tin dipper of water from an oaken bucket. During the intermission the little boys ate watermelon and ran down the railroad bank; young couples talked in top buggies, with Uncle Job vigilantly patrolling the grounds. The men squatted under the trees to consider the fall price of cotton.

"Red spiders got a-foul o' your cotton yet?" Cousin Sim wanted to know.

Uncle Millard answered that what the red spiders didn't damage it, the Republicans would. Cousin Sim warmly defended his party.

The women disappeared into the little house among the pines to dip snuff in a sweet fellowship of flesh.

> *"We're marching—to Zion-n-n*
> *Beautiful, beautiful Zion,*
> *We're marching upward to Zi-on-n,*
> *The beautiful city of God."*

The song floated out from the church, and the groups drifted in. The preacher turned from his tender theme of the morning to challenge Christians to leave the fleshpots of Egypt and come serve the Lord. He launched into an attack upon dancing, theater-going, card-playing, drinking. Kate dropped her eyes, but Garland looked steadily toward the pulpit. Mr. White reared back in enjoyment as the preacher gave it to the church members. Then the congregation sang "I've wandered far away from God," and that same tired, hurt expression settled on the preacher's face as he urged backsliders to leave their fleshpots and come shake his hand.

Uncle Wes was the first to go up. Then the aisle thickened with backsliders—Uncle Job, whose fleshpot was no fleshier than fat domineckers and shoats made them; Dele, whose fleshpot might be Calvin; Aunt Emmie, the vigilant committee, Uncle Millard, Aunt Puss's folks, Babe Landers—to shake hands with a man, was Essie Pear's whispered comment —John the last of all. Oh, if only they would pray now so that Nannie Lou could cry and cry! On the crest of the emotional wave, the preacher invited all who wanted to go to heaven to come forward—

> *"Come then and join this holy band*
> *And on to glory go,"*

sang Cousin Nath and the few who could still control their voices. Even Garland was afraid not to go on that one.

Suddenly the preacher whitened, staggered, and reeled off the platform out a door. He almost went to heaven right then on the throes of acute indigestion. The men placed him under a tree and did what they could to hold him to earth. Nannie Lou's heart was under that tree. For many Sundays it remained a sacred spot.

The brothers and sisters returned home and took up their fleshpots where they left them—milk pails and swill buckets mostly. Garland's cider had lost its savor; it was nearing the dregs anyway; he promised Kate to join in September sure. Husbands and wives over their everyday chores rather sheepishly avoided one another's red-rimmed eyes.

XXXV

THERE WAS ALWAYS a stir of excitement in the neighborhood over the coming of a new school teacher. This year the interest was intense because a young man right out of college had been hired. Uncle Israel, who had employed him and at whose house he would board, had shown his picture around, and the girls secretly began to dream dreams. When Uncle Israel walked into Sunday school the day before school was to open late in September, eager eyes were turned upon him and Mr. Stevens; and fewer voices declared, during the first entrance of the teacher, that when the roll was called up yonder they'd be there. The girls resolved that when the roll was called next morning at school, they'd be there. The boyishness of the teacher went straight to the hearts of the women, though the men shook their heads a little doubtfully on front porches that afternoon. Uncle Millard declared he heard Aunt Airy tell Mr. Stevens the Governor had ridden in her carriage.

The boys felt reassured. "Aw, he couldn't whup nobody. He ain't old enough," Fatty declared from the top of the scuppernong vine.

"Got a sharp eye, though."

"Answered questions in the men's class today. Bet he's smart."

"Wait till I give him that 'xample," challenged Swade, popping a grape into his mouth. "Ain't no teacher worked it yet."

"Aw, women can't work 'xamples. I bet you this marvel *he* can get the answer."

"Bet you this bean shooter." The boys felt glad that Ellis Pate would be away at college. He'd break up their snipe-hunt again, otherwise.

The girls were carried away.

"He looks so good and kind."

"Did you notice how blue his eyes are? Deep, like the ocean was that day," Nannie Lou mused.

"Do, you'd get drowned in 'em," giggled Christine.

"Deep blue, I was talking about," and Nannie Lou began making a mark around her foot.

"Bet he's strict as old Dan Tucker."

"Dan Tucker wa'n't strict. He got drunk."

"I'll be thirteen in November," Nannie Lou absent-mindedly observed, studying the outline of her foot.

"You better tell him twelve tomorrow."

"I shall say thirteen. I soon will be."

"Do, I'll tell him better. I'm thirteen, and I'm nearly a whole year older'n you."

"You're so old, why don't you write your own compositions then?" challenged Nannie Lou. She had Christine there.

"Oh, I don't care how old you tell him. Mamma said after this summer I wouldn't have to go bare-footed no more."

"I won't either."

"You will when you work out in the field, I bet you." She had Nannie Lou there.

Cousin Maggie in a corner of the porch raved on about the new teacher's broad shoulders and handsome face, as though there were no beau in Raleigh. Letha listened in silence, but that night she rubbed buttermilk on her face and arms in the dark.

As the weeks wore on, the neighborhood began to wonder

how it had managed without Mr. Stevens. He organized a literary society, a baseball team, spelling matches, and a Latin class. At recess he played with the boys, or helped some girl with her arithmetic or history. Christine with her "agricola parva" and "amo te" was too much for Nannie Lou; she prevailed on Mr. Stevens to let her take Latin too. Helping her write a sentence into Latin one recess, the teacher noticed a poem on the opposite page of her note book, under the title of which was, "By Nannie Lou Fuller."

"Did you write that?"

"Yes, sir."

"May I read it?"

"It isn't fit for you to read."

Presently he looked up from the poem. "You wrote that?"

"Yes, sir."

"And you're just twelve?"

"No, sir. Thirteen."

"That's rather remarkable. Do you have any others?"

"Oh, a whole book full. I'm working on a novel too."

"Bring some more verses. I'd like to read them."

For the first time in her life, Nannie Lou felt appreciated. When Mr. Stevens picked out one of her song poems, inspired by a picture on the schoolroom wall, and told her it ought to be set to music, she walked with her head in the clouds. The night that John had the teacher to eat supper at his house, he reiterated his opinion that "My Home by the Sea" ought to be set to music. He knew the name of a composer in Chicago to whom the poem might be sent; it would cost only two dollars, and something might come of it. Later, alone with John, Dele thought this song business better be dropped; next the child would be trying to write a novel, and they couldn't afford to encourage her that way; there was no two dollars to spare anyway. John thought he could manage. Secretly he added that it wasn't every man who had a daughter that could write songs; some day she might write

Sunday school pieces, and that would do as much good as preaching. The lines were sent to Chicago. And the two dollars.

In October Calvin came home to help house the crop, baseball season being over. Dele could not keep her eyes off him for days. His bronzed face strikingly handsome, a new light in his eyes and a buoyancy in his step, his new clothes worn with an air, he took all eyes his first Sunday at home. He was himself almost jauntily patronizing among the aunts and uncles, shaking hands all around like a preacher, and he was smoothly debonair with the cousins, remembering every one in spite of having been away to Alabama.

"You know Calvin's a fine chap. It ain't every feller that would go way off to another country and come back familiar as he left," Uncle Hen mused at the Sunday dinner table.

"Why, he shook my hand hard as any preacher," Aunt Puss added.

"Asked Margie wasn't she goin' to kiss him," chimed in little Tiny.

Margie looked at her plate. "He's the best looking thing I ever saw," she thought.

At first Calvin talked incessantly, following Dele around to take the heavier part of her work, pitching ball to the little round-cat batters on Saturday afternoon, pulling down Nannie Lou's curls which she was beginning to pin up, telling Letha about his chum who sent her word he'd like to meet her. Dele missed a whole pitcher of buttermilk that night. In the field Calvin sang as he worked and called old Nellie all sorts of pet names.

XXXVI

AFTER THE FIRST killing frost the potato vines dropped black on their rows, and John prepared to dig his sweet potato crop. He ran his plow deep into the rows, while Calvin raked the furrows, separating the vines and heaping the potatoes into big piles along the plowed ground. Next they separated the cut-roots from the solid potatoes and gathered them in hamper baskets to hill. Then on the ground were scattered thick layers of clean pine straw on which the potatoes were to be laid. Stout pine poles were forked together to form a tent-shaped hill, which was made by the addition of dry corn stalks, several thicknesses of pine straw, and over it all huge shovelfuls of dirt packed firmly in place. A small door frame was inserted at one side, just big enough for a person to crawl through, and a fitted door attached to make the hill snug and warm inside. Potatoes would keep till spring in these hills, growing sweeter and more syrupy with age and providing an abundance to bed for potato slips at planting time.

Dele scratched in the plowed ground for the little potatoes that had been overlooked, loving the feel of the soil on her hands, the acrid odor of frost-bitten vines, the mellow ripeness of harvest, the nearness of Calvin. This morning, not quite free of a tangle of dreams, she had been so unsure of the dear reality of the boy in the house again that before day she had tipped to his door for reassurance. There in the dimness of dawn he lay at peace, his head pillowed under one arm. Inside she was singing all morning; the house, the fields looked special; her heart warmed to the potato hills and the clean dirt of the fields.

Calvin heaped the flawless potatoes inside the big hill and the cut-roots in a smaller one for immediate use. John told him to take the rest of the day to hunt squirrels, but Calvin kept hunting jobs; he helped Letha wring a supply of broom straw, snatched the iron away from Dele and bent his strength to smooth the wrinkles out of a pillow slip, scorching the print of the iron on it, and loaded the two-horse wagon with cotton to take to the gin early the next morning.

Before light next day Calvin set out for the gin. There was

a feel of winter in the late October air; so he eased himself
into the warm cotton and cozily drowsed away the five miles.
A lantern hung outside the gin where two wagons were waiting. Awake now, Calvin burrowed deeper into the cotton
to wait his turn. He fixed his eyes on a star in the west that
was growing less steadfast as the dawn drew nearer and the
other stars flickered out. He and Milly had looked toward
that star from the back porch last Christmas, just before she
had lifted her face to him, and that star had seen. There had
been no sky nor moon nor stars then, just blinding ecstasy
that had dissolved the earth and set them adrift into some
glorious forever. When she had moved in his arms and had
whispered they must go back into the parlor, it had seemed
a long way to come through strange distances before he
had really touched earth again. There had been that same
star brightly steadfast away up there, but it had looked different. Could stars remember? They saw so many things,
so many faces turned up to them, the look in so many eyes;
stars must be wise and sad with so much human rapture and
agony naked before them. Could she look out a window
somewhere and see how lonesome and lost and left that star
was now? Was she sleeping, dreaming, awake maybe and
gazing at that star too, wondering about him? Gradually the
blind despair that had crushed him when he first learned last
February that she was gone had given way to a gentle sad-
ness in his thoughts of her and then to an increasing faith that
even great distances and long silences could not divide them,
born of his own recent knowledge of miles, their futility to
separate. Last month this time he had been in Alabama; now
here he was hundreds of miles away on a gin-yard in North
Carolina watching the dawn appear. What would this day be
bringing to her? Would those sweet brown eyes—
  "Mr. John?"
  "It's me. That you, Jessie?"
  "Mr. Calvin. You back home? I shore is glad to see you. I
234

saw old Daise and knowed her first thing; she knowed me too."

"How you gettin' on, Jessie?"

"Jes' common. Mr. Calvin—" Jessie jumped off his wagon and climbed into the cotton by Calvin—"Is Mr. John aimin' to keep dem white folks another year?"

"Why?"

"'Cause I wants to come back home."

"You don't mean—"

"Yessuh, I does. I means I ain't stayin' wid Mr. Nick no longer, if I has to move out in de road!"

"Why?"

"Me and him don't suit. I's hongry."

"To be sure—"

"Monkey business don't hold you together. I wants hog meat. Look how ga'nt I is."

"Believe you are."

"Wait till good day, and you'll know I is. Mr. Nick say hog meat ain't good for us; he say his wife tell him dat's what de matter wid de South—hog meat and hookworms. Law, Mr. Calvin, dat 'oman all time tinkerin' on de tenants—made we-all take a pa'cel o' free medicine for de hookworms dat got us down so bad we puore staggered in de cotton patch, but Mr. Nick wouldn't let us stop. Miss Joyce eve'y time she see my younguns all time lookin' in deir years and necks to see if dey wash."

"Northern folks are different from us."

"Law, when dey come back from Phil'delphy last Febr'ary she brought a pa'cel o' papers and stuff dat tell how to take keer o' we-alls' bodies, she say, and I never told her we can't read 'cause den she mought want to learn us."

"How about—their girl?"

"Miss Milly?" Jessie was silent an instant. "Miss Milly too good to stay here long."

"It wouldn't be much—" Calvin stopped, suddenly realizing he was thinking out loud. Jessie had paid no heed, so

235

gratefully did his memory flash back to the few simple kindnesses Milly had shown his family.

"She done widout to give we-all. One night when I worked up dere and dey wouldn't give me no sepper—dey don't feed from de table like your folks—Miss Milly slipped her own vittles out to me. I knowed dey wa'n't none left for her neither, 'cause dey don't cook but jes' a piece around at dat place. Miss Joyce say dat what ail de South, waste and dirt and grease—"

"Jessie, did she know she was goin' to Philadelphia, until the night she left?"

"Miss Milly? Well, seem lak she did, and den seem lak she didn't. Her folks was aimin' to go off to Rolly dat night to a big shoo-round, and she was goin' to stay at home and practice her musit. And de next thing I knowed dey had all bundled off sudden and gone up no'th. Miss Milly jes' dat mornin' was laughin' and askin' me how many coons I caught de night befo'— Her folks wouldn't let us ketch coons nor possums neither if dey knowed it, but Miss Milly wouldn't tell— Den she say she was goin' huntin' dat comin' night herself, and I ask her what she was goin' to hunt after, and she say: 'You'll know tomorrow, Jessie.' And den suddenlike she say to me: 'Jessie, don't you rest a lot sweeter when you completely tired?' And I tell her, 'Yeb'm, you does'; and she say, 'I'll know tomorrow.' And look like a bright light shined out'n her face somehow. Dat was de las' I saw of her, happy and shinin' dere in de road."

Milly ... Milly! Calvin was suddenly sick with longing for her; distances were again overpowering, and the world was empty and stark. There was no longer a star to witness the agony of yearning in his eyes, and almost he doubted if there was an Alabama.

The ginner motioned Calvin forward now; so Jessie climbed back into his own wagon as Calvin drove on the scales. He moved the cotton toward the feed pipe from which it was carried to the gins to be separated into lint and seed. When the lint cotton had been baled and marked with lamp-black, he rolled it from the platform into his wagon and started home.

After this Calvin seemed to work without interest, mechanically, perfunctorily; the whistling ceased, the gaiety slipped into soberness; he moved quietly about the house. Then one afternoon about sunset Dele saw him leaning against the crape myrtle tree staring toward the blue haze over Neuse River, and his eyes were somber.

A few cards drifted in from Alabama and one day a letter from a teammate offering him his job, clerking in a small store till the baseball season opened; the job would be open immediately after Christmas, and while the salary was small his room and board would be furnished free. Dele's heart contracted painfully when Calvin brought her the news, but when she saw that the dead stillness in his face had given way to an alertness she hid the ache that never quite let her alone and told him it was a good chance.... A country so far away that if he were sick she couldn't lay him on her bed and see after him, so separated by miles that her hands were helpless to reach out and do for him, so overpowered by dis-stances that her love was helpless to shield him against the small hurts of life. It would be harder this time to see him go; she had known the bitterness of waking to his absence, of trying to sleep with unease tugging at her. She did not stop walking that day; from task to task she went with driving energy, without rest. That was her way to dull the aching thought of Alabama, so far away, so unreal. She sensed that it was important for Calvin to believe in Alabama.

XXXVII

THE HARD FEELINGS that had been smoldering between Aunt Sugar and Aunt Airy for months suddenly blazed into the open just before Thanksgiving. Aunt Sugar had felt aggrieved ever since the school teachers had been boarding at Uncle Israel's and had never let an opportunity to slur at Aunt Airy pass by. She made an opportunity of Cousin Sell. Since summer he had been staying in Raleigh, most of the time with Aunt Nettie. Now Aunt Nettie had no intention of sharing her Thanksgiving feast with Sell Pate; Dwight had bought a turkey and was having his boss man at his mother's on Thanksgiving night; her table was bigger than his, and most of her boarders were away for the holiday. Sell also, according to her plans.

So she wrote Uncle Israel to meet her at the siding on Wednesday before Thanksgiving. When the train stopped, Aunt Nettie bounced off, followed by Cousin Sell and his extra shirt. There was nothing for Uncle Israel to do but tell him to hop in the carriage and take him on home, knowing it would not suit Aunt Airy to have him on hand long. Aunt Airy, however, accepted the extra guests with better grace than had been anticipated. She always relished town company, and this was a chance to show off her city kinfolks before Mr. Stevens; so she temporarily overlooked the implications of the extra shirt Cousin Sell laid on the bed. It wasn't until Aunt Nettie hurried back to Raleigh next day that the full meaning of his presence flashed on Aunt Airy. He was here on her for Christmas. She simply would not put up with him.

"Cousin Airy, I've been under the doctor's hands since last I saw you. I'm not well, not at all well, not at all," Cousin Sell assured his hostess as he buttered his biscuit Thanksgiving morning. Ca'line grunted doubtfully.

Uncle Israel asked him what seemed to be his trouble.

"Why—complications. My doctor said I should lead a sedentary life. I fainted on Cousin Nettie's porch one day."

He did indeed faint one day, and one of the boarders had called the doctor, who had assured Aunt Nettie that the trouble was purely local and had been aggravated by the sedentary life the patient had lived.

Aunt Airy now saw her chance. "I should think you ought to be in Raleigh where your doctor can keep an eye on you. It takes a long time to get a doctor out here. You might die before one could get here."

"I brought some medicine along. My doctor thought I'd be all right if I don't stir too much."

"When did they start givin' medicine for pure stomp-down laziness?" Ca'line, passing around a plate of hot biscuits, wanted to know.

Uncle Israel, trying to hide the grin that threatened, asked if Cousin Sell could eat anything.

"Yes, practically anything. Lots of butter and hot biscuits—" Ca'line emptied the plate at his place—"vegetables, but no cabbage and onions, any kind of meat, preferably chicken in place of hog meat. Cousin Airy always cooked such nice baked hens."

"I suppose turkey wouldn't hurt you either."

"No. Oh, no. My doctor wanted me to have turkey. He insisted on turkey, in fact."

"And a sedentary life?"

"That's right, Cousin Israel, sedentary's right." He seemed pleased that here was a relative who could speak his language. "Sedentary."

"What's that 'ere?" Ca'line demanded.

"It means inactive, Caroline."

"Sittin' down," Uncle Israel amended.

"He didn't need no doctor to tell him to set on it. What ails him—he's set on it all his life. Come out here to the woodpile, and I'll cuore you."

"I'm not able to cut wood, Caroline. I wish I was. I really feel pretty rocky this mornin'."

"Whyn't you take some medicine then?"

"Perhaps I'd better. Fix me a half teaspoonful in a little

239

water, Caroline." The doctor had told him it was merely laxative, mildly.

"Do, you'll be too lazy to tend to it."

But Ca'line went in the kitchen and dumped a half package of the powder into a glass of water. Aunt Airy thought it was the strongest looking half teaspoonful she ever saw. Cousin Sell drank it absent-mindedly and then suddenly looked startled. It didn't taste right.

"Maybe I shouldn't have taken it. Perhaps I don't need medicine today."

"All you need is a corn cob and a jam' of the fence."

"Hush, Ca'line. Mr. Stevens will hear you."

"I don't care nothin' 'bout Stevens. He needs one too, I reckon."

By noon Cousin Sell was ill. He was unable to eat any Thanksgiving dinner, any supper, any breakfast. He felt mistreated, exasperated. Somebody had put something in his food; they begrudged him the little bit he ate. Well, he would just leave. Plenty others would be glad to have him. So about night he slipped away without telling anybody where he was going. By the time he reached Aunt Sugar's he was too weak and dizzy to go on to Dele's as he had planned. Aunt Sugar heard his grievance and pursed her lips in a grim line. This was just like Airy Pate. Hadn't she taken the boarders right out from under her? Her advice was for Cousin Sell to hurry back to Raleigh and let his doctor look him over before he got any worse, advice he decided to act on when Aunt Sugar supplied the money for his ticket.

Then Aunt Sugar began to tell around the neighborhood that Aunt Airy had given Cousin Sell croton oil. It was bad enough to deny him food; the poor fellow was nearly starved when he got to her house, but to try to kill him with croton oil! Well, who was surprised? The report soon reached Aunt Airy. She would have the neighborhood know that she had never had a drop of croton oil in her house, had never seen any croton oil, and that Sell Pate had eaten what he pleased at her house. Whoever said different— Well, who was surprised? Aunt Sugar would have the neighborhood know she said different; Cousin Sell had been given something in his food: if it wasn't croton oil, it may have been poison for all she knew. The poor man looked pale around the gills and fainted on her porch time she opened the door to him. Aunt Airy said whoever accused her of putting poison in food was Ananias and Sapphira; but what better could you expect of Sugar Pate? Hadn't all her folks come from Republicans, and whoever heard of a Republican being thought anything of? The query got around to Aunt Sugar, who wanted to know what was Democrats but just the poor common class of folks? All rich, respectable folks were Republicans all right; look it up in the history book. Aunt Airy was relayed the command and laughed scornfully. A sure thing Sugar Pate's folks hadn't ever been rich; they were so "pore they stunk." Aunt Sugar continued with a "poor but honest" thrust; at least her daddy had never stolen song book funds from the Sunday school treasury to shingle his porch with like Airy's old daddy had one time before John Fuller took charge of the treasure!

The women stopped speaking to each other; they forbade their children to visit; they refused to go to Grandpa Pate's on Sunday afternoon; Aunt Sugar even made Uncle Seth stay at home, the first Sunday he had ever missed seeing his father. Uncle Israel thought the whole thing was a pack of foolishness, but even he grew a little polite toward Uncle Seth. Uncle Job heard about the misunderstanding and reported it to the vigilant committee. The committee waited on the sisters. Their case would have to be brought before Confurnce Saturday.

Saturday afternoon the preacher stepped wearily from the platform, belching as noiselessly as possible the ham and cabbage and huckleberry pie Aunt Cynthy had served for din-

241

ner. Uncle Israel went forward to read the minutes of last Confurnce and to call the roll of the males. The females were called only once a year, the first Saturday in August just before revival meeting—subtle admission on the part of the brethren that the sisters needed reviving too and were eligible to reconsecrate their lives, if not to vote.

"I. C. Pate—U. C. Penny," droned Uncle Israel from the roll book, while a grin spread over the hot freckles of the little boys baking by the stove; that coincidence of initials perennially tickled them.

Old Mr. Penny opened his eyes, raised his head, and glanced around sheepishly at the other Amen-brothers; he always slept through the preaching part of the service. Cousin Sim shouted "Present" in answer to his name, slyly took a chew of tobacco, snapped his galluses over his shoulder, elevated his feet, and settled into solid enjoyment of apple-jack and the business in hand.

Uncle Hen, doubling his chin above his stiff collar, answered, "Here!"

"Pres'nt," responded Cousin Nath with a twinkle toward Mr. Penny.

John said, "Here," without any flourish.

After staying for his "Present" Uncle Millard slipped out to go to the siding for a mess of fish for supper.

Mr. Tom Smith delivered an impressive "Here" through the new false teeth he had bought since his wife died, and then looked over toward the women's side, twisted his mustache, and fingered the fifty-cent piece in his pocket.

On the women's side one mother with a handkerchief spread over her bosom was getting her baby to sleep, while old Miss Becky hovered close, with wistful eyes, moving a palm-leaf fan over the job. Dele passed out tea-cakes from her brown pocket-book to Aunt Puss's fretting child in front of her. Cousin Maggie, stuck tight to her pew, leaned slowly forward and pulled most of the hot varnish off the bench on

242

her new worsted dress. Aunt Puss's Julia, who always managed to slip into the bench next to the men and to sing out of the same book with a nearest man, eased a little nearer to Cousin Ashley, who grew redder and redder of face and yet was too bashful to move. Deck Williams and Kitty Banks were sitting together on the back seat, writing answers to questions in the song book. To "What Will the Answer Be?" Kitty found a suitable response on the next page, "Nearer, Still Nearer" was pointed out to her Swain. He turned a few leaves and pointed out to her "Close to Thee." "I Love Him," she next indicated with her finger.

Aunt Emmie, staring dully out the window at a tiny grave in the churchyard, was calculating how much more butter she would have to sell before she could buy a little marble angel to mark the spot. Aunt Airy glanced toward the tree their gray horses were tied to and saw again in her mind the Governor alighting from their carriage. Aunt Sugar across the aisle sat tense and primed for the vigilant committee's report. Oh, yes, she was going to forgive and forget Airy Pate like the committee had got her to promise, but she'd give them all something to remember first. Uncle Seth, having settled down after his meek "Present" toward Uncle Israel, saw the grim set of Aunt Sugar's lips with dread. Side by side on the back bench, Aunt Sad and Miss Jennie listened very quietly to the Confurnce proceedings, understanding little of it. Miss Charity, as that same burning pain seared her breast, held her breath to suppress a cry that was almost wrung from her this time. This would be her last Confurnce. She would take off her black dress, press it good, lay it away with the bleaching underclothes she was married in, and get ready to die. Dele and Mary Pate should shroud her; she would rather Sugar Pate stayed away at that time, but she didn't want Sugar's or anybody else's feelings hurt. Essie Pear glared at Babe Landers, who had stopped Tom Smith on his way to Confurnce to beat a ride, if he didn't have a load. Her eyes fixed on the torn carpet, Kate sat still, very still.

In the middle aisle Cousin Nick and Miss Joyce waited as patiently as they could for the dull session to be over. They had to stay after the sermon today, for the preacher was going home with them. Miss Joyce, in a brown wool coat suit under her furs, grew a little restless; she whispered to Cousin Nick, who immediately rose to open a window for the much needed ventilation. "Thanks," she nodded to him as he resumed his seat. Calvin watched Miss Joyce with fascinated interest; today was the first time he had ever realized that she and Milly favored; there really were brown flecks in her eyes too. Ca'line, who had been brought along to church today just in case her word about the croton oil should be needed, glanced up at the open window where some "clean pure air" was rushing into the hot church and promptly rose to slam it shut.

Cousin Nath moved that the church buy some new tin dippers. A heated argument ensued. Some facetiously suggested gourds; everybody could spare a gourd. One thought new dippers would be too heavy a drain on the treasury; another thought the church needed to be more concerned about what came out of mouths than what went in, glancing toward Aunt Sugar. One declared it was the wrong time of year to talk dippers; who wanted any water in cold weather? Cousin Nath insisted that the old rusty tin dippers were unhealthy. Cousin Nick nodded approvingly, whispering his firm conviction to Miss Joyce. Pulling away from the varnish on her pew, Cousin Maggie whispered to Aunt Lina that the church ought to remember there was such a thing as germs; the beau in Raleigh had long ago converted her to that belief. Uncle Job moved that the money new dippers would cost be sent to the orphans. The motion was carried.

Then Cousin Sim, shifting his apple-jack to his other jaw, moved that the women give the church a good cleaning be-

244

fore Christmas. There had been some talk of a Christmas tree this year; do, the church ought to be nice and clean for the occasion. The women whispered around among themselves that Sim ought to have to wash up that corner where he spit tobacco juice. A chorus of male "Ayes" put the motion over, and the women kept nursing their babies, distributing tea-cakes, and dreaming of little marble angels.

When the vigilant committee rose to report, Nannie Lou breathed a deep sigh of satisfaction and settled to the enjoyment of the best part of church. The first case to be considered, said the chairman, was that of Brother Garland Miles. Nannie Lou started and blushed. What was this, calling her folks out in church? Did Mama know? Glancing quickly around, she could not tell from Dele's unruffled composure whether she had known that Garland was to be up before the church or not. The committee had waited on Brother Garland, but had been unable to convince him of the error of his way. He was present; what did the church want to do? The moderator inquired if the offending brother would acknowledge that he had been under the influence of strong drink. Garland, unabashed, declared right out that he had sat in Fonnie Bundy's lap the first Sunday night because he couldn't see a seat nowheres in the church; every bench had looked filled to him; so he had taken a seat where there was a seat, in Fonnie's lap. Under cross examination he admitted he had drunk some hard cider that Sunday, well right smart, and it may have affected his eyesight, yes. Take his name off the church roll. Kate, her face a shamed red, kept her eyes on the torn carpet and tried to suppress the little wave of nausea that rose in her throat; hard-burn had tormented her all day, but she had to come with Garland on this occasion just to show folks. Wouldn't Brother Miles say he was sorry? Well, Brother Miles was and he wasn't. Wouldn't he promise not to indulge in any more spirituous liquor? Wine was a mocker, strong drink was raging, and whosoever was de-

245

ceived thereby was not wise. At the last it stung like an adder. Kate looked up hopefully; an adder had bitten Garland at the tobacco barn last summer, and it had been very painful. But Garland would not promise; he might not hold out. The kindly pleadings were renewed; the preacher suggested that the matter be carried over till next meeting. Garland wavered; he glanced at Kate's red face, visualized the cider barrel in the corn crib equipped with a long reed through which to suck the cool twangy amber, and grew firm. No, take his name off the church roll, for a while anyway. (Later, when the barrel was nearer the dregs—) Fellowship was sorrowfully withdrawn. Miss Joyce whispered to Cousin Nick this was absurd, turning the boy out for drinking cider; if cider, then why not eggnog? Cousin Nick assured her hurriedly, nervously, that was different. What time was she? His watch had stopped.

Very low-voiced now the vigilant committee reported the case of Sally Hewitt, "overtaken in a fault." A hush fell over the church; women averted their eyes; girls blushed; the big boys slyly winked at one another, while the little boys looked questioningly at their elders. Nannie Lou still couldn't understand why having a baby entitled anybody to get turned out of the church, and there wasn't anybody to explain. Christine at school one day had tried to tell some of the girls where babies came from, but Nannie Lou had run out of the cloak room in disgust, not believing what she had heard. Misconduct was the charge before Confurnce. Although there was no precedent in this neighborhood, only one course was open; fellowship was hastily withdrawn.

There was one other matter to be called to the attention of the church; two of the sisters had confessed they had been guilty of back-biting each other and wanted the church to forgive them. Mindful that back-biting was forbidden in the church covenant, they had promised the vigilant committee to refrain from further wrong-doing in this particular. The sisters were present, if they had any further statement to make—

Aunt Sugar rose trembling but determined. "Yes, I talked about Airy Pate. I said anybody that would make a servant out of kinfolks and put something in vittles to make a poor innocent old man sick wa'n't fittin' to board the school teachers and next year—"

The vigilant chairman interrupted hastily to remind Sister Pate that she had come to settle strife and ask forgiveness, not—

"Well, I want her to forgive me—and forget."

Aunt Airy was too proud to blaze out what she felt; she was a little afraid of Uncle Israel too; then there was Miss Joyce. Let them go ahead with this forgiveness business; she'd get even; she knew something on Sugar Pate she didn't think anybody knew, but wait till next week! So the misunderstanding was patched up, the sisters forgave each other and forgot, and the moderator adjourned the meeting with prayer.

XXXVIII

A FEW DAYS BEFORE Christmas the Hewitts packed up their broken furniture to move across the river, and Jessie prepared to come back home. John had told Mr. Hewitt early in the fall that he would need his house another year. Dele had demanded it even before Jessie had started begging to move back home.

"Mr. John," he had pleaded, "I's hongry. You got to take me back."

"Filled up, Jessie. Can't take you back."

"Well, you jes' well's to make room, 'cause I's a-comin'. Look here how loose my britches bindin' is."

"I got no white houses on my place."

"Now, Mr. John, you could o' talked all day and not said dat."

"You stay on at the river where there's a-plenty white paint and fish."

"You can't eat white paint, and dat man don't give you no time to fish. He's de hardes' feller ever I worked for. De rashuns he 'low'nces out wouldn't mo'n fill a holler tooth, and no wood to warm by, and—"

"You wouldn't be satisfied with me now, after Nick Pate."

"Mr. John, he's hard. One night when de yard man was sick he dressed me up in de black britches and white coat and made me wait on de comp'ny. I tole 'em sepper was ready, and 'cause I forgot to call it dunner dat man wouldn't le'me have a mou'ful o' sepper. Naw, suh, I's leavin' dere."

"Well, it's a free country."

"How soon can you git dem Hewitts out o' my house?"

"I can't take you back, Jess."

"Send your wagons after me a-Sad'd'y. We'll be waitin'."

So Jessie had hurried back to the cold white cabin to tell Mariah to pack up, for they were moving back home Saturday.

John didn't see that the Hewitt girl's having a baby had much to do with raising cotton and tobacco, but women folks saw things in a different light. The baby was to be pitied, of course, Dele admitted, but she was stern about that kind of sin and relentless about letting that kind of woman live on Fuller land. After Sally's "sin" had become a certainty, there had been no further contact with the Hewitts except through the old man. To him Dele had continued to give food and clothes as she could spare them for his family, and when she heard that Sally had a boy baby she bundled up some baby things to send along with the shirts and dresses she was sparing anyway. But she would not go near Sally.

Aside from bringing the first illegitimacy into the neighborhood, the Hewitts had been disappointing. The men were hard-working enough, constantly driving themselves at jobs, but without much luck. The fields were kept clean, though

248

poor judgment about fertilizing and cultivating made the yield of a normal looking harvest very poor indeed. No care was taken of the house; window lights were broken, boards were ripped off the kitchen to make a pen for the cotton on the front porch, weather-boarding from the stable was slipped off for quick kindling, the yard collected all sorts of debris. (Mariah had kept the yard swept clean of a hint of trash.) The clothes that had been given them to wear to Sunday school were taken for the cotton patch, and no foresight was exercised about food. As the supply increased, they had acquired two hounds that consumed quantities of bread and meat. The hens that Dele had given Mrs. Hewitt soon after they moved, in order that she might supply her family with eggs, were early in the year killed for the table. It had angered neighbors to see clothes that had been good enough for them to wear to church being abused in the tobacco and fodder field. Most of all it had angered the women to see Sally Hewitt's misshapen figure wearing their daughters' dresses in cotton patches along the roadside. She could have worked next to the woods.

It didn't matter any more to Sally who saw her than it did to old Bessie cow, with calf. The vague stirring toward conformity that she had felt at the beginning of the year had abated when Ellis Pate abandoned the trysts with no explanation. Several times she had gone to meet him after his first failure to appear, and then with no hope at all she had gone to re-live those hours with him. When she realized after he passed her one day in the road without answering her greeting that he was through with her, she accepted it as she had always accepted things; the world that had been opening into a splendid place closed down on her again. Then the physical discomfort of her condition had pushed her further into the old rut; she ceased to care and became animal-like in her reactions. It had never occurred to her to reveal the secret meetings; she was afraid, even if there had not been some strange innate delicacy that made her choose to keep those splendid hours forever to herself.

So, when Mrs. Hewitt had asked her who got her in that fix she had declared she didn't know. The women, when they heard the girl didn't know who the baby's father was, were outdone at the implications and a little bewildered at the easy promiscuity of Man.

"Every woman in this neighborhood's mad with her husband," Uncle Millard laughed at Dele's one night. "Just watch till the favor pops out."

The women did not laugh; there were things not to joke about.

When Calvin, who had been very thoughtful and quiet about the whole thing, saw the Hewitts leaving he suddenly remembered the hunt last fall and that strange wild animal with a cry like a lost child's on the night air. The girl might feel like that. Dele, seeing the wagons moving off, breathed a sigh of relief and pity, relief because now her world was cleaner and safer and pity because that little boy baby was homeless. Kate, who was spending the day at her mother's, suddenly wished she could see Garland. Nannie Lou hoped Santa Claus would come to see the little baby and the little girls, whose pale blank faces she would miss behind the window panes.

The procession moved along the bare country road, not knowing or wondering to what they went. Two of the Hewitt boys, clutching the hounds that rebelled against the indignity of homelessness, rode in the first wagon to steady the battered bedstead, the soiled shuck mattresses, the dirty quilts, the rusty tin safe, the barrel of old clothes and shoes, and other odds and ends of shiftless poverty. In the second wagon the family sat listless and passive in the wintry afternoon sunshine, seasoned to move without regret and without hope. The shabby furnishings, the human jetsam were etched in bold relief against the fringe of dusky pines that bordered

250

the road, as exposed as a buffeted old lady before her shrouders.

Preacher Rafe Bliss, helping his wife minister to a sick cow at the pasture gate, moralized at length. "Well, this is what sin brings in its wake. If we sow to the flesh, of the flesh we must reap corruption. It was ever so and will ever be so: the wages of sin is death! If only the youth of our land could realize how transitory, how evanescent, is the fleshly impulse—"

"Yes," Miss Katie thought bitterly to herself, "and a few graybeards, too. If my bed could talk . . ."

Miss Katie was a funny woman.

Aunt Sugar, taking in clothes off the line, turned her back toward the road as the Hewitts passed, and reckoned John Fuller would stick to niggers like other folks after this and keep white share-cropper trash out of the neighborhood.

Buddy inquired wonderingly what would become of folks like the Hewitts if all the neighborhoods in the world felt like that.

"You go tote in some wood!" Aunt Sugar ordered him sharply.

"Well," Aunt Cynthy told Uncle Millard, coming in from the store with a pound of sugar, "they've gone. We've seen the last of the Hewitts."

"Gone, hanh?"

"I know Dele's glad. And I'm glad for her."

"I ain't."

"Why, Millard!"

"Now I won't never know whether that baby's got my favor or no."

Aunt Cynthy wouldn't laugh; she didn't like that kind of joking.

Pulling the curtain back from her window to catch a last look at the Hewitts, Aunt Puss wondered if Sally Hewitt gave plenty of milk. Uncle Hen wondered within himself why one of his six couldn't have been a boy baby.

The wagons jogged along, jolting the Hewitts, who took the bumps as they came. Mrs. Hewitt, swaying lifelessly with the motion, handed a potato to the little girls, who looked somehow more exposed and defenseless away from their window panes. Old man Hewitt on the wagon seat alone nodded now and then. Sally on the wagon floor at the rear opened her shirtwaist to the baby, bundled in a ragged quilt in her lap.

Aunt Airy saw the procession at that instant and thought it was a shame for respectable people to have to look at a loose woman nursing a bastard along the public road, the same road the Governor had ridden along in her carriage. Ca'line mopping snuff over her gums with a new tooth-brush snapped: "If that gal wants to wash hippins,* it ain't nobody's business but her'n."

Uncle Job pitied the sinner while hating the sin. "I'm glad she is moving from our midst. I feel that my son is safer now." And that son, furtively watching the wagons bearing the Hewitts out of the neighborhood forever, lifted his heart in gratitude and silently rededicated himself to the high purpose. "God is very good," he mused with tragic egoism, not relating God's goodness at all to the homelessness of the mother and baby. There had been no room in his thinking for concern over his responsibility for her "ruin," so terrified had he been that she would tell of the secret meetings and ruin him forever in the neighborhood. Night and day he was tormented, convinced that his sin was bound to find him out. He made many a midnight covenant and dedicated himself anew if only Sally Hewitt might disappear forever from his sight. "God is good," he mused gratefully as the wagons jolted down the hill. He turned back to the books he had brought home from college to study during the holidays.

* Diapers.

252

Uncle Wes, watching the wagons pass, was silent for some time. When he finally turned to Aunt Mary he seemed to speak from away off. "I reckon we all had a hand in it."

"In what, Wes?"

"Ruinin' that girl."

"I reckon so, Wes." Aunt Mary had no idea what he was talking about, but Wes was usually right.

"If she *is* ruined."

"She *did* have a baby, Wes."

"We all had that baby I reckon."

"Why—" Aunt Mary could follow no further.

"We all had a hand in it, is the way I see it." But Uncle Wes did not have the words to explain what was in his mind. He was so still that Aunt Mary tipped out of the room.

Miss Joyce, in a plush chair by the fire, looked up from her deck of cards and saw the Hewitts passing. "Oh, that's the girl who was turned out of the church. Mr. Pate, stop the wagons. I'm going to give her a book on child care and the feeding of infants."

"Why, Joyce, I wouldn't bother with that trash. There's nothing you can really do to help a shiftless, mangey crowd—"

"That's the way you Southerners are about the down-trodden. I declare you need missionaries!" She stepped regally into the front yard, throwing her fur around her neck against the chill December air, and commanded the "down-trodden" to come around to the back door. There were a few things—

XXXIX

WITH EXCITED EXPECTANCY the neighborhood gathered on Thursday night at the church for the Christmas tree. After a few recitations by the little girls, Ellis Pate rose to the occasion with a fine Christmas talk, in which he glorified the Mother and Babe. "Motherhood," he assured his listeners, "is a beautiful thing. At this season of the year we bow in humble reverence to the Virgin who said to the angel: 'Behold the handmaid of the Lord; be it unto me according to thy word.' So have mothers through the generations since that blessed hour bowed to the will of the Lord, forgetting self, enduring pain, suffering all things for the sake of little children. (What did Ellis Pate know about women kind of pains? several women asked themselves. They supposed, though, he learned at college; a lot could be learned in four months.) It is especially fitting at this blessed season that we pause to pay tribute to motherhood—" Ellis paused and then paid eloquent tribute.

Aunt Airy for the first time wished that Robin or Swade would study for a preacher. It must feel good, she thought, watching Aunt Lessie, to have a son get up and praise you like that in public. If she and Israel had started earlier they might have whipped that engineer business out of Robin's head. Aunt Lessie was being watched all around, but she was so tired from a heavy washing and ironing that she was unaware of the curious and envious glances, unaware even of the pretty words flowing so smoothly from the lips of her son; she did feel proud that he wasn't the least bit scared any more, that he did not seem lost for a word. She had used to hope that he would some day be a conductor, so that she could ride on the train all she wanted to, but now she was glad he was a preacher.

The gifts had been hung temptingly on the limbs of the cedar Uncle Wes had cut out of his pasture, and the lighted candles were being carefully watched by the tree committee. Cousin Nath, covered in red calico, was an effective Santa Claus behind his door-face, though the little children screamed in fright when he approached them, and clung to their mothers. The Sunday school presents were first handed out—harps, mirrors, combs, brushes, soap dishes, mustache

254

cups, whisk brooms, handkerchiefs, pencils, paper, nothing over ten cents. Then came the "specials."

"Calvin Pate—Special." Santa held up a small package tied with red twine. Calvin raised his hand, and the gift was taken to him. It was a pearl-handled knife with three blades. No name was attached; he turned it over in his hand, mused over it, wondering who the giver was. Christine whispered to Nannie Lou that Margie bought that knife for Calvin; that Margie cried every time anybody said anything about Calvin's going back to Alabama. No, Nannie Lou wouldn't tell; of course she wouldn't tell a soul.

"Millard Pate—Special." A huge shoe-box was deposited in Uncle Millard's lap. He began unwrapping the parcel, finally reaching a small box which he cautiously opened. Inside there was a black doll-baby. He quickly tossed it over toward Cousin Sim, declaring it had his favor.

"Mrs. Sad Pate—Special." There was a home-made pin cushion from Miss Jennie, though nobody would have called it that. Even Miss Jennie decided at the last minute it looked queer; so she had written on the wrapper: "A pin cushion, from Jennie." Aunt Sad's special for her was a towel. Miss Jennie had lain awake wondering if her name would be called out, how it would sound, if she would be very scared.

"Mrs. Airy Pate—Special." She put that on for herself, Aunt Sugar whispered around loud enough for everybody to hear.

"Mr. Calvin Pate—Special." Miss Charity, unable to come herself, had sent this pocket handkerchief by Mr. Bill. She had always thought the world of Calvin since the time he used to haul her sand in his little wagon and she slipped him tea-cakes from her satchel at church.

"Miss Maggie Pate—Special." Cousin Maggie had finally persuaded the Raleigh beau to come to the Christmas tree, and in a flutter she had been waiting for her name to be called. The present was a little glass jewel casket lined with

255

pink satin. Proudly the gift was displayed, the beau beaming with satisfaction at the admiration his gift was exciting. "Maggie ha'n't got a jewel to her name," Uncle Millard laughed to Uncle Hen.

"Mrs. Hen Davis—Special." Aunt Puss rose to receive the interesting package. When she found that it was a chicken craw, she was as mad as fire. There was a time for all things, and enough of a thing was enough, she fired toward Uncle Millard. "Twa'n't me this time, Puss," he declared.

"Miss Kitty Banks—Special." It was a ring from Deck Williams.

"Miss Nannie Lou Pate—Special." Mr. Stevens had left a book for her. Nannie Lou flushed happily and went nearer to the light to begin reading. It was Ivanhoe, and on the first leaf was written: "To Nannie Lou Fuller—From Will Stevens." There were gifts for the other girls too, but hers was the nicest, cost the most. She was going to put up her hair after Christmas.

Dele's special from Calvin was a plain bar pin; he had borrowed the money to buy it, promising Garland to send him the first money he made after his return to Alabama. Dele told Calvin it was pretty, just what she needed, knowing she didn't have any dress nice enough to pin it on.

"Miss Ca'line Pate—Special." Ca'line bent herself to untie the bulky package Cousin Nath handed her and was lost to the world in her concentration. The present proved to be a paper of safety pins, without a name. Ca'line stared at it nonplussed until those around her began laughing. "They must think I wear hippins!" she said loud enough for everybody to hear, just as Uncle Millard expected her to.

There were many other specials that were opened amid much pleased excitement. Since Calvin was leaving Saturday, he told most of the kinfolks good-by at the Christmas tree. Aunt Puss told him not to go down there and take up with some Alabama girl. Well, good-by. He must let them all hear how he was getting on; Margie had thought a lot of that card he had sent her last summer. Well, good-by. Aunt Sugar shook his hand cordially enough, but she did think he better stay around here where there was Sunday school and church and stay away from 'way off yonder where there were so many temptations. Aunt Airy told him still more emphatically that she thought it was just fine for him to be going 'way off to see some of the world, that she reckoned there were Sunday schools and churches in Alabama as well as round here, and that playing baseball was not half as much harm as a lot of things some folks around here did. Uncle Israel wished him good luck. Uncle Hen told him to knock a home run and think of him. Aunt Mary and Uncle Wes just shook his hand and said Good-by like they meant it.

Dele looked on unsmiling but calm. She managed the same dead calmness during the final packing, the supper Friday night, the last breakfast, the good-by handshake. (There was no kissing between men and women around Pate's Siding, even in families.) When Dele heard the train blow, she broke down unexpectedly and had to hide in the dairy till she was composed. Then she swept the yards for Sunday.

XL

When the teacher suggested a box party to raise a little money for baseballs and bats and mitts, the neighborhood heartily responded. Only Uncle Job did not permit his women folks to prepare boxes, for he believed the money could be turned to a better cause. Aunt Sugar was another dissenter; she remarked that if she had all the balls and bats in the country in a pile she'd stick fire to them. And if that was what Stevens was teaching the scholars, they'd better hire a woman next time.

The other women took pride in helping their daughters prepare boxes for the party. Fried chicken, fresh ham, boiled eggs, pickle, cake, pie, were packed into shoe-boxes, tied with fancy ribbon, and carried to the rostrum by the baseball boys so that nobody would know whose box he was buying. Robin was very busy with the boxes.

The program was opened with a song by Nannie Lou Fuller, which she had dedicated to the baseball team. The teacher explained that a song poem had been set to music by a composer in Chicago, and a group of girls would now sing it; he was sure the neighborhood was proud of this little girl, who was showing talent so early. All the kinfolks looked at John and Dele to see how they were taking it; their faces were noncommittal.

Cousin Nath began to sell the boxes. It was not difficult to look at the girls' faces and tell whose box was being auctioned. A few older women had brought boxes too; and much merriment was occasioned when some swain, eager for one particular box, got fooled and had to eat with some old aunt or cousin whose box he had bought by mistake. Robin, who seemed ubiquitous, prompted several purchases.

"Lessie said her box was goin' to be tied with red ribbons, and for you to be sure— There it is now," he whispered to Larry, as Cousin Nath held aloft a fancy box.

"Ten cents," Uncle Millard began.

"Fifteen cents," Larry offered.

"Twenty," promptly came from the rear.

"Twenty-five." The box was Larry's. He looked around for his partner, who was supposed to rise so that the purchaser might identify the owner and open the box with her. Aunt Puss fluttered up. A great shout of laughter followed Larry as he hurried with his box to sit with Aunt Puss and her babies. Passing Robin, he whispered, "All right, sir!" He would get even with Robin Pate.

Without much hope, Letha had prepared a box and covered it with pink paper. She had said several times, once when Mr. Stevens was present, that she was going to fix her box up

258

fancy with pink paper, like she had read about in The Progressive Farmer. She waited breathless.

Uncle Millard started with ten cents. After an embarrassing pause, Garland raised it to fifteen. Letha sat to eat with her brother-in-law; she tore the pink paper into little bits and threw them on the schoolroom floor. "Well," Garland thought, biting into a ham-biscuit, "I can tell Katie I done what she told me to, and I would o' gone to twenty-five on that pink paper." Suddenly he felt anxious to get back to Kate.

A heart-shaped box tied with blue ribbon was held up amid exclamations of admiration. "Whose is it?" everybody whispered. Robin slipped into the bench with Deck, whose marriage to Kitty Banks was expected any Sunday now. "Kitty said tell you to buy her box when it's put up; it's heart-shaped with a blue string— Look, it's up now!"

"Ten cents," Uncle Millard said.

"Twenty," challenged Deck.

"Twenty-five," came from the rear, where a plot was underway among the boys to make somebody pay for that one.

Without hesitation Deck made it thirty, though a quarter was tacitly understood as the limit.

"Thirty-five," shouted a voice at the rear. There were five of them; so they could easily go fifty at ten cents apiece.

"Forty," but Deck was slowing down.

"Forty-five," came the answer.

There was silence. Robin nudged and prompted Deck: "Fifty. Go on."

"Fifty." It sounded very dry and tense and final. That was the last penny in Deck's pocket.

"He's done. Let him have it," was the whispered agreement at the rear. Deck held up the fifty cents and rose.

"Rise, thimble, rise and show your bright eyes," Cousin Nath teased, looking straight at Kitty. Over on the left side Miss Jennie rose. A roar went up from the back seat. Almost blind with rage, Deck bolted for the door, the half dollar tight in the palm of his hand.

There was an awkward pause. Even Cousin Nath could not think of anything to say right off; he held the box aloft until in the sudden silence the sound of buggy wheels and a horse's rapid trot outside were heard, as Deck drove off. Miss Jennie blushed painfully and resumed her seat.

"Fifty-five on that last one," Uncle Wes said as casually as though there had been no interruption. He and Aunt Mary joined Miss Jennie and ate out of her box just like it was a picnic. Later at bedtime Aunt Mary complained of a headache and took one of Dele's native herb pills, so she would feel like fishing next day. Uncle Wes slipped one out of the box, too, but he never mentioned the queer fried something that had caused the severe hardburn.

"Mary, what and all did Miss Jennie have in that funny box last night?" Aunt Lina wanted to know as the two women sat on the bank at Uncle Job's pond next day.

"Sh! I got a bite." Aunt Mary spoke no more till sunset. She took home a nice bucket of fish.

When Nannie Lou's box was held up, her face grew crimson, and her breath almost stopped.

"Ten cents," Uncle Millard began.

"Twenty-five." It was the teacher.

"He's partial to her, my children tell me," Aunt Puss whispered loud enough for Dele to hear.

"Why, he never knew her box from nobody else's," Uncle Hen whispered back.

At recess that day Nannie Lou had looked up from her Latin sentence and had wistfully exclaimed: "I don't believe I'll bring my box tonight. Nobody will want mine."

"Bring it on. What are you having to eat?" Mr. Stevens asked.

"Fried chicken and ham and—"

"I'll buy it."

260

"You won't know."

"I'll guess."

Nannie Lou was ashamed to open her box, ashamed to eat with him by herself, and too happy to swallow. He had guessed right. A sweet secret was between them. Oh, Mr. Stevens, I'll die when you leave— "Have a biscuit, Mr. Stevens."— In four more weeks—I'll die when you leave— "And some more fried chicken."— Oh, when you leave— Mr. Stevens, Mr. Stevens!— He bought four other boxes and spread the contents on top of a desk, inviting the baseball boys and several girls to eat with them. But he had bought Nannie Lou's supper first; she had that to take to bed with her.

"Last, but not least," declared Cousin Nath, holding up a final shoe-box. "Whoever wears shoes out of this box sure mashes the ants where she walks. Buy this one, and you'll over get your money's worth. I smell cowcumber pickle and pound cake and fried rooster—"

Uncle Millard had whispered across to Mr. Tom Smith that this was Babe Landers' box. Lately Mr. Smith had been fanning the daisies on her hat, Aunt Lina had sawed him off so.

"Are you sure?"

"I am. I give her the box my gum-baiters come in. That's it," assured Uncle Millard.

"Reckon she'd eat with me?"

"Eat you, way she's been castin' sheep's eyes over this way."

Mr. Smith twisted his mustache and ran his hand in his pocket. "Ten cents," confidently shouted Uncle Millard.

There was a dead silence. Uncle Millard looked around a little wildly. He nudged Mr. Smith, who suddenly took his hand out of his pocket.

"Ten cents once, ten cents twice—" Uncle Millard poked Mr. Smith in the ribs; he didn't want to eat with any woman

261

—except Cynthy. "Ten cents twice— Hurry up. The rooster inside this box will be crowin' for day. Ten cents once, ten cents— Wake up over there, Mr. Smith. You got a sweet tooth. Ten cents— All right, Millard, it's yours."

The house roared. Uncle Millard looked sheepishly toward Aunt Cynthy and resentfully at Tom Smith, but he arose and took the box over to where Babe Landers was standing. Seated ludicrously on a bench side by side, they were the climax to a night of fun.

Before Dele left the school building, she slipped up to Mr. Stevens and said to him very low: "Mr. Stevens, I wish you wouldn't praise Nannie Lou's writin' no more."

"Why?" he was startled.

"It's best not to raise her hopes."

"But I honestly think the child has talent. Her pen may carry her far, if—"

"That's what I'm afraid of." Then Dele without another word slipped out the side door toward the surrey where her family waited.

The teacher, pondering those words, was puzzled and then very, very sorry for that nice child whose mother apparently did not sympathize or understand. He would write Olive about it and ask her advice.

Nannie Lou turned restlessly on her pillow. Only four more weeks. She would die in four more weeks.

XLI

THE MOON HUNG FAR South, and a vague haze drifted out from the woods. Brush and broom straw had been burned off new grounds, and now the men were shrubbing the hedgerows. A few sassafras bushes were left for tea. The women were fitting new pine straw into hen nests, setting out violets along front walks, sprinkling lime around doorsteps and under houses, making—on the full of the moon—great pots

262

of lye soap out of the winter's soap-grease, and—on any moon at all—lye hominy out of yellow corn.

Dele was gathering the final turnip salad to cook with the last tom-thumb. Dark nights and handful days were near, and she must plant her beans. Across the rock hill Aunt Cynthy limped toward her kitchen with an apron full of spring onions. She was going to fry them in bacon drippings for Cousin Sell's dinner. Cousin Sell, who stayed in circulation among his kinfolks, had been served fried onion greens at every table for the past eight days, but his welcome was too uncertain to risk another menu-ism. He had observed over at Aunt Sugar's that he had eaten onions four days straight, and Aunt Sugar snapped: "The country ain't no place for comp'ny in the springtime." Cousin Sell replied that, from the papers, trading with Japan had picked up some. For the city kinfolks had definitely sent him to the country for a year. Aunt Nettie had told him pointedly she needed her room for her boarders. Since when, very patiently on finding water buckets empty, he had eased back to rocking chairs on front porches till the women folks drew up some fresh water; then he uncomplainingly watered the fried greens and without a whimper carried his onion breath on to the next cousin's. Now from the hickory rocker on the front porch at Uncle Millard's, he glanced without much real hope at Aunt Cynthy's taut apron.

Aunt Sad and Miss Jennie, widow and spinster, who continued to find a strange content, the one in telling and the other in hearing the plain tale of a drab enough married life that death had dressed up almost into an idyl, passed along with a turn of alders which they had wrested from the woods for brush brooms. Yards still had to be kept clean.

Down the road Aunt Puss was scalding and scouring. The quilts on the clothesline made an endless labyrinth of tents for the children. The bedsteads, their minutest crevices flushed with boiling water, were cooling by the smokehouse, while from within Uncle Hen was hauling out his meat to sun. Cousin Ashley at Dele's well for a drink of water and a relay of the news remarked: "Th-th-the b-b-bugs m-m-must have r-r-rousted 'em d-d-down the road at C-c-cousin Puss'." Cousin Ashley *had* ordered patent medicine from way off yonder for stuttering, but it had done little good. This morning he was full of the run-away marriage. Kitty Banks had climbed down a ladder from her upstairs window last night and had run off with Deck Williams. Cousin Ashley, who drove a bay horse like Deck's, happened to pass the Banks' place soon after the elopement. Old Mr. Banks had grabbed the horse's tail, demanded his daughter, and was just laying on the buggy whip before Cousin Ashley finally blurted out: "Y-y-you g-g-got the w-w-wrong man." This morning Mr. Banks was tramping back and forth in his cow pasture, hitting at the saplings with his walking stick. "P-p-practicin' up," Cousin Ashley remarked, as he left the well to resume his work in the field.

Dele went hurriedly to answer the front door. Old Mr. Wall had come for one more dozen native herb pills. "Not that I think anything will do Charity much more good," he told Dele, "unless prayin'. You know, Miss Dele, when she was her worst off the other day, I went out to the corn crib, and I says: 'Oh, Father, let us stay together a few more years.' I went to the house, and I knowed time I laid my eyes on her she was better. I set down and jus' looked and looked at her." Dele's eyes were moist as she handed the pills to the old man. She wouldn't take any pay. He turned at the steps. "Charity has said she wants you and Mary to—to shroud her." Dele turned back to the kitchen, where she was very quiet over the turnip greens.

When the dinner bell rang, Nannie Lou wanted to hide. Meals had become increasingly routine since school closed. The meat was tasteless, the milk had a hint of wild onion in it, the butter was bitter. Pungent odors that a month ago had sharpened the appetite, now brought a faint nausea. Everything she ate went right to her stomach, she told herself. But there was no escape; she sighed her way to the dinner table. Dele looked sharply toward her plate, where the tom-thumb and the turnip salad lay undisturbed. Nannie Lou left the table. A vague restless unease sent her from room to room, with nowhere to sit; there were no sweet fires to gather her in; the hearths were all clayed and cold. She went to the porch and watched the men tearing up the earth; she gazed up the long road stretching toward an empty horizon; she heard the lonesome calling of the doves from the blue mist at the wood's edge, the frogs' chorus from the swamp. She wandered back to the cheerless bedroom; nothing there but a box of bed quilt squares—the school books had been packed away; she slipped from under her mattress her Evangeline, sprinkled with the beautiful "Begins" in the teacher's Spencerian; she laid the handwriting against her cheek. Then from farther under the mattress came Pilgrim's Progress, thickly peopled. Even the paper-dolls between the pages were dull now. In one section there was Chicopee, where the English Orphans had their being—Mary Howard and Ella and George Moreland, cut from stray magazines and the farm paper—and there was a White House, where a President and a Princess Alice consorted with Eugene Wrayburn and Nicholas Nickleby and Dickens' nice young ladies. Every scrap of silk and lace and ribbon, slipped cautiously from Letha's drawer, had gone into the recent marriage of Eugene Wrayburn to Princess Alice, and the finest chairs and rugs and beds from Sears' catalogue into their home at Saratoga Springs.

Now listlessly moving the paper Boffins and Hexams and Roosevelts from Chicopee to London to Washington, Nannie Lou began to plan funerals. There would be some beautiful corpses—the Princess herself—a profusion of crowns and crosses, heart-broken husbands and lovers to mourn constantly at the graves of their loved and lost awhile. Pilgrim's Progress would have many a turned-down leaf, sad, sad mounds beneath which would sleep pale still forms and over which nightingales would vainly strive to comfort the broken-hearted. Nannie Lou closed the book, the world of the paper folk, and strolled down the hill. The first stars were appearing, the "forget-me-nots of the angels." Eloquently, sadly she recited "Sunset and Evening Star" and then—

> *"Break, break, break,*
> *On thy cold gray stones, oh sea!*
>
>   .   .   .   .
>
> *But O for the touch of a vanished hand*
> *And the sound of a voice that is still!"*

Oh, Mr. Stevens. In the gloaming, oh my darling—

On the way back to the house Nannie Lou was ill. Dele overheard her. "Calomel," said John, when Dele started to give the child a native herb pill at bedtime. John measured with his knife blade the right dose of calomel for a girl of twelve—no, thirteen, wasn't it?

"Sassafras tea for a few days after this," promised Dele, knowing how calomel did Nannie Lou.

Nannie Lou knew that calomel and sassafras tea could not bring back the "tender grace of a day that is dead." Something in her had died four weeks ago, and her heart was crushed with longing; what had been could never be. As though sassafras tea could heal a broken heart. Oh, for the touch of a vanished hand, and the sound—

Nannie Lou took her place at the table next night for supper as ordered. A sweetish aromatic fragrance filled the room. At the corner of the table covered with a tea towel was the big white pitcher, and inside a dozen red roots were seeping in boiling water. Into her cup with a little sugar added to taste was poured the reddish amber liquid, and Nannie Lou

266

drank—against the blue calomel bottle behind the clock. Gradually Nannie Lou found a place to sit again. She started a morning glory quilt. The graves in Pilgrim's Progress opened, and joy reigned among the husbands and lovers in Chicopee and Washington and London. Nannie Lou began to memorize a long verse to say at roll call Sunday.

Dele believed in sassafras tea.

XLII

Miss Charity sighed wearily as the clock struck one. "Just one," she thought. "Five more hours till good day."

At her side Mr. Bill was snoring contentedly, the springs of the bed vibrating with every noisy exhalation. These vibrations increased the nightly torture that wracked Miss Charity more and more frequently and left her often in a cold sweat of exhaustion, the faint odor of sickness tormenting her senses. That was her secret so far, the searing red pain through her breast with no mercy at all, the insinuating smell of dissolution creeping from under the cover. She had never been to bed a night in her life with Mr. Bill that she had not washed away the sweat of the day's toil with sweet soap. There was a special lavender cake that she kept hidden in the machine drawer, and her subtle fragrance had been unfailing through the years. Even though Mr. Bill had often been too tired or too used to her to wash more than his feet, Miss Charity had vigilantly kept her own flesh sweet and clean for bed. Till now. She could stand herself, the sweetish acrid smell of pain and medicine; it was a thing that had to be stood. But to be stripped bare of her decentness before Mr. Bill— If only she had a bed to herself.

For another hour Miss Charity lay braced and tense against the return of the wrenching agony, fearful that, dropping off to sleep, she might be seized unawares and shake so with the spasm that Mr. Bill would be aroused. He needed

267

sleep and rest, with the spring plowing ahead and no help. Uncle Wes had given a day's plowing, and John had sent Jessie to help bed up the corn rows, but neighbors had their hands full, too.

Exhausted, Miss Charity finally slept a little, but was mercilessly awakened to suffering that tore at her like something alive; a cold ague held her powerless. Mr. Bill, startled out of deep sleep, sprang from the bed and bent over her. She tried to choke back the cry that was forcing itself out before she was fully conscious.

"Charity, what is it? What ails you?" His voice was frightened; he swallowed hard.

She braced herself, tensing her arms and legs. "Why—bad dreams I reckon— Bein' as you're up, give me a swallow of medicine."

"Plant Juice?"

"It'll answer."

"It ain't helpin' you much as it did at first, is it? It was recommended high for rheumatism."

"Just a little to wet my throat. There."

"Le'me rub you in mothers' salve. That use to ease you off."

"No." The sour odor of her damp flesh insinuated itself even through her suffering. She held the cover tight around her neck. "Just Plant Juice this time."

"I'm goin' to order some more Dr. Parry Davis's Pain-killer. It holp you, and—"

"Le's use up what stuff's on hand before you waste any more money on me."

"Puss was tellin' me about a remedy she saw advertised—"

"I'll be all right. You go back to sleep now."

"I rather rub you or do somethin'—"

"I tell you— Go drop down in the other room—"

Without a word he quickly climbed back in bed with her. "Now call me if—"

"But you can't rest none with me gruntin' and carryin' on all hours."

"Don't bother me none. Grunt all you feel like it."

Once a year ago, when pain was beginning to creep up on her during the night, Miss Charity had suggested that she sleep in the shed room or that another bed be moved into their room so that her restlessness would not disturb him. He had looked at her for several minutes, absent-minded, as if not quite understanding. Then with an emphatic, "No, sir, we'll sleep together like we always have, no matter what," he had abruptly left the room.

Last week, with the spring planting and their little cooking, too, on him, Miss Charity had suggested that he would be bound to get a good night's sleep every day or he could not hold out till stuff was planted, adding that nobody could rest in the bed with her any longer. This time there had been a half-frightened look in the eyes that turned quickly to hers and then as quickly looked out the window across the plowed ground.

"I rest good a-plenty.... You reckon that little corner yonder will do us for sweet potatoes this time, without any extra rows in the garden?"

"It ought to do you."

"Just two of us—one potato hill ought to be a-plenty."

"Yes—"

"You don't eat much sweet stuff noway, with your rheumatism."

"No. I shan't eat—much."

Miss Charity had known for a long time it was not rheumatism, and with the knowledge her desire increasingly was to retreat into herself, to withdraw from the quick—to yield to the importunity of disease, to have her agony alone. The intimacy of ravaged flesh even Mr. Bill could not share, with whom she had shared everything. Separate beds would avail more than patent remedies now. Was it that separate beds

269

suggested to him a sinister separation he sensed inevitably approaching?

After a sleepless miserable night Miss Charity could not eat the bite of breakfast Mr. Bill brought to her bed—coffee, fried egg, flour hoe-cake. She tried, but her faltering was too plain.

"I'm goin' to get Mary Wes to fix you a stew pan of chicken soup for your dinner. I'll catch one of your spring bitties—"

"We call on Mary so much."

"Rather get Miss Jennie to stew you up one of her receipts?" She smiled wanly, trying to respond to his forced cheerfulness. "Last dish she brought the dog wouldn't eat it. What'd she call it?"

"Blank mange. Has her dish been sent home?"

"Glad you thought me of it. Things slips my mind so bad now'days."

"You ain't gettin' enough sleep, Bill. You can't get no rest with me gruntin' and carryin' on all night and smellin' of mothers' salve and truck. We'd both be better off apart. Le's move that spool bed in here and—"

"I ain't never been above lyin' with you, have I—even when your babies was born, like some men would—and I ain't goin' to leave you now, don't care how you smell, unless you run me out. I couldn't stand—I rather lay on the pure railin' than—"

He stormed suddenly at the dog, lying quietly in the hall, and abruptly left the room. The bluster had not altogether concealed the hurt trembling in his voice, but it kept him from crying on the untasted fried egg and flour hoe-cake—before her. So Miss Charity gave up the hope of a bed to herself, till nearer the last, of course. She would have to brace herself against the onslaught of searing pain a little harder, till spring plowing was over, and somehow nights would pass.

270

That night Uncle Wes brought Mr. Bill and Miss Charity a plate of fried chubs for their supper. Aunt Mary had caught a nice chance at Whiteoak that evening, more than they knew what to do with. Miss Charity sent Aunt Mary word that the fish tasted good to her.

Then Aunt Nettie, who was Miss Charity's niece, left her boarding house in Raleigh in charge of her son Dwight's wife and came out to visit her kinfolks in the country a few days. Her last day and night she spent at Miss Charity's. At once she saw that the older woman was sicker than the neighborhood realized, and she sensed, too, her mental distress.

"Nettie, get that lavender cake of sweet soap out of the machine draw and bring me a pan of hot water," she had directed Aunt Nettie as soon as Mr. Bill had gone to the field. "If I don't scald and scour a little every day—" Miss Charity with an effort sat up in bed.

"Why, I wouldn't, weak as you are. Dele will come and wash you often as you need it."

"I rather tend to myself as long as I can." She had sent Aunt Nettie from the room while she tried to wash off the night's staleness.

Mr. Bill came to the house for a drink of water at ten o'clock. In the doorway he looked eagerly toward Miss Charity, who was propped on pillows in the middle of the bed.

Aunt Nettie stopped washing the window and turned to Mr. Bill. "Aunt Charity needs to lie to herself, Uncle Bill. Some good old gal sleep will do her more good than medicine."

"We've always lay together," Miss Charity defended weakly, dreading Mr. Bill's hurt eyes.

"It's goin' out of style to lie together anyway. Why, my boarders always wants to know first thing if I can furnish 'em twin beds. I've had to put single beds in every married couple's room. Dwight's wife told me to. She and Dwight don't lie together, neither."

"Dwight's wife don't sleep with him?" Miss Charity's voice was shocked.

"Why, it's goin' out of style—"

"It's style here," Mr. Bill remarked dryly.

"Aunt Charity's got to rest, and with you snorin' and log-icin' all over the bed—I heard you last night."

When Mr. Bill returned to his plowing, Aunt Nettie very efficiently and positively moved the spool bed in the other corner of Miss Charity's room and told Mr. Bill at dinner time there was where he would sleep. "Till Aunt Charity is better," she added significantly. Then she cooked up a supply of nourishing food and went on back to Raleigh to see about her boarders.

All day Miss Charity's relief was tempered by the hurt, lost expression in Mr. Bill's eyes. Yet in the cool fragrance of fresh linen that smelled of sun and air and starch, with her head on a pillow that was still warm from sweet April sunshine—Aunt Nettie had been thorough-going and had cleaned and cooked her visit out—she seemed brighter by night and ate with relish the broiled chicken and custard Aunt Nettie had left prepared. She even showed interest in the farm and garden, suggesting that Mr. Bill send to Dele's for some bunch butter beans and some pepper plants. She would need red pepper about seasoning the sausage next fall, and Dele always had plants enough for the neighborhood. Mr. Bill's face brightened when she mentioned seasoning sausage "next fall."

"Nobody can't season sausage like you, unless Dele, and you learnt her."

"Puss puts too much red pepper in hers, and Airy don't put enough. I grind me a boll every now and then along with sage and meat—no rule for me—just mix and taste. Then I always grind in a little thyme and bay; it gives it a

272

special flavor. I never told nobody that, not even Dele, but what's the use to keep it a secret any longer?"

A shadow suddenly fell between them. He could reach out across the foot of the bed and touch her; yet he knew she was not there. She was away again—'way off yonder where sausage meat didn't matter, where even he didn't matter— and there was no reaching her. But she was back sooner than usual.

"Nettie says Dwight's boss man give him another raise. He took Dwight to ride in his automobile Sunday."

"I wouldn't ride in one of them things— But law, I reckon the country will be full of 'em some day."

"Apt as no. But I won't be here to see it."

"Me neither. And don't care if I ain't. I don't like to meet one of the things in the road myself."

They talked on awhile of homely, everyday things—of the heifer that would be fresh in June, of the May cherries that Dele would preserve for them, of the rose bushes in the back yard that were budding out pretty, of the soap grease that needed to be made into lye soap, of new pine straw he would haul tomorrow for the hen nests and cow stalls. When Miss Charity began to speak drowsily, Mr. Bill tipped out of the room and sat for some time on the front porch near her window.

Miss Charity, in the middle of the big feather mattress, yielded to the sense of relief that a bed to herself brought. She could be as bad off now as she pleased in the dead hours when well folks were asleep, and she wouldn't have to strain and hold back when pain took her. Wrapped in darkness it could be borne now. And she needn't wash as often. She could stand herself. It was a strange thing that her own babies' hippins had never been offensive to her, when other folks' babies had sometimes turned her stomach. And Mr. Bill—his sweat and dirt had always smelled healthy and almost clean, while some men—The preacher had taken off his coat

273

at the dinner table one hot Sunday after a long service in a thick suit, and she had nearly heaved before she thought. The preacher had told her when he stopped by after March Confurnce that the Lord loved those whom He afflicted and exhorted her to count her blessings, to name them one by one. Well, a bed to herself was a blessing— Oh, another one, Pain!

Mr. Bill came in. She almost held her breath until she heard the springs in the opposite corner yield to his weight. Then she sighed with relief and sank into the burning whiteness of the agony. It passed sooner, giving up to it: it spent itself, and she lay exhausted. Sleep held her then awhile, until another stab began to burn through her. At first she held herself tense and strained to keep from shaking with the spasm and arousing Mr. Bill. With the realization that she was alone, she gave way, letting the wrack work its will and spend itself. In the relief that followed she closed her eyes. She knew now that nights would never have the same terror again, since she need no longer conceal from the quick the ravages of the flesh.

Suddenly a peculiar quality in the breathing on the other bed arrested her. A quick fluttering intake of breath, and then Mr. Bill blew his nose, like a head cold. She listened tensely.

Mr. Bill was crying, crying like a little boy after a bad dream. The minutes passed. The clock struck one. . . .

"Bill—"

"Hunh?"

"I wish you'd come over here and lie with me. I been havin' bad dreams again, and—and I'm scared."

"That's foolishness. Ain't nothin' goin' to hurt you, with me right here."

But he came with alacrity. Soon he was snoring contentedly by her side. She braced herself against the next wave of pain.

274

XLIII

With ten dollars in her worn purse with which to buy the family's summer supply of dry-goods, Dele was on her way to town to do her spring trading. Sitting silently by John on the front seat of the surrey, her eyes on the rim of trees beyond which was Raleigh, she was figuring the yards of household homespun, of voile and lawn and gingham for the girls' dresses, of striped madras for John's everyday shirts, of batiste for Kate's baby, of some nice white goods for Calvin a Sunday shirt. John speculatively studied the fields along the road, wondering how much fertilizer had been put down, what the cotton yield was to the acre, how many hands there were to chop the cotton.

On the back seat Letha glanced passively at the farm-houses where breakfast smoke still wavered from kitchen chimneys, where women came from smokehouses with chunks of meat or from cow-lots with buckets of milk, where men were hitching mules to plows or distributing guano from trumpets. Nannie Lou saw everything with eager eyes. Dressed in her best spring percale, she could not identify herself with the farm folks and the dull routine in evidence along the way. It seemed unreal that only yesterday this time she too, barefooted and in faded gingham, had been sweeping the yard, that an ordinary breakfast was behind her and an ordinary day ahead; that the churning was waiting, the hearths were to be clayed, the lamps washed and filled, the water-shelf scrubbed. Yonder a girl drew water for the chicken trough; a woman walked from the garden with an apronful of pusley; a child swept the front porch. Nannie Lou felt very sorry for them. Christine, who had begged John into letting her come along, was chattering excitedly about what they would see at the Museum and the park, though nobody paid any attention to her.

They had left home before sun-up after a hasty breakfast

by lamplight. They would eat dinner at Aunt Nettie's, though Aunt Puss had told around in the neighborhood that Aunt Nettie said her country kinfolks put up on her a lot. Packed in a box in the foot of the surrey were spring onions, garden peas, cabbage, and a dozen eggs which ought to pay for their dinner if Aunt Nettie did say that.

Nannie Lou hoped they would get to Aunt Nettie's before the city folks were stirring much; she was not ashamed of their turn-out, but a protective instinct somehow made her self-conscious and eager to shield the things that were dear and familiar. She could not help projecting herself to the sidewalks and observing the surrey and Daisy as they would look to strangers—John and Dele on the front seat, neatly dressed and unobtrusive, yet so patently alien to city streets; the girls on the back seat suddenly timid and hushed as the city rushed on them; old Daisy popping her feet noisily on the unaccustomed pavement, like the country mule she was.

"Yonder's the rock-quyrry. Le's stand up and see if we can see the bottom."

Nannie Lou paid no mind to Christine, for the Yankee cemetery with its green grass and daisies and flag floating in the early sunshine had challenged as always her fervent partizanship and poetic loyalty, arousing goose bumps of patriotism for the "Lost Cause" for which Grandpa Pate had eaten fat meat for Christmas dinner.... "Let drums beat loud (of course there were not any drums really) and flags float high, O'er Yankee graves 'neath Southern sky (that was pretty) While loyal hearts their (some nice poetic word here) pour, On Southern dead forevermore." One stanza was securely tucked away in her mind by the time the German bakery on the outskirts of the city was reached. There would be others.... For heroes bled—

Christine dug her elbow sharply into Nannie Lou's side and whispered, "We're at East Raleigh. Le's look."

Flushing, Nannie Lou averted her eyes as she had always

276

been told to do when passing through East Raleigh. Very erect and stiff Dele kept her eyes straight ahead, quivering inwardly with anger that there were such places to lure boys like Calvin into wickedness; thinking suddenly of the clean order of her house, the restful shade of the trees in the grove, the white sand around the kitchen door, the cold well water, the fresh coolness of the bay blossoms in the pasture lane; wishing that the day had passed and they were on their way home again. Calvin was nearer there.

John glanced indifferently toward the rows of houses and wondered if the women were pretty sure enough, if they were still asleep, and what a man could see in That.

Christine furtively watched the doors and windows with fascinated interest, hoping to see Something. Only once did she spy any sign of life: a fat woman wearing a soiled dress-ing sack, came on the porch to water a box of pink geraniums, but her face was not painted, and her neck was not too low.

Aunt Nettie, just starting breakfast in her basement kitchen, was surprised and not too cordial at the arrival of the country kinfolks; for they meant five extra plates, and she had no smokehouse or garden or henhouse to step out to in emergencies. John breezily assured her they had come to put up on her a week, but Dele hastily made it clear that they had come just for the day's trading, that they had eaten break-fast, and that the food in the boxes was for her if she could use it. Aunt Nettie, peeping into the boxes, told them they had to eat dinner with her anyway. That, Dele promised, they would do, after the boarders had eaten, if Aunt Nettie would not put herself to any trouble.

At eight o'clock they walked up the street together, to look at the show windows till the stores were open. Then Dele, taking Letha with her to help carry the bundles, began the tiresome job of pricing yard goods and looking for rem-nants and bargains, while John with Nannie Lou and Chris-tine went according to his promise to the Museum. A quiet unreal world with strange odors, unbelievable sights: stuffed animals so lifelike that they actually moved before wondering eyes; snakes so large and terrible that even a grown man caught his breath and jumped back from the glass cases; birds so natural that it was unnatural for them not to be startled by human observers; the ugly giant turtle with his painted back; the skeleton of the whale—Jonah could certainly have stayed three days in this one's insides—things like this made you believe but the more in the Bible; the butterflies, bugs, colorful rocks and stones, different kinds of wood, of fish; ladies' dresses worn during the war, the Confederate flags, guns, uniforms—it all made you believe but the more in history too. Without words they stood looking a long time at the fountain in the middle of one room, the splashing of the water emphasizing the stillness of the silence. Even Christine was subdued by the vastness of another world so different from the everyday of her experience. The morning passed. Almost it seemed odd, on the street again, that horses and dogs were moving, that people should be hurrying, that the squirrels on Capitol Square were frisking on the ground.

When they reached Aunt Nettie's, they found Dele with her shoes off, resting her aching feet and counting the money left for the evening's trading. Letha was checking over the bundles to see if all the goods were there, while Aunt Nettie was in the dining room waiting on her boarders. When John glanced over the table he suddenly felt very sorry for town folks. The cabbage were not half seasoned—where was the meat anyhow?—the potatoes were boiled in clear water, when the only way to bring potatoes to the table was smothered in butter gravy; the beef hash was good enough, what little bit there was of it, as Cousin Nick said about the butter; the drinking water was warm as branch water, and the with-it tasted like sawdust, whatever it was. It all just made his stomach mad, he told his family, stopping on the way back up the street after dinner to buy two dozen bananas and some little fig cakes.

"Now le's find a empty bench on Capitol Square and quieten our stomachs," John suggested leading the way. "My hash is lonesome."

Dele sat with them a few minutes and then hurried back to the stores to finish her trading. There had been some pretty white silky broadcloth at Stronach's that would make a nice Sunday shirt for Calvin, but it was too high, twenty-five cents in the yard more than the percale she usually bought. It was hard to turn away from it; the clerk said it was the thing for young men's shirts. She must try elsewhere though. Buttons, lace, machine needles, braid, quilt lining, apron checks, baby batiste, a black and white lawn for her-self—these were left for the after-dinner search. The madras for John's shirts, the girls' lawn and gingham dresses, long cloth, unbleached domestic, thread, tin plates, a new dipper had taken all the morning, but she had saved thirty cents by trying at different places and finally "jewing" down the man in the department store. Thirty cents was nearly half enough for her lawn dress. Her feet were sore from walking the hot pavement in her Sunday shoes, and the stores were beginning to be crowded and oppressive. Her throat felt dry and parched; but city water, even if she knew where to get any, availed nothing against thirst. Home seemed a long way off. Paved streets, strange folks, East Raleigh, a long slow road, miles and miles of thick woods, Walnut Creek, and Big Branch were between her and Home. And between her and Calvin what strangers, what long roads, what thick woods, what miles and miles, what city streets, what rivers, what— everything! Her throat tightened; she couldn't bear it. There was an impulse of panic as the sense of distance overwhelmed her.

The clerk came forward. "Can I help you?" Dele looked at her, bewildered an instant. "Something for you?"

279

Dele had to think. "Yes. I want to price some shirt goods."

"Any special material?"

"Le's see your percale, something nice, but not high."

The prices would do, but the patterns were not suitable, the goods didn't have enough body; Dele knew to herself that it just wasn't silky enough. "Much obliged, though," she nodded as she turned toward the door.

"I should hope so. She fingered and patted every piece on this shelf."

"And—priced! Must have been somebody's wedding shirt."

Stronach's. Nothing less than the broadcloth there would do. Calvin was bound to have a nice white Sunday shirt down there among strangers. After all she really didn't need a lawn dress now; maybe later in the summer— With the silky goods tucked under her arm and the white and black lawn marked off her list, Alabama didn't seem quite so far; this cloth would cross the cities and rivers to him; she would make the shirt Monday, finish the particular work and the button-holes Tuesday, and mail it so that it would reach him by Sunday. This very goods that she carried at her side, that she would finger and hold in her hands, would touch Calvin in a week's time, would actually touch him.

When she had finished her trading, Dele hurried on to Aunt Nettie's to wait for her folks, completely worn out as a day in the field never tired her. It was so late before they started for home that Aunt Nettie had begun to worry about five extra plates for supper. John explained that they had stayed at the park too long and then had had to walk back to town part of the way before they could catch a street car. On the way out of Raleigh John bought two pounds of cheese and a loaf of bread at the bakery to do them till they got home.

The surrey moved along slowly past the Yankee cemetery, the rock-quarry, the straggling houses, into the country road, flanked by dense woods. The smell of earth and trees and wild flowers was incense to Dele, and she silently thanked her Maker for having fields and country life in His plan. The May moon lighted the road, and the sweet breeze blew some of the city weariness off. The girls, worn out by their day of rest, became drowsy by the time they crossed Big Branch and settled back in their seat for a little nap.

A bright light far down the road aroused John first. Alert, he suddenly pulled on the reins and stopped old Daisy. The others sat up startled.

"Somethin' afire?"

"The woods, you reckon?"

"Looks like the whole elements is on fire."

"It seems to be movin'. It is movin'."

"An automobile." Nannie Lou and Christine were awake instantly.

"Daisy'll run away sure."

"Le's don't meet it. Turn out—"

"I don't want to meet it, but with woods on both sides of us—"

"Drive on to the Todd place. It's close."

"If I can make it." John slapped Daisy's rump with the reins, urging her on. "If Daisy was to meet that varmint she'd tear this surrey all to smash. Get up there, Daisy."

The dazzling light drew nearer. Daisy jogged along. The old Todd place finally appeared, its crumbling walls and broken porch lighted sharply by the on-coming machine.

"Jump out," John ordered as he swung into the Todd grove. On the ground he seized Daisy's bridle. "I'm goin' to lead her behind the house till that thing goes by."

The girls, holding to the remaining bananas, fig cakes, and cheese, sprang from the surrey and involuntarily hid behind the big box-bushes in the deserted yard. Only Dele remained seated with her bundles. Back in the country with the trees and plowed ground and—room, she was steadfast again.

Nannie Lou was never to forget that picture of her mother sitting calmly on the front seat, holding to her packages, while John tore through the grove toward the back of the house.

The automobile roared by, the fierce lights receded, faded, were gone. The moonlight with its soft healing held again the decaying house so rudely bared. "Here, hold the reins. And if she starts to run frail her good. I'll learn her to run away!" Dele took the reins as John went to help the girls find the bananas and cheese and the string of blue beads that Christine had lost somewhere in the Todd grove.

Daisy, knee-deep in the dewy grass, grazed steadily. Dele tore the paper of one bundle and touched the silky goods inside.

XLIV

Miss Charity had been dying for days.

"How is Miss Charity this mornin'?" neighbors inquired from front porches of the women who were taking turns sitting up with the sick woman, hoping the answer would be: "She's dead, poor soul—at last." The whole neighborhood waited, tensely expectant, not quite in the mood to make ordinary plans with a funeral so definitely in the air.

Now and then when Miss Charity through her wracks of pain recognized some neighbor, she whispered that she hated to bother folks so. Aunt Sugar brought her to consciousness more often than the rest. When the tired eyes closed with a weary finality and Miss Charity settled down to die, Aunt Sugar was the one to stand over the bed and summon her back.

"Miss Charity, do you know who this is?—Miss Charity, who is this?—Do you know—?"

And the tired woman came back, polite even in her extremity, and whispered, "It's—Sugar."

For days she had begged those who ministered to her to

282

slip the pillow from under her head. Dele, Aunt Puss, and Aunt Mary who were spending what the doctor had said would be her last night—"She can't possibly live till morning"—held a conference on the back piazza at midnight, after Miss Charity in an agonizing wrack of pain had pleaded with Aunt Mary to take the pillow from under her head.

"I don't believe it would be no sin, myself." Aunt Puss was crying in her apron. Aunt Mary and Dele stared at each other in the lantern light with troubled eyes. "Do you think it would be a sin, Dele?"

"I don't know. What do you say, Mary?"

"I don't know either."

"Mortification has already set in. The odor is bad, all over the house. Carbolic acid don't keep it down no longer."

"And Miss Charity always kept such a clean house. Now when she can't help herself—"

"Le's talk to Mr. Bill. If he says do it—"

"I can't."

"I can't either."

Aunt Puss knew she couldn't either. Still she called Mr. Bill from the shed room. He was trembling so violently when he got to the back piazza that Dele, in pity, asked him for some camphor gum.

"Is she—any worse?"

"About the same," he was told. He tipped to her door to torture himself again with her suffering.

The women returned to the sick room. "She seems easier," Mr. Bill observed, moving over to the bed. "Quieter. Maybe she'll get some sleep and wake up feelin' better." Her low moan from the pillow was echoed involuntarily by the husband, who laid his hand pityingly on her head and whispered something. Urged by the women, he went back to his vigil in the shed room.

"He ought to know death struck her two days ago. The doctor has told him how bad she is."

"Sh, Puss. She's of herself. Here, le's sprinkle a little camphor and turpentine around the room."

They added the sweetish odor of camphor and the pungency of turpentine fumes to the carbolic acid already permeating the house. Aunt Mary stood by the bed quietly, not disturbing the patient, but just there, if Miss Charity should open her eyes and feel by herself. The odor of honeysuckle from the ditch bank back of the lot drifted in on the spring breeze and became an insistent note in the medley of the sick room odors. Aunt Puss saturated her handkerchief with camphor and inhaled frequently, while Dele sat in a corner quietly watching the pillow. She hoped Calvin was fast asleep.... Wonder what he had for supper down there in Alabama. As long as he stayed satisfied and well—

The silence of the vigil was broken by a weak exclamation from the bed.

"Look!" The women rose quickly and stooped over Miss Charity. She raised her hand feebly to indicate the window. "Look...Do you—see it?"

"What, Miss Charity?"

"There— Look." The dead eyes had come to life. Beads of moisture gathered on the lined forehead, on the ravaged neck where a thin pulse flickered feebly. A clammy hand touched Aunt Mary's. "You—see—it?"

"It's all right, Miss Charity. Just shut your eyes and—"

"Doves— When did—I—ever—see—" Her eyes followed the doves as they flew from the window and perched on the foot of her bed. "Watchin'—of—me."

"They won't hurt you," Aunt Mary soothed her. "Doves won't hurt nobody."

"Her last words," Aunt Puss whispered to Dele. "She's gone this time. I'm goin' to call the family."

But next morning when the women, hurrying home to get a little sleep, were stopped by eager inquirers from front porches, they had to admit Miss Charity was still living.

284

"Mortification has set in, though," Aunt Puss assured the inquirers. "And she saw doves in the middle of the night."

Pressed, she had to own that Miss Charity was still of herself.

Aunt Cynthy, Aunt Lina, and Cousin Maggie sat up the next night, and they also had to admit the following morning that Miss Charity was still alive, "Just livin', and that's all."

Dele hurried back into the kitchen, where Letha was frying chicken and Nannie Lou was churning on the milk, and began packing bread warm from the oven, ham, jelly cake, and pickle into the August meeting basket.

"How was she?" Letha placed a browned wing in the dish and hastily sprang away from the pan from which the frying liver had just popped hot grease on her hand. Nannie Lou paused eagerly in her rhythmic swing of the churn dasher.

"Still livin'."

Nannie Lou impatiently plunged the dasher into the churn and splashed a spray of milk on the porch floor. She was so certain Miss Charity would be dead this morning. They said she had been picking at the bed covers for a week, that death had struck her three days ago, that she had seen doves, that mortification had set in. If Mama had to leave home another night— Darkness was so thick and smothery these nights, with death hovering down the road, that it pure smelled. She was afraid to get up in the heavy darkness, even though the chamber was right under the foot of her bed.

Dele put the dish of hot chicken into the basket, spread a white fringed napkin over the top, and told the girls to have dinner ready for their Papa at twelve o'clock if she wasn't back. When she turned into the lane leading to Miss Charity's, she noticed the doctor's buggy in the grove. Circling the front yard, she went to the kitchen, where Aunt Sugar was making a fire to heat some water. The doctor soon joined them.

"What you think of her this mornin'?" Aunt Sugar demanded, a little reproachfully.

"She's been dead some time, except—"

"What? I heard her breathin' when I come through—"

"Yes. Still breathing. I'm going to turn her. She has lain—in that position—long enough. Will you two come in with me?"

They followed the doctor into the sick room. He had asked Mr. Bill about turning Miss Charity and had told him what it would mean. White and shaking, Mr. Bill left the bed and sat in the hall outside the door, waiting. He had not long to wait. Dele was the one to tell him.

"She's gone, Mr. Bill."

Aunt Mary was sent for. The neighbors arrived quickly, shocked and subdued. With a handkerchief soaked in camphor tied across her mouth and nose, Aunt Sugar threw the cover off the bed and stripped Miss Charity, while Dele went to the kitchen for water and soap. When Aunt Mary entered and saw Miss Charity naked on her bed—Miss Charity who never would even let anybody see under her arms—she blushed red up to her ears and hastily threw a sheet over the still form. Aunt Sugar soaped her bath cloth and threw the sheet over the foot-board as she set to work vigorously washing the ravaged face and neck.

"Ain't she one skeleton though?"

Aunt Mary eased the sheet back over the wasted body and washed the feet and legs carefully, as though not to hurt Miss Charity. Dele gently soaped the flat yellow breasts which had once given sustenance to lusty life. "Dear Calvin," she would write, "Miss Charity is out of her suffering—"

"She had a lot of moles," Aunt Sugar observed under her handkerchief. "There's one right at her neighbor." *

Dele put a towel over the exposed flesh and helped Aunt Mary with the feet and legs.

* Navel.

286

"I never saw a corpse in no worser shape. She'll be purgin' before mornin'."

"Get the clothes out of the trunk, Sugar, and—hush." Dele spoke before she thought.

The clothes were placed neatly in the tray of the little tin trunk—long open drawers with a draw string around the waist, a cambric "body" with heavy darts designed to "keep a woman from flopping."—"You know, Mary," she had once whispered behind her palm-leaf fan at church, "before I'd flop like Puss does I'd tie 'em down with hard home-spun"—a short chemise with a hamburg ruffle around the neck, two bleaching underskirts, and the black dress folded away in moth balls. Under the clothes were a handkerchief, two sheets, a towel, a comb.

Miss Charity's fine gray hair was so tangled that Aunt Sugar got the scissors to cut some off.

"Take 'ere, Sugar. You fix the cot." Aunt Mary got the tangles out all right and rolled the hair down over the ears like Miss Charity had always worn it. Mariah helped the women take down the bed and carry it out in the sun and pile the bed linen in the wash-house. The empty space provoked echoes as the women walked.

"Mr. Bill, you can—come in now," Dele said. "She's ready."

Mr. Bill came in to look at her. He stood at the cot a long time, calm now after days of agitation.... "She looks good." He put his hand on her head, her hair. "Her hair still shines like silk. Cut me off a little piece, Dele—to keep." His eyes were dry, though Dele had to blink away tears as she stooped to shear a lock. "It's just as pretty white as 'twas brown, though I thought when I saw her hair down the first time that her brown plait was the prettiest thing I ever saw.... She looks good."

Then he glanced at the empty space where the bed—his bed and hers—had been so long and for the first time broke down.

287

"It's the Lord's will," Aunt Sugar comforted him. "The Lord doeth all things well. He knows best."

It was a ghastly night. The odor of disease and death, of neglected lamp-wicks, of honeysuckle, surmounted the disinfectants with which the house reeked; but the neighbors, sitting on the porch through the long hours of the wake, were as casual as at a corn-shucking.

"I'll take my shaddin' in a boat. Seinin's all right if you're in a swidget, but watchin' a pole is more like it—to me."

"Runnin' pretty good this week?"

"Neuse River's full of 'em. Puss had a baked shad last night. I caught two, but the biggest one—I reckon he weighed seven pounds—jumped back in the river."

"Hen always catches the jumpin'est shads!"

"He was every bit o' two foot and strong as a ox. He finned me; it's done started festerin'." Uncle Hen displayed a sore thumb. "And itch—I never had nothin' to itch like—"

"You ought to have smallpox one time—sore thumbs all over your face, every one a-itchin' the same time and you darin' to scratch."

"This here new vaccination claims to do away with smallpox, but blest if they're goin' to scratch my arm." Uncle Hen took a chew of tobacco.

"If you had waded in scabs in a pesthouse ankle-deep—"

"Why, Millard!" Uncle Job chided. The house of death was no place to stretch things in.

"Millard shore went through somethin'. Measles is bad enough, or chicken-pox."

"Ch-ch-chicken-pox i-i-itches p-p-plenty for m-m-me. I s-s-set in the h-h-hen house half th-th-the night," Cousin Ashley testified.

"Changin' the subject, I'm going to start shinglin' my tobacco barn tomorrow—or next day." Mr. Smith remembered the funeral tomorrow. "Be glad of any help, on a swap of course."

288

"I'll help you half a day, soon as I catch up with my plowin'."

"Wait till Monday, and I'll help. I'm goin' shaddin' tomorrow—or next day, now."

"We ought to all take a day off and clean up the graveyard. Several graves have caved in bad, and the weeds got a right good sling," Uncle Job reminded them.

John and Uncle Wes were reminded. They arose quietly and went through the hall into the room where the light was burning dimly. They took a bottle of red liquid, opened the coffin, and sponged the face and hands of the corpse; the undertaker had shown them how.

"She was a good woman." John hoped Dele was resting good at home on their bed. They ought to take more work off Dele; no woman was made out of iron. What would a man do if— He set the bottle on the mantel and went to wash up at the water-shelf on the back piazza.

The other men left the porch to file into the dining room where ham, cheese, biscuits, cake, and pickle had been spread by the neighborhood women for the midnight snack. John tasted Dele's jelly cake.

Early next morning the men shouldered spades and shovels and set off to the graveyard. Uncle Millard laid off the grave, and soon the red clay was heaped on one side of the opening, as the men relieved one another. Women gathered roses and cape jessamines and tied them with white ribbon from last summer's hats. Aunt Lina and Dele worked all morning on wreaths and a crown cut out of pasteboard boxes and covered with pink roses and ivy. Aunt Mary found a white rose from Miss Charity's bush in the garden to place in the hand of the corpse—"To take along with her," Aunt Mary said to herself, looking at the neglected flowers in the garden.

At one o'clock the black hearse with its tassels flying in the May breeze was driven to the door, and Miss Charity was moved out of her room for good. The procession of buggies—

Uncle Israel's carriage with the Family in it followed the hearse—wound out of the lane, creaked up the sandy road, across the railroad, up the hill to the church. Uncle Millard, Uncle Wes, Mr. Smith, John, Uncle Israel, and Cousin Sim lifted the coffin from the hearse and bore it down the aisle to the altar. Mr. Bill, his suit brushed and his shoes blacked, followed with the Family and sat sort of dazed and lost on the front seat.

> *"Nearer, my God, to Thee,*
> *Nearer to Thee,*
> *E'en though it be a cross—"*

The preacher paused, looking out over the congregation, and then in a clear assured voice he repeated without once glancing at the Bible Her favorite chapter... "The Lord is my Shepherd, I shall not want; He maketh me to lie down in green pastures.... And I will dwell in the House of the Lord forever."

Cousin Maggie was playing the organ again, and faltering voices were trying to assure the Family that She was "safe in the arms of Jesus, safe on His tender breast." Mr. Bill was thinking not about Jesus at all—Jesus was in the Sunday school lesson, and he knew there was such a Thing—but his thoughts were back in that empty corner at home where he and Charity had lay together and had their secrets—Charity wouldn't care about bein' in nobody's arms, not even Jesus's, she was so modest.... She looked good. He was puttin' her away nice. Well, that was one of the things everybody had to do—die—when their time come. It was a relief to know she was out of her suffering, at rest. She had worked hard in her life. The biscuits she had made, let alone— He saw her bending over the bread tray kneading biscuit dough; lots of women didn't know how much grease to put in biscuits, but Charity—where was his handkerchief? Seems like lately he never could find a handkerchief. Charity had always kept

290

them in the little drawer on the bureau and always remembered to think him of puttin' one in his pocket. Not that he cared who saw him cry, but his nose was goin' to need wipin' and—

"Let us pray."

This was his chance.... A half plug of tobacco, three nickels, a shoestring, a collar button in one pocket, and in the other a big hole. No handkerchief.

"For we know that Thou doest all things well, and we submit our wills to Thine. Even in our darkest hour help us to look up into the face of our loving Father and say, 'Thy will be done on earth even as in heaven.' Be with the bereav-ed family and make them conscious as never before—"

Mr. Bill wiped his nose furtively on his coat sleeve; it would not wait any longer. Nannie Lou who through her tears was furtively peeping to see how the Family was taking it, saw him and all but sobbed right out. If she could just get to herself and have one more bait of crying. Suppose it was Mama—

"We thank Thee for the life of this good woman, for her faithfulness, her devotion—" The preacher was winding up his prayer; always he praised the corpse just before the amen. The crying must quit before the folks raised up from praying, don't everybody would look at her and wonder why she was taking it so hard. She would just taste the tears to see if they were salty— Come on, tears, fall fast as you please. I want to see if you are salty. I bet you're not. Flow! ... Nannie Lou was bearing up when the prayer ended.

John had not been praying either.... They could all take a lot of work off'n Mama. The three nights she had sat up at Miss Charity's had been the lonesomest he ever spent. She had no business workin' in the field noway, now that he had other help; no woman was made out of iron. Mama sure had stuck to him, gettin' up before day and wadin' dew waist-deep into the cotton patch. What would a man do—?

Dele sat bent over with her head resting on the bench in front of her. Right now Calvin was on the baseball field knocking home runs maybe, and everybody rooting for him. It seemed strange to think of him playing ball while they were sitting here at Miss Charity's funeral. Miss Charity used to hand him biscuits from her black satchel when he got restless during sermons; she had always made a lot of him even when he got too big to eat her biscuits at church. June, July, August, September, October—no, she wouldn't count May and October, for some of May was already gone, and he would come home in October. If only Calvin could get over Milly. Nobody round the neighborhood ever heard anything from Milly; folks believed she had written and her proud folks up there in Philadelphia had done away with her letters. Milly had never acted a bit stuck up, though. If it were Calvin up there in that coffin—no, she wouldn't think about that; she'd never have that to go through, for she wouldn't be able to draw another breath if he—Think of Kate a little. Kate would get along all right; it would be nice to have a baby in the family again. Calvin would be surprised; if it was a boy, maybe Kate would name him Calvin, and maybe he'd have little ringlets all over his head like Calvin did when—

A green fly circled over the heads of the congregation.

"Thine shall be the glory forever and ever. Amen."

> *"Sleep on, belov-ed, sleep and take thy rest,*
> *Lay down thy head upon thy Savior's breast.*
> *We love thee well, but Jesus loves thee best.*
> *Goodnight, goodnight, goodnight."*

At the grave the coffin was opened so that friends might take a last look at the remains. Mr. Bill looked just an instant through the glass plate and then let them shut her up. She had changed; this was a stranger.

With the handle of the shovel John smoothed the mound, flattening the ridge at the top so the flowers would stay on.

The women covered the red clay with roses and violets and cape jessamines and turned with chastened tenderness to go home with their families.

XLV

"Job R. Pate."

"Be not deceived; God is not mocked. For whatsoever a man soweth that shall he also reap."

"Ashley Pleasant."

"J-J-Jesus w-w-wept."

"John Fuller."

"The Lord is my Shepherd; I shall not want."

"Sim Bryant."

"F'rGods'lovedtheworldthatHegaveHisonlybegottenson thatwhosoeverbelievethonHimshouldnotperishbuthaveeternal life." Cousin Sim sat down in a lather.

"Henry H. Davis."

"Follow me." Uncle Hen blew his nose as he resumed his seat by Uncle Millard.

"Israel Pate."

"I beseech you therefore, brethren, that ye present your bodies a living sacrifice, wholly acceptable to God, which is your reasonable service."

"Wesley Pate."

"God is love."

It was roll-call Sunday, and the secretary was finishing the men's class before turning to the intermediates. Every second Sunday in May it was a custom, handed down from Grandpa Pate's young days, to call the names of the Sunday school scholars, who were expected to respond to the roll-call by a verse of Scripture. There had been of late years a little murmuring of protest against the custom, for grown men and women did not like to stand up and say a piece before one another and less before their children, who could say their verses so much more glib than their parents. But the tradition was too firmly rooted for protest to flourish. John, though he was mildly against the annual roll-call, always memorized a new nice-sounding verse and never said it. The past Sunday night he had selected, "Let us press on to the mark for the prize of the high calling of God in Christ Jesus," and had practiced it up and down the cotton furrows during the week. When he rose to say it in Sunday school, however, it fled from him; and he found himself repeating as annually, "The Lord is my Shepherd."

The secretary turned a page.... "Christine Pate."

"Remember now thy Creator in the days of thy youth, while the evil days come not nor the years draw nigh when thou shalt say, 'I have no pleasure in them.'" Christine's glance toward Nannie Lou was triumphant. Nannie Lou had told her in class that her verse was going to be "Let there be light," which was easy as anything. Two or three women at the front were whispering and nodding approval of the pretty verse Christine recited.

"Margie Davis."

"Behold the Lamb of God."

"Lessie Pate."

"Cast thy bread upon the waters."

"Nannie Lou Fuller."

"They shall be afraid of that which is high, and fears shall be in the way, and the almond tree shall flourish, and the grasshopper shall be a burden and desire shall fail; because man goeth to his long home, and the mourners go about the streets: Or ever the silver cord be loosed or the golden bowl be broken, or the pitcher be broken at the fountain, or the wheel broken at the cistern." In a clear sweet voice Nannie Lou delivered hers, glancing as she sat down at the women near the front. They were whispering to Dele: "That was fine," "That beats everything yet," "I know you are proud of that child." The child could tell what they were saying.

After Nannie Lou's the verses all seemed routine. The women tremulously responded to their names, some of them forgetting. Aunt Emmie in almost a whisper said, "Suffer the little children to come unto Me," and sat trembling for minutes afterwards. Dele testified that "Joy cometh in the morning," thinking of poor Mr. Bill. Aunt Cynthy, bashful before Uncle Millard, managed "Come unto Me all ye that labor," only to be reminded on the way home that she left out the "rest." Miss Jennie bravely offered, "Man proposes, but God disposes," which she had found in an old Sunday school quarterly, and sat down blushing in confusion as she noted some whispering among the school girls, though she was too timid to ask if she got "pro-" and "dis-" mixed as she had done several times during the week's practice just before settling to sleep. With a thump Aunt Sugar warned the young folks: "Be sure your sins will find you out." After the infant class lisped a few "Follow Me"'s or "Jesus wept"'s the roll-call was over till next second Sunday in May. On the way out of church several women stopped to tell Nannie Lou how smart she was to learn such a long piece. Aunt Puss whispered to Aunt Lina that she didn't believe there was such a verse in the Bible.

While the Fullers were eating dinner, Garland sent word for Dele to come at once; Kate was sick. Quickly assembling a basket of food and a few home remedies, Dele hurried to the buggy waiting under the cedar for her. She found Kate washing dinner dishes, bending at intervals over the table as pain tore at her.

"How long you been—sick, Kate?"

"I felt the first one when I went to the smokehouse for a tom-thumb to cook with the turnip salad. They're coming faster now."

"Take 'ere. I'll finish. Go on strip and wash, and I'll come fix your bed—"

"Garland helped me fix the bed before he went for the

295

doctor." Kate had to stop in the hall and lean over a table when the next pain seized her. "I can't stand many like that," she thought, feeling the moisture at the roots of her hair and biting her lips to keep from crying out. She had made up her mind not to cut up, and as long as she was of herself nobody should hear her grunt. Pouring water into the pink-flowered bowl, she sponged her body quickly, put on the cambric nightgown, and tried to braid her hair. It was moist, and her hands were damp and clammy.

By the time Garland and the doctor came, it didn't make much difference to Kate who heard her grunt. Elevating her knees so that she could press against the foot-board with her feet, the doctor stood close and held her hand, advising her best how to bear with the pain. Kate heard nothing; instinct guided her. Garland hovered near, in spite of Dele's plea for him to go into the kitchen. Kate's white face, her eyes dark with suffering, her low moan as she pulled with the wrenching agony were suddenly too much for Garland. He fainted. Dele felt like slapping him. The doctor had to leave Kate and attend to him, though Kate did not seem to notice.

It was over in three hours, and Kate was eating a piece of milk custard. "I said I wasn't going to grunt and carry on, and I didn't," she boasted. "Did I?"

"I done the cuttin' up, honey," Garland assured her. "Everything begun to turn black, and next thing I knowed I fell over and—"

"You take this plate and get out of here awhile," Dele commanded, her patience at low ebb. "You ain't the only man ever had a baby."

"She's got my nose; don't you think so?" Garland stopped in the doorway to ask. "My nose sure as you're born," he answered.

"Garland wanted a boy so bad I didn't know whether—"

"You always want what you get. Now go to sleep."

"Maybe my next one will be a boy. Your second one was."

296

"Calvin was a pretty baby—fat as a butter ball. Everybody said he was pretty."

"She's going to be pretty. Her hair's got to curl, if I have to use curling irons."

"Calvin had more hair than most babies, and it curled up around his little neck—"

"Her little hair will curl too, just like Calvin's. I'm going—"

"It don't look like Calvin's. He had ringlets all over his little head, and—"

"When did you hear from Calvin?"

"Yesterday."

"All right?"

"Sounded real satisfied."

"I hear that Miss Joyce's folks up in Philadelphia are trying to marry Milly off to a Yankee. Seems they won't tell anybody her address."

"Nobody don't want to know it."

"She does have Garland's nose. I hope her hair is curly."

"You're goin' to sleep now. Hush talkin'."

"I want another teeny piece of custard or—"

"When you wake up; not before."

"Well, watch my baby then. If she cries, wake me up." Kate closed her eyes in a blissful aura of motherhood. "I'm going to name her Swannanoa Virginia."

Dele drew the shades and sat down by the cradle. Kate dozed.

"It'll seem good not to be tootched out in front," she said drowsily. "Though—I want five more."

XLVI

THE FIRST SUNDAY in June Kate brought little Swannanoa Virginia home sixteen days after she was born into the world. At Confurnce the day before, Garland, begging forgiveness, had been restored to full fellowship with the

297

church. The family made no reference to his restoration, but Dele cooked the things he liked for dinner, and John made a great fuss over his baby. "Little Swannie favors you some," he even conceded to please Garland.

"Now, Papa, she's Swannanoa Virginia," Kate begged.

But Swannie she became and soon was an important member of the family. To Letha she grew to be the center of things. Late at night by dim lamp-light she worked dainty stitches into batiste and made more little pillows than Kate laughingly hoped she would ever need. Half the money she earned for her own scant wardrobe went into presents for Swannie.

Nannie Lou liked the baby all right, but the pallets and baby clothes strewed around on the chairs and rose bushes in the back yard irritated her. Suppose somebody should come. The kinfolks didn't matter, for they were used to babies' habits. But if Somebody—There was little prospect, but one had to hope. "I may run down one Saturday this summer as Mr. Israel and Miss Airy asked me to, and if so I shall certainly see you and read your current verses," He had written.... One Saturday.... After that brief note Nannie Lou developed a passion for clean hearths and immaculate yards. Early Saturday mornings she would find a brush broom and sweep the front and back yards, her eyes constantly on the bend up the road; once as she leaned on her broom and studied the road wistfully, Dele sighingly looked toward the river haze, not quite understanding, but identifying that otherwhere look in her daughter's eyes. Then late Saturday afternoons Nannie Lou would put fresh flowers in all the vases and, dressed in a spotless gingham, would sit on the front porch—waiting, posed with Ivanhoe, his gift, in her lap—"I shall certainly see you"—Certainly. Had he meant You? She slipped his note from between the pages of Ivanhoe to find new meanings. "Read good books, practice your writing if it gives you pleasure"—That might mean he

liked her for herself, not her poetry—"Read good books"—
Fit herself to be his equal? Ten years would not be too much
difference if you read good books—"And don't be easily discouraged in your ambitions"—Don't give up heart even
though distance divides? Days were so lonely, years were so
long, though; she wanted him only, him and his song. In the
gloaming oh, my darling, when the lights are dim and low—

The Sunday afternoon topic this particular June day was
Milly. Cousin Nick had told Garland with his own lips that
Milly was going to be married at the end of the summer and
would soon be home to get ready. Garland disremembered
the fellow's name, something with a Mac to it; he lived up
there in Philadelphia, had a big job of some kind, and Cousin
Joyce was figuring on a big church wedding with waiters
and a long trail and decorations. Milly would be home by the
last of July, and a dressmaker from Raleigh had already been
engaged to spend a month at Cousin Nick's making up the
wedding finery. Matter-of-fact Kate inquired if Calvin was
to be written about it.

John thought it wouldn't make so much difference now.
Calvin had got weaned off from Milly and wrote like he was
real satisfied down yonder.

Letha thought Calvin should be told. If the marriage was a
certain fact he ought to know; they had no right to keep it
from him.

"It's a sure fact all right. He's hired me to help paint up
around his place—the barns and out-houses," Garland assured
Letha.

"Write him, some of you, if you think best. What was it
in his last letter about the fellow that got married and had to
give up his job?" John asked Dele.

Nannie Lou hurried to get Calvin's letter from the mantel
and to read an extract: "I rather play baseball than anything
I ever did. I won't get in the big leagues probably, but as
long as I make enough to live on I'd play just to play. The

299

cap'n told me he was going to use me in an exhibition game with a team from Texas, and there will be a scout from the majors to see that game. You all think of me, so I'll hit good that day. Well, anyhow, I'm satisfied like things are, only I wish I made enough to send more home. I couldn't live any better than I am, but there's little money in it yet. Felt sorry for one of my team mates the other day. He jumped up and got married on a spur and had to give up the team and go home to make enough to support a wife. All the girls here are good to we baseball boys."

"Sure, write him; let him pick him up a girl down there and forget all that buck-boy foolishness over Milly." Garland was now a father.

Nannie Lou wished Calvin would find a girl so rich and pretty it would make Milly look like two cents with a hole in it. She began building air castles in Alabama.

"Milly's all right," Dele said quietly. "Who knows what she's been through?"

"That's right," Kate agreed. "Nobody has heard a word from her as I've heard of since she left. She may have been pretty miserable up there away from everybody."

"Swannie's awake." And Letha dashed into the house to attend the voiced urgency within, followed by Kate and Dele. Aunt Sugar and her girls, Uncle Millard and Aunt Cynthy, Cousin Sim's folks came to see what Kate's baby looked like. Later Aunt Nettie and her boy, whose boss man had just given him another raise that the kinfolks had not heard of, drove up. Her chief news, though, was an item that she had found in a Raleigh paper: "Mr. and Mrs. Nicholas Whitington Pate announce the engagement and approaching marriage of their daughter, Milly Victoria, to James Monroe MacWilson of Philadelphia, the wedding to take place early in September."

After a longer than usual letter to Calvin that night, Dele added: "And Milly's going to marry a man from Philadel-

300

phia in September. Everything happens for the best. Milly never had no health. You keep all your money. Wait till you play in the big leagues to talk about sending money home. Everybody is proud of how good you are playing. They all ask about you every Sunday. I'm going to send you a pound cake Saturday. From Mama. P.S. Write soon."

Anxiously Dele watched the bend in the road for the mail man, even before there had been time for a letter to come from Alabama. Nannie Lou, discouraged and down-hearted that there had been no further word from Mr. Stevens, still looked with hope and renewed interest when she saw the mail man coming.

"It's a race between Mama and Nannie Lou these days to see who can get to the mail box first," Letha observed, herself never looking up from the baby cap she was crocheting to see whether the mail man stopped or passed on. Often John waited under the buggy shelter, peeping from between the boards to see if there would be a letter; if the carrier stopped, John, with a hint of triumph in his glance toward the house, met him and took the mail, waiting interminably to take it to the house.

The July days seemed very long and depressing. A week passed, ten days, two weeks since Dele's letter to Calvin, with its urgent "Write soon." Dele went about her work as usual, but she lay awake at night and lost some of her steadfastness. Letha found her pouring hot damson preserves from the kettle on the table. "Why, Mama, the jar's full; you're spilling damsons all over—"

"What am I thinkin' about?" Dele pulled herself together then, but later in the garden she caught herself pulling up young collards along with pusley for her cow. Why didn't they hear from Calvin? Had she done right to tell him about Milly, going on three weeks ago? If there was no letter tomorrow she would write again, and still there would be the long tedious waiting before time to expect an answer to her second letter. Why didn't John mention Calvin's silence? Seldom had there been three weeks between letters. Were they all uneasy, too? At night she began to plan to send John down to Alabama to visit Calvin. He had never been anywhere but to Morehead City, and it would be a nice chance for him to see how they raised cotton in another state. The money part could be managed some way, and she and Garland could handle the cantaloupes. In the morning she would mention it to John, and with the girls' help try to persuade him it was the right thing to do. When day came, she knew her plan would sound too absurd; they would all stare at her, and she might break down. One more day, and then—

So feverishly did she work that the morning chores were finished by nine o'clock. An hour to wait before mail time. With a sort of desperate patience she went to the cantaloupe patch across the road where John and Nannie Lou were loading the wagon for Pate's Siding. She helped pull the ripe cantaloupes and lay them in piles for the next wagon load. Lifting two choice Rocky Fords, she hurried to the mail box with her gift for the carrier, not realizing it was for the gods. The mail man began smiling when he saw Dele standing there at the road. Often he had inquired after that ball player of theirs in Alabama, and as often had called to anyone in sight that the postmark was Alabama this time, as though he did not know how seldom another postmark found its way into their box! Dele's heart stood still; she could not smile, with that sick anxious tightness in her throat. Grimly she held out the two cantaloupes.

"Much obliged. Very much obliged." He made room for the gift near the mail bag. "Rocky Fords—the sweetest that grow. We like them for breakfast with red ham gravy. Very much obliged." He slapped the rein gently over his horse and moved off.

"A letter—don't you have a letter?" Dele called tensely after him.

"Bring you one tomorrow." He smiled and drove on.

Why had he smiled then? He had no business smiling if there was no letter. Resentment filled her heart. Maybe there was a letter, and the cantaloupes had made him forget. Let night come, and she would write a scolding letter to Calvin, telling him she couldn't sleep unless he wrote regular; and if he had worried any over what she put in her last letter, to quit, for it wasn't worth the snap of his fingers, and he was old enough now— She knew there would be no scolding letter.

Her firm resolution to do something definite after one more day bore her through that Tuesday. Over the dinner pot, rolling the pastry for the chicken pie, cutting watermelon rind for pickle—Calvin's favorite—seeding damsons for preserves, canning corn and tomatoes, Dele composed lines that would have been classic. They were never written.

As she rang the bell for supper, the lonesome whistle of the seven o'clock train passing Pate's Siding drowned her summons. On that very train there might be a letter. Never mind, the one she would write tonight would bring an answer; it would be possible to hear in five days; she could bear it five days, with preserving and pickling, washing and ironing, Kate and little Swannie coming, to fill the time. Tuesday would bring an answer. Unless on that very train that just passed— Almost cheerfully she washed the supper dishes, strained the milk, put her canned vegetables in the pantry, weighed the fruit and sugar, filled the preserving kettle, and put the melon rind in lime water. In five minutes she would sit with Calvin. . . . "Dear Calvin: It has been three weeks—" As she locked the back door and hung up a clean towel, Nannie Lou tore into the kitchen wildly excited, incoherent.

"Guess—guess—" She seemed unable to finish.

"What?"

"Guess—who's—in yonder!"

"Who?"

"Calvin!"

"What!"

"He's married. She's with him."

Dele sat suddenly by the table and looked at Nannie Lou helplessly.

"Her name's Winnie. She's pretty. She kissed Papa."

Steps through the hall, across the back porch. Dele kept staring at Nannie Lou helplessly. Calvin stood in the door.

"Brought you somethin'." Calvin stepped toward Dele, shook hands with her, and reached back for the girl who had lingered in the doorway. "Somethin' from Alabama. This is Winnie, Mama. We're married."

There was a brief hesitation. Dele did not move. Winnie suddenly came forward, threw her arms around her neck, and whispered something. Dele could not hear for the funny roaring in her head; she saw before her a sweet brown-eyed child with little white hands.

"We come on the seven o'clock train—walked from the depot. We been married a week today," Calvin added. Still Dele could not speak. She looked toward John and Letha, who were standing in the kitchen door.

"I'd met you if I'd known," John was looking at the little stranger.

"Decided to steal a base on you. She wanted to send a telegram, but of course you wouldn't got it—out here."

"Please like me." The appeal aroused Dele. Impulsively she arose and put her arm around Winnie, she who had never hugged her own daughters; she somehow felt very sorry for the child from Alabama.

"Come on let me fix you some supper. We can talk afterwards."

"Plenty of it, such as it is," John smiled at the Alabaman.

With a warning glance at her husband, Dele led the way into the dining room. John ought not to have quoted Cousin Nick the first thing, reminding Calvin of things. But maybe

Calvin had forgotten that joke about Nick's "plenty-of-it butter such-as-'tis"; for he was very lively at the table and on the front porch afterwards, where he told about the exhibition games, batting averages, and big league scouts. Now and then Winnie confirmed a statement and praised Calvin's ball record every time there was an opportunity.

Before light next morning Dele tipped through the back porch, intent on dressing a chicken to fry for breakfast. She did not tip lightly enough. Before her first fire had burned out, Calvin tipped into the kitchen and sat on the wood-box behind the stove.

"Fried chicken for breakfast?"

"You didn't have to get up. You need to sleep after that long trip."

"Oh, I slept good. Wanted to see around in daylight. Winnie's still asleep.... Make many cantaloupes this year?" Calvin watched her salt the chicken.

"Nice chance." Was it only yesterday that she had given two Rocky Fords to the mail man? "Watermelons too. Do they raise many in Alabama?"

"Not any better than ours. There ought to be some money in raising melons—shipping them up North and hauling them to town. Maybe trucking a little on the side."

"He has shipped right smart this year."

"I was wonderin'—maybe Papa would let me have some patches by myself, make me a little money to kind o' get a start."

"You mean—you're tired of baseball?"

"Tired? I'd never get tired! I'd rather play ball than—" he checked himself. "But two can't live on what I got, not when everything's to buy like down there. I thought maybe I could stay here, help house the crop, and then next year Papa might be willin' to let me tend some land—"

"He will. I'll talk to him." Dele sifted flour. "Set the damsons on the stove and let them start cooking. I've got a cup

305

tin full of rind to pickle and a pantry already full of canned stuff."

"I aim to work hard and try to get along."

"Winnie got many folks?"

"She's the only child. Her Mama's a widow. She sews."

"That was a pretty dress Winnie had on last night."

"She's got a lot of pretty dresses. She wants to learn about cookin' and cannin'—like you. I told her about you."

Dele gulped before she could speak. "She's sweet-lookin'. I'll give her some biddies. I raised over a hundred and fifty this year; seemed like all the hens wanted to set."

"They called me the Tar-heel slugger down there. Tar-heel stands for North Carolina. I'll be satisfied here. Course I'll miss ball practice, but— They rooted every time I come to bat."

"They did?"

"Did you show my picture in the baseball suit?"

"Yes. Everybody thought it was fine."

"The boss said I'd make the big leagues."

"Peel these apples, and I'll fry some for breakfast."

Calvin took the dish. "I some kind o' hated to leave down there. Course I think the world and all of Winnie, but—I'll be satisfied here all right. I was raised to farm. I sure know how to plow."

"And there's always plowin' to do."

After breakfast Jessie, who was going to the siding after the trunks, waited under the crape myrtle tree to see the lady from Alabama. "You knocked a home run dat time, boy," he told Calvin. "Clear 'crost de fence. You couldn't knocked one no purtier."

"You ought to have seen one he did knock that last game; he could knock fast balls and curves that bothered everybody else," Winnie declared with pride.

"You'll bat curves behind old Nellie mule awhile now, won't you, Mr. Calvin?"

"Aim to, Jess."

"He's going to keep up his ball practice too, so he can play in the big leagues some day." The little wife was firm about it.

"Bes' thing's to turn in and raise you a whole crap o' baseball players of your own," Jessie said low to Calvin, winking at Mr. John. "I better git along after dat trunk 'fore I git hit." Jessie started toward the wagon. "Mariah'll be down to see de new lady by-'n'-by. She won't believe till she do see." He laughed. "Naw, 'cause I don't, lookin' right at her!"

Nannie Lou could not keep her eyes off Winnie. She flushed with pride at the thought of taking her to Sunday school. Calvin's wife was the prettiest and stylishest girl that had ever been in the neighborhood! That little pink dimity, made up very simple and dainty, was better'n most Sunday dresses. When they walked in church— She did hope Cousin Nick and Miss Joyce would be there. When Milly got home she'd see somebody else could marry, too, same as herself. Winnie had the smallest feet she had ever seen on a married person, and such pretty patent leather slippers. Sunday she would go in and sit with Calvin and Winnie and introduce her to all the kinfolks. "Yes'm, I'm coming," she answered the kitchen call.

From the handbag in the hall Winnie took a ball and glove and ran into the yard, challenging Calvin to "play ball." He followed slowly without interest and caught her pitches with one hand. When the mail man came they were still mechanically tossing balls to each other in the grove.

"Here it is," called the mail man, waving a letter and stopping his horse. Calvin walked to the road. "Told your mother yesterday I'd bring a letter today."

Calvin took the letter.

"How you getting on?"

Calvin was staring at the envelope.

"Needn't ask though, for you're looking top-notch." He

307

slapped the rein gently over his horse. "Tell your mother we enjoyed the cantaloupes." The mail man drove on.

"Play ball," Winnie challenged from under the big oak tree. Then she noticed the whiteness of his face. "Calvin, are you sick, darling?"

"No. Why?"

"I just asked." She studied his averted eyes and the pallor around his lips. "It is a hot sun." She drew him in the shade with her. "I just love these trees, Calvin. They're like ours."

He missed the note of wistfulness in her voice. "Um-humph," he agreed.

"Mother is bending over her flowers just about now and cutting some for the house. Can't you just smell the warm odors of her pink roses?—I'll like it here," she added hastily.

"You better go in and write your mother. And I'll go help Papa with his load of cantaloupes."

"All right." She held up her face. He kissed her.

When the wagon was loaded, Calvin slipped through the lot, down the lane, into the shaded privacy of the pasture. Without meaning to, he sat under the sweet gum tree where once M and C had been carved. His hand shook as he opened the letter.

"Dear Calvin," he read. "I'm coming home. You're my home now. And always. There has never been anybody else. If you have heard so, you knew in your heart it was just one of the things I couldn't help. Nobody knows where I am now. I got some work last week, and tomorrow when they pay me I'll have enough to buy me a railroad ticket straight to you. I've worked in a factory, Calvin, and I'm tired. I want to be completely tired when I find you, so I can rest. We'll rest together and work together. I'll go to the field with you, follow your tracks in the furrow, plant the seed, and wash your dear tired body at night. I have soothed the tiredness from you and put my head on your pillow and breathed with you so

308

many nights that it will not seem strange, not strange at all, but so sweet I shall be afraid to sleep. It has been a dream so many mornings. Oh, Calvin—soon now. Always—Milly."

XLVII

On his way to the siding for the trunks, Jessie stopped at every field where there were workers to tell about Calvin's marriage. Kate and Garland came home to welcome the bride and groom, bearing little Swannie like a banner.

"We're goin' to give you a supper," Kate whispered to Calvin, "at our house."

"How's this for a home run?" Garland wanted to know, proudly displaying his daughter.

Winnie gently put her face against the sweetness of the baby's cheek.

"She's some kind o' pretty," Garland whispered all around.

Almost impatiently Letha took the baby away from Winnie and went in the house to fit the new cap on the dear little head.

Soon Uncle Millard came up the walk, Aunt Cynthy panting on behind, a little bashful at meeting a stranger from so far.

"Cynthy got me into my Sunday pants, but 'twas wuth it," Uncle Millard assured Calvin, his eyes glued admiringly upon Winnie. "If Cynthy dies, I'm a-goin' to Alabama to play ball sure."

Uncle Hen drove his surrey into the grove, and Aunt Puss fluttered hurriedly toward the house to stay till bedtime with her brood.

"Law, Calvin, you sure took us all on surprise! Everybody thought you was so wrapped up—"

309

"Look, Puss! Tiny will be in the bee gums," Dele hastily interrupted, preparing to stick close to Puss the rest of the evening.

"You sure knocked a home run this time," Uncle Hen offered, as he shook hands with Calvin, "clean over the corn patch. Millard, le's me and you practice up on our curves."

Aunt Sugar was the next one to come bustling into the porch to see the bride and groom. "You've done the right thing now, Calvin. Settle down on the farm and put your mind on somethin' some account. I bet that child can't make a biscuit."

"She helped Calvin load a wagon full of cantaloupes this evenin' to take to town in the mornin'," Nannie Lou defended.

"Pitched right in, hunh? Well, that's a credit to you."

"Calvin ought to excuse himself and get to bed soon, for he wants to leave by three o'clock in the mornin'." Dele in the general confusion could not tell whether Calvin was just tired from his afternoon's work or too quiet. At supper he had been too quiet, and he somehow looked much older than at breakfast.

"Yes, go on to bed, Calvin. We'll excuse you," the women insisted.

"Sure, we'll excuse you," and suddenly for no reason at all Uncle Millard and Uncle Hen were laughing heartily.

But Calvin sat with the kinfolks till bedtime, very still, saying little. When he and Winnie had gone upstairs, Dele followed with a glass of water and a native herb pill. "It won't hurt anything. You pitched in and worked in the sun too hard today, not used to it."

Calvin swallowed the pill in silence.

By three o'clock Dele had a hot breakfast waiting when Calvin came down. "I didn't want you to get up for me."

"I get up soon every morning." She buttered him a biscuit. "You ought to get five or six dollars for your load of cantaloupes today." From the sideboard she sliced jelly cake for his lunch box. "Your Papa is goin' to give you the rest in the patch. Even the culls ought to bring you five dollars a load, and there ought to be four loads. Twenty dollars is no bad start."

Calvin ate the buttered biscuit.

"You don't have anything to worry over. We're all goin' to help you get a start. Winnie's a nice girl.... You'll be back by three o'clock this evenin', I reckon.... Won't you?"

"Should."

"Here's your bite of dinner. We'll pull you another load while you're gone, to take back to Raleigh tomorrow." Dele held the lamp for him as he hitched old Nellie to the wagon. "Soon as you sell out, hurry on back home so you can sleep some."

"You go back to bed and try to get a good nap—gettin' up this time of day."

"I will." She held the lamp till he was out of sight up the road. Then she sat in the dark at the shed room window, as though to keep him company on the lonesome ride.

It was a long day. Frequently during the morning, Winnie set her pan of peaches on the floor and went to look at the clock. Nannie Lou helping her peel peaches to can, admitted to her sister-in-law that she could write poetry, that she had a whole book of poems and a novel started, that Mr. Stevens was the best teacher anywhere, that he wanted her to get an education, that he thought her pen might carry her far—

Dele carried the peach peelings and seed to the pigs, and long before time to expect Calvin she began to watch the road anxiously. At three o'clock the women went into the cantaloupe patch to pull another load for Calvin. Winnie soon cut her hand pulling too hard on the vine, but she did not stop. Her little white hands were stained and bloody— for Calvin.

At four he came home. The load had netted him seven dollars. He handed the money to Winnie. "Put it away," he told her, "with the last of the baseball money. For you."

"For us," she answered proudly.

"You go get some sleep now, if you aim to haul another load tomorrow," Dele instructed. "I'll wake you at supper time."

"Yes, for we're going to finish this load ourselves," Winnie told him. Calvin looked at her hands, all stained and bloody; she put them out of sight behind her back. "And tonight I'm going to make my first biscuits."

"You go rest now, Winnie. Me and Nannie Lou can finish here. You've worked hard all day."

"I want to help. I love to."

"Change your dress then; that one's too nice—"

"I haven't anything more suitable, I'm afraid."

"Nannie Lou, bring here one of your dresses for Winnie to wear in the field."

Much too large, faded, ill-fitting, the gingham dress somehow added immeasurably to Winnie's appeal. It was her simple attempt in symbol at adjustment to his way of living. Calvin kissed her impulsively, not knowing that he was saluting the unassuming gallantry of the funny little figure. At first Dele and Nannie Lou had to laugh a little at her; then the tears rushed unexpectedly to Dele's eyes as she turned to the field with Calvin's wife.

At supper time when Winnie was sent to wake Calvin, the family sat waiting at the table. Winnie came to the dining room door and spoke very quietly, but she was white and trembling.

"Come upstairs. I can't wake Calvin."

Dele laid her fork calmly across her plate and followed Winnie upstairs. Bending over the bed, she called Calvin. He did not reply. She shook him gently, violently. There was a shuddering sigh from the bed.

"Call John quick," Dele instructed Winnie.

312

Soon Winnie returned with John.

"What is it?"

"There's something wrong—here."

"How?"

"I can't wake him."

When John raised Calvin to a sitting position, the pillow slipped to the floor. Under it was a bottle. Quickly John examined it, sniffed the odor.

"You and Winnie hold him up like this. Keep shakin' him. I'll ring the farm bell."

"What is it?" Winnie whispered brokenly.

Dele could not speak.

"Was it medicine—an overdose? He said he had headache—"

Soon the farm bell was sending out its summons.

John reëntered. "Le's stand him on his feet. We got to keep him awake."

With the strength of desperation Dele lifted the boy to his feet.

"Let's get the doctor," Winnie begged.

"Soon as help comes. We got to keep him roused."

"Calvin—oh, Calvin!"

"Hold up his head there."

"Oh, Calvin—please!"

They moved him away from the bed. John shook him roughly.

"I—want—"

"He's tryin' to say somethin'."

"What, Calvin? You want what? Speak, son."

"I—want—to—sleep—a thousand years—"

"No, no. You mustn't. You can't. You can't!"

"Fight it, boy. Don't give way to it. Take a step. Walk. Come on now."

But they moved dead weight along the bedroom floor. The next half hour was confused terror. Uncle Millard and

Aunt Cynthy came first. The house was soon filled. Uncle Israel's carriage and the two gray horses that had carried the Governor were dispatched the five miles for the doctor. The men moved Calvin downstairs to the front porch.

"Cover me up— Blow—out—the—light, and—leave—me," Calvin begged drowsily as he was carried carefully down the steps.

Dele was alone with John an instant then. "Let me see that bottle."

"It was laudanum."

"How much?"

"Enough."

The women took Winnie into the parlor and tried to divert her mind from the steady walking on the front porch. Once she ran out and tried to get Calvin to speak to her. Then she sat very still and white and lost in the big rocker, still wearing the ill-fitting gingham, after Aunt Sugar had told her the men could do more if the women folks kept out of the way. Aunt Mary came and sat by Winnie, not speaking, just sitting there close. In the corner Letha and Nannie Lou were noiselessly crying. When Kate arrived, Letha took little Swannie and went out in the back yard with her. Aunt Sugar, moving from the parlor window to the front door to speak to the men, stopped long enough to say to Kate: "I know you hate now he went off to play ball." Kate went to the kitchen and began heating water. "'Twouldn't never happened if he hadn't left here. You know it, and I know it," Aunt Sugar followed her with.

The doctor came and did what he could, little enough by the time he got there. "The doctor says his stomach is paralyzed," the whisper went around in the parlor. The men by turns kept walking Calvin up and down the porch, beating his bare legs and arms with keen little switches from the sugarberry tree.

Uncle Millard and Uncle Wes moved Calvin's lifeless arms

from around their necks to Garland's and Uncle Job's. Calvin flinched not at all from the little switches now.

"I hate to see him tortured any more," Uncle Wes told the men.

"Better here than hereafter," and Uncle Job applied fresh switches. Two hours passed. Uncle Wes spoke very gently to John who was sitting on the doorsteps by himself. "John, I'd have it stopped."

"What?"

"The switches—all of it."

"Do all you can." John was too dazed to make a decision. Uncle Wes mentioned it to Garland; Uncle Job overheard.

"You don't mean quit?"

"I mean—let him rest."

"But there's a hereafter. There'll be no rest if—"

"I'd lay him down now."

"If we give up, we'll be held accountable. Millard, go get some more switches. Walk faster, Garland."

Up and down, up and down with the limp figure of Calvin between them walked the two men. Garland was crying a little.

Suddenly Dele appeared in the front door, a quilt on her arm.

"Stop!" All eyes were turned on her. Uncle Job paused momentarily.

"What for?" he wanted to know.

"Lay him in here on my bed."

Uncle Job resumed the walking without a word.

"Bring him on to my room, Garland." Something in her tone stopped the men.

"You don't want to be guilty—"

"I want him to have—peace."

"Peace, when—"

John found his voice. "Do like she says," he nodded to Garland. Uncle Wes and Uncle Millard straightened him on

Dele's bed, where he had been born and had had pneumonia three times. She smoothed the pillow and spread the quilt over him.

"He wanted us to cover him up and blow out the light and leave him to himself." Dele resolutely went to the table and blew out the light. "He got so little he wanted."

John walked off to the lot alone in the darkness. He gave old Nellie an extra bundle of fodder.

Dele, going over Calvin's clothes, came across the little sailor suit he had worn in the school picture years ago. There was a hole in the pocket. She mended it. Then she handed Uncle Wes the clothes she wanted Calvin buried in.

So, late that night, alone and completely tired, Milly came in and found Calvin.